monsoonbooks

RADIKAL

Olivier Ahmad Castaignède has been living in Southeast Asia since 2000. In 2015, he decided to quit his salaried job in a multinational to focus on writing and travelling. He has since published two novels in French, completed an MA in creative writing – and gone back to work in the IT industry. He also writes plays (staged in Singapore) and creative non-fiction, often inspired by his travels around the world. His short pieces in English have been featured in literary journals *Joyland Magazine, The Crab Orchard Review, Business Mirror, WanderLust* and *SARE,* and also published in the anthology *Letter to My Son* (Marshall Cavendish, 2020).

Scan a QR code to listen to a playlist of tracks appearing in this book on Spotify or Apple Music.

Spotify

Apple Music

Radikal

Olivier Ahmad Castaignède

monsoon

monsoonbooks

First published in English in 2023
by Monsoon Books Ltd
www.monsoonbooks.co.uk

No.1 The Lodge, Burrough Court, Burrough on the Hill,
Melton Mowbray LE14 2QS, UK.

First edition.

ISBN (paperback): 9781915310101
ISBN (ebook): 9781915310118

Cover design by Cover Kitchen.

A Cataloguing-in-Publication data record is available from the British
Library.

Printed and bound in Great Britain by Clays Ltd, Elcograf S.p.A.
25 24 23   1 2 3

In memory of Tino

Glossary

Indonesian

Ayah	father
Baru	new
Begedil	fried patty made of potatoes and minced meat
Beef rendang	a beef dish, slow-cooked in a mixture of spices and coconut milk
Bule	Caucasian (literally means albino)
Cewek	girl, chick
Kukun	witch doctor
Goblok	stupid, fool
Ibu	mum, mother
Ikan bakar	grilled fish
Jenggot	bearded person (used pejoratively to refer to a Muslim zealot)
Kakek	grandfather
Kebaya	traditional blouse-dress combination
Kobokan	bowl of tap water used to wash hands before and after eating
Nenek	grandmother
Ojek	moto taxi
Pak	abbreviation of bapak, mister

Pancasila	core ideology of the (secular) Indonesian state – means five principles
Pelacur	prostitute
Pontianak	female vampiric ghost in Indonesian folklore
Pribumi	native Indonesian (generally meant to exclude Indonesians of Chinese ancestry)
Sambal goreng	fried chili paste
Sayang	dear, honey, a term of endearment
Waria	third gender (biologically male) individuals (also used for transgender women)

Arabic

Asr	one of the five mandatory daily prayers in Islam, falling around late afternoon
Bidah	religious innovation
Dhuhr	one of the five mandatory daily prayers in Islam, falling after the sun has reached its zenith
Hadith	the corpus of teachings, deeds and sayings of the Prophet as verbally transmitted by some of his assumed companions and recorded in writing by early Muslim scholars. The Hadith constitute the major source of guidance for Muslims apart from the Qur'an.
Isha	one of the five mandatory daily prayers in Islam, falling when complete darkness has been reached
Kafir	(plural Kuffar) miscreant, infidel

Maghrib	one of the five mandatory daily prayers in Islam. As the Islamic day starts at sunset, it is technically the first one since it coincides with sunset.
Mujahid	(plural mujahideen) one engaged in jihad
Qiyam	standing position in Islamic prayer
Rakat	(plural Rakaat) prescribed set of movements and words which constitutes the basic unit of Islamic prayers
Salat	Islamic prayer
Salaf	the pious predecessors (taken to be the first three generations of Muslims). By extension, a pure one.
Subuh	one of the five mandatory daily prayers in Islam, which coincides with sunrise
Sujud	prostration position in Islamic prayer
Surah	one of the 114 chapters of the Qur'an
Subḥānahu wataʿālā (often abbreviated as SWT)	
	'Glorious and exalted is He', mention placed after the name of God (Allah) in Islamic texts
Wudu	ablution

Prologue

The Islamic State soldier lowered his torch and ignited the oil trail leading to the caged prisoner in the middle of the desert. Flames gushed forth, racing across the kerosene-soaked sand, but even before they reached the cage the pilot collapsed face first and his body did not so much as flinch when the fire gripped his orange jumpsuit.

Part I

To Excess

Jakarta, May 2014

1

'No, not tonight,' said Hendra.

He had promised Jasmine that he'd go slow on ecstasy pills.

'Come on, Radikal!' the clubber insisted, rolling the r in Hendra's stage name like Indonesians do. 'One X never hurt no one! This stuff's the bomb, believe me, man. When you're back in your cage, we'll all fly together!'

Ignoring Hendra's renewed protests, the Caucasian clubber beckoned to one of the passing mamasans – easily recognizable in her glowing canary-yellow ultra-tight dress. She moved towards them, smiling at Hendra, and unfolded before the clubber's eyes the famous triptych menu of XS nightclub, pointing at the different panels with a small torch: on the centre one, the drinks menu; on the left one, a shortlist of girls with photos, services and prices; and finally, on the right panel, all the varieties of ecstasy, shabu and ice available for sale that night.

'Two Bart Simpsons,' said the clubber, confidently.

'Don't want a girl to go along with that?' the mamasan suggested, while searching for the pills inside the money belt around her waist.

'Thanks, *mami*,' replied the clubber, with a wink. 'But I already got what I need for the night.'

In a foreigner's mouth, mami, a slang for mamasans in local

Jakarta lingo, was a telltale sign of regular visits to the capital's numerous massage parlours. Though tonight the clubber had indeed already found company; for behind him, Hendra noticed a teenager who smiled suggestively in the Caucasian clubber's direction while jumping like a gazelle to the fast-paced techno music. Her low-cut jeans and torn t-shirt revealed a belly button from which a huge piercing protruded, almost menacingly.

Hendra did not like Caucasians at XS. They were only interested in the young, sometimes underage, girls who sold their bodies just to get their fill of X and ice for the night. They were seldom there to listen to music – to his music. And when they approached him, it was often to get their names added to the guest list for private parties. But this clubber, hopping on the dancefloor like a boxer skipping rope, had grabbed his arm while Hendra was weaving his tall and muscular frame through the ecstatic crowd after finishing his DJ act, inching towards the bar where his girlfriend Jasmine was working. The clubber had insisted on offering Hendra a drink in appreciation of his great performance. Since topping the DJ charts for almost a year now, Hendra, or DJ Radikal as he was known, had become a sort of celebrity in the clubbing world and even bules – albinos in Bahasa, as Caucasians were called locally – now recognized him. By the time they had reached the bar, the drink had become a pill.

Reluctantly, Hendra closed his fist around the X that the clubber was pressing into his hand.

The bule introduced himself in heavily accented English. His name was Alessandro. Thirty-five years old, Italian, he had been living in Jakarta for a year and spent all his weekends at XS. Which certainly explained why the man's face looked vaguely familiar to Hendra.

'For all my life, I tell you, I never seen a place like this. XS, the club where *all excesses* are permitted, isn't that what your slogan says in Bahasa?' He swallowed his pill. 'Only excesses of religion are forbidden here, right?' he continued with a laugh after washing down his X with a gulp of water. Then, pointing at Hendra's closed fist, 'Hey, man, why are you not taking yours?'

'Umm, maybe later,' replied Hendra, irritated.

He observed the bule's face. Alessandro's eyelids were shut like two perfectly aligned piggy bank openings, a clear sign that he was already stoned. He wore a shirt with a large unbuttoned collar that offered a glimpse of the top branches of a geometric tattoo on his bony torso. A tuft of short, scruffy black hair. A skinny, willowy body. Hendra thought of a scraggy camel – but a tastefully dressed one, sporting a pair of tight white trousers that ended just above the ankle, a deep blue jacket and black loafers without socks.

'You know, I really love your music, Radikal,' the clubber shouted over a sudden explosion of bass. DJ Violetta's set followed Hendra's and she specialized in hardcore techno.

The bule explained that just like Hendra he was a big fan of 80s and 90s European electro-body music. He told Hendra to listen to Tribantura, especially their ground-breaking song 'Lack of Sense'. Over the bule's shoulder, Hendra could see Jasmine smiling and winking at him. At 1.75m, she towered over the other waitresses and was hard to miss with her metallic blue hair and her full hips accentuated by the red form-fitting skirt of XS waitresses (to differentiate them from the yellow-attired mamasans). Her long slender legs were hidden by the bar but Hendra's mind had no problem filling in the gaps. All he actually wanted now was to spend whatever was left of his break talking to her.

But first, he had to get rid of the intruder and he knew this guy would not leave him in peace until he gobbled up his Bart Simpson. He grabbed one of the small water bottles that lay on the bar top and swallowed the pill.

'Thanks for the dove. Sorry, I really need to go now. My turn soon,' he lied.

'Can't wait, Radikal. Blast things off, OK?'

'Count on me,' replied Hendra. Then, while shaking the bule's out-stretched hand: 'By the way, what are you doing in Jakarta?'

Hendra's question was simply a courtesy, a sudden impulse that he would later regret.

'I'm an accountant with a German company,' replied Alessandro. 'My office is at the Intiland Tower … you know that freakish building built by an American architect?'

All Jakarta residents knew Intiland. It was one of the most hideous buildings in town. Depending on whom one talked to, the tower looked like a disembowelled plane engine or the torso of a man being tortured. And yet (or maybe because of that infamy), Intiland was also known to be one of the most expensive places in the CBD.

'I thought there were just banks there?'

'And a few European MNCs. TMM, my company's TMM. It's a big German firm. Ever heard of them?'

Hendra gasped inwardly. 'TMM? Yes, my mother worked there … and my father. My father used to be the head of your factory in Batam.'

'You're kidding me. What's your father's name?' Alessandro

was laughing. 'Who knows, maybe he's my boss now!'

With a brief hand gesture, he signalled to the impatient teenager jumping next to him that he would soon join her.

'He doesn't work at TMM anymore,' said Hendra finally.

'Why? He retired?'

'No. Not really …'

What had possessed him to talk to a complete stranger about his father? He wasn't about to tell him that he had never even met his father.

The young Indonesian girl approached again, pulling on Alessandro's arm to take him to the dancefloor. She looked totally stoned. And underage. No doubt about it.

'Now I *really* need to go,' said Hendra, extending his hand.

Alessandro left the bar area and joined his prey for the night, who swayed like a boat in high seas. But instead of going to the dancefloor they walked towards the exit. Most likely Alessandro had decided that he had more urgent needs to satisfy. The thought sickened Hendra, who felt a sharp squeeze between his temples. Clearly the discussion with this bule had upset him and, to make things right, another ecsta was in order before his next set. He waved in the direction of the mami and asked her for a 'love' pill – one of the pink ones with a little heart etched in the middle. The ecstasy factories were so proud of their products that they liked to print their logos (a Bart Simpson head, a heart, a blue dolphin, etc.) on each and every tablet as if they were minting their own money.

For Hendra, Xs were always free at XS, whether offered by a customer or not. He also ordered a Red Bull (sugar-free so as not to dampen the effect of the MDMA). He would gladly have downed a vodka shot with the Red Bull, but he knew from experience that under X, it was best not to drink alcohol to avoid dehydration. Then, as he raised his eyes, he met Jasmine's cold and disapproving gaze.

***

After his break – during which Jasmine pretended to be too busy to talk to him – Hendra returned to the cage where he was suspended during his sets, four metres above ground. On his whim, the cage could slide along a rail across the full diagonal of the room.

Hendra scanned the hysterical crowd, jumping in sync with the infernal rhythm imposed by DJ Violetta who was still mixing. The loudspeakers vibrated so much that it sounded like they might explode at any moment. One of Hendra's favourite French electro-house artists, Vitalic, would make for a perfect transition, he decided – provided that he doubled the speed, that is.

While digital technology had long supplanted vinyl records, mixing panels still consisted of two (or more) turntables in the form of digital music players (called CDJs) with a back-lit top cover rotating at the same tempo as the music of the CD (or MP3 file) underneath. Like the good old turntables, these modern versions could be hand-controlled for beatmatching, scratching or box-beating. Yet Hendra often found himself missing the real thing – like how he preferred the antiquated ceiling fan in his apartment to the sleek air-conditioning system.

Headset to his ear, he adjusted the beat of his chosen track to the hardcore music before switching to Vitalic with one quick push of the mixer. When he lowered his gaze, he saw a young Indonesian with a rapper cap raising his arms in his direction and coordinating all his moves with the binary rhythm of the French composer. Hendra smiled at him. Some days he thought he only lived for these moments when he was in perfect communion with his public. He closed his eyes and started to dance, his left hand tweaking the bass slider, adjusting it to his mood like a surfer who orientates his board to catch the best waves.

Clearly, he was already flying high, sky high, and he knew that later the comedown would be all the tougher because he had no ketamine to cushion it. Fortunately, Jasmine had promised to sleep at his place tonight, and so, should he experience a crash landing, he would be able to seek comfort in her arms ... What a joy this Vitalic track. He could never get enough of its formidable raw energy. But now the music was almost over and to choose the next piece he would have to scan the floor and check the pulse of the room. Did the crowd seem like it wanted to dance to something more aggressive? Or faster? Hendra opened his eyes.

He felt the blood leaving his face. Empty. The dancefloor was totally empty. Could the clubbers have vanished because they didn't like his music? No, no, impossible. It had to be a hallucination. Not a common effect of X pills, especially when they were as pure as those sold by XS, but it could happen. He blinked and turned in his cage to face the circular central bar – nobody there either, except for the waitresses in their red uniforms. He squinted and realised that they were huddled in the middle, their mouths wide open as if they were screaming – but with the music drowning all other noises, he couldn't hear anything, and for a fleeting instant he thought they looked like giant gasping goldfishes. All of sudden, they all pointed at something in front of them, before diving behind the counter.

Under X, the reel never spins at the right speed, it's either too slow or too fast. But despite being in full slow-motion mode, Hendra finally understood that something wrong was happening at XS. He turned his head in the direction the waitresses had pointed and saw three men, dressed all in black but for white hoods, pushing forward and swinging baseball bats before them.

At last, thought Hendra. At last, they were getting a visit from the White Brigade, the vigilante organization which had taken upon itself to contain the unbridled expansion of vice activities in the Indonesian capital. Not that Hendra welcomed in any way this intrusion which interrupted his mix and his ecstasy high, but he had always wondered why they had never been targeted before. The White Brigade tended to come down very hard on clubs like XS that didn't shut down or at least scale down during Ramadan. Nicknamed the White Brigade because of the colour of their members' hoods, the militia was popular with certain sections of the local population who viewed favourably their vice-cleansing operations.

Hendra himself wouldn't have minded an XS with fewer prostitutes – and maybe even fewer drugs – but Pak Kelvin, the club owner, had once told him that if they stopped these 'little side businesses', they might have to close shop because 'many people only came to XS for *that*.' (Hendra also knew that his boss was in cahoots with one of the X and shabu factories which flooded Jakarta's nightclubs with their products.) The 60-year-old ethnic Chinese regularly boasted about his excellent connections with the police and had convinced himself that he was untouchable.

That XS would never be attacked by the White Brigade. But when he had defied them a few months earlier by keeping his club open during Laylat al-Qadr – the 27th and most sacred night of the fasting month – Hendra had thought that Pak Kelvin was playing with fire. And tonight's events were proving him right.

Hendra finally noticed the clubbers cowered behind the large sofas surrounding the dancefloor while the three White Brigade members carried on with their 'clean-up' operation. Material damage only, whether it was the bar tops or bottles of alcohol exploding under their battering. The aim was to frighten and purify without any bloodshed.

Hendra was beginning to wonder why he couldn't hear any sound from all the glass breaking around him, when he realised that he still hadn't stopped the music. 'Join in the Chant' by Nitzer Ebb, a 90s English EBM song and the next piece on his USB key after Vitalic, was now playing, with the three-word shout chorus – 'muscle and hate' – punctuating the militiamen's forceful blows. Hendra decided to interrupt his mix while the storm wreaked havoc. Later, he would play again for those clubbers still brave enough to dance – or too stoned to go home.

He paused the music on his control panel although the turntables continued to spin – he had never understood how to turn them off without powering down the whole DJ deck. Closing his eyes, he started to float away, carried off by the sounds of breaking bottles which had replaced Nitzer Ebb's screams of hatred, feeling like he was listening to a gamelan orchestra in the midst of tuning. He was brought down to earth when a shout, louder than the others, startled him. He opened his eyes, blinded momentarily by the bright lights now flooding the nightclub, and quickly understood that the White Brigade attack was about to go awry. Momo, one of the XS bouncers – who Hendra had long suspected of popping X pills during his work shift – had decided to interfere. Facing the three hooded members, he was challenging them with a switchblade, drawing large Os in the smoky air.

Hendra heard one of the White Brigade members scream: 'Get the fuck out of the way, *goblok*!'

But Momo lunged forward and plunged his knife in one vigilante's thigh.

A scream of pain resonated throughout XS, but the bouncer's victory didn't last long. A second militiaman came to the rescue and struck Momo in the stomach with his bat. Momo bent over and crumpled to the floor.

'You're going to pay for this!' screamed the injured man, who was already back on his feet.

Straddling the club bouncer lying supine on the floor, the hooded vigilante struck Momo's head with repeated swings of his baseball bat, wielding it as effortlessly as a conductor's baton. Cutting through the clubbers' and waitresses' screams of terror, Hendra thought he heard the sound of a ripe jackfruit exploding as it crashed to the ground. As two more vigilantes grabbed their frenzied accomplice around the waist and forced him towards the exit, the man continued to scream: 'Next time we'll bomb this place! Sons of Shaytan!'

Understanding that the night was definitively over, Hendra removed his USB key of techno tracks and slipped it into his pocket. For a while his gaze lingered on the mixing console with the two spinning turntables – where the hell was that on/off switch? – until he finally gave up and started descending the ladder.

By the time he reached the dancefloor, a crowd of traumatized clubbers was walking in the opposite direction, towards the club exit, under the reassuring guidance of the XS security team. Hendra reached the place where Momo the bouncer was lying in a pool of blood with his eyes wide open as if imploring people to help him. Stuck to the bar's zinc top, Hendra thought he could make out fragments of brain, but he also knew it might well be his own imagination running amok under the effects of X. Especially since it was the first time he found himself inside XS with all the lights on. The harsh white colours bathing the club seemed so surreal. Like in a dream.

'There's nothing we can do for him,' said Pak Kelvin after failing to detect a pulse in Momo's neck.

Jasmine had left the bar to join Hendra at the site of the slaying. With the fluorescence effect under the UV light of a nearby projector that nobody had thought to switch off, her red dress had taken on a weird hue that looked similar to coagulated blood. She was shivering. And crying. Hendra held her in his arms. Caressing the contour of her ear, he brushed the roots of her blue curls where the hair was thinner than a baby's.

'Why did they kill Momo?' she asked. 'He was a nice guy. He has two children, you know?' Jasmine took an interest in the personal lives of all her colleagues.

Momo, a nice guy? wondered Hendra. That's not what he would call a family man who routinely hooked up with underage girls … The security head was known to let undocumented female teenagers enter the club in exchange for 'extras'.

'But why did he have to interfere?' he said. 'If he hadn't provoked those guys, he'd still be alive!'

Jasmine released herself from his embrace, staring at him with outraged eyes as if he had said something totally egregious. Then, kneeling, she took Momo's right hand and recited the usual Muslim prayer for when someone passes away.

'*Inna lillahi wa inna ilayhi raji'un.* Verily we belong to Allah, and verily to Him do we return. O Allah, forgive Momo, raise his degree among those who are rightly guided, grant him a successor in his descendants who remain. Forgive us and him, O Lord of the Universe, and make his grave spacious, and grant him light in it.'

Twenty minutes later, the medics finally arrived. They tried to carry Momo's body out on a stretcher but the metal frame wouldn't fit inside the lift, so, with the help of Jasmine and Hendra who were making sure the body didn't slip, they cautiously climbed down four flights of stairs.

After the ambulance left, Hendra and Jasmine went back up to the club. Loud voices filled the main hall as they walked in. The police had arrived and things didn't seem to be going well for Pak Kelvin.

'What do you mean it's just an accident? One of my bouncers is dead, and you're telling me it's just an *accident*?'

'A very unfortunate accident,' answered one man – short-legged, overweight and with sleek black hair – who behaved like he was the squad leader. 'X overdose. His head exploded. That's terrible.' He burst out laughing, and his colleagues joined in.

'Think you can fuck with me like that?' Pak Kelvin crushed broken glass under his feet. 'Tomorrow, I'll talk to the chief of police!'

'Talk to your chief of police if that makes you happy. But let me tell you something, Pak. If you want to me to search for the perps of a beating gone wrong, I might also have to look into all those thriving little traffickings of yours. But we can certainly close XS if that's what you want. *You* choose ...'

***

Half an hour later, after Jasmine was done comforting the other waitresses, they made their way home to Hendra's apartment. He lived in Glodok, the same old Chinese neighbourhood as XS, and his flat was less than ten minutes away on foot, so he generally walked back home. But tonight, Jasmine insisted on taking a taxi.

'Did you hear the guy's threats before he left the club?' she asked, as they sat in the back of a Bluebird.

Hendra just nodded.

'And he was completely gone, you know. I saw his eyes through his white hood and that totally freaked me out. His right eyeball was like ... frozen.'

'Really? I was too far from the fight. Couldn't see much, you know.'

'Hmm ... Or maybe, you were just too fucked up to see anything clearly? Look at yourself, you look like a zombie!'

He stared at his image in the rear-view mirror: his face was as white as a sheet and his green eyes were wide open like he was about to scream. He was indeed not at his best. Certainly not the 'model good looks' that Jasmine liked to praise.

'How many pills did you take tonight? And why wait so bloody long to switch off the music?'

Hendra remained silent, mechanically drawing his 'signature' on his handphone, as if wanting to unlock it. All his girlfriends before Jasmine were also hooked on drugs. Some were even more of a junkie than him and had dragged Hendra far down the dope route. But Jasmine hated drugs and wanted him to quit everything. To be fair, he had been totally off K and heroine for the past six months, only contenting himself with some harmless X from time to time. But tonight he wouldn't have minded a bit of ketamine; the evening had been cut short and without anything to bring him down he would probably not be able to sleep before 7 or 8 am.

As the taxi pulled up in front of his apartment building on Jalan Mangga Besar VIII, Hendra put his phone back in the front pocket of his denim jacket – a new one from Pot Meets Pop that he had purchased the previous weekend at a factory outlet in Bandung. Now that he had stopped buying all sorts of powdery dust to complement XS's free pills, he had more money to splurge on fancy clothes.

Back in the flat, while Jasmine was taking a shower, Hendra searched desperately through his bedroom nightstand drawer where he used to stash his dope, hoping to find any left-behinds. There was nothing, not even an empty sachet. He licked his index finger before running it inside the drawer, but as soon as he brought it to his mouth, he realised that he had only collected dirt. Feeling totally hopeless, he swallowed one Lexotan pill and lay on the bed.

When Jasmine joined him in the room, her anger seemed to have abated. She was all smiles and had even removed the new nose piercing he didn't like. Hendra laid his hands on her breasts, always so supple, so gracious, so exciting. One day, she had told him that she had to massage her breasts every morning for ten to twenty minutes to prevent the silicon from hardening. Ever since making love to a *waria* for the first time at 20 years old, Hendra could not get enough of the feeling. The sex was always so pure, so intense, so *radical*. In his eyes, warias were not transgender women – they formed a real third sex[1]. He loved Jasmine as she was, with that wonderful male organ embellishing her woman's body, investing it with an irresistible sensuality. He didn't want to hear about the gender reassignment surgery that some warias kept talking about. He didn't want Jasmine to become female.

They started to make love, but although his penis was incredibly hard – probably harder than the baseball bat which had smashed Momo's head – he had absolutely no sensation on the glans, as if his sex had been plunged into a bowl of cocaine. After penetrating Jasmine for thirty minutes without getting close to ejaculating, he conceded defeat. He knew that if he insisted, he might find himself in the morning with his foreskin covered in blisters – as had happened a couple of times in the past. He apologized to Jasmine who was staring at him with a reproachful look, having no doubt guessed the reason behind his anorgasmia problems. To redeem himself, he offered her a blowjob but she told him that she wasn't in the mood anymore and switched off the light.

In the dark, next to the sleeping form of Jasmine, the other event of the night suddenly came back to Hendra's mind. TMM, his father ... That looming bad trip was now inescapable.

---

1 The term *waria* in Indonesia is traditionally used to describe third-gender biologically male individuals, although it's also now commonly applied to transgender women. In this book, the pronoun 'she' has been employed when referring to Jasmine in the English language – in line with the gender with which she identifies. But it should be noted that in Bahasa Indonesia, third-person pronouns are all gender-neutral, which means that trans and genderqueer people do not have in principle to pick a specific gendered pronoun.

2

With a black skullcap folded in his hands, Hendra rushed down the stairs of his building two steps at a time. It was already 11.30 am and he didn't want to be late for Friday prayers at Masjid Arrahim.

The mosque, located in the same side alley as XS, was where he usually attended the compulsory weekly sermon. He liked Haji Ahmad, the imam who officiated there: a gentle 70-year-old man who had long ago stopped complaining about the noise and other disturbances caused by the club and its rowdy clientele. On the contrary, he welcomed with open arms all those who wanted to perform the Fajr prayer before heading home after partying all night long – so long as they weren't intoxicated.

Hendra walked briskly along Jalan Mangga Besar Raya, hoping to reach the mosque before the gathering storm above his head exploded. Halfway down the busy road, a street vendor planted herself in front of him.

'Boss, can you buy me something, please?' she said, shoving beauty cream samples in his face.

When Hendra's eyes met the young girl's, his stomach instantly churned. The countless filiform warts on her face gave her skin the appearance of a lava field – one that would have put to shame Krakatau's rugged slopes. Hendra shook his head and resumed his walk, quickening his pace. He couldn't wait to hear what Haji Ahmad would say about last weekend's events. Surely he would bring them up in his sermon.

Hendra reached the mosque entrance. From the outside, Masjid Arrahim's corrugated Islamic dome looked like an overgrown brown mushroom whose symmetry was broken only by a diminutive minaret which barely rose above the neighbourhood's three- or four-storey buildings. Similarly unassuming, the mosque's interior was mostly bare except for the worn-out prayer mats, the *minbar* from where Haji Ahmad pronounced his sermons, and the few rusty fans hanging from the walls. Such frugality was not wholly intentional; for its upkeep, the Arrahim mosque had to rely on the generosity of the public but outside of Ramadan the *zakat* box placed in front of the *mihrab* often remained empty. In the Glodok neighbourhood, people were not well off and those who had some money were usually ethnic Chinese – and therefore mostly Buddhist or Christian. That didn't prevent the muezzin's powerful call for prayer from rising five times a day over the street hubbub, forcefully reminding believers of Allah's greatness.

Skullcap now on his head, Hendra removed his Doc Martens and socks before joining the crowd of people massed in front of the three-foot-high sliding gate. Half-shut outside prayer times, the blue metal barrier with its paint peeling off in ragged strips, had been pulled aside to let the faithful stream in. After performing his ablutions at the dedicated *wudu* area, Hendra passed under an arched ceiling standing on green pillars adorned with Arabic inscriptions and finally reached the main prayer hall. He sat cross-legged on the floor in the front row, a few metres away from the *minbar*, before deciding to perform a few *rakaat* while waiting for the sermon to begin.

His religious observance might not have been perfect, but it was steady. He prayed at least twice a day – at dawn, for Fajr, and at sunset, for Maghrib – dutifully fasted during Ramadan and paid *zakat*, the mandatory Muslim alms, every year. It was in the area of *haram* substance consumption that he regularly strayed from the right path, although for the last few months he had cut down considerably on his past excesses. Even so, Hendra knew that total abstinence would most likely always be out of reach for him. How could DJ Radikal not take an XTC pill from time to time? Jasmine, on the other hand, was way stricter than him. Unless under exceptional circumstances, she never missed any of the five daily prayers. And she never consumed alcohol – much less any sort of drug. Her only real misconduct, as far as Islam was concerned, was that she engaged in pre-marital sex with Hendra. And even this was through no fault of hers, because warias had no legal existence in Indonesia, which made marriage a rather unlikely, if not impossible, proposition.

Having been seated on the floor awaiting Haji Ahmad's arrival, the congregation stood up as one when the imam walked into the praying hall, donning his usual *Haji* white cap – worn only by Muslim men who had made the pilgrimage to Mecca. The old man was balding and along his temples the remaining salt and pepper hair was so thin that Hendra often wondered how it had not already fallen out. His short goatee was almost as sparse, although this state of affairs probably had more to do with Indonesian genes – not really conducive to beard growing – rather than with the imam's advanced age. Above his square glasses, in contrast, his eyebrows were surprisingly thick, as if through practice, devotion and concentration, the reading of the Quran had created some sort of hair callus around his dark brown eyes.

Haji Ahmad ascended the *minbar* before launching into a recitation of Al-Fatihah, the Quran's first *surah*. The old man's strong and melodious voice filled the room, warmly enveloping the faithful in its religious fervour. The out-of-season storm Hendra had avoided earlier had just started, and as the mango tree's thick foliage covering the mosque's roof couldn't totally insulate it from the heavy tropical rain, from time to time the corrugated dome emitted sonorous plinks which seemed to punctuate the imam's incantation.

After they finished reciting Al-Fatihah together, Haji Ahmad cleared his throat a few times, while striking the wooden floor of the raised platform with his pilgrim stick in order to indicate the beginning of the sermon.

'*Allahu akbar, allahu akbar, Ma'asyiral muslimin wal muslimat,* O believers, let us first express our gratitude to Allah, the Almighty, for His unconditional love for us. May He continue to guide us and bestow upon us the strength, patience and courage to rise above each obstacle with which we are faced.'

He took a long pause before hammering the pulpit's floor again with his stick, much more forcefully this time. Sitting cross-legged on the prayer mat, Hendra could feel the vibrations all the way to his stomach. The old man resumed talking, his voice swelling with anger.

'Why, my brothers, why is the peace message from Allah *subḥānahu wata'ālā* insulted, perverted and violated every single day by people who call for murder in the name of Islam? Who are these so-called Muslims who commit hideous crimes, who kill men, women and children alike, supposedly to serve Allah? They are assassins, miscreants, damned souls; that's what they are! The real martyrs are all the innocents who die at their hands, whatever their race or religion, while the coward terrorists who blow themselves up will go straight to Hell!'

The imam stopped and scanned the room. Hendra felt that the congregation was holding its breath. Even the rain appeared to have paused. At last, Haji Ahmad continued his sermon with the same raw rage bloating his words. Like always, he first recited passages of the Quran or the Sunnah in Arabic before translating the sacred words into Bahasa.

'As mentioned in one hadith in Sahih Al-Bukhari, our Prophet, peace be upon him, once said: "There will appear some people among you whose prayer will make you look down upon yours, and whose fasting will make you look down upon yours, and whose deeds will make you look upon yours. They will recite the Quran, but their words will not exceed their throats and they will go out of Islam as an arrow goes out through the game." My dear brothers, you must ignore all these preachers of hate who declare that if you don't join their jihad, you are not real believers. Because *they* are the apostates, *they* are the ones who have repudiated their religion!'

Usually more restrained, Haji Ahmad was speaking with unabated frenzy today, staring at the audience with such intensity that when his gaze met Hendra's, the XS DJ instinctively lowered his eyes.

'What is jihad, this sacred word that malicious people use and abuse to push lost souls into hatred and senseless violence? Jihad is first and foremost the spiritual war that we have to wage every day against temptations, against our inner demons, against evil, so that we can continue to follow the straight path.

'Jihad is also the fight for the common good and the betterment of our society. A fight, if you undertake it, which will earn you many rewards on the Day of Judgement. And there are plenty of organizations in Indonesia with noble causes that you can certainly join to make our world a more caring place.

'Yes, this spiritual fight can sometimes turn into a physical one, but only if you are forced, under duress, to abjure your faith. And even in this situation, our Prophet, peace be upon him, said: "Stop, O people, that I may give you ten rules for your guidance in the battlefield. Do not commit treachery or deviate from the right path. You must not mutilate dead bodies. Neither kill a child, nor a woman, nor an aged man. Bring no harm to the trees, nor burn them with fire, especially those which are fruitful. Slay not any of the enemy's flock, save for your food. You are likely to pass by people who have devoted their lives to monastic services; leave them alone."

'Jihad is not a divine commandment to expand Allah's kingdom by force and war. If we want to spread Allah's words, we must do so with compassion and love, and not through murder and *terror*.'

Straightening himself, Haji Ahmad adjusted his skullcap, which had slipped onto his forehead, before continuing in a slightly calmer tone: 'Last week, a tragedy happened not far from here, in a nightclub that I'm sure some of you know about or even patronize. Pretending to be acting in the name of Islam, three assassins beat our dear Momo to death. Yes, there are so many things forbidden by God taking place at XS every day. But do we have the right to kill other persons just because they engage in haram activities? Isn't this Allah's responsibility, and only His, to decide upon these sinners' fate on the Day of Judgement? We must all have the courage to denounce the murderous impostors who want to usurp God's place. Now, let's say a small prayer for our Brother Momo.'

They all recited in unison. 'May Allah place him amongst those that He mentions in the surah Al-Fajr: "O soul at peace, return to your Lord, well-pleased and pleasing; enter among My righteous servants; and enter My Paradise."'

After the congressional two-*rakaat* prayer following the end of the sermon, everybody shook hands. Some who recognized Hendra offered their condolences for Momo's death, and he thanked them absentmindedly.

How different were spiritual and physical jihads, he couldn't help wondering. Could you really do one without the other? Picking up his boots in front of the mosque's sliding entrance gate, he headed towards XS. He was supposed to start mixing at 2 pm. Weekends started early at Pak Kelvin's nightclub.

3

'*Sayang*, can you give us two gin and tonics?' Hendra asked Jasmine. 'On the strong side, please.'

'For your friend,' replied Jasmine, winking at Alessandro, 'I'm going to pour a double dose. But for you, my dear, it'll be tonic only. You're on duty tonight if I'm not wrong.'

Hendra had once again run into the bule during his break and this time Alessandro said he had a surprise for him.

Tonight, the girl at his side was a bit older. Early twenties, with a transparent sequined top glittering under the laser flashes, she also looked much less stoned than Alessandro's conquest the other day. She stood behind him, motionless, like she was waiting for a bus. Maybe not a fan of techno, thought Hendra. Yeah, come to think of it, she didn't appear to be one of those hopeless teenage ravers clinging to bules at XS, expecting them to bankroll their X consumption in exchange for sex. This girl simply looked like she was after Alessandro's real hard cash. Was she one of these *cewek*-for-hire on the fourth floor, whom this bule would have picked up before going dancing?

As was the case every time Hendra was confronted with what some Indonesians called a night butterfly – an expression that was way too poetic for his taste – he started to experience a strange feeling that he never quite understood. The closest word that he could find to describe the sensation coming over him was disgust – even though he didn't actually despise the girl in any way. In practice, Hendra carefully avoided XS's top floor which was nothing more than a giant brothel where prostitutes seated on red leather sofas waited for johns to choose them. Sometimes, though, he would bump into one of the girls in the lift, or on the dancefloor like right now, when a clubber invited his catch to dance with him. 'Men want to be able to empty their balls when they go clubbing,' Pak Kelvin had once told him, always so attentive to his clientele's needs. 'This is a service that we have to offer.'

Their drinks arrived. 'This is for you,' Alessandro said, handing Hendra a collector's edition CD of Front 242 – one of the most famous EBM bands from the 80s and 90s.

'Wow, thank you!' said Hendra, beaming as he read the album's title. *Geography*, his favourite from the Belgian band.

Alessandro explained that it was his way of congratulating Hendra for being crowned DJ of the year by RCTV. Unfortunately, the bule added, he would not be around when Hendra received his title next weekend, as he would be partying at a friend's villa in Bali.

Alessandro – who, tellingly, sported a skinny white t-shirt bearing the slogan 'Zombies don't like fast-food' in Bahasa – seemed to have become even thinner since the first time they had met. Tonight, thought Hendra, he looked more like a parched camel than an elegant one. A camel losing his humps under the daily fire of the MDMA, the main ingredient of X pills and a derivative of amphetamine. A few drops of acid were often added to provide a more psychedelic high, but the overall effect remained the same: an intoxicating sensation of invincibility combined with a potentially dangerous loss of appetite. After popping their pills, the clubbers would dance like madmen (or madwomen), going without food, and sometimes even water, for hours on end.

Only a year ago, Hendra had dropped to 125 pounds on his five-foot-ten-inch frame (despite often arguing with Jasmine that, in his case, Xs were no more harmful than caffeine because he had everything under control). Fortunately, he was now back up to 150 pounds. Alessandro still had a few more humps to lose before hitting rock bottom but he was making fast progress and would be there in no time. Would he bounce back? Hendra doubted it. Very few bule clubbers like Alessandro ever bounced back. As far as he could tell, they just disappeared one day – hopefully having been repatriated to their home country.

'Care to do some K with me?' asked Alessandro. 'I found some *very*, *very* good ones.'

A sure giveaway of someone flying high on X, he kept clenching his jaws and grinding his teeth. Like a proud camel, thought Hendra.

He was never a fan of taking K when he still had to mix for the night. Under the powerful anaesthetics (normally used to put horses to sleep), he often became too mellow and risked losing the aggressive edge that was DJ Radikal's trademark. But it would have been impolite to turn Alessandro down after the present that he had just received. Never mind, he would just sniff a tiny speck, and with a bit of luck Alessandro would be too fucked up to notice.

'Thanks for the offer,' said Hendra, 'that'd be nice.' Then, seeing that the bule was searching through his pockets, he quickly added: 'No, not here! They'll kick you out if you powder your nose at the bar. Let's go to the toilets.'

('Too dangerous,' Pak Kelvin had replied one day when Hendra had asked him why snorting was forbidden inside XS. Hendra couldn't tell whether his boss was referring to the risks of overdose or to possible police intervention.)

'I see, so we're going to lock ourselves in the john like two faggots,' said Alessandro, laughing as though it was the funniest thing he had heard in a long time.

He whispered something into the girl's ear and she took off with a sour face before pressing the nearby lift's *up* button, confirming Hendra's suspicion – yes, she was returning to her quarters on the top floor. Raising his hand to catch Jasmine's attention, Hendra left his new CD with her while he 'went to the toilet'.

It took them a while to cut their way through the thick crowd to the restroom area on the other side of the club. Only ten days had passed since the White Brigade attack but it was as if nothing had happened. XS was already packed to the brim and it wasn't even the weekend yet.

They squeezed together inside a cubicle before bolting the door. Straightaway, Alessandro knelt in front of the bowl and set to wiping the lid with toilet paper. And as there was almost none left on the roll, he had to finish the job with the sleeve of his silk shirt. That's when Hendra noticed Alessandro's hair was even more slicked back than Leonardo Di Caprio's in *Gatsby*. Long locks were stuck to the top of his head, maybe to hide the early signs of baldness.

'Tell me,' started Alessandro, while carefully tearing a K

sachet above the now sparkling clean toilet lid, 'didn't you say your old man was the head of the TMM factory in Batam in the 80s?'

'Yeah. Why?'

'So, your padre's Hadi Harsono, right?' the bule asked, turning around and facing Hendra with the expectant smile of a good pupil who has just answered a tough question. Except that Hendra was never going to give him – or anyone else for that matter – any stars for trying to guess his father's name. 'Hey dude, don't stare at me like that. It was very easy to find your padre's name, I just had to ask our managing director's personal assistant. She's been with TMM for thirty years and she remembered who was the Batam factory's boss for much of the 80s. I even did some research on LinkedIn and found your father's full résumé.'

'But how's that your business?' asked Hendra, who actually felt more stunned than angry. Yes, Hadi was his father's first name although Dini, his mum, had always told him that his Indonesian-Chinese surname was Wijono, not Harsono. Could it be the same person?

Alessandro stood up, looking apologetic, and gave Hendra a gentle tap on the shoulder.

'Don't get upset, man! I just found it so funny that your old man had worked in the same company as me. I'm very curious by nature. In Italy, I was nicknamed the *donnola*, the weasel, because I liked to snoop around.'

'I see,' said Hendra, still in shock.

'And your father's a big shot now,' continued Alessandro as he knelt again and started drawing lines of K on the lid. 'He's the CEO of TCC, our biggest competitor.'

Hendra's head started to spin. The former manager of the TMM factory in Batam in the 80s was still alive while his dad was supposed to be long dead and buried.

'*Sprechen Sie Deutsch*?' asked Alessandro, a stupid smile splattered across his face.

'What?' replied Hendra.

'You don't speak German?'

'No … why?'

'Didn't you pick up a few words of German when you lived in Munich as a young punk?'

'Munich? Why would I have lived in Munich?'

Alessandro frowned. 'You mean you didn't follow your padre after Batam, when he went to work for several years in our Munich HQ?'

'But how do you know all this about … Hadi Harsono?'

'It's all on LinkedIn!'

'What's LinkedIn?'

'Wait, what, you've never heard of LinkedIn? In what world do you live, dude! LinkedIn, it's like Facebook but for your professional contacts.' Then pulling out his latest Samsung phone: 'Look, here's your old man's full CV online.'

Hendra almost snatched the phone out of Alessandro's hands, accidentally locking it as he pressed the side button. But he had already noticed Alessandro's Z signature on the screen and managed to unlock it. After anxiously browsing through Hadi Harsono's CV, he finally calmed down – this man could not be his dad. Hadi Harsono had left Batam for Germany in January 1987, eighteen months before he, Hendra, was born.

'Not my father, for sure,' he said, returning Alessandro his phone. 'My father was based in Batam until well into 1988.'

'Really? He must have been Hadi Harsono's successor then.'

'Maybe. For all I know, he might never have been the factory head.'

Hendra was lying. He just had to close his eyes to picture his mother's face washed with tears and hear her pleading voice when she repeated: 'Sayang, your dad was the big boss in Batam, the *manajer umum*. What more do you want to know?'

But right now, he just wanted to cut short this grotesque discussion with Alessandro, a discussion which should never have started in the first place. And so he quickly added, hoping to placate any further questioning, 'I know very little about my dad as my parents divorced when I was very young.'

'I see,' said the bule. Then after a pause, 'Do you know that this chap, Hadi Harsono, had quite a reputation, according to the PA? She told me he was a helpless womanizer, and that's why he was sent to Germany.'

Alessandro snorted with his loud, obscene laugh, making Hendra's blood boil almost beyond the point of no return. Yes, the bule was snooping around way too much, and at this rate, he was going to end the night with Hendra's fist in his face.

'So, what are we waiting for?' he said. 'Let's fucking sniff this K, OK!'

Alessandro finished preparing two lines of K, making them as thin as possible with his credit card. 'The Flazz Card to get a flash!' he said, waving his plastic.

Flazz was the marketing name that the local bank, BCA, had given to its new contactless payment cards, and the card was plastered on billboards all over town.

By now, Hendra was totally fed up with Alessandro and his stupid jokes. Let's get it over and done with, he thought, while rolling the brand-new 10,000 rupiah note that Alessandro had given him. Hard to find, crisp new notes were junkies' favourites because all too often with older ones a little bit of powder would remain stuck within the creases during the upwards drug transit, and so after sniffing one had to unfold and lick the note or, more radically, swallow it.

In one go, Hendra sniffed the full two lines. A bitter taste quickly flooded his mouth. What was it again that he had told himself ten minutes ago? Oh, yeah … only a tiny speck.

'Wow, dude,' said Alessandro. 'That was a big one up your schnoz! In my country, we call that a beam! Guess you're going to have a very nice trip very soon … My turn, now!' And he pulled out another sachet of K, getting ready to make new lines on the toilet lid.

For Hendra, the high was already kicking in, as sudden as it was violent. Explosive. Blood was rushing to all his extremities, and he could almost feel his scalp trying to separate from his skull. Groggily, he sat down, right on the floor, not bothering about the piss stains everywhere. A profound feeling of well-being was running through his whole body. The tightening of the stomach, the difficulty breathing, the palpitations, all these painful sensations that the evocation of his father had brought on were quickly fading away. He floated in happiness.

A bang on the door pulled him out of his high. Security was telling them to come out right away. Most likely, they had been locked inside the cubicle far too long and Budi, the young transvestite who supervised the toilets, had alerted the bouncers.

'It's OK, we're coming out!' Hendra screamed, hoping that the bouncers would recognize his voice and not break the door down – as they were instructed to do to prevent ODs.

He staggered out of the cubicle and, without waiting for Alessandro, started up the stairs to return to the main hall. His mother's radiant face was flashing in front of his eyes. How beautiful she was with her high cheekbones, her delicate thin nose like a doll's, her chiselled chin. And her gorgeous dimpled smile. More beautiful even than Sandra Dewi or Nadine Ames. Had she been taller, she could have been a model. Hendra had been devastated by her death four years ago when she was run over by a *mikrolet*, a local minibus, while crossing the street.

Minutes later, as he leaned unsteadily against the bar, Jasmine stared at him in silence, her eyes full of anger and disappointment. She refused to serve him anything and forced the CD into his hands before addressing the customer next to him.

That's when Hendra felt someone pulling at his right arm. He turned his head, it was Pak Kelvin.

'What the hell are you doing here, DJ Radikal? Don't you know it's your turn to mix!'

***

'Holland Bakery on Jalan Mangga Besar Delapan,' said Hendra to the taxi driver as he eased himself into the back of the car.

'Think it's not open yet,' said the man, turning around to look at Hendra.

'I know, Pak … I live upstairs.'

The driver looked hesitant. 'Don't want no puke in my car, ok?'

'Just take me there, Pak.'

The man shrugged before switching on his (likely tampered) taximeter and driving off.

DJ Radikal's set had been an indisputable disaster. He had sniffed way too much K, especially after staying clean for six months. Completely spaced out – to the point that he could hardly see a thing – he had found himself incapable of making a proper transition between tracks. As soon as he had concluded his performance, at 5 am, he had decided to head straight home without waiting for Jasmine who only finished her shift around 9 am. And because of his blurred vision, he had opted to take one of the overpriced TransCab taxis always waiting in the early hours at the corner between XS's back alley and Hayam Wuruk, Glodok's heavily polluted artery.

During his set, Hendra's mind kept returning to the discussion with the *donnola* and that certainly didn't help with his mix either. Growing up, he had learned to push away all the painful thoughts about the mysterious circumstances of his father's death. His mother was hiding things from him, that much was clear, but there was no point torturing himself with endless questions for which there would never be any answers. Still, the doubts were always there, lurking at the back of his mind, ready to resurface at every turn. Like that day when Alessandro had pronounced the name of the German company where his father had worked until his tragic death right on the threshold of both fatherhood and marital life.

His mum, who was a simple factory worker at the TMM

facility in Batam, had fallen in love with the manajer umum, and despite their liaison being rather illicit – his father was ethnic Chinese and non-Muslim – they had planned to get married. But alas, Allah had decided otherwise; barely three weeks before they were supposed to tie the knot (and six months before Hendra's birth), Hadi had died during a horrific fire that had burned down the entire factory. Or so his mother always said whenever he plied her with questions. Already from a young age, he had found his mother's story somewhat puzzling. And one thing really bothered him: she didn't have any portrait of his dad, much less a photo with the two of them posing together.

At 14, he had consulted the archives of the weekly *Tribun Nongsa* at the central public library in Jakarta but for the whole year of 1988 he couldn't find any mention of a fire that would have ravaged Batam's TMM factory. He had read and reread the papers so many times that he ended up almost memorising all the articles. One day the librarian had even asked him what it was that he was looking for so intently that these yellowed pages might soon fall to pieces under his daily perusal. Finally, he had confronted his mum with the results of his research, accusing her of lying. But she had maintained her version of events, insisting that TMM had blocked all news articles in a bid to cover up the scandal.

Much to the cab driver's displeasure, Hendra lowered the window on his side to let in some fresh air and to try and stem the flow of his thoughts. Could this Hadi Harsono be his father? Or was the same first name really just a coincidence and, as suggested by Alessandro, Hadi Harsono's successor at the helm of the factory was none other than his father, Hadi Wijono? Hendra could have easily assuaged his curiosity by simply asking the bule to check with the PA who it was that had come after Hadi Harsono. But he had no intention of going down that route, and not just because he'd rather rot in hell than talk to Alessandro again. No, whatever it was, it didn't matter anymore and the only thing to do was to silence his restless mind, to drag all doubts back beneath the surface of his consciousness where they should have stayed but for that snooping bule.

The taxi finally stopped in front of his building. Hendra paid the driver his inflated fare and got out of the car, realising at the same time that the sun hadn't yet risen and that he had fully recovered his vision. Now that the most acute K effects were over, he knew that a more relaxing phase would kick in. That was the nice thing with ketamine: unlike many other drugs, the comedown tended to be a gentle affair.

Upon entering his flat, he completed his ablutions before performing the Fajr prayer. Then he went to bed and tried to fall asleep. But, despite the gentle waves of endorphins that the K was now spreading in his tired body, he could barely close his eyes. At 8 am, after spending two hours on his back inspecting the water seepage on his bedroom ceiling, he gave up. He got out of bed, walked to the living room and inserted a Nusrat Fateh CD into his sound system. (One year ago, he had become enthralled by the spiritual and physical trance states that the whirling dervishes could reach through their mystical music, and that's how he had discovered Nusrat Fateh, an amazing Pakistani singer who masterfully interpreted devotional Sufi songs.)

Hendra switched on his laptop that was lying on the low coffee table, first pretending to read his emails before connecting to LinkedIn. He easily relocated Hadi Harsono's public profile and again convinced himself that the dates didn't add up. The ethnic Chinese man had left the Batam factory a good few months before the time when he had been conceived.

Despite the ceiling fan spinning at full speed, sweat continued to stream down Hendra's skin. For once, he decided to switch on the aircon.

He had tried searching for his father on the Internet in the past – especially on Facebook when it took Indonesia by storm in the 2010s – but hadn't found any trace of a Hadi Wijono, a factory manager in Batam who would have died there in 1988. Only a few men of the same name who were mostly born after Hendra. This was hardly surprising though; his dad had passed away long before the rise of the Internet, and his only claim to fame, so to speak, that might have etched his name into online memory was his death in such tragic circumstances. Circumstances which, assuming his mum was telling the truth, TMM had tried so hard to cover up. But maybe LinkedIn, as a social network focused on professional lives, would be able to unearth *something* about his dad's time at TMM?

Hendra typed 'Hadi Wijono', the name he knew his father by, into the LinkedIn search box, more out of curiosity than with any real hope of finding his progenitor. Still, his pulse quickened when eight profiles came up: Ryan Hadi Wijono, a '23 yo student'; JK Hadi Wijono, sales supervisor at PT Indomarco, Jambi; Koes Hadi Wijono, etc. All way too young to be his dad – who anyway was supposed to be dead, wasn't he?

So, what now? He decided to read through all the CVs he could find belonging to past and present managers at TMM

Indonesia. Who knew if an ex-colleague or subordinate of his dad might have mentioned him in a post? He spent a lot of time researching the profile of a certain 'Winanda Prima', who had been the security manager of TMM Indonesia from 1986 to 1990, even browsing his Facebook account and other social media profiles, but no, he couldn't find a single reference to his dad – or even to Hadi Harsono for that matter. In the end, after more than two hours of poring over numerous LinkedIn profiles, he still hadn't uncovered any information about his father. Now he was ready to sleep, ready to slam shut the Pandora's box that Alessandro had cracked open the night before. And in the future he would make sure to steer clear of the bule.

He was about to close the last LinkedIn window when his attention was drawn to a selection of profiles on the right side of the screen, under the heading 'people also viewed'. In particular, that of a woman called Yasmina binte Ahmad, MD of Putra Electronics. Malay probably, going by her name. Until now, he had barely glanced at women's résumés; judging by their photos, the female professionals whose profiles popped up on his screen were way too young to have worked at the Batam facility at the same time as his dad. But this Yasmina binte Ahmad looked much older. In her 60s, probably.

He clicked on her thumbnail and enlarged the photo. The woman was really beautiful. Coquettish with ravishing black eyes enhanced by black eyeliner and mascara, and a matching black hijab that framed a radiant face with porcelain skin. In a way, it seemed as if the red lipstick was only there to prove that this wasn't a black-and-white photo. And just by looking at the screen, Hendra could almost smell her heady perfume. A perfume that was probably without alcohol, like his mother's, so that it had to be applied in large quantities to make sure the fragrance would last until the end of the day. In her profile summary, he saw that she had been educated in the US. Maybe the daughter of some rich Malaysian tycoon? Had she worked at TMM prior to joining Putra Electronics, was that why her profile had popped up? He scrolled down to her work experience and saw that she had done a stint at TCC – maybe together with Hadi Harsono? He continued to look through her résumé ... and suddenly froze. '1988-1990, Manajer Umum, TMM, Batam factory.'

For a long while he remained supine on the sofa, gripping the black fabric as if trying to cushion the fall. But the black hole swallowing him was bottomless. A sheer emptiness into which he could only disappear. He grabbed his phone. He was going to call his grandfather, scream his pain, demand explanations. Hands shaking, he dialled his grandparents' house number in Medan but hung up after two rings. How could he forget? His grandfather was sick. Very sick. He had been diagnosed with lung cancer eighteen months ago and although Hendra had not seen him since last year's Lebaran, his grandmother kept lamenting, over the phone, how fast the disease was spreading.

He felt like crying but the tears wouldn't come. All these years he couldn't help but hope that if his mother had lied it was only about the circumstances of his father's death – maybe to protect Hendra from some truth even more painful than a work accident. But no, she had also lied about his very identity! Because if his father hadn't been the manajer umum of TMM factory in Batam, who knew if he was even called Hadi Wijono? Maybe it was just a random name that his mother had picked up to keep him quiet when he had started to hassle her with his questions. Or maybe not so random ... since Hadi was also the factory manager's first name when his mother had joined TMM in late 1986. And a womanizer at that, according to the bule ...

But hadn't he always suspected there was a deeper secret than simply the facts surrounding his father's death? As a kid, he'd often had the impression that people went quiet whenever he entered a room. He had learnt to be discreet, sometimes even to tiptoe, to catch things that people wanted to hide from him. But to no avail. On the contrary, over time, his mother and grandparents continued embellishing the story, telling him countless anecdotes about his father such as his craving for *kue lapis*, the famous layered cakes from Batam; his meteoric rise at TMM despite his young age; his cycling feats; his love of Malay cooking and, of course, his green eyes, like Hendra's. As a teenager, Hendra would close his ears as soon as his mother and his *kakek*, his grandfather, began a new charade, sounding like second-rate TV actors in an Indonesian soap opera. And today, with just a flick of his fingers, Alessandro had brought down the house of cards that his family had so painstakingly built all these years.

What if his father was indeed Hadi Harsono? Even after his relocation to Germany, there was no reason why he couldn't have seen his mum again whenever he came back to Indonesia for work or on holiday.

That's when Hendra realised that his neck had become stiff. Fearful, he pressed his hand against his right temple and felt the blood vessel pulsating under his fingertips. What the fuck! Maybe because of the K still streaming inside his body, his extremities were just too sensitive? He tried again, barely brushing the temple this time. The throbbing was definitely there. Panic engulfed him. The fall wasn't over yet.

Hendra stood up, overwhelmed by a feeling of profound hopelessness. He had been free from these terrible headaches for almost four years, and now all of a sudden they were back. The headache was rapidly rising in severity, and he started pacing the corridor that led from the living room to the bedroom as the pain was already so severe that he couldn't stay in place. His head was like a fully inflated football, ready to burst. And yet, more air was being pumped inside. No mercy. It might explode, but who cares? His left eye was closing, shedding tears like a sponge being squeezed.

A few minutes later, Hendra felt that he had finally reached the point of peak pressure. Which meant that he now had to endure this state of absolute suffering – as if someone was trying to gouge his left eye out using a chisel from inside his skull – for maximum one hour. During moments like this, the only thing he could cling to was the knowledge that the pain was time-bound. The fluorescent dial of the mural clock indicated 11.05 am. So, at the latest by 12.05 pm, his ordeal would be over … until the next one. When he was in an acute phase, he could have up to five attacks a day.

The first time Hendra had experienced this type of headache eleven years ago, he had woken up his mother in the middle of the night. Shaking uncontrollably. Convinced that he was about to die. They had taken a cab to the emergency department, yet by the time they arrived his headache had disappeared. So they went home without seeing a doctor. But less than three hours later, a new attack struck and this time he was hospitalized. The doctor who examined him quickly excluded a migraine diagnosis. Yet he wasn't able to determine the cause of Hendra's headaches. Or rather, he mentioned to his mum before discharging him the next day, that his pain was likely 'psychosomatic'. Hendra didn't know what the word meant but after checking his dictionary at home he vowed never to talk about his suffering to any doctor again.

Taking a pack of ice from the freezer, he wrapped it inside a cloth before applying it to his temple. Then he started to pace in quick circles, focusing his attention on counting his steps to try and fool the pain. Unfortunately, he knew all too well that these strategies were no better than pissing in the wind. Because there was only one thing that worked in his condition: to snort something powerful like heroine or ketamine. But, bloody hell, since he was supposed to have quit months ago he had no dust whatsoever to put under his nose right now.

It was by chance that he had discovered K's calming effects on his headaches early one morning at a friend's party just as a new attack was looming. Some guys next to him had invited him to sniff K. Hendra, who had never heard of the drug, was told it was a hallucinogen originally developed as an anaesthetic for horses. And that's how he had done his very first line, betting that K wouldn't have any effect on his impending headache ... Well, he hadn't felt anything – in his head or in the rest of his body – for the next few hours. A miracle! After that, he began to take anything and everything he could lay his hands on – K, X, shabu, amphetamines, heroin, you name it. His attacks had ceased four years ago – a few months after his mother's passing – but by then he was already too much of a junkie to even think about cutting back.

From the corner of his eyes, Hendra saw that the clock indicated 11.30 am. He still had another thirty minutes to wait but he didn't know if he would be able to hold out until then. He wasn't used to this kind of excruciating pain anymore! Two pulsations – the throbbing of his head and the quickening of his heart rate – now resonated against each other.

He felt very thirsty and went to the kitchen, reaching for a glass on the rack and grabbing a fresh bottle of Aqua in the fridge. Suddenly, the chisel struck his eye even more violently and he swayed, quickly grasping the fridge door handle to avoid falling. Dizzy with rage, Hendra smashed the glass on the kitchen countertop, removed the leather armband that concealed the countless scars on his wrist and made a quick incision. It was another trick that he had discovered when he had no drugs or if they were failing to stem an attack; after cutting himself, the pain in his head would quickly ebb away. The complete remission of his headaches over the last four years meant that his past wounds were now fading and – until tonight, that is – he had hoped that he would soon be able to ditch the ugly armbands that gave him a hardcore rocker look.

Blood trickled down his forearm and he placed it above the sink so as not to stain the kitchen floor. Progressively, the throbbing moved from his head to his wrist, the soccer ball deflated and a few minutes later, the headache had vanished completely, replaced by another pain, of much lower intensity, where he had slashed his skin. He applied a plaster to the wound before returning to the living room and collapsing onto the sofa.

How he had prayed to be rid of these fucking headaches for good! Between his DJ-of-the-year award by RCTV and his passionate love affair with Jasmine, he should have been oozing with joy. Why had this abominable pain come back all of sudden? He had never been able to clearly identify a trigger. Attacks would occur anytime, whether he was asleep or awake, happy or miserable, stressed or relaxed. But he had learned to detect the moment when his neck stiffened. That was the warning sign that an attack was imminent, and if he sniffed a good dose of K or hero right then, he was often able to kill it in its tracks.

Tonight, though, he couldn't help wondering if it wasn't Alessandro's revelation which had awakened the beast. Yes, that's right, the headaches were back because of that fucker! The next time he saw him at XS, he would flatten his snooping nose. He grabbed the blue clay ashtray lying on the coffee table – a hideous souvenir from Bali, in which he liked to stub out his joints – and threw it against the wall. The ashtray bounced before hitting the shelves where he stored his CDs and *angklung* collection. Some of the instruments started to slide, but he managed to catch them just as they were about to crash onto the floor.

Hendra's grandfather was a passionate player of angklung, a traditional Indonesian musical instrument made of bamboo tubes clattering together to render a single note. From the age of six, each Lebaran, Hendra had received a new angklung from his grandfather, beginning with miniature bamboo tubes and moving progressively to taller ones each year. Hendra had recently joined together the first twenty angklungs on a black teak console, ordering them by height so that he could play entire melodies.

Spontaneously, he started shaking the bamboo bells and the deep sad sounds emitted by the angklungs quickly calmed him down. He sat back down on the sofa with the soothing image of Jasmine now in his mind. The attack was only an accident. There wouldn't be a second episode, simply because he would stop digging into the past. His mother had died long ago, and whatever her secret was, it had died with her.

Part II

The Inner Demons

Jakarta, May 2014

4

'One *roti abon sosis pedas*.' Hendra pointed at the pastry. Cindy, the shop assistant at Holland Bakery, nodded and picked up an empty cardboard box to pack the *roti*.

The shop occupied the entire groundfloor of Hendra's apartment block. The building's crumbling façade – which had evidently not had a facelift since colonial times – didn't deter the bakery's enthusiast clientele from lining up, often in droves, to buy the delicious pastry creations, which combined Dutch baking tradition with the Indonesian taste for spices. Hendra himself had quickly become a regular soon after the business had opened two years ago, not least because he liked to chat with Cindy. He found the young ethnic Chinese quite sexy in her form-fitting orange *kebaya* topped by a mysterious headdress – as if she were wearing on her head one of those boat-shaped Batak houses that could be found on the shores of Lake Toba. The *roti abon* was his favourite, a spice-laden loaf with sausage bits and strips of melted gruyere cheese laid over a thin layer of sambal.

He left the shop while already biting into the soft, warm bread and headed in the direction of XS.

The nightclub was open every night of the week, except on Mondays, and from Thursday noon till Sunday noon it didn't close its doors. Hardcore clubbers would be holed up inside the entire weekend, consuming X after X to keep jumping. Hendra himself, now that he had become the star DJ, mostly mixed on peak days: Thursday and Friday nights, and non-stop from Saturday evening until Sunday morning. Sometimes he also came back on Sunday afternoons when Pak Kelvin organised one of his 'tea parties'.

Tonight – Saturday 17th May 2014 – was *his* night. Around 1 am, an emcee from RCTV, one of the most popular Indonesian TV channels, would crown him DJ of the year, an award that was the outcome of an extensive online vote organized amongst Jakarta's main nightclubs. For the occasion, Hendra had slipped on a pair of skinny fit black leather pants together with a white flannel shirt that Jasmine had given him last year for his 25th birthday. Making it seem like the shirt had just been ripped, strips of clothes hung down from the long sleeves, undulating when he DJed or danced. He had also mixed up his two pairs of Doc Martens: a black shoe on the left foot and a red one on the right.

It was thanks to music that Hendra had not completely disappeared down the junkie hole when, at the age of 16, he started to seek refuge in drugs to soothe his headaches (among other things). Not only had his grandfather passed on his passion for angklungs but he had also taught Hendra how to play other percussions, like the *kendang* in gamelan ensembles, or the *rebana*, a large tambourine of Malay origin whose four-beat rhythms were often heard at weddings or dance celebrations. And when Hendra had discovered on the Internet the EBM, a European artistic movement which also worked on a binary beat, he had experienced an aesthetic shock of sorts and taught himself to mix. He started by playing in small clubs and private parties but soon he established his reputation amongst the initiated with his unique, uncompromising music style, leading his very first fans to call him 'DJ Radikal'. In 2008, he had been the first in Indonesia to start mixing European Electronic Body Music; since then, lots of DJs had followed suit, but Hendra remained the undisputed star of what electronic music fanzines in Jakarta had nicknamed the 'electro revival movement'. He spent his days listening to, classifying, analysing, adapting and memorising techno recordings from all over the world. He also searched endlessly for new sounds within the inexhaustible treasure trove of traditional music and had just started composing himself. His dream was to be invited one day to play in one of the most famous clubs in Amsterdam, Ibiza or Berlin. On some nights, when his music flowed like a pulsating waterfall, it quenched his thirst for the absolute, and he might even have forgotten to pop ecstasy pills.

In his glory days, he could gobble up to three or four Xs a day, seven days a week. No wonder that afterwards he had to take large amounts of heroin, sometimes through injection, to come down and sleep. Thank God, with Jasmine's help and love, he had finally found the strength, one year ago, to start cutting back. Now he occasionally took some X – and that too only when he was mixing – and in rare moments of weakness he succumbed to the temptation of K, like that ill-fated night with Alessandro. But the smack, no more. He had vowed never to fall into the trap of heroine again. It had been too painful to wean himself off the 'orgasmic powder' (as he used to call it).

Hendra soon reached Jalan Hayam Wuruk, the main artery that ran across the Glodok neighbourhood from north to south.

Located halfway between the CBD and the historical port of Sunda Kelapa, Glodok was known for its major role in the riots of 2000 that had engulfed Jakarta during the time of Suharto's fall. Hundreds of ethnic Chinese had been lynched by an angry mob of *bumis* consumed with racial hatred. (Never mind that the rich descendants of the Straight Chinese who had initially settled in the area centuries ago had long deserted the old ghetto and were now living in plush villas in Menteng.) Today, Glodok was, first and foremost, the epicentre of the unbridled nightlife of which XS was the icon. Alcohol, drugs and prostitution held sway over the entire district, under the complicit watch of the police who collected their share of the illicit trades.

Six years earlier – long before starting at XS – Hendra had moved to Glodok because he really felt in his element there, much more so than in the more modern districts towards the south of town, chock-a-block with shopping centres all trying to outdo each other in glitz and tack. Jakarta's old Chinatown had remained intact, untouched by the gentrification that was swallowing more and more swathes of the city every day. Only the omnipresence of sex workers disturbed Hendra but as most of them tended to remain hidden behind their gilded storefronts, he rarely actually saw them.

Divided along its middle by Batang Hari canal, six-lane Jalan Hayam Wuruk carried heavy traffic all day long, surpassed only by the teeming commercial activity taking place on both sides of the sidewalk. Shortly after he walked past the hotel Mercure Jakarta Kota, Hendra reached its most crowded stretch. There, at night, the street vendors would take possession of the entire pavement, turning even a leisurely walk into an obstacle course.

Resellers of pirated CDs, illegal restaurant operators washing their dishes in the middle of the road, hawkers of durians, rambutans and jackfruits, peddlers of fake Viagra pills, the odd chess players – they all unabashedly blocked the passage. Illuminating all the stalls was the same crude light emitted by bare overhead light bulbs, siphoning electricity from the nearby Wisma Hayam Huruk. The only modern office building in the area, the 14-storey Wisma Hayam Huruk seemed to rise like a UFO above the dilapidated low houses covered in red graffiti that crowded the neighbourhood.

All sorts of smells collided inside Hendra's nose as he wove along the thoroughfare: exhaust fumes, rotten fruits, *ikan bilis*, over-cooked BBQ meat, refuse stench coming from the Batang Hari which, over time, had been become more of an open sewer than a canal. Some days he almost felt like puking but he also knew that if he didn't smell these smells for more than a few days, he would start craving them. He would start craving for home.

As he passed the fish store, Toko Sinar Laut, Hendra saw the large crowd that had already started to gather at the mouth of the narrow alley leading to XS. He strode on and entered the Arrahim mosque where he found himself almost alone on the central carpet. Most believers tended to perform the Isha prayer at home before going to bed.

Less than ten minutes later, Hendra exited the mosque and made for XS. Right at the corner with Hayam Wuruk, a giant denture hung two metres above ground signalling the presence of a dentist – a comical signboard which had been a source of countless hallucinations whenever he left XS under acid. As he raised his gaze towards the denture and smiled, a quick, sharp pain, like a low-intensity electric shock, radiated through his neck. Hendra froze and pressed his left temple for a long time. Long enough to convince himself that there was absolutely no pulsation under his fingers. It was a false alarm. He was being over-cautious but there was no reason to worry; since that terrible attack a few days ago, he hadn't experienced any new episodes, whereas in the past his headaches always came in clusters of three or more in one day. Clearly, that upsetting incident had only been an isolated relapse.

He resumed his walk, circumventing the gazebos belonging to the unlicensed restaurants that sold seafood right on the sidewalk and gave off a smell of acrid oil all the way to the club's entrance. He used to enjoy eating mussels there when leaving XS on Sundays around noon, until one day he had lost three kilos in one night after a bad case of food poisoning.

In front of XS, he was welcomed by Ari, the 40-year-old former boxer hired by Pak Kelvin to replace Momo as head of the security team. Following the White Brigade attack two weeks ago, Ari had supervised a complete overhaul of the safety protocols. Now, starting some fifty metres before the club entrance, barricades had been erected in the middle of the street to prevent any vehicle from passing. This new arrangement had irked the restaurant owners who were losing part of their 'terrace' in the process, but the plan had been officially endorsed by the district's chief of police. Ten more bouncers had also been added to the team, with some of them posted right before the main door, forming a human rampart. And a few assault rifles were now kept behind the cashier's desk. Just in case …

Hendra entered the main hall where DJ Violetta was mixing.

He wasn't a big fan of her ultra-hardcore sets where the BPM – beats per minute – sometimes exceeded 180. But clubbers under X were generally very fond of this kind of musical violence. On stage, go-go dancers in skinny red shorts and transparent tops were trying to follow the infernal rhythm, though unfortunately for them, the laws of gravity ensured that their breasts always bounced back with a significant lag.

Hendra strode towards the central, circular bar where Jasmine was waitressing that night. On the dancefloor a large crowd hopped madly, in sync with the music. To the side, Hendra noticed an ethnic Chinese man in his fifties wearing a black leather jacket and a pair of mirrored sunglasses, who kept rocking his head from left to right, without a break, at the same crazy speed as DJ Violetta's beat. If that guy didn't feel seasick, thought Hendra, then Xs ought to be really good tonight. The thought made him smile and when he spotted Jasmine his smile turned into a wide grin. He sat down at the bar and ordered a Red Bull without alcohol. Jasmine was still upset about his recent excesses with the bule, and he had promised to her that tonight he would keep off all haram substances. They spent the next hour whispering sweet nothings into each other's ears whenever Jasmine wasn't serving someone's drink, until it was nearly time for Hendra to take over from DJ Violetta. He blew Jasmine a kiss and headed for his cage.

It was Pak Kelvin who had thought of this set up for the DJ after attending a Cirque du Soleil performance in Singapore. He had discussed the idea with the head of set design at Aula Simfonia Jakarta Concert Hall and the latter had proposed he install a track on XS's ceiling. Hanging four metres above ground like a cable car cabin, the fully-fitted enclosed DJ booth could slide from one side of the dancefloor to the other. But the resident DJs had found the new cage both ridiculous and dangerous and had refused to set foot in it. Instead of bowing to the sensitivities of his artists, Pak Kelvin had clung to his vision and searched for a new DJ. And, just to get hired, Hendra had accepted – despite his fear of heights. Since then, the hanging cage had become DJ Radikal's trademark.

Climbing up a small ladder hidden at the back of the room, Hendra reached the cabin and actioned a command next to the mixing table to slide himself above the centre of the dancefloor.

For once, he decided to debut his mix with a sung piece. Other than when he played Front 242 or Nitzer Ebb classics, vocals were relatively rare in his sets because he preferred the violence, the minimalist purity, of the techno sound without any human voice to soften it. But sometimes – especially coming after DJ Violetta – lyrics provided a magical counterpoint to the fury of the bass sounds, like with this particular track from French DJ The Exorcist, where a Siren-sounding feminine voice chanted a mesmerizing refrain: 'Amphetamine, cocaine, caffeine, heroin, morphine, nicotine, mescaline.' He knew that Jasmine didn't like these 'junkie rhymes' as she called them, but it was certainly way more subtle and inspiring than the Spanish hit 'Ecsta si, Ecsta no, Esta me gusta, me la como yo' that DJ Violetta mixed ad nauseam.

A commotion on the dancefloor interrupted his reverie. The on-site medic team was carrying someone away on a stretcher. Probably a clubber in 'overheat' mode who had fainted. X-fuelled hyperthermia was a common occurrence at rave parties. The inevitable dehydration that resulted from long hours of non-stop dancing under the influence was often compounded by the woollen caps that ravers liked to wear, at times bringing the temperatures below their skull into zones that could be fatal. After a few deadly incidents, Pak Kelvin had decided to hire the services of two medics specifically trained to spot and treat clubbers in a state of hyperthermia. Getting high in complete safety, Pak Kelvin had explained, was a very promising segment in which he intended to become a pioneer.

Hendra slowed the music down. He was nearing the end of the build-up, the moment of maximal tension in a mix. The moment when, dizzy with excitement, and full of shared religious fervour, the crowd is waiting for the denouement, the explosion, the apotheosis. The moment when music becomes voyage. In one go, Hendra released the bass sounds and all the clubbers climaxed together. Ecstatic screams flew in from all sides. Dancers hopped like kangaroos across the dancefloor. That's when Hendra launched a series of strident beeps, creating a sensation of near panic, of sheer urgency, inside the club.

As he lowered his gaze towards the euphoric crowd, he saw Eddie, the emcee from RCTV, nodding approvingly in his direction. Hendra waved in return and would have been walking on air but for the increasing stiffness in his neck that he could no longer ignore. But no throbbing temple yet, fortunately. In between his two sets, Pak Kelvin and Eddie were to present him with his award (in the form of a pair of small golden turntables). Hopefully, the looming attack would only strike *after* the short ceremony.

'Destroyer of Worlds' by Death Cycle, the last piece of his first set, was playing. Hendra was about to reduce the pulsating bass sounds when he suddenly felt a different kind of pulsation in his left temple. His hand froze around the balance button. The headache was taking hold so quickly now that, at this rate, in a matter of minutes his head would be near the explosion point and he would not be able to receive his award! His vision became blurred. He knew he had to go to the toilet straightaway. Hurt himself. Stop the attack and then come back.

While letting the music of Death Cycle finish its course, he ripped the headset off his ears and pressed on the command button to bring the cabin back to its base. As he stumbled down the ladder, Hendra heard rather than saw Pak Kelvin come on stage to announce that Radikal had been elected DJ of the year. Loud applause reached his ears, muffled, drowned out by the ringing in his head. He didn't have the strength to stay, not even for one more minute. He rushed to the back of the club, grabbing an empty glass on his way to the toilets, before running down the stairs and locking himself inside a cubicle.

'What the fuck are you doing?' screamed Pak Kelvin, banging on the door.

Hendra didn't reply. In one hard knock against the wall, he broke the glass, removed the armband on his left wrist and made a quick incision. Sliding to the ground, eyes closed, he waited for the attack to pass. Blood oozed into the toilet bowl, taking away the pulsating pain in its brown trail. A few minutes later, the attack had been thwarted.

When Hendra finally came out of the toilet, Jasmine and Pak Kelvin stood in front of the door staring at him suspiciously. The RCTV presenter was long gone, Pak Kelvin informed him while his eyes lingered on Hendra's wrist where traces of blood were still visible. Hendra flatly apologized, explaining that he had experienced a sudden migraine attack. Now he just wanted to go home as he felt too weak to go back into the cage for his second set. Pak Kelvin shrugged and walked away, leaving Hendra alone with Jasmine.

Without a word, Jasmine grabbed his hand, holding it as tight as possible while she walked him to the exit. There, she hugged him for a long while before helping him into a taxi. He was devastated. His crowning night had been a fiasco. Worse, he had probably convinced all the people present, including the RCTV emcee, that DJ Radikal was a hopeless junkie.

5

'Why are these idiots blocking the way?' Hendra snapped, in the back of a taxi that was bringing him home, several days after the failed award ceremony. At this rate, he would never have enough time to prepare his mix for that night!

Now that he wasn't high all the time he felt like his days were getting shorter and shorter, whereas on X they seemed longer and more intense, as if one kept adding thrilling new scenes to a (rather drab) short film. Only the ending disappointed (in general).

They were stuck in a demonstration of so-called 'jockeys', who were protesting against the lifting of the '3-in-1' regulation. Implemented ten years ago, the '3-in-1' made it compulsory for motorists to carpool on congested roads during peak hours, imposing hefty fines whenever there were fewer than three people in a vehicle. But what had initially seemed like a good idea had led to the creation of a new profession, the 'jockey', who, for less than a dollar, rode along with the motorist so that the latter didn't have to pay a penalty at police checkpoints. Finally taking stock of the failure of the '3-in-1' system, the governor of Jakarta planned to rescind it, but that decision threatened to put out of business the more than one thousand jockeys who plied the streets of Jakarta during rush hour – most of them poor women with children in tow. And so, today, the soon-to-be jobless were blocking the streets around Monas, the Indonesian 'Statue of Liberty' – which some Jakartans referred to as 'Suharto's last erection' – while also burning effigies representing the evil governor.

A woman knocked on Hendra's window, and he lowered it just enough to be able to hear what she wanted from him. Horrifying tales abounded of jockeys mugging motorists – but also of male drivers molesting their defenceless female co-riders.

'What d'you want?' he asked.

'You alone?' said the young woman who carried a baby in a sarong sling tied in her back. 'Don't want no company?'

'No. Why?'

The '3-in-1' system didn't apply to taxis, which were officially considered part of the public transport system thanks to the influential Blue Bird Taxi Group's lobbying.

'Dunno. Maybe you need someone to help you relax during the ride ...'

How could she have the nerve to make this kind of proposal with a baby in her arms, thought Hendra.

'My baby hasn't eaten for the whole day,' she added when he didn't reply.

He saw a chance. 'Listen, I'm late for my appointment. Think you could ask your friends over there to let us through?'

Hendra slipped her a 10,000 rupiah note through the window gap. She smiled, swiftly hiding the money inside the sarong sling, before getting everyone to make way for Hendra's taxi.

He was on his way back from a pointless appointment with a neurologist in the south of Jakarta. To be nice to Jasmine, he had agreed to see this specialist recommended by her brother – a surgeon at Pondok Indah hospital, one of the most well-regarded in Jakarta – but he had wasted his time. After Hendra had described his symptoms, the neurologist had given him a funny look and asked if he had felt 'anguished or anxious lately'. In the end, Hendra had left the doctor's office with a full-page prescription for painkillers. Well done, doc ... but if painkillers were the answer, he already knew of the best ones in the world – except that they were now off-limits to him.

Sadly, after a four-year respite, his headaches were back with a vengeance; since the last incident at XS, he had had attacks every single day, sometimes as many as five daily. But he just had to hang in there now and hope that sooner or later he would enjoy a new remission period.

After his disastrous award ceremony at XS, Hendra had had a hard time convincing Pak Kelvin that it really was a painful migraine episode rather than a bad trip that had forced him to harm himself inside a locked toilet cubicle. On giving him his set of miniature golden turntables, Pak Kelvin had recommended that Hendra send his apologies to the RCTV presenter. Which he had done, via WhatsApp, without getting a reply.

When the taxi reached the intersection between Jalan Mangga Besar Raya and Jalan Hayam Wuruk, they ground to a halt. Mangga Besar Raya was already chock full with the usual bumper-to-bumper late-afternoon traffic. Hendra decided to walk the last 500 metres home and paid his fare. As he exited the car, he felt drizzle on his face but shrugged it off. In Jakarta, such a trickle of water hardly constituted rain.

As soon as he reached his apartment building, Hendra climbed to the third floor, two steps at a time. As he opened the door, he was surprised to find Jasmine waiting for him in the living room watching TV. Even though she had keys to his flat, she hadn't said she would drop by before starting her shift at XS.

'What are you doing here?' he asked Jasmine after giving her a perfunctory kiss on the lips.

'What a nice welcome!'

'Sorry, sayang ... I'm a bit stressed. I've yet to prepare anything for my mix tonight.'

'I was on my way to XS and thought I'd pay you a surprise visit and maybe more ...' she said with a suggestive smile. 'But first, what did the doctor say?'

'He's given me a long list of painkillers. But honestly, sayang, I've been there before. I don't think it'll have any effect on my headaches.'

'Just give it a try, please.'

Hendra shrugged and sat down next to Jasmine on the sofa.

'And, if needed,' she said while getting closer to him, 'I know of something else to relieve your pain.'

She started caressing his crotch, but he gently pushed her hand away.

'Please, Jasmine ... I need to prepare my mix. Once this is done, maybe ...'

'Fine then ... tell me when you are free ...'

She resumed watching her RCTV *sinetron*. As far as Hendra could tell, it was another episode of *Bawang Merah Bawang Putih*, a local Cinderella adaptation set in modern Jakarta that had been captivating her for months.

Hendra set to work. Like all DJs these days, he prepared his sets on a computer before downloading his music selection onto a USB key that he would later insert inside the cabin's DJ deck.

He had learned to mix with vinyl records at 16, but the CD was already coming up, and he'd only played a handful of times with real turntables. And five years later, CDs themselves disappeared, replaced by computers and USB keys.

He decided that tonight he was going to include a few pioneering 80s electro tracks from Aphex Twins' *Selected Ambient Works* and Front 242's first full record, *No comment*. Since he had not played these albums in a while, he first had to transfer the music from the old LPs to his laptop. He easily located them in his collection of vinyl and CDs. Ordered by artist and in alphabetical order, they pretty much filled the three-foot-high shelves that lined the four walls of his living room. The only exception was the one corner dedicated to his Angklung collection, now with the recent addition of his RCTV award. He used to hang portraits of his mother above the shelves, but a few years ago he had replaced them with Qur'anic mother-of-pearl inscriptions, each reading one of Allah's 99 names. His mother's precious photos were now safely stored in a drawer in his bedroom. Maybe one day he would pull them out, but for the moment it was too painful for him to see his mother look at him whenever he raised his gaze. Not to mention answering the questions of visiting friends who wondered who the beautiful woman was.

After taking his pair of old turntables from the shelves, he placed them on the coffee table in the living room and knelt in front of them. He put Aphex Twins on the left turntable and Front 242 on the right one.

Jasmine had switched off the TV and was watching him.

'Never seen you mix with these kinds of old … discs. How does it work?'

She was teasing him, of course. She had seen him mix many times, including with vinyl records. But he played along and launched into a demo.

Mixing with LPs was the best school to learn the art of DJing. Many of his colleagues who only used computers barely knew how to beat-match two songs. They simply switched from one track to the next without bothering so much as to work on a real transition or any sort of overlap. Like this English celebrity Carl Cox, whose success Hendra could never understand. To his eyes, these guys were just jukeboxes, whereas a real DJ was someone who could mix two tracks (or more) together for five to ten minutes in a row to produce an entirely new piece. A DJ was a musician and a composer rolled into one, with others' songs as his endless repertoire of notes.

He had isolated the masculine choir in Front 242's music and was now superimposing Aphex Twins' chorus. Then he started to scratch and stutter under Jasmine's admiring gaze. Each and every of DJ Radikal's sets was an artistic improvisation offered live to clubbers. Real techno fans could tell the difference.

'Hmm … really amazing,' said Jasmine, embracing him from behind while he was mixing. She had no panties on under her cotton dress, and her erect penis brushed freely against his back. Unable to resist Jasmine's hard-on, Hendra turned around and grabbed her cock in his hand.

'Please,' said Jasmine, 'can you remove your armband? It's painful when you jerk me off.'

Hendra just smiled and kissed her. He only removed his armband when he was safe from prying eyes, making sure that even Jasmine never caught a glimpse of his many scars. He certainly had no intention of breaking the rule tonight – especially with all his fresh wounds.

* * *

Hendra arrived at XS at 9 pm, barely fifteen minutes before the start of his first mix. He was in a foul mood. They had made love twice before Jasmine had finally left his flat around 7.30 pm to start her shift. By then, he had no choice but to rush through his song selection. Except for the intro, he could not even remember now what tracks he had hurried to record on his USB key. He knew Jasmine meant well to visit him like that ... but didn't she know that he was mixing early tonight? How could she not understand that the quality of his performances depended on his careful preparation?

As soon as he entered the main hall, he started to look for Pak Kelvin – whom he had unsuccessfully tried calling before coming to XS – hoping that he could convince his boss to postpone his set by one or two hours. That would give him enough time, alone in the cabin, to get his mix together. Scanning the dancefloor, Hendra desperately tried to spot Pak Kelvin's silhouette. He usually liked to stand by the side, observing the comings and goings, hands on his hips, his oversized stomach bulging forward. But on top of the artificial vapour generated by the fog machine, there was so much of that stupid *kretek* smoke around the dancefloor that it was nearly impossible to pick out anyone. The clove cigarettes didn't just spread a revolting smell, they also emitted a very thick smoke, thicker than regular cigarettes. No wonder that his grandfather, who used to smoke up to two packs a day of that junk, had developed lung cancer at 62 years old.

Stress compressed Hendra's breathing and he could feel his neck stiffening by the minute. To hell with his promises to Jasmine! He beckoned to one of the ubiquitous yellow-dressed mamis and asked for an X. It would take a while for the full MDMA effects to kick in, but it was better than mixing completely clear. Clear and unprepared, that is. He quickly swallowed a 'Spice' pill – red-coloured like sambal – and then knocked back three gin and tonics before crossing the dancefloor to the cabin.

He inserted his USB key into the sound system and activated the CDJ turntables which started blinking on both sides of the mixing desk. At the same time, lights came on around his cage followed by thumbs ups all over the dancefloor. Anxious whistles cut through the smoky air. For the beginning of his set – the only part that he had managed to finalize after Jasmine's departure – he had chosen 'Der Mussolini' from the electropunk German band D.A.F, which he was going to remix with Project Pitchfork's 'Rain'. Headset on his ears, he increased the trebles coming from the D.A.F. track and synchronized its beat with the insipid piece that DJ Argo was playing (that guy was a real bore with his forever cheerful jungle sets). At the right moment, Hendra pushed the fader to switch off DJ Argo before increasing the volume of 'Rain', already spinning on the left turntable.

Fans raised their heads in his direction, smiling, their eyes full of gratitude. A nice warmth spread to Hendra's stomach, the same sensation of well-being that he experienced after eating a plate of sambal goreng prepared by his grandmother. The X promised to be good. He looked up and made his neck crack; any kind of discomfort was already gone. He finally let himself be carried away by DJ Radikal's music …

He was near the end of his first one-hour set and, given the context, he had done a pretty decent job. Now the time had come to push his fans to their limits. He had always dreamed of blasting Laibach at XS, and tonight he was going to make the leap. While Jeff Mills' 'Hatsumi' was playing, he searched for the Slovenian band's German remix of 'Life is Life' on his USB key. But he couldn't find the title on the computer monitor even though he clearly remembered pre-recording it. Had he saved it under the wrong name? Oh, there it was! But 'Hatsumi' was already almost over and he didn't have time to make a proper transition, so he just suddenly pushed the mixer knob to the new track. The deep, martial voice of the lead vocalist Milan Fa's singing 'Lieben heist Leben' resonated in the room. Lowering his eyes, Hendra saw the expressions of shock, of near panic on the clubbers' faces. What's more, it could take a while to adjust to Laibach's irregular – sometimes almost random – beat and so the crowd quickly froze. No need to upset them, thought Hendra who concluded his mix a bit abruptly. But he certainly wasn't going to let them get off the hook so easily!

During his break – despite his set's less than stellar ending – he was treated to countless vodka shots by his fans. And he gobbled a blue-coloured X (a 'Smurf' according to the *mamasan*) as well as one hit of acid, graciously pressed into his hand by a young male admirer. Although mostly invisible during the day in Jakarta, homosexuality was on full display at the popular nightspots around town. Avid lovers of both X and techno, gays were quite a crowd at XS, and Hendra often had to keep his distance from them as they could quickly turn even more clingy than Alessandro.

When he went back up into his cage for his second set, he was completely stoned. Electric. Free like a bird roaming the sky. 'In the club of all eXcesseS, the DJs fly,' the *Jakarta Post* had titled a recent article on XS, with an accompanying photo of the hanging cage. It had been a while since he'd last mixed in this state and he had to be careful. Even with the safety grill around the cabin, one wrong move and he could fall into the crowd four metres below.

He was bursting with so much creative energy tonight, he was going to show everyone what Radikal was capable of. As soon as he took over again from DJ Hargo, Hendra resumed right where he had left off, mixing Laibach with a jerky Thai pop track for a record ten minutes! Talk about cultural shock. He was ecstatic, in full musical trance. People kept leaving the dancefloor one after the other, but he didn't give a fuck. He was going to teach them a lesson in music and then they would come back for more. Tonight, Radikal would be true to his name, no holds barred! From time to time, he emitted a small scream into the mic to cheer himself up since the silent room denied him the applause that he truly deserved.

At some point, he noticed Alessandro sitting on the right side of the dancefloor, not far from his cage. Once again, he was in the company of a young girl. Way too young for him, with a gothic look and bluish braids. She smiled in Hendra's direction, unveiling braces flickering under the stroboscopic light. Hendra and Alessandro's gazes crossed and the bule threw up his hands, as if asking 'What the hell are you doing?' before giving him the thumbs down. 'Who the fuck does he think he is, this retard?' screamed Hendra to himself inside the cabin.

When he finished his set, there was nobody left on the dancefloor – except for that spaced-out ethnic Chinese senior citizen in the leather jacket and mirror-glasses he had first seen on the night of his calamitous crowning. But Hendra was in heaven; at last he had mixed Laibach at XS – and not just one track, four of them! He was so excited; he would have to cool off or he risked going into overdrive very soon. Well, there was something that would help him come down, and he had an idea who to get it from.

He walked up to the Chinese man and spoke into his ear. Did he know where to find some Kit Kat? The 60-year-old patriarch lowered his glasses and looked at Hendra with a huge smile on his lips. Digging inside his jacket, he pulled out a small sachet of K and slipped it into Hendra's palm. 'On the house.'

Without wasting time with long thank yous, he rushed to the toilets and sniffed a three-ply line inside a cubicle. But when he came out, he felt even more restless, more febrile, as if about to blow up. Was the K cut with other stuff? Or maybe he was just too ecstasied already.

He decided he wanted to chat with Jasmine and started across the dancefloor to get to the other side of the club. It was DJ Violetta who was now in charge, and the ground under his feet seemed to have acquired a life of its own while the air kept vibrating against his face as if a shockwave was reverberating across the room. In the middle of the dancefloor he bumped into Alessandro who held him back by the arm. A bit too brusquely for Hendra's liking. Not a good start.

'That was the shittiest music ever, Radikal!'

Hendra could tell from the bule's bloodshot eyes that he had taken some very strong dope. Maybe crack, as pure cocaine was hard to come by in Jakarta. His eyes kept moving in all directions, like a pair of broken autofocus lenses unable to fix on any point.

'Shittiest music? You mean fucking greatest EBM of all times!'

'Well, my girlfriend and I, we didn't like that Nazi music,' replied Alessandro. His gaze was directed at some imaginary spot above Hendra's head.

Sudden hot flushes came over Hendra. He knew too well the sensation and should have gotten away but he couldn't help himself.

'I don't know about you, but as for your *friend*, it's normal that she didn't like the music. She's not even sixteen, she knows fuck about music.'

'Seventeen,' replied Alessandro with a snigger that pushed Hendra to his breaking point. 'She's seventeen. It's her birthday today.'

Hendra was seeing red. Just leave. Leave before it's too late.

'By the way,' continued the bule, 'I checked, and after Hadi Harsono it was a chick that became the factory head. I guess she can't be your padre, right?'

Slap! Hendra heard the noise of his hand whacking Alessandro's face before he felt the impact in his arm, all the way up to his shoulder.

'What are you doing, man? Are you crazy or what?' screamed Alessandro, nursing his cheek.

'Shut up and get the fuck out of here.'

'I'm going to report you to the s–'

Hendra didn't let him finish his sentence and delivered an uppercut to his chin. Looking more surprised than hurt, the bule staggered. With all the kilos that Alessandro had lost, he was a real lightweight but, still, what a pleasure to punch him! Such a pure and intense feeling that Hendra couldn't help prolonging it. He landed another hit, a direct jab between the eyes. Alessandro's legs gave way, and he crumpled to the ground, blood pouring from his nose.

The crowd of clubbers quickly parted. Many still looked on, but not the bule's girlfriend who was nowhere in sight. Hendra stared at the crawling form in front of him: a long, wiry mammal with a thin head, a white stain on the throat and a crimson muzzle. A weasel ... yes, a weasel bleeding from the nose! Vermin hunting season was open! Hendra jumped onto the animal that was trying to stand on its hind legs. With one hand, he seized the slick hair and with the other, he punched the whining mouth. Soon, there wouldn't be much left of the *donnola* ... He could hear rising squeaking sounds but they had no effect on him. He felt so liberated, so happy, at last relieved of the cast-iron weight that had been pressing on his chest. Alessandro was the best punching ball ever. A perv who deserved a good hiding. An arrogant bule who dared to criticise his music. A fucking snoop who had triggered his new headache attacks. Yes, it was the bule's fault if his crowning night had been a disaster. He started to strike harder and harder until someone – Ari, judging by the man's voice – tackled him from behind and pulled him away. For a while, Hendra's fists continued to kick in the air.

A tacit rule in the clubbing world is that security always stands with the personnel whenever there is a fight between a patron and an employee. The bouncers grabbed Alessandro and dragged him away by the arms and legs. The bule wailed and screamed, his face and torso covered in blood, with shreds of his torn shirt floating to the sides. But there was nothing he could do about the fact that he was being thrown out of the club via a backdoor often used for that purpose.

***

Ten minutes later, Pak Kelvin went to see Hendra while he was savouring his trip, lying down on the semi-circular sofa hidden in an alcove, where Ari had installed him after the fight.

'You really messed up that bule,' said Pak Kelvin who had pulled over a footstool and sat level with Hendra's head.

'Hmm,' he replied.

He was fixing on the ceiling's spotlights, which seemed to blink in tune with DJ Violetta's fast-paced beat. For once, he rather liked her hardcore mix. Pure unabated happiness flowed through his dilated veins. An adrenaline burst in the middle of an X-cum-K high, that was totally insane. He was burning up, almost delirious, only vaguely aware of the presence of Jasmine seated next to him.

'You won't see him here again,' continued his boss. 'I told him he was blacklisted from XS. But maybe now you can tell me what happened?'

Hendra forced himself to come down a little bit to be able to talk to Pak Kelvin.

'He was with some kiddo,' he said, turning his head in his boss's direction.

'What?? What the fuck are you talking about?'

'This bule is a perv who bangs underage chicks. He hangs

around with a different one every time he comes to XS.'

Pak Kelvin had better hurry, thought Hendra. He wouldn't be able to restrain his mind for very long. It just wanted to continue flying. High, very high.

'And that's why you trashed him?'

Hendra just smiled.

'So you rearranged this guy's face because he was going out with a hooker you thought was underage? I can't fucking believe this!'

What Pak Kelvin didn't know was that it wasn't Hendra's first time. Two years ago, he had been fired from The Liquid, a smaller club where he was DJing before XS. He had demolished the face of another perv, a 60-year-old bule who seemed to want to spend his retirement groping young girls on Jakarta's dancefloors.

'You think like these bules now, Pak. But they're not hookers, these kids. Not like the girls that work for you on the top floor.'

'Really? I don't see the difference. Sorry, my bad, yes, they drive down the prices! And how do you know she was a minor? You saw her ID?'

'No need, boss. The bule said so. Totally dissssgusting!' He pretended to vomit on the red leatherette sofa. 'And that retard thought he could criticize my music!'

'I didn't like your last mix either, Hendra. You sure had your own fun, but you emptied the dancefloor!'

'You're right, Pak. Just like before a tsunami. And you know when will be the goddamn tsunami? During my next set!'

Hendra burst out laughing, almost choking on himself. Pak Kelvin forced him to sit up.

'Listen to me, you little fucker. I don't need my staff to beat the shit out of my patrons. Even if they fuck around with young girls. That's not our problem. We already have enough on our hands with the White Brigade.'

Hendra didn't reply. The sofa had become a surfboard. He was gliding effortlessly over the waves. Radikal was truly the best.

'You're totally fucked up. Look at me when I talk to you!' Pak Kelvin grabbed Hendra's shirt and shook him. 'What the fuck is wrong with you? This, after the fool you made of yourself when RCTV was around! I should fire you on the spot.'

Pak Kelvin let go of Hendra who fell back on to the sofa where he resumed his surfing competition.

He heard some whispering. Laboriously, he opened one eye and saw Jasmine who seemed to be pleading with Pak Kelvin. *What was she telling this fat prick?*

'OK,' his boss said into his ear after some (unknown) time. 'Your girlfriend Jasmine's convinced me to give you another chance. But you're suspended for the next three months. Hopefully by then, your "migraines" will be over and you can come back to mix at XS. But let me warn you, you try your little vigilante act one more time and you're fired for good.'

Pak Kelvin left Hendra alone with Jasmine, who was now holding his hands. Hendra closed his eyes but the red light continued blinking on his retina.

Jasmine whispered into his ear. 'I think it's time for you to get home. I'll go with you.'

Down the back alley leading to XS, a group of key-waving taxi drivers on the lookout for unsuspecting customers blocked the intersection with Jalan Hayam Wuruk. Hendra followed Jasmine as she elbowed her way through to hail one of the more honest taxis travelling down the avenue. Just as they started along Hayam Wuruk, one driver shouted after them.

'Hey, *deejay*, have fun with your girlfriend! Or should I say your boyfriend?'

Hendra stopped walking despite feeling Jasmine's hand trying to pull him forward. He turned around just when the cabbie was addressing his fellow drivers.

'Look at this hot waria, men! I'm sure our little DJ friend is gonna have a very good one tonight!'

Hendra freed his hand from Jasmine's and pounced on the driver, throwing a massive blow that sent the man flat on the ground. He straddled his chest and tried strangling him but he couldn't close his hands around the man's neck which was even thicker than a pig's. Not halal, the fucker. He resumed the head bashing instead, impatient to put an end to the squealing.

Behind him, he could hear Jasmine pleading: 'Sayang, please stop. Just stop.'

Hendra paused, his fist suspended in mid-air. The red light kept blinking faster and faster in front of his eyes.

'Enough, sayang,' said Jasmine.

Her voice was reaching him from far, very far, as if he were in a comatose state, and she was calling out to wake him up. Jasmine pulled forcefully on his arm and he stood up. Pushing their way through the crowd of onlookers, they walked away from the driver. The guy was shouting like a fishwife, covering his nose with two hands. Like the *donnola* just now.

'Let's take a walk,' said Jasmine. 'You need a bit of fresh air.'

While crossing the street to walk along Batang Hari canal, they almost got hit by an *ojek*, a moto-taxi, then continued straight before turning left into Jalan Mesjid Kebon Jeruk. They were taking the back route, Hendra realised, without understanding why.

'If we take small streets,' said Jasmine, as if she had guessed his thoughts, 'we can spot them more easily should they try to follow us to find out where you live. Because they'll want to get even, for sure.'

He looked at her, puzzled.

'They? Who?'

'The taxi drivers just now, of course!'

He searched his mind but couldn't remember anything. Well, that wasn't his first time losing short-term memory after sniffing K. Everything would be back to normal in less than 24 hours.

They continued walking in silence, hand in hand.

***

The *azan* resounded in the distance. With the warm colours of the rising sun lighting up the sky, the clouds of pollution had taken on iridescent, poetic hues.

***

At an intersection, Hendra saw a public bus from the Transjakarta network, probably starting its shift.

***

A *tuk-tuk* honked at them as they walked past Gereja Glodok, the shining new church in the neighbourhood.

* * *

Still hand in hand, they passed in front of run-down Lokasari Plaza, near Hendra's place. He wished they would take this kind of lovers' stroll more often.

* * *

'Here ... put this around your fist,' Hendra heard Jasmine say.

Ice-cold water dripped onto his face. He shuddered.

'What's that?' he asked, opening his eyes.

'It's a towel with ice inside. Your hand's all swollen. And bleeding.'

He looked at his hand. Indeed, it was all red. Then again, he was seeing everything in red right now – the sofa on which he lay, Jasmine's face, the walls of the living room. He brought his hand to his tongue and gave it a sweeping lick. A metallic taste invaded his mouth as if ... as if he had just gobbled up a hit of acid. Could it really be blood? To be safe, he still grabbed the towel and pressed it against his knuckles.

He stared at the mother-of-pearl inscriptions hanging above the shelves. It took him a while to adjust his vision and read some of God's 99 names in Arabic: '*Al-Qayyum*', the Self-Existing One; '*As-Salam*', The Source of Peace; '*Al-Halim*', The Most Kind.

He closed his eyes. Smiling. Floating in happiness.

With a long sigh, Jasmine sat down next to him.

'Are you going to tell me what happened?'

'Why? Something happened?'

'Yes, you beat up a clubber tonight at XS and Pak Kelvin suspended you for three months.'

'Three months? Really?'

'Go to bed, sayang. And try to sleep. We'll talk tomorrow after you've come down.'

Hendra reopened his eyes: '*Al-Muntaqim*', The Avenger; '*Al-Hakkam*', The Judge; '*Al-Munit*', The Taker of Life.

A wave of sadness engulfed him. Jasmine was right, soon he *was* going to come down. He would be washed ashore, naked and defenceless, and then swept out again, pulled down to the bottom, drowning in the clear waters without any chance to escape the truth. And he had no more K to avoid a total meltdown, only some fucking Lexotan pills. After the triple dose he had snorted inside XS's toilets, there was nothing left of the Chinaman's gift.

In the room, he started sobbing. To cheer him up, Jasmine offered him her erect penis, but after making her come, he felt even more dejected. Dejected and hopeless. Everything was going to disappear. His demons were back.

6

'What is it, sayang? Please. Talk to me. I know something's happening. And I don't just mean your headaches.'

'Just because I punched that bule? I told you, I hate these pervs who sleep with kids at XS.'

Jasmine hadn't left the flat after walking him home in the morning. To be able to stay with him the whole Sunday, she had even cancelled her attendance at some family event. As Hendra lay in bed, coming down from the insane high of the night, he could sense her entering the room to check on him every once in a while. Now that he was awake, she was questioning him and wouldn't give up until he told her what was wrong.

'And why did you have to beat up the taxi driver like that?' she asked.

Yes, now he remembered the brawl with the driver. He'd been riding high on the crest of the wave then. Last night's climax for sure ...

'You know I hate it when taxi drivers disrespect you.'

Her face softened. That's how they had met one and a half years ago, while he was waiting for a cab near Plaza Indonesia. In front of him in the taxi queue stood a ravishing waria whose incredibly long slender legs, moulded in tight Levi's, gave him vertigo.

After stopping next to them, a driver pretended to ignore Jasmine, inviting Hendra to climb into his taxi instead.

'Got a problem with the lady in front?' asked Hendra.

The driver's answer – which lady? – made his blood boil and he confronted the man who just cut and run without taking any passenger. Naturally, he started chatting with Jasmine after that and learned that she worked as a waitress at XS, the best techno club in Jakarta. She also told him that the club owner was looking for a DJ ready to try out a 'new concept' – while he, Hendra, had just been fired from Liquid after trashing an old perv there. Barely one week later, Hendra performed for the first time in the hanging cage.

'You're not going to fight with all the taxi drivers in Jakarta who poke fun at me. Leave it to Allah to punish them for their pride!'

Hendra remained silent.

'Anyway, I don't believe you. If there's nothing wrong, why are you taking all that junk again? And how come you have so many cuts on your wrists?'

That's when Hendra realised that he wasn't wearing his armbands anymore. Jasmine must have read the surprise in his eyes for she said: 'You removed them last night when we were walking home. You told me that you were so happy with me around that you didn't want to hide anything from me anymore. This also you don't remember?'

'Jasmine. I've told you, this is just to stop my headaches. When I cut myself, the pain in my head goes away.'

She took his hands and turned them upside down, exposing all the fresh cuts on his wrists.

'How many new scars have you got? Five? Ten? How can you do that to yourself?'

'Because ... the headaches are back ... like crazy. I have two, three episodes a day. It's this or getting trashed ... like last night.'

'Wow. What a programme! And do you know why your headaches are back after all these years?'

'I don't know.'

'Do you even realise that DJ Radikal won't be mixing at XS for the next three months?'

He could feel that Jasmine was growing more and more impatient. But what would have been the point of telling her about his mum's lies? He wasn't even sure it was the reason behind his latest bout of headaches. And even if that was the case, even if Alessandro had triggered all of this, wouldn't he feel all the better if he just stopped stirring up the past?

They heard the azan. It was already Maghrib. Already the end of the day. After they performed their ablutions, Jasmine put on her praying hijab, a long piece of white cotton cloth covering her body from head to toe like a veil of purity. Standing side by side on the carpet, they started to pray, with Hendra reciting Al-Fatiha, the first surah of the Q'uran. During the third and last *rakat*, as he was in the *sujud* position with his front touching the ground, Hendra felt his neck stiffening. Here it was again ... even after he had taken enough drugs for one whole month. Whatever he did, the headaches didn't leave him in peace. How could opening up to Jasmine make things worse?

As soon as they finished praying, she said (without trying to hide the weariness in her voice) that she needed to go home – to her brother's place, where she lived – as she had no change of clothes. Hendra stood in front of the door, blocking her way.

'OK, I'm going to tell you what that bule told me. Maybe ... there's a link.' He pulled her down next to him on the sofa.

'You already told us last night ... he didn't like your music ...'

'It's something else, something about my mother. Remember how I told you I never met my Chinese Indonesian father? You know, this story about my mum dating the head of some factory when she was working in Batam. She got pregnant, they were planning to get married and then he died all of a sudden in a freak accident just before my birth ... Do you remember?'

'Yes of course, how could I forget that?'

'But it doesn't ring true, does it?'

'Sayang ...'

'As far back as I can remember, I think I've always known that this story was just a pack of lies. Just how did I get these green eyes? Mum always said I had my dad's green eyes, but how many people do you know in Indonesia who have green eyes? At school, I was called the Afghan ...'

'That's cute.'

Hendra frowned. That wasn't exactly a good memory. At some point, he had even imagined that Dini wasn't his mum, after doing some research on the genetics of eye colour and understanding that *both* parents must carry the green allele, even recessively, for their offspring to be green-eyed. However, the presence of this allele was very rare in Indonesia – less than one or two percent according to geneticists – and his grandparents, when probed, said they didn't know of any green-eyed ancestor, like a Dutch colonizer for instance. Only after managing to get his hands on a copy of his birth certificate – clearly stating Dini as his mother and 'unknown' for the father – had Hendra somehow put to rest his doubts on his mother's side. But what were the odds that his father was also one of those very rare Indonesians to carry the green eye allele? Wasn't he, more likely, a foreigner from a country where green eyes were a familiar sight? Over the last few days, that question had come back to haunt him with a vengeance.

'Well now,' continued Hendra, 'thanks to that moron, I am one hundred percent sure my mum lied to me about everything.'

He told Jasmine about Alessandro's revelations that night, his own search on the Internet and the conclusion he had reached. Then his decision not to go any further and to stop torturing himself with his mum's secret.

'But why?' asked Jasmine. 'Why should you give up the truth?'

'Because now that my mother is dead, there's no chance anymore to ever understand what happened. It's totally hopeless.'

'And your grandfather?'

'He's so sick, why would I torment him with this story? And he might not even know anything.'

'But that must be the reason why your migraines are back, don't you see that?'

'I have told you, these are *not* migraines ...'

'Whatever.' Then after a pause: 'To be honest, I think Alessandro might have done you a big favour –'

'Please Jasmine, it's not funny!'

'He's given you a key piece of information from where you can start your search again. Hadi Harsono might not be your father but he must have known your mother at the time when she was dating your dad. Maybe this man can give you some leads that will help you trace him.'

'My father's supposed to be dead, Jasmine.'

'But you need to know who he is to free yourself from all this … suffering,' she said, holding his wrists.

'Are you suggesting that I meet up with this Hadi Harsono?'

'Whatever you'll find out, sayang, it's better than not knowing. Better than running away and … drowning. And in a sense it's sad but you don't have to worry any more about hurting your mum by digging into her past.'

Hendra closed his eyes. The attack had started.

Part III

The Saving Hand

Jakarta, June – July 2014

7

Hendra exited his building and got into the first empty taxi driving past. Just a week ago, Jasmine had urged him to talk to Hadi Harsono, and here he was, on his way to meet the former TMM manager at Pacific Place, one of Jakarta's swankiest mega malls.

Getting in touch had been surprisingly straightforward. Hadi Harsono's LinkedIn profile included an email address to which Hendra had simply sent a message. His mother, he had written, had been a worker at Batam's TMM factory at the time when Hadi Harsono was the local GM, according to his online CV. Certain events had apparently taken place in his mother's life while she was employed with TMM, events which he now wanted to understand better. Sadly, she was no longer around to explain, but he believed, or rather hoped, that Pak Hadi might have information that could help him in his quest. Hendra had braced himself for a long, unbearable wait, knowing that most likely the former TMM manager would just ignore his email. Best case, he would politely turn him down after a few reminders. But to Hendra's surprise, Pak Hadi had reverted in less than 24 hours, and in the same email – without even asking a single question about the so-called 'events' – proposed that they meet the following weekend. Hendra knew he should have rejoiced at this quick and favourable outcome but he couldn't quell the uneasiness he felt in his stomach after such a hasty reply. Increasingly nervous, he had been plagued with even more frequent headache attacks over the last few days while he waited for the meeting.

Hendra instructed the taxi driver to drop him in front of Pacific Place's southeast gate. There were no fewer than eight entry points and if he took the wrong one, it could mean a very long walk to Le Garçon de Paris, the restaurant that Pak Hadi had selected. Located in the CBD, within a stone's throw (by Jakarta standards) of some of the most prestigious five-star hotels in town, Pacific Place was a gigantic temple of consumerism that bore witness to the Indonesian middle-class's rising wealth – and one of those heralded icons of the city's newfound modernity that Hendra emphatically disliked. One day when he was high – way too high – on X, he had lost himself in Pacific Place and experienced one of the worst bad trips of his life. Dizzy with vertigo as if he were standing at the edge of a precipice, he had teetered around the infinite maze of shops for hours, anxiously pacing corridors and escalators without finding an exit.

Today, he sauntered straight into Le Garçon de Paris. With its round marble tables, stylish wicker chairs and well-groomed waiters, who had exchanged their batik shirts for plain white ones with crisp black aprons, the chic restaurant tried hard to reproduce the atmosphere of a Parisian brasserie. One garçon asked if Hendra preferred to sit inside or on the terrace. The 'terrace' was actually the seating area in front of the café, inside the central airconditioned concourse along which many of Pacific Place's restaurants were spread out. Hendra opted for the terrace and asked the waiter for *air bandung*. That was his favourite drink during the day, a mix of condensed milk and rose water which left a delicious taste of sweets, reminiscent of childhood, in his mouth. Originally from Malaysia, *air bandung* was becoming more and more popular in Jakarta. Unfortunately the waiter informed him that they only served French beverages, suggesting that Hendra try instead their famous *diabolo menthe*, lemonade flavoured with mint syrup.

Hendra's phone buzzed. A message from Jasmine to tell him that she was on her way from her psychology class – a new interest she had picked up recently – and she would see him at Le Garçon de Paris very soon. She had offered to be around for his meeting with Hadi Harsono and he had gladly accepted.

In the mid-afternoon the café was almost empty except for a few wealthy, over-perfumed matrons chatting over tea. To take his mind off things, Hendra started eavesdropping on their animated discussion about the latest price increase of Hermes' scarves. One particularly upset ethnic Chinese woman kept waving her wrinkled hands in front of her face, making her bangles ring like a Balinese chime.

Just then, Hendra saw Jasmine walking along the concourse towards him. In her platform shoes she was a head taller than those around her, her gaze gently moving to the rhythm of her swaying hips. As she neared, resplendent in her yellow dress with black polka dots, Hendra's lips parted in an awed smile. Warmth spread through his body and the tension that he had been feeling since morning receded a bit.

'Hello, sayang.' She kissed him noisily on the left cheek.

Hendra breathed in her intoxicating perfume, briefly closing his eyes. When he reopened them, he realised that the matrons had interrupted their discussion and turned their heads in Jasmine's direction, looking (truly or affectedly) scandalized.

Jasmine sat down and asked the waiter to serve her the same drink as Hendra.

'You mean you've drunk this stuff before?' he asked.

'Nope, but it sure looks delicious.'

She lent in to stroke Hendra's freezing hands, revealing the top of the tattoo that covered her upper body – a rose with petals blooming on her collarbone. The tattoo was a very rare instance of Jasmine not strictly following Islam's code of conduct which forbade all types of permanent body alterations. She never even wore any sort of colour on her long, thin nails, despite polishing them almost every day. Hendra couldn't help thinking that this tattoo was maybe the relic of a childhood more troubled than she was ready to admit.

His phone rang. As he was about to pick up, a man approached their table.

'Are you Hendra?' the man asked.

'Yes, I am, and you are ... Pak Hadi Harsono?'

His heart beating in his mouth, Hendra stared at the man's eyes. They were brown. Unmistakably brown.

The former TMM manager took a seat. He was a jovial man. Mid-sixties, fat, bald and short, with a warm handshake. Hendra introduced Jasmine as his girlfriend, and if Pak Hadi guessed that she was a waria he didn't let it show.

'I really like this place,' he said. 'A perfect replica of a French bistro. Not even the cedilla in "garçon" is missing!'

He showed them what a cedilla was before ordering a cappuccino.

He smiled at Hendra. 'May I ask your age, young man? You

do look rather young to be born in the 80s, if I understood your email.'

Hendra replied that he was going to celebrate his 26th birthday at the end of the month.

Pak Hadi's face brightened. 'Happy early birthday then!' Then, after a pause: 'You know, the years I spent in Batam are some of the happiest in my life. I was only 35 when TMM entrusted me with the job of setting up their new factory. At that time, Batam was still a rotten hole, if you'll forgive the expression, with only a few Malay kampungs, two or three mosques and lots of buffalos! But since I was born there, I pulled strings at the governor level and we managed to build this factory in less than twelve months. Five years later, it had already become the biggest production site of the electronics industry in Indonesia. Really a wonderful time for me.'

He took a quick short sip of his steaming hot coffee.

'If I can be of any help, I'll do so with great pleasure. Do you have any photos of your mother so we can first confirm that I've actually met her?'

Hendra pulled out a picture of his mother in her thirties from his shirt pocket, a face portrait that she had given him years ago. In the yellowing photo, her black hair was pulled at the back into an elegant bun that heightened her delicate features and, maybe because of the flash, her fair skin had an almost magical glow. Hendra could have tried searching for an even older photo among his mother's possessions, which were stored in his bedroom cupboard, but everything – her clothes, books, souvenirs, letters – was still in the same Cosmo boxes that he had jumbled the belongings into when he'd emptied her tiny apartment on Jalan

Pahlawan Revolusi. Every time he wanted to unpack them, a feeling of deep sadness descended on him and he gave up before he started.

A thin smile formed on Pak Hadi's lips as he looked at the picture.

'Yes, I do remember your mother a little bit,' he said, raising his eyes. 'A real looker, for sure ...'

Hendra shuffled in his seat and turned his head away.

'I think she arrived towards the end of my stint in Batam. Hmm, let me think ...' He broke off and examined the photo again, a bit more closely this time. 'Yes, that's her, that's your mother who came to my office one day, crying. She was upset after receiving her first salary. She had been promised much more, apparently. Sadly, there were quite a few unscrupulous recruiters who would lure workers with promises of totally unrealistic wages.'

Pak Hadi looked up, and in his eyes, Hendra thought he saw some relief.

'But, apart from that sad episode, I have, unfortunately, very few memories of your mother. In your email, you mentioned some "events". Maybe you could tell me more?'

As suggested by Jasmine, who thought the best strategy was to be as candid as possible with Pak Hadi, Hendra told the TMM manager the exact same story that his mother had always told him. As he talked, it was like every word coming out of his mouth was further tightening the knots in his stomach.

'So, Hadi Wijono would be your father's name?' asked Pak Hadi, once Hendra was done talking.

'Yes.'

'This name doesn't ring a bell, unfortunately. And let me tell you, there's never been any accident or deadly fire in *my* factory, I'm quite certain of that.'

Hendra lowered his eyes.

'I'm sorry, young man.'

Now was the time. The day before, when they had discussed this meeting, Jasmine had insisted that, if necessary, he ask the question bluntly. They had to dispel any doubts, even if that meant forcing Pak Hadi into a corner. But Hendra hesitated. What if the man got upset?

'And you ... couldn't you ... be my biological father?' uttered Hendra finally, his last word no more than a murmur.

Pak Hadi seemed unfazed.

'I was expecting this question, this is a perfectly legitimate one after what you've just told me. But no, this cannot be, I can assure you.'

Hendra kept quiet.

'In January 1987,' continued Pak Hadi, his voice finally exuding all the aplomb that one would expect from a former senior executive at an international company, 'I was transferred to Munich and I didn't return to Indonesia for three years. As you said you were born in June 1988, it's ... impossible for me to be your father.'

There was a long uneasy silence disturbed only by the chattering voices of the matrons behind them, until Pak Hadi finally resumed talking.

'While my career was definitely booming during my time in Batam, my private life was far from exemplary and I've certainly committed a few youthful indiscretions ... If there was any chance that you could be my son, I would tell you.'

In Germany, explained Pak Hadi, he had rediscovered Jesus' teachings and put an end to his philandering ways. Then, upon his return to Indonesia, he had tried to atone for his past sins by 'doing the right thing' – whenever it was still possible. Hendra understood implicitly why it was that Pak Hadi was here today: to make sure this young man wasn't the fruit of one of his 'youthful indiscretions'. It finally became clear to Hendra that the former TMM manager was telling the truth. That he wasn't his father and had no idea who he could be. The knots in his stomach loosened somewhat.

'But if you want,' said finally Pak Hadi, 'we can also do a paternity test.'

'No,' replied Hendra. 'I believe you.'

Pak Hadi finished his coffee. 'I'm so sorry that I couldn't help you more. Let me pay for the drinks.'

'No, please,' said Jasmine, talking for the first time. 'We'll take care of that. It's already so kind of you to have accepted this meeting!'

'Are you sure? Well, if I remember anything else, I certainly have your email, young man.'

He stood up and shook Hendra's hand before respectfully inclining his head in Jasmine's direction as a way of parting.

After Pak Hadi left, Jasmine tried to comfort Hendra by insisting that at least they had ruled out one possibility. Feeling rather numb, he simply nodded, rose to his feet and went inside to pay the bill.

Moments later, as they were walking away from Le Garçon de Paris, they heard someone calling Hendra's name. They turned around and saw Pak Hadi running towards them.

'Sorry, I suddenly remembered something,' he said after finally catching up with them, visibly out of breath. 'When your mother was living in Batam, she was often in the company of another woman. A family member, if I'm not wrong. And just now it all came back to me that this woman was the one who had gotten your mother's hopes up with promises of whopping salaries.'

'A family member?' asked Hendra. His mother had always told him that she was all by herself in Batam.

'Yes, a sister or maybe a cousin, around the same age. Also, quite a stunner. But in a different way ...'

Pak Hadi's eyes brightened at this evocation. Another one of his youthful indiscretions? couldn't help wondering Hendra.

'Her name slips my mind. Tall, short-haired with clear Chinese features but darker skin. I mean darker than your mother.'

'M ... Maia?' asked Hendra, incredulous.

'Yes, that's it. Maia! Have you asked her? I mean, she might know about these "events", I suppose.'

Hendra felt he was being sucked into a drain hole. Pulled down all at once, powerless, defenceless.

'No ... I haven't. But I will,' he replied in a flat voice. 'Thanks again for your help.'

Pak Hadi seemed to be about to add something but after a moment of hesitation, he quickly took his leave again.

Shivering, Hendra sensed that someone was holding his hand.

'Let's just go home now,' said Jasmine.

***

'Now can you please tell me, who is this Maia?' asked Jasmine, after they reached his flat.

Hendra hadn't uttered a single word during the whole ride home and she had respected his silence. But now she was anxious to know.

He sighed painfully 'She's my aunt, mum's foster sister. Mum never told me they were together in Batam.'

'Maybe because it wasn't important? Are you still in touch with this aunt?'

Jasmine rose from the sofa and switched on the side lamps. Though the daylight was quickly fading in the living room, Hendra would have preferred to stay in the dark. He thought about protesting and then just started down the frightful memory lane.

'Maia's biological parents were ethnic Chinese who lived in the same village as my grandparents. They only wanted a son for their first child, and so when Maia was born they gave her up for adoption and my grandparents took her in.'

He stopped for a while and Jasmine waited, looking at him with a solicitous smile on her lips.

'My grandfather,' resumed Hendra, 'threw her out of the house after an … incident. I was six or seven when it happened. My mother had gone shopping with my grandparents, and some distant cousins and I were left behind in Maia's care. We were playing on the swing in the garden and at some point I fell backwards. When I stood up, the wooden seat was swinging back at full speed and hit me flat in the face. I lost one tooth and my upper lip was split in two. The neighbours had to bring me to the village dispensary.'

'Oh, so that's the origin of the sexy little scar that I can feel when I kiss you. And I always thought it was because you had gotten into a fight ...'

'Please, sayang, don't make fun of me.'

She was probably trying to lighten the mood but just bringing back those memories had made Hendra very fearful. He continued:

'When my grandparents came back, they learned that Maia was talking to a man standing on the other side of the garden fence when the accident happened. Maybe my cousins ratted on her, I don't remember. But I know there was a loud fight, with my grandpa screaming that Maia was leading a sinful life. He told her to never come back till she had changed her ways.'

'A sinful life? How could you even catch and remember those words if you were only six then?'

'I suppose my grandparents must have filled in some blanks when I was growing up. I kept asking questions about Maia as I often saw her image in my mind.'

Hendra stopped. His neck was already stiffening.

'You could say she really left a mark on me, so to speak ... Even today, twenty years later, I can still remember her lipstick when she kissed me after picking me up from the ground. The traces on my cheeks were so thick, I couldn't wipe them off. And it was such a weird colour. Deep orange, almost ochre. Never seen it on any other woman.'

'Maybe because this colour only exists in your dreams, sayang.'

Hendra stared at her, vaguely offended. Of course this colour existed.

'Anyway ... Did you ever hear from Maia after that?'

'I kept badgering Mum to find out what had become of her. But she was always very evasive. Said she worked in a bule restaurant in Pondok Indah. Then one day I overheard a discussion between my grandparents, and I understood that things had really gone south for Maia ... She had become a mamasan in a massage parlour in Jakarta. That was five, maybe six, years ago. Since then, I don't know anything.'

'You mean you didn't even try to reconnect with her when your mum passed away?'

'No.'

'But I think now you have to look for her. She is probably the only person to know what happened to your mum and dad in Batam. Did Dini ever mention which massage parlour?'

Hendra sighed. 'Fortune Spa. But I'm not sure I want to do this, sayang. If Mum never told me she was with Maia in Batam, she must have had her reasons ...'

'Sayang, what's worse? Knowing the truth, whatever it is, or letting this secret endlessly torture you?'

Hendra didn't reply. The nerve in his neck was already more tense than a bowstring ready to loose its arrow.

Jasmine stood up. It was time for her to start her shift at XS. She gave him a long kiss, urging him before closing the door to contact the spa where his aunt had last worked. She hadn't realised that he was about to suffer a new headache attack. One of these reverse 'trips' only he had the knack for, which always started with the comedown.

What Hendra had been too ashamed to reveal to Jasmine was that before becoming a mamasan, his aunt had learned the trade hands-on. Based on discussions between his grandpa and Dini that he had eavesdropped on when he was a kid, Maia used to work as a *pelacur* in bars frequented by bules. He had searched in a dictionary for the word *pelacur* but hadn't really understood the definition. Still, from the way grown-ups said the word, he knew it was very dirty. Immoral. And in his child's mind, Maia had quickly come to symbolize evil. She was the wicked witch who terrorised him in his dreams, armed with a swing seat and a giant lipstick.

It was only around the age of fifteen, during his first night-time expeditions with his gang of friends, that he had finally understood what profession his aunt was engaged in. Was she already a *pelacur* when she was working at TMM with his mother? Hendra remembered Pak Hadi's clearly nostalgic smile when he had pronounced his aunt's name. Nausea washed over him and he rushed to the toilet, just in time to deliver half-digested viscous pizza bits into the bowl.

He had never grown out of his feeling of disgust in the presence of prostitutes, even after starting on his DJ career and getting to know every nook and cranny of Jakarta's underground nightlife. It was like an allergic reaction, and no matter how ubiquitous prostitution was in his world, he could not be desensitized. Some days, he felt like a surgeon who couldn't bear the sight of blood.

The headache was getting stronger by the second. In a few minutes the pain would be intolerable. He decided to listen to Tantrum, a new dark techno band that he had discovered recently. He had noticed a few days ago that their subtle blend of techno and gothic metal, with the odd satanical scream in-between, tended to soothe him when he put it on full blast through his headphones. He also turned on the TV – he needed both sound and image to distract him as he paced the living room.

Flipping through the channels, he came across a video showing the beheading by ISIS soldiers of a combatant loyal to Bashar el-Assad.

The camera zoomed in on the butcher knife as it slowly but surely sliced through the hooded enemy's throat. Hendra stopped walking. Howls of pain and terror managed to filter through the rare pauses in the techno music. The headless body finally collapsed to the ground, still writhing, with blood spurting from the neck and splattering the execution room's white walls.

The ISIS soldier had applied the same technique that Hendra had been taught as a kid to slay the sheep during *Idul Adha*, the Feast of the Sacrifice. On that day, Muslims all over the world celebrated Abraham's boundless faith when, on Allah's order, he had set to kill his own son, Ishmael. At the last minute, an angel had appeared in front of the patriarch, ordering him to sacrifice a sheep instead of his son. Well, today, no angel had come forth to save the ISIS enemy.

Hendra switched off the music in his headphones just as the camera panned around to capture the ISIS soldier proudly brandishing the miscreant's severed head. That's also when the journalist (from TVPI, an Indonesian cable TV channel specializing in religious and educational programmes) spoke up and condemned the abominations committed by the ISIS 'terrorist'. Hendra waited, hoping for a replay, but the next program was a sermon by Rizieq Shihab, a famous Muslim preacher and native of Jakarta. Never mind. These images were probably available somewhere on the internet. Hadn't he been able to watch again and again Daniel Pearl's execution by the Taliban in Karachi in 2002?

He started up his laptop and browsed web portals linked to ISIS, quickly tracking down the clip in question – and many others. After a while, he moved to the ISIS official website itself, which was a mine of gory images depicting decapitations and other physical punishments meted out by the Shariah courts. Thieves' hands were cut off, murderers' heads chopped, adulterous lovers stoned to death. The red colour of the blood contrasted with the omnipresence of black, ISIS' official colour and his own favourite – like the grooves of his vinyl records. He continued his exploration, reading up the commentaries that accompanied the images and justified every punishment with a verse from the Quran or a hadith. His heart started beating faster and faster, his hands were damp, his breathing irregular … Suddenly, he slammed his laptop shut, as if he had just been caught red-handed watching porn movies.

He realised that he was feeling much better. Without having to peak first, his headache had miraculously disappeared, replaced by a pleasant floating sensation in his head. Even the feeling of suffocation he had experienced after his meeting with Pak Hadi was gone. He finally fell asleep on the sofa, but not before locating Syria on Google Maps.

8

The shrill noise of a saw slicing through steel pulled Hendra out of his sleep. The Indonesian megalopolis had become one giant construction site; even now in Glodok they were erecting more condominiums. Without some sort of sleep aid, it often proved impossible for Hendra to stay in bed beyond 9 am.

He sat up and massaged his mouth. The scar on his upper lip hurt as if a fast-moving swing had been smashing his face the whole night. No doubt he had dreamt of Maia after leaving the sofa for his bed around 1 am. Deciding that some Lexotan – his lifeline, in the absence of a more powerful drug, when he felt a bit too anxious – was in order, he opened the nightstand drawer but the plastic box wasn't there. He remembered he'd had it with him when he'd left the house to meet with Pak Hadi. Most likely, on his return, he had tossed it into the glass bowl in the living room where he usually emptied his pockets.

Two geckos slipped between his feet as he walked along the corridor from his bedroom. Just like him, they were probably disturbed by the non-stop vibrations of the floor and walls under the jackhammers' relentless battering. As soon as he entered the living room, Hendra switched on his sound system. He picked a CD by Sami Yusuf, and soon the Sufi poet's spell-binding voice singing all of Allah's 99 names started drowning out the racket.

Hendra plunged his hand into the bowl. The glass container from Ikea was overflowing with the loads of 100- and 200-rupiah aluminium coins that he removed every day from his wallet because they took up so much space. After a while, he would grab a handful of them and give them to kids begging in the street. Amid the coins, he also felt a comb, a few of Jasmine's hair clips, condoms, and business cards admirers gave him during his breaks. At the bottom of the bowl, Hendra finally found the green box, opened it and swallowed two pills in one go. Then he sat down on the sofa and closed his eyes.

What if Jasmine was right, he asked himself as he began to relax. What if the best thing for him to do was to confront his fears and talk to Maia. He switched on his laptop and launched a Google search for 'Fortune Spa'. The place had its own website detailing the different types of massage that were offered (Swedish, shiatsu, hot stone, deep tissue) as well as the profiles of the 'therapists' (*yeah, sure …*) photographed in skimpy outfits. About ten of them, all very young and each sexier than the last, but there was no trace of Maia. Hardly surprising, even assuming she still worked at Fortuna Spa. Hadn't she been promoted to mamasan? And even if she still serviced customers from time to time, she was probably too old to be featured on the spa's website. The only way to know for sure was to make a call. Hendra dialled the phone number shown on the contact us page. He tried a few times but kept getting the busy tone. Too many customers, maybe … He finally hung up, telling himself that he would make another attempt later.

Hendra lifted his eyes from the screen and saw one of the geckos staring at him from the ceiling, motionless. That's when he realised that the noise of the jackhammers had stopped. Most probably the workers were on their break. He might as well watch some TV while it lasted.

He switched off the music and grabbed the TV remote, which had slipped between the sofa cushions. When he pressed the standby button, it was TVPI that opened on screen, the same station he'd watched the night before. The religious channel was showing what seemed to be a sermon by a Muslim preacher. His name and qualifications were blinking on the screen's bottom left corner: 'Dr Jusuf Salim, fundraising director at the association The Saving Hand'.

Dressed in a long black djellaba, leaning against a wooden pulpit, the elegant man in his fifties spoke in a convincing yet gentle voice. He liked to raise up his right index finger to stress his words – that is, whenever his hand wasn't busy smoothing a greying pointed goatee as if trying to stretch it out. Dark sunglasses masked his eyes, hinting at potential blindness.

Hendra increased the volume.

'My dear brothers and sisters, look at these photos. I took them at the morgue last Saturday. These youngsters had their beautiful lives taken from them after overdosing on the drugs that freely circulate in Jakarta's nightclubs. This is JAsri, 17 years old. Budi, 19, Dwi, 16 …'

New images kept appearing on screen, showing the bruised faces of lifeless teenagers with eyelids swollen shut. Dr Jusuf listed their names and ages in the manner of a cop enumerating the victims of a serial killer.

'And this young girl here, the face so battered that she could not be identified, the police think she was killed while prostituting herself to "get her fix" – as they say.

'Do I need to show more photos to burst your bubble?' he asked in a sudden accusatory tone, while keeping his calm demeanour. 'How can you remain oblivious to the plight of our children ravaged to death by vice and drugs before our very eyes? Is it because of all the worthless material possessions that you accumulate in your luxury homes that you cannot see the suffering around you?

'My dear brothers and sisters, every weekend you go out and gorge on haram goods inside the swankiest shopping malls. When you come home at night, chloroformed by these earthly pleasures, driving in your SUVs along Jalan Hayam Wuruk, you force yourself to close your eyes lest you see all these neon lights that are redder than hell itself. But how long can you pretend to ignore the moral devastation unfolding in our very town every single day of the week that Allah *subḥānahu wata'ālā* gives us? Are you going to wait for your own child to become a victim before you start taking action?

'These daily tragedies could be avoided with a minimum of education and prevention. And that's what we do at The Saving Hand. We inform young people about the dangers of drugs and warn them against sexual relationships outside marriage. We show them how the pervasive and perverse influence of western media propagates values and ways of life which are against our Islamic teachings.

'Our Prophet Muhammad, peace be upon him, once said: "He who has no compassion for our little ones is not one of us." You can send your donations to saving_hand@paypal.com. Or should you want to volunteer with us, please call the number that appears at the bottom of the screen.'

Hendra remembered seeing The Saving Hand at XS about two weeks before the White Brigade's attack. Truth be told, he couldn't help finding them comical that day in their white t-shirts with a large printed hand on the back. Under the club's fluorescent lights, their singular outfit took on a rather ominous appearance. At first, he had even thought that they were part of one of those tacky shows that Pak Kelvin sometimes organised between sets – like, once, that troupe of Romanian performers walking around the dancefloor looking for Dracula.

But today, Dr Jusuf's forceful words resonated with Hendra. They brought to mind Imam Haji Ahmad's sermon of a few weeks ago. Hadn't he exhorted the faithful to wage their 'spiritual jihad' and 'fight for the common good and the betterment of society'? Every night at XS, Hendra met so many of these kids falling into drugs and prostitution, each time feeling more indignant and powerless. Why not make the most of his three-month suspension by volunteering for The Saving Hand? For sure, having brushed with an OD a few times, he had a certain 'expertise' as far as drug abuse was concerned.

Hendra dialled the number shown on TV and it was Dr Jusuf himself with his mellifluous voice who answered. Very quickly, after learning that Hendra wasn't working that day, he suggested that they meet at his house around noon and have a light lunch together. He lived on Jalan Perbanas in Menteng – the most exclusive district in Jakarta – right opposite the Bank Mandiri branch. Hendra felt both surprised and sort of honoured by the proposal. It wasn't every day that he was invited to some rich guy's villa.

He decided to wear his pair of flannel pants together with the batik shirt that he reserved for such (rare) formal occasions. He tried again to call Fortune Spa but the line was still busy – or maybe it was down. It seemed there really was no other option than to go there in person. But first, he would meet with Dr Jusuf.

* * *

One hour later, Hendra was sitting on a line 6 TransJakarta bus. Thanks to that first (and so far, only) public transport system in the Indonesian capital, he was going to reach Menteng on the other side of town in less than thirty minutes. They sped effortlessly down TransJakarta's reserved lanes, as if taunting the helpless motorists stuck in the city's infernal traffic jams. In an aerial photo of Jakarta taken at the peak of rush hour that Hendra had seen in *Kompas* one day, it looked as if a sculptor had carved these busways right through the gridlock with his chisel.

As expected, the amateur musicians who played guitar in the streets to earn their keep had expanded their field of operation to the Transjakarta, and one of them, a young guy in his twenties, now faced Hendra. He was singing with enthusiasm, and talent, 'Ada apa denga Cinta?' – a rather sad love song which was one of Hendra's mother's favourites. His lanky body floated inside an oversized faded yellow t-shirt soaking up the beads of perspiration dripping from his gaunt face. Clearly he wasn't getting enough to eat every day, but he seemed genuinely happy. Which maybe wasn't a good thing in his profession, thought Hendra – one might want to look a bit more pitiful for commuters to reach for their wallets.

Hendra realised that they were already driving through the posh district of Menteng. Just before getting off, he dropped a 5000-rupiah note inside the guitar case at the singer's feet, and the young musician shot him a large smile, revealing red-stained teeth. He might not have enough money for a good meal but that didn't prevent him from chewing betel nut all day long!

A few minutes later, just before noon, Hendra presented himself in front of the two-metre-high solid-steel gate marking the entrance to Dr Jusuf's villa. An outer wall of similar height, topped by barbed wire, surrounded the residence, and prominent signs warned would-be intruders of the risk of fatal electrocution. Quite a fortress, thought Hendra.

After having confirmed that he really was expected inside, the two guards opened the door and submitted him to a body search even more thorough than the one newly imposed on clubbers at the XS entrance. Then one of the guards led him along the gravel path that cut across the garden towards the house.

'*Assalamualaikum*, Brother Hendra,' said Dr Jusuf, who was standing on the doorstep waiting for him. Just like during the TV sermon, his right hand kept smoothing his rather short and sparse goatee.

He had changed into a tapered white djellaba that suggested a slender and athletic body. On his head, he now sported a red and white checked turban while still wearing the same dark sunglasses. But given how naturally he turned his head towards him, Hendra understood that the religious man was not blind.

'*Waalaikumsalam*, sir,' replied Hendra. He had taken Dr Jusuf's right hand in his and brought it to his forehead while bowing at the same time.

He followed Dr Jusuf into a plush living room that reminded him of the lavish reception hall of the Hyatt, one of Jakarta's classiest five-star hotels. His eyes focused on a large curtain splitting the room in half.

'On the other side is where my wives live,' explained Dr Jusuf, who had followed Hendra's gaze. 'When I have visitors, we pull the curtain – in accordance with the Islamic purdah requirement that is unfortunately largely ignored nowadays in Indonesia.'

Hendra was intimidated by the solemnity and the opulence of the place, hesitating to even step onto the richly adorned carpets with their sophisticated geometrical patterns. In fact, after hearing Dr Jusuf's TV sermon – and despite the prestigious Menteng address – he would have expected more austere-looking living quarters. In some strange way, he couldn't help feeling relieved when he noticed the familiar 99 Koranic inscriptions hanging on the walls – one of which, Al-Latif (The Kind), was cut in the middle by the purdah curtain.

A servant knelt in front of Hendra and offered him an icy hand towel.

'So, what can I do for you?' asked Dr Jusuf, after inviting him to sit down. Smiling and almost too solicitous, he was doing his best to put Hendra at ease. He had also removed his sunglasses and Hendra realised that indeed he wasn't blind but one-eyed – his right eyeball was motionless.

Hendra replied that he was willing to volunteer with The Saving Hand. He had some free time over the next few months and wanted to do something useful. What exactly were they doing on the ground? he asked without admitting that he had actually once seen them in action at XS.

Dr Jusuf first repeated what he had explained on TV. Though without the photos of victims to support his speech, thought Hendra, it felt much less convincing. Then he went into more detail about their actions, in particular how in nightclubs they handed out leaflets to as many youths as they possibly could. The main difficulty in their outreach efforts was in fact to convince the owners of these places of perdition to open their doors to the NGO members. He gave Hendra one of their leaflets, which the XS DJ noticed, had the same format as a flyer for a rave party. The first page covered the dangers of drug consumption and the risks of addiction together with some practical advice on avoiding accidents and ODs: drink water regularly, do not take alcohol at the same time, make sure to dissolve the heroine with enough citric acid to prevent phlebitis, never shoot up alone, etc. The other side of the flyer was dedicated to the lure and deception of transactional sex. As Hendra read through the text, he couldn't help noticing that there was no mention of the word prostitution itself.

'These teenagers,' explained Dr Jusuf, when Hendra expressed his surprise at such an omission, 'often refuse to accept that going out and sleeping with strangers in exchange for alcohol and drugs is already a form of prostitution. So if we use this term with them, they'll just stop reading and throw our flyer away. And we'll have lost our chance to keep them from going down the slippery slope.'

At last, Dr Jusuf's warm voice started to have its soothing effect on Hendra, as it had that morning, and he was beginning to relax.

'How do you identify underage patrons in the clubs?' he asked.

'But why should we, my dear brother? Isn't the security supposed to check everyone's IC and bar anyone below the age of 20 from entering?'

At that same moment – probably by coincidence – women's laughter filtered through the curtain.

Hendra kept quiet.

'Of course, everybody knows this is a blatant lie,' resumed Dr Jusuf with palpable bitterness in his voice. 'But what can we do about it? Anyway … we give our brochures to everyone – a bit of education has never hurt anyone, has it?'

Dr Jusuf explained that he himself was only a volunteer member in this association founded by Umar Bin Talib, a venerable imam in his seventies, who officiated at Al-Amin Mosque in Tangerang, 25 kilometres to the west of Jakarta's city centre. Dr Jusuf was in charge of fundraising and recruitment at The Saving Hand but in 'real life' he headed the Department of Shariah and Koranic law at the University of Indonesia in Depok. Hendra speculated that this function probably explained the official doctor title attached to his name, as well as the grand residence in which he was being received.

Two servants entered the room carrying large trays that they set on trestles. Palms turned upwards, Hendra and Dr Jusuf said a prayer together before one servant came forward with a golden jar and poured water onto their hands. Hendra rubbed his fingers under the runnel while the water flowed into a silver bowl, a *kobokan*, placed to that end on the table below. Finally, he plunged his right hand into the plate in front of him and rolled a mixture of *begedil* and beef *rendang* inside his palm. No sooner had he inserted the food into his mouth than the spicy sauce melted on his tongue, deliciously engulfing his entire palate. Instinctively, Hendra nodded his head in appreciation.

'What do you do in life, dear brother?' asked Dr Jusuf.

Hendra had prepared for this question. And he knew that he had to lie if he didn't want to be thrown out on the spot ...

'I work in a pizzeria at Plaza Senayan,' he replied. 'But they're closing down for renovations for three months.'

'Three months?' asked Dr Jusuf.

'Yes ... they really want to revamp the whole place.'

Dr Jusuf didn't say anything for a moment, staring at Hendra in a way that seemed both inquisitive and puzzled. Then he bent forward and grabbed Hendra's wrist.

'*Alhamdulillah*, my dear brother! Allah wanted us to meet, this is fate. Together we're going to defeat the forces of evil in Jakarta!'

A shudder run down Hendra's spine.

Dr Jusuf let go of his hand before asking in a calmer voice: 'How would you define your religious practice, dear brother?'

'Good ... I mean I fast, I pray five times a day whenever possible. I ...'

'Whenever possible? And you think that's OK?'

Hendra kept quiet, avoiding Dr Jusuf's gaze.

'You're like so many Muslims in this country who think they can just interpret and adapt God's teachings as they see fit. But the objective is to follow the Salafs, Hendra, the pious Predecessors – that is the first three generations of believers and only them! Unfortunately, all over Indonesia, people are taught an Islam corrupted by *bidah*, innovation. The messenger of Allah, peace be upon him, once said: "Beware of the new practices because every new practice is a religious innovation; and every religious innovation is an error, and every error leads one to the fire of Hell."'

Dr Jusuf spoke with passion and virtuosity, constantly quoting in Arabic from the Sunnah or the Qur'an. His fervour was infectious, and Hendra listened in awe and silence. But when he mentioned the strict application of Shariah Law in Indonesia, Hendra couldn't help protesting. In today's world, hadn't some parts of Shariah become inapplicable?

'Bidah again!' Dr Jusuf flared up. 'And what an arrogance! How can human reason judge if God's laws are still applicable or not? The only source of law is Allah; the Shariah is immutable, uncreated! But don't worry,' he continued, returning to his usual soothing voice, 'you'll learn everything again once you start volunteering at The Saving Hand. We have religious classes to erase all these wrong teachings and guide lost souls like you back onto the right Path. The journey that leads to Him is long and arduous but we'll take you there!'

***

Night had already fallen when Hendra left Dr Jusuf's house. How could time have flown so fast?

They had eventually agreed that Hendra was to start his volunteer work with The Saving Hand as soon as the following week. Before he left, they had prayed one last time together, for Maghrib, and Hendra could hear Dr Jusuf's wives – probably three of them judging by the number of distinct voices – following their husband's oral instructions, hidden behind the black purdah curtain.

Hendra decided to take a cab. The overcrowding of the Transjakarta during the evening rush hour risked disrupting the deep sense of inner peace so exquisitely enveloping him after spending the whole afternoon in Dr Jusuf's company. He flagged down a passing Bluebird, and just as he was about to give the driver the directions to his flat, he realised that he had forgotten about the other task that he was meant to accomplish that day: to pay a visit to Fortune Spa. Half-heartedly, he asked the driver to take him to Blok M, an enclave in South Jakarta with a large cluster of bars and massage parlours – mostly patronized by bules – where Maia's last known place of work was located.

Fortune Spa – the mere evocation of that name was enough to bring back all the anxiety that his long session with Dr Jusuf had freed him from. Very quickly he felt his neck getting stiffer and stiffer and in the end he told the taxi driver to turn back and drive north towards Glodok. He would visit Fortune Spa another day.

9

Over the following weeks, Hendra, under Dr Jusuf's tutelage, became more and more involved with The Saving Hand. He had imagined that the well-groomed fundraising director would shy away from any involvement on the ground, but to his credit, whenever possible, Dr Jusuf joined the NGO volunteers on their nightly expeditions to Jakarta's 'dens of perdition'.

Yet the XS DJ continued to wonder, as when he had first seen The Saving Hand in action at the club, whether their operations really served any purpose. Way too high to understand anything, many of the youths that they approached at night just threw the NGO's flyers to the ground without even a side glance. Even when the music inside the clubs wasn't too deafening and the volunteers could try to engage in a discussion with those few who did not seem hopelessly wasted, they only elicited loud laughs and contemptuous shrugs.

'What matters,' explained Dr Jusuf to Hendra one day, 'is that these youngsters remember us and our name. So that the day when they need our help, they will search for The Saving Hand on the Internet and find their way to us.'

These marketing ambitions probably justified the ostentatious t-shirt that they wore on their nocturnal walkabouts. 'We are here to help you' proclaimed the slogan on the back, directly below the large right hand with open palm and spread fingers that Hendra had seen the first time. The double meaning was now obvious to him: the NGO didn't just try to *save* but it also wanted to *stop* all the trafficking. However, the only actual religious symbol in their attire was a black skullcap – to avoid coming across as too intimidating, Hendra had been told.

Once or twice a week, Hendra followed the classes given by Umar bin Talib at the madrassa located within the Al-Amin mosque compound. Often it took him more than an hour by bus or even by cab to reach the place, but he never regretted making the trip. The imam delivered incisive, fiery sermons in which he denounced the innovations introduced into Mohammed's teachings by Muslims across Southeast Asia.

'There are exactly 320,015 letters in the Qur'an, a number that has always been the same ever since the Book was revealed by God to Prophet Mohammed, peace be upon him. If we cannot even *change* one single letter in God's words, how can some fake believers out there arrogate to themselves the right to *interpret* His commandments as and when it suits them?'

Like Dr Jusuf, Umar bin Talib considered that all the arrangements with Allah's teachings, all the concessions to the modern world, explained in themselves the moral wanderings of the youth these days. And so The Saving Hand carried its actions on two parallel fronts: the preventive work in nightclubs and the promotion of a purer form of Islam within Indonesian society.

In his sermons, Umar bin Talib often liked to clear the air on the question of the hijab. *Of course* it was compulsory for women to wear a veil. And a real one, not the local version which was more a decoration, a fashion accessory enhancing the facial features instead of hiding them: the true hijab was supposed to be the *niqab* which completely covered the face, shielding it from men's leering eyes. Also when she left the house, the woman's clothing had to be of black colour, with strictly no visible jewel or embellishment that might arouse males' lust in the street. Even the hands had to be hidden in black gloves. As for men, Umar bin Talib insisted that they had to grow a beard because, as narrated by Nafi Mawla ibn Umar, the Prophet once said:

> Do *the opposite of what the pagans do. Keep the beards and cut the moustaches short.*

And never mind if for some the potential for hair growth was limited by genes, and no matter how hard they worked at it they still looked like pubescent teenagers, it was the intention that counted.

Dr Jusuf didn't agree with Umar bin Talib about this and advised Hendra against donning a full beard (even if he could grow one). A goatee was enough, especially since the *jenggot* – the bearded men – were not very well-accepted in Jakarta. A similar disagreement arose on the question of men's clothing: the qamis, the long robe worn by Umar bin Talib, wasn't necessarily the most appropriate attire in all circumstances, said Dr Jusuf. It depended on the social environment. In fact, as long as trousers stopped right above the ankle, the Sunnah was upheld.

In some cases, Umar bin Talib's teachings clearly veered to the unconventional, like the recommendation to use a miswak – a twig made from the Arak tree – to cleanse one's teeth, or to adopt the practice of segmented sleep like the Prophet in his time. Still,

Hendra couldn't help warming to this idea of going back to the roots and the rejection of modernity that it implied. One point in the cleric's teachings initially had him quite worried though: the outright ban on music. For, according to Umar bin Talib, music and singing were included in those 'idle talks' that the surah 31.6 mentioned:

There are some people who prefer idle talks over God's message in order to lead those without knowledge away from God's path, and to ridicule the Qur'an. They will have a humiliating punishment.

Fortunately, when Hendra had casually questioned Dr Jusuf, the university professor's reply had placated his concerns. It wasn't music per se that was forbidden, Dr Jusuf had said, it was all the haram activities that people indulged in while listening to music: drinking alcohol, taking drugs, fornicating.

Thanks to these classes, Hendra also discovered the lives and works of famous Sunni scholars. He found the figure of Ibn Taymiyya, in particular, totally fascinating. The 13th-century Syrian theologian – one of the first to consider the Shiites as apostates because of their idolisation of the fourth caliph Ali – had on multiple occasions risked his own life on the battlefield to fight the Mongol infidels. He was legendary for his inflexibility in his interpretation of the Qur'an or the hadiths. No amount of cajoling or arm-twisting by the rulers of the day would make him endorse any kind of corrupt ruling – even when thrown in jail, he would continue to issue fatwas against the Vizier's decisions. Ibn Taymiyya's thirst for the absolute resonated with Hendra, like a powerful echo reaching him through the centuries.

And there was tangible proof that he was doing better: Hendra now had fewer headache episodes (sometimes only one every other day) and he was able to cope with them without taking any drugs. Admittedly, his temporary estrangement from XS significantly reduced the temptations, but at the same time, if he really had wanted to, it would have been fairly straightforward for him to buy any kind of substance – especially during his night missions with The Saving Hand.

* * *

Fasting month was already upon them.

During this sacred period, the NGO's operations in nightclubs were suspended, not so much because the 'dens of perdition' were closed – sadly for too many of them it was business as usual – but because, luckily, youth patrons themselves were few and far between then, presumably thanks to tighter parental control. So Hendra joined the ranks of volunteers roaming the streets to further the advancement of a non-corrupted form of Islam within Indonesian society. In the company of Dr Jusuf, who continued to mentor him, Hendra would walk around shopping centres to encourage women, young or old, to wear at least the local hijab version – the niqab being seen at the moment as a rather unrealistic target by Umar bin Talib.

As soon as they spotted a woman who wasn't dressed according to Islamic requirements, they would approach the sinner and hand her a brochure reminding her of the rules of modesty as established in the surah Al-Azab:

O Prophet! Tell your wives, your daughters, and the believing women to draw their veils over them. That is better so that they will be recognized and not annoyed. And Allah is Forgiving, Merciful.

At the bottom of the page, the Saving Hand's phone number and email were indicated (for those who needed more information), while at the back of the flyer was written a hadith from Sahih Al-Bukhari forbidding men from wearing trousers that dragged on the floor:

The part of the garment that hangs below the ankles is in the Fire.

However, since even amongst teens in Jakarta the grunge look wasn't particularly in fashion, most of the people that they approached on these missions tended to be unveiled women.

Hendra's view on the hijab had always been one of free choice. Wasn't Islam supposed to mean *voluntary* submission to God's will? If some Muslim women didn't wish to cover up, it was their decision, and if indeed they were in the wrong, they would have to account for it on the Day of Judgement. But after attending Umar bin Talib's religious classes, Hendra had changed his perspective. Weren't the hadiths the imam drew on abundantly clear on the obligation for Muslim women to wear the hijab? If so many of them dressed so impudently, how could it be of freewill? No, it was because God's words had become inaudible amongst all the modern discourses and The Saving Hand's mission was simply to make sure that Allah's message could again be heard loud and clear.

One day around 1 pm, Hendra was to meet Dr Jusuf at Pacific Place for one of these missions. The professor had told him that he would be waiting at the Starbucks near the north entrance. At first, Hendra couldn't find him and started wondering whether he had again lost his way inside the mega mall – until he realised that despite the scorching noon sun, Dr Jusuf was seated on the *outdoor* terrace of Starbucks. He should have guessed, of course. Hadn't the professor insisted the other day that if one spent all day in the air-conditioned atmosphere of Jakarta's shopping centres, one would miss out on the real meaning of Ramadan, which was to get Muslims to experience the sufferings of the less fortunate? At the time of the Prophet, he had told Hendra, the Salafs of the Arabian Peninsula held occupations that were significantly more arduous than theirs these days and would carry on with their jobs even when the fasting month coincided with the summer season and its peak desert temperatures of 50 degrees.

Hendra and Dr Jusuf started their tour of Pacific Place. At this hour, the mall was full of ethnic Chinese wives on shopping sprees, who were strictly off limits even if they didn't wear a veil because there was not an insignificant chance that they might be Christian. The Saving Hand members were to avoid sparking any kind of friction with any of the other five officially recognised religions in Indonesia: that was Umar bin Talib's unequivocal instruction, to the dismay of Dr Jusuf who thought that the founder of The Saving Hand was way too tolerant in this regard.

'Isn't the veil *also* supposed to protect men against impure visions!' would protest Dr Jusuf.

They approached a female student with a pretty face, long black hair and an ankle-length denim skirt. At first, she looked at them in surprise when they handed her one of their brochures. But after quickly reading through it, she hastily apologized for her carelessness, reached inside her handbag and pulled out a striped green-and-blue hijab. She gave Hendra a wide grin that deepened her dimples, before asking with a laugh if the phone number at the bottom of the page was his.

As they continued their rounds, they came across an unveiled middle-aged woman with the smart looks of a senior executive – and a skirt that stopped right above the knee.

'A mini-skirt!' gasped Dr Jusuf. 'And why not a bikini while she's at it! This debauched woman is going to get it from us!'

Hendra was more reluctant. From his own limited experience of such field operations, older, richer women who bared their legs in shopping centres were often unrepentant. And what swiftly followed proved him right: their target, after barely a cursory glance at The Saving Hand's brochure, lashed out at them.

'What gives you the right to tell me how I should dress? *I* choose how I dress. And nobody should judge a woman based on the length of her clothes.'

They quickly left lest the argument escalate. The Saving Hand's proselytist activities had the tacit endorsement of the local authorities so long as nobody made noise.

Finally, after a few hours working the Pacific Place grounds, Dr Jusuf suggested that they get on the Transjakarta to deliver their moral lessons to commuters. The hijab was becoming rarer and rarer within Jakarta's working classes too. Cut off from their villages, immersed in the anonymous life of the megalopolis, young female migrants often ended up distancing themselves from religious practice. As far as The Saving Hand's groundwork was concerned, there was also a big advantage in targeting unveiled women of a more humble extraction: they were much more easily convinced, often reacting as if they had been caught red-handed, and then duly committing to dressing more appropriately the next day.

As they were handing out their flyers to passengers, they noticed, seated at the back of the bus, a young hijab-wearing girl fondly holding her boyfriend's hand. Dr Jusuf lost no time in scolding the couple, who quickly untied their hands without even a word of protest. After that, the lovebirds didn't dare even look into each other's eyes. They finally got down at the next stop with deeply mortified expressions as they passed in front of Dr Jusuf.

'Good riddance,' mumbled the latter.

One hour later, they hopped off just as they were reaching Masjid Istiqlal on the edge of Glodok. As the sun was about to set, Dr Jusuf suggested that they perform Maghrib together inside the mosque and then break their fast in the company of the faithful. But Hendra excused himself – he was supposed to have dinner with some friends. (One friend in fact, Jasmine, whom he knew was waiting for him at his flat.)

'Thanks,' he said, as he was bowing and holding Dr Jusuf's right hand, 'thanks for welcoming me at The Saving Hand. Every day I get to fight this jihad against vice ... I feel so alive ...'

'Don't be absurd, Hendra. You're not fighting any jihad right now. The real *mujahideen* risk their lives in the name of Islam. Not us.'

'But ... what about the spiritual jihad?'

'The spiritual jihad is just another invention from the modern world, another of these bidah without any basis in Islam. There's only one form of jihad, OK?'

The annoyance verging on anger that Hendra could sense in Dr Jusuf's words took him by surprise. Hadn't Umar bin Talib himself mentioned the spiritual jihad in one of his sermons?

But Hendra quickly forgot about the day's only sour note, feeling wonderfully light-headed as he walked in the direction of his flat, about twenty minutes away. Not eating and drinking anything from sunrise to sunset was such a magical and powerful way to clear his mind and eliminate all the toxins that he had accumulated in his body. Fasting, together with his active involvement with The Saving Hand, was fast purifying him and for the last three days he hadn't experienced any headache attacks. More discipline and more rigorous religious practice, that's what he needed – not trying to uncover his mother's secrets.

In fact, he kept postponing his visit to his aunt's last-known workplace, Fortune Spa, and had even lied to Jasmine about it, pretending he had been there but that Maia had quit the massage parlour without leaving so much as a contact number or forwarding address. It certainly didn't help to bolster his resolve that on some nights he still experienced nightmares in which Maia chased after him and tried to forcibly kiss him with her orange-painted lips. He would wake up panting, sweating, and then rub his eyes for a long while to get rid of the ochre colour blinding him, before having to swallow Lexotan pills to fall back to sleep.

When he reached his flat, Jasmine had already set the table, with the radio switched on to make sure that they wouldn't miss the azan. A few minutes later, the muezzin's voice resounded, proclaiming Allah's greatness and signalling the end of the fast. They first ate a date before drinking water and then started savouring all the *nasi* Padang dishes that Jasmine had bought.

After a while, she cleared her throat, looking at Hendra with an ironic expression that, at first, he couldn't place.

'Tell me … do you want me to start wearing the veil?'

'No … why? I mean, it's your choice.'

Anyway, since in his eyes warias were not women but belonged to a third gender, he also believed that the koranic injunction didn't apply to them. But of course, he knew he couldn't tell Jasmine that.

'Then … why did I find *this* among the magazines in the living room,' she asked, pulling out one of The Saving Hand's brochures about proper Islamic dress code.

He had intentionally left Jasmine in the dark about his new activities. Even when she had started to notice, recently, that he was out quite often in the afternoon, he had made up a story, telling her that he was volunteering at a mosque, taking care of a fundraising drive to help the inhabitants of the Mentawai Islands who had lost everything in a recent earthquake. He had assumed – and rightfully so, it seemed, judging by the simmering anger in Jasmine's eyes right now – that she would strongly object to his involvement with The Saving Hand if she ever got wind of it. Already that day, when The Saving Hand had visited XS, he had heard her voice her surprise that Pak Kelvin would let a '*jenggot*' association distribute flyers inside his club.

'I can explain,' he started. 'I …'

'How can you even hang around with The Saving Hand! All these Saudis, they want to kill trans and warias, but you … you who like to fight with taxi drivers about me, you don't have any problem with that?'

Hendra averted Jasmine's eyes. She was exaggerating – The Saving Hand had no links whatsoever with the Wahhabis in Saudi Arabia – but she wasn't totally wrong either. Umar bin Talib had explained several times that the Indonesian tolerance towards 'transsexuals' was an aberration, a deplorable influence from the West. He had been very clear on the fate that was reserved for such deviant individuals: 'Unless they repent, the sodomites will be sent to the fires of Hell on Judgement Day.' Hendra couldn't help thinking that the imam was mistaken, if only because Indonesian warias had nothing to do with these transsexuals in *buleland*, but this time he knew better than to ask Dr Jusuf for his opinion. He was all too aware that he would be expelled on the spot from The Saving Hand if people had any inkling of his liaison with a waria.

'They can be a bit critical about you,' Hendra replied, finally. 'But no, they don't want to kill you, that's not true.'

'You mean … to kill *us*, right?'

'In any case, I'm only involved in their preventive actions to educate and protect minors. I am just fighting my spiritual jihad as recommended by Haji Ahmad.'

'Are you sure you really understood what Haji Ahmad meant? He certainly didn't want you to associate with *jenggots*! I can't wait for you to start working at XS again, so that you'll stop mixing with these evil people!'

Hendra didn't want to tell her that he dreaded his planned comeback to XS in early September when his three-month suspension ended. Now that he was with The Saving Hand, he felt reassured, almost taken care of. The religion had given him new bearings, like a moral compass that helped him keep drugs at bay. He was afraid he would get lost again once he was back playing at the club.

10

Hendra's grandparents were waiting for him at the doorstep, beaming. Without uttering a word, his kakek stretched up from this wheelchair and held him tight in his frail arms, his entire body shaking with emotion. Then, as soon as Hendra had freed himself, his teary-eyed *nenek* nearly smothered him as she covered his face with kisses.

He had not seen them since the previous year's Ramadan celebrations. Nenek had a few more wrinkles and white hair than he remembered but overall, she looked good. His grandfather's health, however, had noticeably deteriorated, as evidenced by this new wheelchair, and Hendra felt a pang of guilt at not having come earlier.

Like every year, he was visiting his grandparents for Lebaran, the week-long festivities at the end of the fasting month. He had flown into Medan from Jakarta, and then bused his way for more than two hours to Pasar Rawa, the village where Kakek and Nenek were born, had always lived and would die one day. A long journey, tiresome, full of delays, which he had accomplished alongside millions of Jakarta residents undertaking their yearly pilgrimage to their hometowns. At the Medan bus station, it had taken more than one hour just to secure all the presents meant for relatives onto the roof of their battered vehicle.

'What's this goatee for?' Hendra's grandfather asked, no sooner had they entered the house.

Trying to sound as casual as possible, Hendra explained that since joining an Islamic NGO a couple of months ago, he had become more observant; in particular, he was now praying five times a day without fail. His kakek just kept observing him, intensely, quizzically, his eyebrows joined above the nose.

'Well, I think that this new beard suits you very well,' Nenek said, patting Hendra's cheek.

What would his grandfather have said, thought Hendra, if he had taken to wearing the Salafi trousers, stopping just above the ankle, like a few of The Saving Hand members (against Dr Jusuf's advice).

They sat around the large dining table where Nenek had already laid some of Hendra's favourite Padang dishes: beef *rendang*, *bagedil*, *ikan bakar*, *sambal goreng*. Night had fallen by now and one could hear the large leaves of the palm trees outside swaying gently in the breeze. Hendra wondered whether it was going to rain.

'And what do you do exactly in this religious organization?' his kakek asked after a while.

'I distribute leaflets to the youth to remind them how people should dress according to the Prophet's teachings.'

'Hmm … You mean the hijab, don't you?'

'Yes, among other things. Too many women don't cover up these days.'

'What are you talking about?' exclaimed his grandfather. 'Women are free to decide whether they should wear the veil or not. What do you think, Ani?'

Hendra regretted not mentioning first The Saving Hand's less proselytizing activities like their preventive actions in nightclubs. Hadn't he realised by now how unorthodox his grandfather's religious views were? In his childhood, every time Hendra went back to the kampung for the school holidays, his kakek would spend entire afternoons complementing or correcting the religious education that he was receiving from the *ustads* at the madrassa in Jakarta. But his grandfather, Hendra saw it all too plainly now, had taught him a corrupted strain of Islam in which the *adat*, the Indonesian village customs, prevailed over Shariah law. An Islam filled with innovations contrary to the Qur'an, like the matriarchal organization of the Minangkabau societies in West Sumatra near Padang, from where this kakek's parents had hailed.

'If it makes my grandson happy, I support the veil!' said his grandmother, evidently trying to quell the brewing argument.

But his grandfather carried on, unfazed: 'According to the Qur'an, women are men's equals and for women and men, what matters is to behave modestly. A woman certainly doesn't need to wear the veil to look modest. Your grandmother only started covering her hair when she turned 40. And that was her own choice.'

Hendra had no intention of spoiling the joy of the reunion by getting into a heated discussion with his grandfather. 'Kakek, I brought you a present,' he said, while rising from his chair. 'Don't you want to see it?'

Without waiting for his grandfather's reply, he went to fetch in his luggage the wrapped box containing the bulky orchestra angklung that he had bought at Sarinah Department Store, right before leaving Jakarta.

The oldest shopping centre in town, Sarinah stood at the corner between two of the largest arteries in Jakarta, Jalan Thamrin and Jalan K.J. Walud Hasyim. Built in the 60s, the grand old dame had survived the assaults of the new mega malls although nobody knew exactly why people still went there to shop. Maybe the need to keep some familiar landmarks against the modernity that was fast engulfing the whole city? As a proof of its attachment to the past, Sarinah had dedicated the entire top floor to traditional musical instruments from Indonesia. Angklungs, percussions from *gamelan* ensembles, *rabena* (drums), *cak* and *cuk* (stringed instruments) and *calung* (xylophones) displayed their heteroclite shapes on three- or four-tiered shelves rising above the shoppers' heads. Angklungs themselves were organized by size: the smaller ones, with only one octave, generally meant for kids – like those his kakek gave Hendra when he was younger – then were the mid-size ones, used in orchestras, with two rows of bamboos so that the instrument could play on multiple octaves and finally, giant angklungs that could measure up to 1.5 metres. For 100 USD – a small fortune, given his dire financial situation – Hendra had managed to buy a very rare piece, a *two-pitch* orchestra angklung.

Kakek quickly forgot their discussion about the hijab. He felt the box with his two hands for some time before tearing the blue-teddy-bear wrapping paper – the only one the sales lady had in sufficient quantity. As he pulled the instrument out of the box, he gasped in awe and, wasting no time, started to shake the bamboo frame from left to right. The angklung vibrated, producing several notes that brought tears to his grandfather's eyes. He asked his wife to bring two other instruments from his study. Three was the minimum number of bamboo bells required to play a melody, and when Dini was alive, they could almost form a full orchestra if the whole family went at it together.

After his nenek came back with the two other pieces, they played for a long time, emitting that soft, aerial sound, characteristic of angklungs, which, according to the Javanese tradition, appeases men and ravishes Gods.

After dinner, his grandmother wanted to flip through the old photo albums, one of her favourite activities when Hendra was around. For her, it was more an occasion to evoke cheerful memories associated with her daughter than a way to cry over the past. His grandparents were fatalist: if Allah had called Dini back to Him, she was definitely happier in Heaven. But for Hendra, these moments were always so painful that he only allowed himself to be part of it to please his grandmother. He had not been able to attend his mum's funeral as he was crying so convulsively on that day that his grandfather had asked him to stay at home with the womenfolk. In the Muslim tradition, it was forbidden to weep during the burial, for fear that it might delay the journey of the deceased's soul back to the Creator. Relatives had twenty-four hours to dry their tears, after which the dead ought to be buried peacefully.

Standing up, towering over his grandmother who sat in the sofa, Hendra merely pretended to be looking at the photos. He knew that if he so much as glimpsed at them, an emptiness starting in his stomach might soon swallow him entirely and he would want to flee from there. His nenek kept turning the pages, making some light-hearted comments now and then, and from the strong, damp odour that emanated from the album, Hendra gathered that these were probably very old pictures. Then, all of a sudden,

Nenek jerked and raised her hand to her mouth. She seemed to want to flip quickly to the next page but intrigued despite himself, Hendra held her wrist and stared at the photo. It was an old black and white picture that had almost turned yellow – there was his mum, who could not have been more than twenty then, grinning widely at the camera, and next to her, he recognized Maia pulling a long face. While his mother had kept quite a few photos of her foster sister in her flat in Jakarta, it was the first time that Hendra saw any in the albums of his grandparents. They had probably removed all traces of the 'shameless' girl in the years that followed her banishment from the family. Except for this picture, that is.

'Maia was with Mum when she was working in Batam, wasn't she?' Hendra said.

'Who told you this?' asked his grandmother.

'One of mum's former colleagues at TMM.'

His grandfather, who had been flipping through the newspaper all this while, raised his eyes and met Hendra's stare. For a long moment, his kakek didn't say anything, and an uneasy silence filled the room.

'Leave the past alone,' his grandfather eventually said, while his grandmother closed the album.

Hendra barely moved his head in acknowledgement but that was enough to send a painful jolt down his neck.

* * *

Hendra was looking out the window of the bus bringing him back to the airport in Medan. In the fading light of dusk, the trees were casting green shadows on the reddening clouds.

He felt lost, helpless. His headaches had not left him in peace after the photo incident. A few times, hiding from his grandparents' eyes, he had been forced to slash himself on the wrist to stem the unbearable pain.

They had not talked anymore about Maia but the profound malaise had remained, as if the secret was suspended in the air that they were breathing. A secret his grandparents knew all about, Hendra now firmly believed, but intended to keep hiding from him.

Part IV

The White Brigade

Jakarta, August 2014

11

In Hendra's dream, DJ Radikal was mixing on a beach in Ibiza.

He had never been to Ibiza – he had actually never left
Indonesia – but as the world's techno capital often served as
the backdrop for the Fashion TV clips projected on XS's giant
screens, it had come to epitomize his vision of paradise: a magical
encounter between sea and techno. Since he was a kid, he had
always been fascinated by the sea, and he could have spent hours
listening to the soothing sounds of crashing waves. Never mind
that the beaches closer to Jakarta tended to lack charm (not to
mention clean sand), he didn't hesitate, whenever he had time and
means, to go to Ancol, a sea-side park in Jakarta North, or even
further, a one-hour boat ride, to one of the islands of the Pulau
Seribu archipelago.

Arms raised above their heads, their bodies gleaming with
sweat under the rising sun, the thousands of clubbers in trance
in Hendra's dream cheered him on as he slowed down the music.
Strident screams, together with quick whistle sounds, flew in
from all corners of the beach. Unfortunately, the music's build-up
wasn't even over when all of a sudden, a foghorn started to blast,
drowning his music in its thick, powerful noise. Some clubbers
covered their ears with their hands, while others ran away
frightened. But despite the increasing pain in his own head, DJ

Radikal had no intention of giving up. His fans would not believe their ears! After raising the bass sounds, he accelerated the beat and performed a few spectacular scratches but to no avail ... he had to admit defeat – the party (and his dream) was over.

Now fully awake, he sat upright in his bed, two fingers pressed to his left temple. The throbbing pain was there again. It was the third episode that night, and he had probably slept less than two hours since the last one.

Following his return to Jakarta, one week earlier, his life had resumed its pre-Ramadan routine between Umar bin Talib's religious classes at Al-Amin Mosque during the day, and the preventive operations at night inside the clubs patronized by Jakarta's wayward youth. Yet, something had changed that completely undermined the enthusiasm of his first days with The Saving Hand. The lull in his headaches that he had been experiencing had been just that, a lull, and the attacks were now back in full force. Yesterday, the pain was so excruciating that he couldn't hold back anymore and had bought a few doses of K. But did he have a choice when he was again at three or four attacks a day? As long as he stopped at K and didn't plunge back into heroin hell, it was a lesser evil than the increasingly self-destructive behaviours he was drawn to in those helpless moments.

Hendra opened his nightstand drawer and pulled out a sachet of Kit Kat. Then he grabbed from the floor the bound edition of *Sequence*, Jeff Mills' anthology on which he often prepared his lines when he sniffed in bed. But just as he was about to tear open the sachet of K, his left eye started to cry, and he understood that it was too late – the attack had already progressed so much that whatever the quantity of K he snorted, he would not able to defeat it. He would just be wasting dope. Angry at himself for not acting fast enough, he threw the sachet back inside the drawer and slammed it shut before going to the kitchen.

At last, after an incision on his right wrist with a paring knife, the attack subsided. But it was already 4.45 am, and it would have been pointless to go back to bed – his sleep and his Ibiza dream would not return. So he performed Fajr prayer before taking a scalding hot shower. For a long while, he let the water glide over his body and soothe his soul. Then, as he came out and brushed his teeth with a miswak twig, hoping to find further comfort in the millennial gesture, Hendra observed his face in the mirror. His goatee was growing longer and longer – soon it would be even longer than Dr Jusuf's – and probably because he had stopped popping X pills, his complexion had taken a less pimply texture. But with all these attacks and the lack of sleep, he was also becoming very pale. Was this why his eyes seemed even greener than normal?

He remembered that fearful day when, for hours on end, he had repeatedly begged his mother to tell him the truth. She had come to pick him up from school after he had fought, no holds barred, during recess because of one taunt too many about his green eyes. She had stuck to her usual story: his dad was ethnic Chinese with eyes the colour of jade. His whole body shivering with anger, Hendra had toppled the shelves where his mum stored her fragrance samples, and their tiny flat had reeked of strong perfume for weeks on end after that – an overpowering reminder of his mum's lies.

Now that he had started to unravel the truth, was it really the right decision to stop midway? Jasmine kept telling him (even after he pretended that Maia had disappeared without a trace) that he couldn't spend his life fleeing, that one day or another, the secret would come back to haunt him.

Hendra rinsed his face. He had made up his mind – tonight, after his religious class at the madrasa, he would ask Dr Jusuf for guidance. He felt an increasing connection with the university professor whose lucid and clear opinions he often found so reassuring. He had already thought about confiding in him but he always dreaded the prospect of telling Dr Jusuf that he didn't know who his father was. Tonight, he would put his shame aside and take the plunge. After all, this story wasn't his fault.

***

That night, Dr Jusuf wasn't attending Umar bin Talib's religious class. But as Hendra was about to leave the Al-Amin compound, he spotted the professor on his own, in a corner of the mosque, performing Isha prayer. Hendra approached him as soon as he finished his last *rakat*.

'*Assalamualaikum*, Dr Jusuf, could I … speak to you in private?'

'*Waalaikumsalam*, dear brother. Sit next to me and speak with no fear. Only God can hear us.'

Hendra hesitated. But Dr Jusuf was right, the mosque was deserted now that all the students had left. He sat down cross-legged next to the professor.

Staring at the mihrab in front of him, he spoke softly, interrupting himself from time to time to avoid being over-whelmed. Without hiding anything, he told Dr Jusuf about the unanswered questions which surrounded the circumstances of his birth and kept tormenting him. Should he try to find Maia, as he was urged by 'some friend'? Should he, at all costs, chase the truth about his father?

Dr Jusuf grabbed his hands. 'I knew all along that something was standing in the way of your spiritual awakening. I'm so happy that you finally opened up to me, dear brother, for now I know how I can help you. Yes, you must free your mind of all the worries that burden you. And that means you have to get to the bottom of your mother's secret.'

'So, you too think that I should pay a visit to my aunt at her … massage parlour?'

'I understand and share your disgust, dear brother. You'll have to purify yourself after your foray into such a den of vice. Nevertheless, I tend to share your friend's view: in the end, the truth can only be lighter on your shoulders than the secret's infinite weight.'

Hendra lowered his head and Dr Jusuf briefly touched his hair.

'And I'll be here to help you. The Prophet, peace be upon him, once said: "The one who passed his hand on the head of an orphan, only for the sake of Allah, will have as many acts of virtue recorded in his favour as the number of the hair on which his hand passed, and the one who housed and catered for the needs of an orphan boy or girl, will stand in Paradise with me like this." And upon saying this, the Prophet joined his two fingers together.'

***

After he exited Al-Amin Mosque, Hendra first sought out the nearest ATM and withdrew one million rupiah to cover his potential field expenses. Unfortunately, the ATM had no more 100,000-rupiah notes, and he found himself with a thick wad of twenty 50,000-rupiah notes that made his wallet swell like an angry frog. Then he stood by the side of the road and waited until an empty Bluebird taxi finally passed by. Sure, Bluebird cabs were more expensive, but their drivers were more reliable, and given his feverish state, he didn't want to run the risk of getting a maniac and experiencing a new headache episode as a result.

When he gave his destination, the taxi driver – who wore a white Haji skullcap – turned around and looked at him with a knowing smile. Hendra wanted to protest, but what could he possibly tell him was his motive for going there? After a one-hour drive, the car pulled up in front of a shop with a large banner promoting the benefits of shiatsu and other Japanese massage treatments. In the photo, a woman lay on her stomach with an ecstatic look on her face while two strong, elegant hands worked on her shoulders. The establishment seemed quite respectable and Hendra was about to tell the driver that he must have taken him to the wrong place when he noticed the words 'Fortune Spa' on the top right corner of the banner. As he paid his fare, he felt his stomach tighten even more and he had to take a deep breath before ringing the doorbell.

A kimono-clad young woman with braces greeted him with a salutation that sounded Japanese. She handed him a menu where different types of thematic rooms were featured – the classroom, the hospital ward, the prison cell, etc – while apologizing because the toilet and jungle options, being currently under renovation, were sadly not available. Without a doubt, he was at the right place ... After pretending to be poring over the menu for a few moments, he raised his eyes and asked if he could see a certain 'Maia'.

The kimono looked confused. 'Once you've settled into your room, we'll send over the girls who are free right now, and you can choose the one you like. But you need to select your room first. May I recommend the classroom? It's just been refurbished.'

'But is Maia still working here?' Hendra insisted.

The kimono didn't reply, just looked at him with an embarrassed smile. Hendra decided to bluff.

'I've not been back here for a long time. But a few years ago, I had a great experience with one of your ... masseuses called Maia.'

'I'm sorry,' replied the kimono finally, 'I'm new here. Let me look for the manager.'

A few minutes later, she came back in the company of a middle-aged woman who had the airs and looks of a mamasan.

'Sounds like you're looking for someone called Maia, right' asked the woman, revealing a row of golden crowns as she opened her mouth. 'What does she look like?'

'She must be around forty. Short hair, high cheekbones, Chinese looking. And ... she often wears orange-coloured lipstick.'

The Fortune Spa mamasan smirked. 'Yes ... some Maia that would fit your description worked here until 2011. But I doubt she would have given you a massage, my dear She was the mamasan here before me. And so, she was managing the girls, not taking care of customers! Unless ... she went the extra mile just for you ...'

Hendra looked away.

The woman had now moved to the other side of the reception counter, standing less than ten centimetres from him. Every time Hendra breathed in, he had to inhale her acrid cigarette smell.

'Would you happen to know where Maia would be working now?' he asked finally.

'Seemed she really made an impression on you, sayang,' the mamasan replied with a hearty laugh that deepened his growing malaise, before coming even closer to him. Her chest was now brushing against his shirt and he could feel her skin's warmth against his face. 'We do go beyond the call of duty sometimes, especially when the customer is young and handsome like you … I suggest we take the classroom. Just renovated and I can find a uniform.'

'Please,' said Hendra, stepping backwards, 'just tell me where Maia is!'

The mamasan moved away, looking annoyed.

'Your Maia, she's dead, OK?'

'Dead?'

'Yes, counting the worms, you know. That's what they say in mamasan circles.'

And she took off, leaving him alone with the kimono who still had the same inane grin on her face.

Without another word, Hendra walked out of the door. Despite having learned squat about his aunt's whereabouts (or maybe because of that), he was breathing much better now than when he had pushed the same door open ten minutes ago.

A man called out to him as he was about to hail a taxi by the side of the street: 'Hey, you!'

'It's OK, I'll just figure it out myself,' replied Hendra, thinking that he was one of those touts who tended to congregate around nightspots. One had better stay away from the taxis they flagged down, as the drivers had to pay them a hefty commission which inevitably inflated the final fare.

But the guy continued: 'I heard you talk inside. You're looking for Maia, right?'

That's when Hendra noticed something like a badge around the guy's neck. Did he actually work at Fortune Spa?

'Yeah, right. Why? You met her before?'

'She ain't dead, your Maia. She just had a fallout with the boss, she's now working at Palladium.'

'Palladium, are you sure?'

'Hundred percent positive, my friend.'

Hendra gave the man a generous tip before slowly moving away, still reeling from the shock of what he had just learned. How could Maia stoop so low? Situated right in the heart of Glodok, a stone's throw from XS, Palladium was one of the most popular massage parlours among Jakarta locals, having built its reputation over the years for having the freshest girls in town – sometimes not even 16 or 17. Spotted by recruiters in search of 'new talent' who roamed the poorest villages near the Javanese towns of Indramayu or Malang, the girls were sold into bondage by their parents, often under false promises of employment as factory workers or domestics. They were only freed of their bond after serving a minimum of five to six hundred customers – a quota that the prettiest girls might manage to fulfil in less than six months, but for many others, less fortunate or too shy, it often meant that they had to turn tricks at the Palladium for at least two years. Amongst connoisseurs, the place was held in particularly high esteem for its new arrivals after the end of each Lebaran, a time of the year when cash-strapped families were more tempted to give in to recruiters so as to raise money for the customary celebrations. According to Pak Kelvin, Palladium paid heavy protection money and never had any problems with the police.

As Hendra walked down the street, the night's sultry and exceptionally humid air – even by Jakarta's standards – enveloped his face like a warm flannel. Still, he was shivering. Where was he going to find the strength to visit another Jakarta brothel, especially one with such a sinister reputation as Palladium? But now that he had started, he had to see it through.

He jumped into a Bluebird taxi and asked to be taken to Lucky Plaza – the mid-range mall in Glodok where he remembered Pak Kelvin saying Palladium was located. Upon reaching the place, he browsed through the shop directory at the entrance, hoping to find Palladium's floor number but the establishment wasn't listed. Shrugging – could Pak Kelvin have gotten it wrong? – he headed towards the central lift.

Inside stood a liftboy in uniform and white gloves who was a perfect example of the latest craze in Jakarta's shopping centres (even among the second-tier ones like Lucky Plaza): the hiring of staff whose only mission was to push lift buttons all day long. When Hendra told the boy that he wanted to go to Palladium, the young man initially paused, looking confused, before pressing the '10' button. In his twenties and obviously *pribumi*, Hendra probably didn't fit the image of Palladium's usual clientele.

Unlike for the other floors, Hendra noticed as they started their ascent, no shop name was written against the '10' button on the lift command panel – some semblance of discretion was maintained. As they rose, muffled bass sounds reached a crescendo until the lift slowed down and jerked, before coming to standstill. By now, the entire cabin vibrated under the assault of a powerful sound system. When the doors opened, Hendra found himself face to face with a human-sized mermaid seated sideways on a white-marble unicorn whose single horn pointed down a narrow corridor to the right.

'That way,' said the lift boy, stretching out his hand in the corridor's direction.

As Hendra exited the lift, the air was so thick with the stench of kretek cigarettes that it almost made him gag, but he carried on and soon found himself at Palladium's entrance. Two bouncers searched him while a hostess in a thigh-high slit blue dress attached a numbered plastic strap around his wrist. He wanted to know if this was the number of his assigned locker – he certainly had no intention of undressing – but before he could even ask any questions, the hostess had pulled aside the thick black curtain. The tobacco smell and the sound waves intensified, but apart from the white beams of the projectors playing with the cigarette smoke, Hendra couldn't discern much. He knew it would take a good few minutes for his eyes to get used to the extremely dim lighting that in nightspots in Jakarta was meant to guarantee a certain anonymity. Indeed, so far – apart from that strap – the place had more the look and feel of a cheap nightclub than a brothel.

No sooner had Hendra walked a few steps inside Palladium, than he was surrounded by two different hostesses who each grabbed one of his hands. They led him through the dark towards a better lit area and sat him at a raised table by the stage. There, two girls, way too young to be doing this, were stripping while shaking their hips to the beat of 'I Love to Love'. A sudden rush came over Hendra and he felt his cheeks burning. He needed a drink, and fast.

'Vodka Red Bull,' he ordered from the first waitress passing by.

Hendra turned around towards the back of the room. Squinting, he counted no fewer than fifty girls spread over five or six rows of red couches. Some smoked and laughed; a few were focused on their phones, while still others were smoothing their hair, impatiently shaking their legs at the same time. The colour and shape of their attire seemed to depend on the row where they sat as if each row corresponded to a different 'team'. But there was a clear common denominator between them all: the mini-skirt, whose length was inversely proportional to that of the stiletto heels. The girls' heavily made-up faces glowed eerily under the small spotlights placed above them. Like sad clowns, thought Hendra, and based on those closest to him, whose features he could make out, most couldn't be more than eighteen.

At some point, a girl raised her eyes from her handphone and met Hendra's stare, smiling timidly. Did she think that he was a potential customer? wondered Hendra, horrified, quickly turning his head away, and when the waitress brought his vodka Red Bull, he gulped it down in one shot.

A woman in her forties wearing denim jeans and flat shoes hoisted herself onto the free stool next to Hendra. He noticed that she held a small notebook in her hands, where names arranged in a column were flanked by vertical bars – probably her system of keeping track of each girl's assignments, he thought.

'Like her?' she asked, using a red laser beam to point at the chest of the girl who had looked in his direction. She was doing her best to speak above the deafening music. 'Good choice, fresh from the village but already –'

'I'm looking for someone called Maia.'

The mami stared at him, flustered. 'We have a few Maia here, you know. How is she, your Maia? Tall? Petite? Big tits? Bean-bags?'

'She's not a ... I mean she doesn't give massages.'

The mami smiled. 'You know, we have lots of girls here who do other things than massages.'

'I mean ... . she doesn't take care of customers. She works ... like you.'

'Oh, I see she's a farmer?' Then, probably noticing his incredulous stare, she added: 'She farms chickens, what!'

At last, Hendra understood the mami's dubious play on the double meaning of *ayam*, which in Bahasa could mean both chicken and prostitute.

Bursting into a laugh, the woman touched Hendra's hand and he pulled it away faster than if a cockroach had brushed his fingers.

'Yeah, right, there's a mami called Maia who works here. But I'm not sure if she's in today. What do you want with her, anyway? I also have many sweet young things who can service your engine, you know ... What do you like? Threesomes?'

Disgusted, on the verge of exploding, Hendra pulled two 100,000-rupiah notes from his wallet and thrust them into the mamasan's hand.

'Go get me Maia, please.'

The mamasan slipped the notes inside her blouse, briefly revealing a black bra, and left the table without a word.

A powerful, melodious voice suddenly filled the room. Hendra looked to his left and saw a middle-aged man singing at the top of his lungs that he was 'counting the days, second by second'. It was the chorus of a famous love song by the Indonesian diva Krisdayanti which the patron must have requested in its karaoke version. Hendra wondered what was more obscene: the underage girls undressing on stage or this man declaiming heart-wrenching lyrics while pinching with his free hand the breast of the girl seated on his lap.

'You're the one who wants to see Maia?' asked a hoarse voice behind his back.

Hendra turned around and came face to face with a Chinese-looking woman who was probably nearing fifty. He recognised Maia's sour gaze and inimitable orange lipstick, shivering as childhood memories started flowing back into his mind. She stared at his upper lip and then at his eyes – even though it was probably too dark for her to see their colour.

'H ... Hendra?'

'Yes.'

'What ... what are you doing here?' She sounded more flustered than angry.

That's when Hendra realised that the headache attack that had been looming for a while was rising very fast. There wasn't any time for an emotional reunion (not that he had wanted one, anyway).

He took a deep breath. 'I want to talk to you about things

that happened years ago when mum was in Batam with you.'

'What … ?'

'You were together in Batam, right?'

'How did you find me? Dini knows you're here?'

'Tell me what happened in Batam, Maia!'

'I don't know what you're talking about.'

Now Hendra had to go home as soon as possible and do a line before it was too late, before his head was ripe for the final explosion. Anyway, this whole expedition was a huge mistake, he saw it all too clearly now.

Pulling out an XS business card, he handed it to Maia. 'This is my number; call me if you want to talk.'

Without waiting for his aunt's reply, he rushed towards the exit, but the bouncers blocked his way, sternly reminding him that he first had to pay for his drinks and 'any other services as well'. Hendra finally understood the purpose of the numbered strap around his wrist when a hostess came up to him, removed it and passed it to a cashier. Then, upon settling his bill, he was given a card with the word 'EXIT' written on it – the open sesame that the bouncers took from his hands before letting him out of Palladium. He ran along the smoky corridor towards the lift, where the boy stared at him with eyes that seemed to ask 'Already?' At last, they started to descend, the cheap techno music fading into the background, soon becoming nothing more than an annoying murmur.

Outside Lucky Plaza, Hendra jumped into the first free cab that he found. Sure, he was less than fifteen minutes away from his place by foot but he had no time to lose if he wanted to have a chance to derail the attack.

As soon as he reached home, he sniffed a large dose of K. And even after the threat of the headache receded, he continued snorting. To see his aunt again in this disgusting place, that filthy bordello where every minute young girls lost their innocence, had filled him with rage and hatred. Why didn't the White Brigade visit these whorehouses where Shaytan paraded in total impunity! All these degenerates hanging around at Palladium, mamasans included, deserved to be subjected to the harshest punishments imposed by the Shariah law. And first of all, Maia!

12

'One *air bandung*,' Hendra told the waiter.

'Make it two,' said Jasmine with a wink. 'I'm also starting to like it.'

'So, how was your appointment?' Hendra asked her after the waiter left.

They were at Batavia Café in Kota, Jakarta North. Steeped in Dutch atmosphere, the café-restaurant was located a few streets away from the hospital where, once a month, Jasmine had a follow-up appointment with an endocrinologist for her hormone therapy treatment. She wanted to become more feminine so that people in the street wouldn't be able to tell she was a waria, and that meant taking increasing doses of oestrogen and blocker. Unfortunately, to Hendra's dismay, it also meant that it was getting more and more difficult for Jasmine to ejaculate. Anorgasmia, it seemed, was the price she had to pay to be passable. Only if she went for a genital reassignment surgery – and plunged Hendra into despair at the same time – would her testosterone level lower without the need for such an intensive hormonotherapy.

'Nothing, sayang. I have to continue with the same blocker dosage. It can't be reduced.'

'I see ...' said Hendra, sighing.

For a while they pretended to listen to the music from the old player piano.

'You know, I thought about Maia,' Jasmine broke the silence after their glasses arrived. 'Don't you think there should be a way to find her on social media? I checked Facebook and Instagram and there are thousands of Maias in their fifties living in Jakarta. To narrow it down, I tried your *suku* name[2], Chaniago, but, nothing.' She shrugged.

Hendra hadn't told Jasmine about his visit to Palladium the previous week. In part because of his initial lie but also because Maia hadn't contacted him anyway. To be honest, he couldn't say he was totally unhappy about his aunt's silence. The more he thought about it, the more he was convinced that he had better stop this search before it was too late, before the minefield of his mother's lies left him with a field of ruins.

'Very few people in the family use that name anymore and certainly not Maia, I imagine.'

'Maybe your grandmother would know what nicknames she liked when she was a kid?' she insisted. 'Sayang, I can tell, you still have all these headaches everyday … You have to find a way to get to Maia.'

Perhaps, thought Hendra, he had better tell Jasmine the truth: that he had already seen his aunt and that she simply didn't want to talk to him. That would close this Maia chapter with Jasmine once and for all.

'I saw her …'

'What? When?'

---

2 Minangkabau people have clan (*suku*) names although in recent times, most, like many Indonesians, only use one name (or adopt their father's given name as a last name).

'Last week.' Then, lying through his teeth: 'That Fortune Spa manager I met previously, when she heard about Maia the other day, she remembered my visit and sent me a message to say that Maia now worked at Palladium.'

'But why didn't you tell me anything?'

'Because … I learned nothing.'

He mentioned how Maia had not even admitted to being with his mum in Batam.

'But did you tell her at least that your mother had passed away?' asked Jasmine.

'I didn't have time. I was starting to have a headache attack and I left the place as fast as possible.'

Jasmine raised her hand to call for the waiter and asked for the bill.

'Wait, we're leaving already?' asked Hendra. 'Isn't it a bit too early for dinner?'

'We're going back to Palladium together!'

'What? But they'll never let you enter!'

***

Twenty minutes later, they were already inside the Lucky Plaza lift. When the liftboy, who seemed to have recognized Hendra, saw Jasmine next to him, his good-natured smile quickly evaporated. He clenched his jaw and pressed the '10' button without a word. Yeah sure, thought Hendra on seeing his disgusted look, a waria coming to the Palladium with her boyfriend certainly had to be up there in the ranking of perversions that he had been the silent witness of.

Hendra was convinced that the security would deny them entry but Jasmine quickly took matters into her own hands. She approached the bouncers, who were already observing them inquisitively, and whispered something into the ear of one of them. Seconds later, the man looked at Hendra with a mocking smile and beckoned to a hostess who came forward and tied a plastic strap around Hendra and Jasmine's wrists. As soon as they walked inside, another hostess came forward like the last time but on this occasion Hendra insisted they be seated as far away as possible from the stage. He was already rattled enough; he didn't want, on top of that, to put himself through the distressing spectacle of minors stripping. The hostess made her way through the thick crowd of customers – despite the early hour, the place was already heaving – and after having installed them at a table at the back, she said she would call for a waitress to serve them. To which Jasmine told her, in a gentle but firm tone, that they first wanted to talk to the mamasan called Maia who worked here.

A few minutes later, Maia arrived at their table.

'Listen, Hendra,' she said straightaway, without so much as a hello, 'I have nothing to tell you.'

While staring at Jasmine with an intrigued look, she drew intently on a kretek cigarette and Hendra noticed the (probably fake) ruby ring on her right forefinger.

'Hello Maia, I'm Jasmine,' Jasmine said, holding out her hand.

Maia briefly shook it before addressing Hendra again: 'Your grandparents threw me out fifteen years ago. I want nothing to do with this family anymore. I hope you understand.'

As she was about to turn around and leave them alone,

Jasmine took her arm. 'Maybe you should know that ... Dini has already returned to God.'

Maia paused. 'When was that?'

'Four years ago,' Jasmine replied.

Maia seemed to hesitate before shaking off Jasmine's hand and moving away without another look at them.

***

Hendra was jolted awake by shrill birdsong, as though his bedroom had been invaded by a flight of raucous birds. Upon his return from Palladium, he had fallen asleep after successfully sniffing K to repel a fast-approaching headache attack. Luckily, as Jasmine had had to go to work, she hadn't followed him up to his flat and he had been able to snort at will, without having to hide.

He stretched his arm and grabbed his phone on the bedside table. He still hadn't gotten used to this new ringtone that Jasmine had set up on his Samsung. Looking at the screen, Hendra realised that he had received an SMS from a number which wasn't in his directory. Probably spam for some stupid lucky draw. He swept his finger over the screen, unlocking the phone, and opened the message.

'Where's your place?' he read.

'Who's that?' he replied, heart beating.

Seconds later, the birds started singing again but he shut them up as he anxiously pressed on the incoming message: 'Maia.'

Hendra sat up, panting, even more awake now than if he had received a pail of ice water in the face. After a brief moment of hesitation, he sent his address to his aunt and she replied that she would drop by around 1 am, after finishing her shift at Palladium.

Shivering, Hendra placed his phone back on the bedside table. Then he picked it up again to call Jasmine but quickly put it back down. He needed to meet Maia one-on-one now. He ought to try and wash his own dirty laundry before airing it in public. He also resisted the urge to snort more K to relax – he couldn't afford to be flying too high for the impending face-off. Reluctantly, he turned to the cannabis offered by his dealer and, sitting in the living room, smoked a few joints, one after the other, promising himself to sniff a real beam à la Alessandro after his meeting with Maia.

One hour later, the birds sang again – they sounded like the bulbuls in his kakek's garden, Hendra thought fleetingly as he snatched his phone from the low table.

'I'm here. Which floor?'

He gave Maia his apartment number and watched through the peephole. Despite all the cannabis that he had smoked, his heart pounded so heavily in his chest that he could feel the throbbing all the way to his throat. Even before she could ring the bell, he opened the door.

It had been too dark at Palladium for him to get a good look at his aunt but now, under the glow of the artificial light, Hendra had to admit that despite the age and the wrinkles, she was still a beautiful woman, seductive and curvy in her tight blouse and skirt. Like the girl in a formfitting *kebaya* he had seen in the photo at his grandparents' place. And he couldn't help noticing with some relief that Maia had removed her make-up. Her lips had a natural, light pink colour instead of the orange of his nightmares.

Not saying a word, Hendra shuffled aside to let Maia enter. She walked in and continued straight to the living room at the end of the tiny entrance corridor. Without being invited, she sat on the sofa just as Hendra followed in behind her.

'Mind if I smoke?' she asked, pulling out a packet of Gudang Garam.

Not waiting for Hendra's answer, Maia pulled a lighter from her handbag and lit one of the disgustingly sweet-scented kretek cigarettes. Hendra pushed the ashtray on the low table towards her.

'I knew it,' she said, pointing at the joint butts in the ashtray, 'the cannabis smell is everywhere, even outside your flat!'

He had tried airing the place before Maia's arrival but a very strong wind was whipping Jakarta's streets, so much so that he'd had to close the windows almost immediately and hadn't gotten rid of the heady smell.

'That's what I thought when I saw you with your girlfriend,' continued Maia, 'you seem much more *fun* than your mother.' Then after a pause. 'So ... what are you waiting for? Aren't you going to offer me a joint?'

Hendra didn't say anything. He was paralyzed.

Outside, the storm was gathering speed and pressing against the windows, as if trying to enter.

'And can you please stop looking at me as if I were the *pontianak*!'[3]

How could Maia and his mum be sisters, even if only foster sisters? Hendra couldn't help wondering. They were so ... different.

'Hey, I'm not joking,' continued Maia after trying, but without much success, to blow smoke rings in the air, 'I'd really

---

3 A *pontianak* is a female vampiric ghost in Indonesian folklore.

like to smoke a joint. I didn't have a minute to myself since 8 pm today.'

'OK,' Hendra nodded.

And why not? Maybe after one spliff, Maia would open up more easily. Not to mention that he himself could also do with another joint.

'You know we have this new show now after 8 pm with two girls who make out on stage. And it was total madness tonight!'

A close shave, thought Hendra as he knelt in front of the low table and started rolling a joint. If they had arrived later with Jasmine, he wouldn't have survived the sickening sight of underage girls caressing each other in front of everyone.

Once he was done with the joint, he used his tongue to wet the handmade filter cardboard at one end and burned the twisted paper tip on the other. After briefly puffing on the spliff to test it, he handed it to his aunt and then grabbed the remote control of his sound system. David Bowie's Ziggy Stardust CD album was still inside. Hopefully Maia would appreciate that old rock music from her youth days.

With her left hand, Maia parted her long, black silky hair and placed the joint between her lips. Making the tip glow and crackle, she took a long drag before blocking her breathing for a few seconds to let the cannabis permeate her lungs. Then she exhaled the smoke very slowly, almost with regret.

'How did Dini die?' she asked when it was Hendra's turn to smoke.

Between two puffs, he explained that his mother had been fatally hit by a mikrolet while she was crossing the street near her office. She was already dead by the time the emergency services arrived.

'That's so sad … Why didn't anyone tell me anything? But I guess Kakek didn't even have my number. He never wanted to see me again after … you know.'

Maia started telling him her own version of the swing accident, how while she was talking to a boy from the village, Hendra had slipped his hand out of hers and run towards the swing. Why had he badmouthed her when everyone came back from the shopping trip? Because of him, she had been banished from the family.

Hendra was quite sure he hadn't betrayed her – his cousins had taken care of that, hadn't they? – but he didn't try to contradict her. He could only think of one thing, yet so intense was the fear that compressed his chest that he couldn't even bring himself to open his mouth, let alone ask his question.

Maia kept rambling and rambling. Then all of a sudden, she stopped mid-sentence before adding: 'Are you really sure you can take cannabis? Because you're whiter than a bule right now, you know!'

Hendra lowered his eyes to the ground, as if hoping to find there the courage that he lacked.

'Who's my father?' He had finally managed to spit out the words stuck in his throat.

'I can't say I didn't expect that question but …'

Her voice trailed off.

'So, *who* is he?'

'Back then, he was the manajer umum of the TMM factory in Batam.'

'You mean a guy called Hadi Wijono or maybe Hadi Harsono … ?'

'I don't remember his name after so many years, you know. But you do know that he passed away in the fire of the factory, right?'

'Liar! There was never any fire at the TMM factory! I met this Hadi Harsono who was the factory head when you were there. He has very fond memories of you, by the way …'

He paused for effect but Maia just stared at him stone-faced.

'And why did mum never tell me that you were together in Batam? What were you doing there?'

'Exactly what are you accusing me of? I don't know why Dini never told you we were together. Or actually,' she continued with anger suddenly bloating her words, 'I do know. Like everyone in this family, she was ashamed of me!'

'Maybe she had good reasons!'

Hendra saw the moment when Maia was going to slap him. 'You haven't changed! You're still that same nasty little brat!'

Hendra grabbed her arm. 'Who is HE?'

Maia shook his hand off. 'Your mother said she slept with the manajer umum. I didn't go and check, OK?'

'Cut the crap, Maia! Hadi Harsono left Batam to work in Germany eighteen months before I was born and the person who came after him was a woman!'

Maia kept a straight face.

'Now tell me who is my father!' screamed Hendra, feeling his pulse racing faster and faster.

'I don't know. And now I'm going to leave. I thought … you were really sincere in wanting to reconnect with me, but clearly I was wrong.'

She grabbed her handbag from the low table and made for

the door before turning around:

'And what does your kakek say about your recent findings?'

'He's very sick … Now is not the right time to talk to him about this and … there might never be a right time anymore.'

She looked pensive. Her plucked eyebrows moved into a frown, drawing above her dark brown eyes like the delicate silhouettes of two conical hats.

'I see,' she said finally. 'But I'm sorry, I can't help you.'

He couldn't let her go like that! For she knew everything, that much was clear. He had to hold her back, convince her to talk.

'Sorry to have gotten mad at you just now,' he said, pretending to be contrite. 'All these secrets, it's getting to me.'

'I can … understand. But I don't know anything, really.'

He suddenly had an idea. 'How about doing some K before you leave?'

Who knows? If Maia smoked joints, perhaps she also liked to snort now and then and she might become more talkative after a line of K …

His aunt stared at him, looking both amused and sceptical.

'You sniff K?'

'Yeah, sometimes to come down after taking X at rave parties.'

'And you go to rave parties?' she asked putting back her bag on the low table.

'Yes, I'm even a DJ.'

'Hence the business card and … all these discs,' she said, pointing at his collection of vinyl on the shelves. 'Never taken K but always wanted to try. So, yeah … why not?'

She grinned widely, and for the first time her open lips revealed two rows of perfectly white teeth.

Hendra went to his bedroom and fetched a sachet of Kit Kat. Then he prepared two thin lines directly on the low coffee table in the living room, drawing what looked like white marblings across the transparent glass. He only cut a quarter of a normal K dose, after which he rolled a 100,000-rupiah note – the only one he had that wasn't too crumpled – and showed his aunt how to snort. Matching words with action, he quickly finished his own line, without experiencing much of a rush as the dose was really too small. He handed the money straw to his aunt who knelt and sniffed everything in one go. One long inhalation. Clearly not her first time snorting powder. If not K, she had probably done speed before; it circulated quite freely at night in Jakarta.

Maia closed her eyes, her face flushing while she smiled blissfully. Realising that she was about to fall backwards, Hendra positioned himself behind her. She crumpled into his arms, laying her head on his shoulder. Her body emitted a vanilla-based perfume with floral undertones, mixed with strong notes of tobacco.

'Come, Maia, stand up. You'll feel better if you lie down on the sofa.'

But she seemed completely unable to move and so he lifted her by the armpits and dragged her to the sofa. Her full chest stretched the fabric of her pale green blouse while he hoisted her up. Maia just let herself slide to the side – she was really stoned.

'Don't worry,' he said, taking her hand reassuringly. 'It's just going to last a few minutes.'

'I'm not worried. On the contrary, I feel so good …' she replied as the smile on her lips widened.

Hendra went to the kitchen to fetch a glass of water and then forced her to drink. Still lying down on her side, she slowly came around and opened her eyes, staring at him. Then all of a sudden, she burst into tears – an abrupt mood swing which was quite typical of K newbies. For a while, Maia was going to be tossed around from one emotion to another; right now she was hitting rock bottom but she would soon bounce back.

Between sobs, she asked: 'Dini … what did she tell you about me when you were growing up?'

Her voice had cracked and it was hard to ignore the pain in her pleading eyes as she was looking at him. Then, without waiting for his answer, she sprang to her feet like an excited child.

'No crying, Maia!' she said to herself, drying up her tears with the sleeves of her blouse, while a large smile spread on her face.

She was climbing high again. Hendra seized the opening.

'Who is he?'

She stared at him with glassy eyes. 'I don't know where to start, Hendra.'

'What do you mean?' he asked, hardly hearing his own voice. His heart's frantic pumping was producing an intense buzzing in his ears, like his head was going to explode.

'Factory workers like me and your mum didn't earn that much at TMM, you know,' she said with a very soft voice. 'So sometimes, to complement our salary, some of us would go out with customers in a bar. The Cock & Bull in Nagoya, one of the first that opened then …'

Hendra stopped listening. Stopped breathing. Everything froze around him: the trembling shadows cast by the lamp, the blinking lights of the sound system, the blades of the ceiling fan. The bees in his head panicked. He blacked out.

13

When Hendra came to, the wind's howling had stopped, giving free rein to David Bowie's artistry. Opening his eyes to 'Starman waiting in the sky', he saw Maia leaning over his face, looking alarmed.

'You scared the hell out of me, you know! I was about to call for an ambulance.'

How long had he been unconscious? wondered Hendra. It couldn't be more than five minutes as right before passing out, he remembered hearing 'Moonage Daydream' – the track before 'Starman' on Bowie's album.

Maia's shocking revelations quickly crept back into his mind and he felt like he was going to short-circuit again. The Palladium mamasan might have removed her orange lipstick before visiting him, but she was still a witch. Yes, she *was* a Pontianak that brought desolation into his life.

'Get out,' he said.

'Listen, Hendra. I'm sorry, I was never supposed to …'

He cut her off. 'Get out!'

'I'll clear out, but first, I need to tell you that …'

'Get out of here!' he screamed, cupping his ears with his hands. 'I don't want to listen to you anymore! I never want to see you again, you're not even my aunt!'

Maia stood and grabbed her handbag. Before leaving, she turned around, about to say something, but Hendra shouted at her again and she left without another word.

What more was there for him to learn, anyway? He could easily fill in the blanks. His mum had been a ... night butterfly, and he was the fruit of an unwanted pregnancy, his birth from an anonymous father the consequence of 'professional hazard' – although not a factory fire ...

He curled up on the sofa. Burning everything in its path, the mental pain was spreading by layers inside his head, already attacking the deeper recesses of his mind, including his most cherished memories with his mum. Until when had she been a ... ? All these years, she always said she was working as a secretary for that American MNC she had joined right after giving birth to him. He could still picture her in the mornings, holding the thick red satchel where she kept all her diaries. How many times had she chided him because he liked to write on the blank pages, childish inscriptions, love notes, tiny hearts, that she only discovered once at the office. Perfumed, always elegantly dressed in a blouse and matching long skirt, she would drop him at school before going to work. In so many years, he had never seen her in the company of any man, and for as long as he could remember, whenever she stepped out of their small flat on Jalan Pahlawan Revolusi in Jakarta East, she always wore a hijab. Had it all been a façade to hide more immoral activities?

But why hadn't she had an abortion? Although officially restricted to situations where the pregnant mother's life was in danger, abortion was widespread in Indonesia and considered non-haram by many local Muslim clerics if performed before eighty days.

Hendra stood up, swaying.

He let out a cry of despair and kicked the low table. He resented his mother for making him suffer again with all her lies – even after her death. His neck was already so stiff, like a spear threatening to pierce through his skull. Fortunately, he had his darling little K to help him get better. Everything would stop immediately after that: the questions, the fears, the headaches. With a pang of envy, he remembered Maia's beautiful flash earlier. Now it was his turn to fly high and in order not to waste any of the precious dust particles, he was going to inject himself. As with all drugs meant to be snorted, it could be a bit dangerous, because of the impurities, to fix K. But so much more powerful. The best way to relive the emotions and the intensity of the first trips.

He picked his sole compilation of old country music, placed it in his CD player and searched for 'Waiting Around to Die', Townes Van Zandt's soul-crushing blues. He may not have listened to that song in a long while but now was the perfect time.

His name's codeine, he's the nicest thing I've seen
Together we're gonna wait around and die.

He tied an elastic tourniquet around his upper left arm before inserting the needle in the direction of the blood flow inside one of the bulging veins. He pumped out a bit of blood and once satisfied with the colour of the mixture inside the syringe, he released the elastic. But his thumb had not even pushed the plunger half-way into the barrel when he stopped, his finger suspended in mid-air. A second later, he pulled the syringe out of his arm, threw it to the floor and tore off the tourniquet.

Surely there were other ways to alleviate his suffering than succumbing to the fleeting relief of a fix. Hadn't he learnt that by now after his two months with The Saving Hand? Hadn't he experienced for himself that comforting throwback to the purity of the Salafs? He also remembered Dr Jusuf's words of the previous week and the hadith he had quoted about the Prophet's unconditional love for orphans.

He checked his watch: 4.20 am. Soon, it would be time for Fajr prayer. Dr Jusuf was probably already awake.

'*Assalamualaikum warahmatullahi wabarakatuh*,' said Dr Jusuf, picking up the phone on the second ring.

His warm voice enveloped Hendra who felt as if someone was stroking his hair.

'*Waalaikumsalam*, dear Professor. I'm sorry to disturb you at such an early time. But … I need to talk to you.'

'Of course, dear brother. Come to my house. I'm waiting for you.'

***

Hendra waited until 8 am to take the Transjakarta to Dr Jusuf's place, by which time he felt slightly better and able to travel. The professor had sent his wives and servants on a shopping trip and the purdah curtain that normally divided the living room into two was lifted up, so that Hendra could speak without fear of anyone eavesdropping. Observing him with his sole good eye full of solicitude, Dr Jusuf did not interrupt Hendra while he told him what he had learned about his mother.

'It's better for you to know the truth, dear brother,' said Dr Jusuf when Hendra finished talking. 'Have no fear: Allah the most merciful will lend you His support and heal your wounds. Pray 7, 10, 20 times a day, as many times as you need to feel better. But please remember that it is not your mother's fault: the real culprit is the loose morals exported by the Western World. Without the *kuffar*'s lustful obsessions and evil influence, our women would remain pure, and tragedies like your mother's wouldn't happen. So please keep up your engagement with The Saving Hand to help us rid Indonesia of these scourges.'

Hendra tried to wipe the sweat dripping from his forehead, but his hands themselves were clammy.

'I mean no disrespect, Professor, but what we're doing doesn't seem to be very useful. I mean ... nobody reads our brochures, and many people make fun of us in the clubs. We should be more ... more ...'

'More heavy-handed, you mean?' said Dr Jusuf. A faint smile had formed on his lips.

'Yes, maybe. I don't know ...'

'But you'd be right ... With all due respect to our imam, he doesn't understand a single thing about our modern world. He thinks we can win the war against vice and drugs with some flyers and a hotline. But his spiritual jihad is an invention from the miscreants to keep Muslims at bay, to turn us into meek little lambs ready to be slaughtered. Only the real physical jihad against the enemies of Allah will ever work!'

'You mean you think we should ... *attack* nightclubs?'

'Attack? But we would only be defending ourselves! They are the ones who attack us with their purulent debauchery ...'

Dr Jusuf grabbed his arm. 'Have you ever heard of the White Brigade?'

'Yes, of course. Who hasn't?'

'What do you think of their actions?'

'I ...'

'Would you be willing to join them?' Dr Jusuf interjected.

'What? You mean you're connected to the White Brigade?'

'You said it yourself ... The Saving Hand is useless.'

'But why ... why did you hide this from me?'

'I was waiting for the opportune moment to tell you.'

Dr Jusuf went on to explain that The Saving Hand was the front organization that collected donations under its NGO status. But unknown to Umar bin Talib, a large portion of the funds were diverted to finance the White Brigade, while the vigilantes also often used The Saving Hand's operations to survey places that they planned to attack.

'But we only cause material damage,' Dr Jusuf insisted. 'Scaring people away without bloodshed, that's our philosophy.'

'Then what happened at XS, two months ago? Didn't you kill one of the bouncers there?'

'You seem to be well informed, dear brother. Because I don't recall any newspaper mentioning this ...'

'It's a ... friend of mine who told me about it.'

'Then let me tell you that your friend patronizes *very* haram places!'

Dr Jusuf told him that XS was a highly symbolic target. The cream of Glodok's nightclubs and one of the most immoral places on Earth. During The Saving Hand's only visit there – as the evil Chinese owner generally turned the volunteers away –

they had found so many underage customers and even overheard one bouncer – Momo, Hendra guessed – propositioning a very young girl who wanted to go in but didn't have her ID. To teach him a lesson, the first thing the White Brigade had done, as they arrived to attack XS a few weeks later, was to beat him up at the entrance before going inside the club. They had absolutely no intention to kill him, said Dr Jusuf, but the stupid bouncer had flown off the handle and followed them into the club to get even. Unfortunately, it had proven to be a fatal move for him.

'We're not terrorists, if this is what you're worried about. We've got nothing to do with the Jemaah Islamiyah or Al-Qaeda. Bombing a bar or a nightclub like Paddy's in Bali is not our ambition.'

***

Hendra's first mission took place one week later. At Palladium itself.

He had not hesitated long before accepting Dr Jusuf's invitation to join the White Brigade. Even the connection that he had eventually made between the professor's dead eye and Jasmine's comment on the frozen right eyeball of Momo's murderer had not dissuaded him. With three or four headache attacks a day, he could not have been faring worse and he needed to blow off steam. Since the White Brigade's goals were righteous and Momo's death was, after all, only an accident, why would he think twice?

At 11 pm, Hendra met up with Dr Jusuf and another White Brigade member, Sunakin, at the entrance to the Lucky Plaza

Shopping Centre. An old boxer who had hung up his gloves two years before, Sunakin looked like a bouncer turned imam. He had a very thick chestnut-brown beard, even thicker than a Sikh man's, and always dressed in a white Arabian djellaba.

A few metres before reaching the lift, they put on the White Brigade's trademark white hood. Sure enough, the lift boy must have recognised them because after his initial surprise, he gave them his warmest smile and then quickly pressed on the tenth-floor button without their asking. Regardless, to ensure that he wouldn't alert the Palladium's security staff, Sunakin still relieved him of his talkie-walkie.

As the lift started its ascent, Hendra could only think of one thing: the fear on Maia's face when, in a few minutes, they started swinging their baseball bats inside the parlour.

Dr Jusuf had had to ask for specific approval from the Jakarta governor's office to indulge Hendra's request to attack the bordello where his aunt worked. As the professor had explained to Hendra, the local authorities – who felt increasingly powerless to contain the expansion of vice activities in the Indonesian capital – had privately agreed to turn a blind eye to White Brigade's operations on the express condition that they confined themselves to nightclubs patronized by minors. Which meant that, in principle, massage parlours were off-limits. Nonetheless, an exception had made for Palladium as the establishment had *clearly* gone overboard with the recent organization of live sex shows. Jakarta was no Amsterdam.

As soon as the lift doors opened, they rushed out and, brandishing their weapons, pounced on the security staff barring the Palladium's entrance at the end of the corridor.

'Everyone to the ground,' screamed Sunakin, while Hendra prevented the front hostess in her blue dress from going in and raising the alarm.

'Guys, I think you're making a mistake,' said one bouncer, the bulkiest. 'It's a massage place here, not a nightclub! Ain't no drugs.'

Not holding back, Sunakin hit him in the legs. The man's knees gave in while pain registered on his face.

'Just tell your boss to stop his porn shows, OK?' said Dr Jusuf. 'If not, we'll come back.'

Hendra himself was feeling more and more pumped up. Before coming, to give himself courage, he had popped the two X pills he had bought the day before at XS – as a customer, since his return as DJ Radikal was still two weeks away. And the X trip was exceptionally good. Or maybe that was just because he wasn't as used to the stuff anymore.

They put handcuffs on everyone's wrists and then tied the handcuffs to the external water piping running at floor level. Since the accident at XS, the White Brigade always neutralized the security staff before getting started on their cleansing operations.

They tore open the black curtains and burst in. On stage, one naked girl was wiggling around a pole while another was giving a blowjob to a volunteer from the crowd seated on a chair. The dense throng of people massed in front of the sex show were so transfixed that they had not yet noticed the White Brigade's arrival. Well, tonight they were about to be taught a lesson that they'd never forget!

Two hostesses came towards Hendra and his two accomplices, but on seeing the baseball bats in their hands, they fled, screaming.

Panic quickly spread inside the room and people started running in all directions, like cockroaches surprised by light.

The vigilantes marched towards the stage where the naked pole dancer stood, paralyzed, covering her nakedness with her arms – as if her nudity had suddenly become obscene just because of the White Brigade's intrusion. As for the girl performing fellatio, she had bolted, while her male volunteer, jeans pulled-up in one hand, looked around desperately for his belt. He gave up and started to run, but tripped on his loose pants and fell heavily at the foot of the podium. That's when someone finally had the good sense to stop the music.

The crowd parted to let the surprise guests occupy the stage. Their baseball bats artfully swinging in the air, as if choreographed, they smashed everything that they found on the raised platform: the now lonely chair, the sound system, the fluorescent light bulbs which exploded on impact. Then they moved to the main room, Hendra following in the steps of Dr Jusuf and Sunakin. He based his actions on theirs, savouring the adrenaline rush gushing through his veins as they destroyed everything in their path: the high chairs, the wooden tables, the oversized Gudang Garam-branded ashtrays, the whisky and vodka bottles chilling in ice buckets, the waitresses' abandoned trays of tequila shot glasses, the half-full jugs of Bintang beer. They were like an unstoppable tornado sweeping through the room. Soon they were left with the biggest prize, the bar itself, and they set to work meticulously, making sure that there wouldn't be anything left to drink after their passage.

On his left, Hendra noticed a kind of recess where clients and staff alike, united in their fear of the White Brigade, had sought refuge. Unfortunately, Hendra didn't recognize his aunt there. Could she have managed to flee already? Or maybe she just wasn't on duty that day! He felt rage rise in him. Maia wasn't going to see him destroy her work place.

'Let's attack the rooms,' he said, in desperation.

'What rooms?' asked Dr Jusuf.

'There must be some rooms where all these fuckers gèt laid!'

Dr Jusuf looked at his watch. Hendra knew that they had thirty minutes to finish their raid. Thirty minutes during which the police were instructed not to send any patrol even if someone called them for rescue.

'Must be up there,' said Sunakin, pointing to a staircase to the right of the bar.

'I'll stay here and watch over these vermin,' said Dr Jusuf. 'You have five minutes. Just scare them a little bit, OK?'

Followed by Sunakin, Hendra rushed upstairs and reached a corridor with numbered rooms on both sides. He tried to open the first door but it was locked.

'Stay back,' screamed the former boxer before shattering the door with a single strike of his baseball bat as if the door were made of cardboard.

A few johns had sought refuge inside the room, with some holding a terrorized cewek in their arms. They all started to scream as one.

That's when Hendra noticed his aunt, seated on the bed and staring at him with a defiant gaze. Once again, she was wearing this ochre orange lipstick that he abhorred! Raising his bat, he rushed forward and was about to smash that obscene mug when a blow to the legs sent him sprawling to the ground.

'You moron!' screamed Sunakin. 'Only material damage, remember! Now we clear out. This operation's over.'

Part V

Off Course

Jakarta, September – October 2014

14

As soon as Hendra approached the steel gates, the guards opened them and let him in.

'Come on in, mate!' joked one of them, Ali, who had lived in Australia.

Since joining the White Brigade one month ago, Hendra had become a familiar face at the professor's residence – the vigilantes' unofficial HQ – where every Monday, they would pray, train and plan their next actions.

Dr Jusuf had explained to Hendra that he'd joined The Saving Hand two years earlier as he wanted to wage a 'personal war' against drugs and prostitution in Jakarta. But just like Hendra, he had quickly realised that the NGO's strictly pacifist stance rendered its efforts painfully futile. Yet, he had refused to back down and, without the non-violent imam knowing, had created the White Brigade.

The White Brigade was now like a secret elite club within The Saving Hand, with each new member recruited and inducted by the professor himself. So far, there were only six of them amongst the fifty or so NGO volunteers whom he had considered worthy of his trust: Agung, the very first member, a plumber who Hendra was told had left for Syria a few months ago; the former boxer, Sunakin; Agus, a schoolmaster whose daughter lived in sin with an American expat in Bali; Yatib, a taxi driver originally from Surabaya; Ahmed, a white-collar worker in a logistics company, and Hendra, the latest recruit. All the other Saving Hand activists, including its founder Umar bin Talib, were supposedly ignorant of the fact that Dr Jusuf was the leader of the infamous White Brigade. The week before, the old imam had even *officially* condemned the militia's violence, declaring that even though the White Brigade's cause was perfectly respectable, its means of actions were un-Islamic.

How could Umar bin Talib be so clueless about the activities of his right hand when the Jakarta governor's office itself was in the know? Dr Jusuf had smiled when Hendra had asked this question. The 'pure amongst the pure', as he nicknamed the imam, was too preoccupied by the length of his trousers to notice anything going on in the organisation he had founded in 2001 to promote the expansion of a purer form of Islam in Indonesia. It was in fact only at the suggestion of one of his students then, a former drug addict, that he had embarked on these educational campaigns in nightclubs after being convinced that the protection of minors was a much more marketable cause than the enforcement of the hijab or the lobbying for the ban of rock concerts. Since then, the association coffers were always full. But the imam – who had actually never stepped into a nightclub – couldn't care less about the concrete actions of the volunteers on the ground, the responsibility of which he had now entirely delegated to Dr Jusuf while he devoted himself to the teaching of the pristine Islam of the *Salaf al-Salih* to the NGO members. Umar bin Talib had this utopian conviction that his newly enlightened followers would in turn spread the message among the corrupted youth, and that would be enough to bring about change within Indonesian society.

The guards let Hendra pass without searching him and he made his way to the central porch. There, one of the servants welcomed him in for the White Brigade's Monday session.

Monday had been chosen, as per Dr Jusuf's explanations, because it was – or should be – the most sacred day of the week for all Muslims, the day when it was considered *sunnah* to fast if one could. The Prophet Mohammed had been born on a Monday and it was on a Monday that he had left Mecca and started the Hijrah, the flight to Medina. Upon his return from Medina, it was on a Monday again that he had defeated the Meccans. And, Peace be upon him, he had passed away on a Monday.

As far as Hendra was concerned, the choice of Monday for The White Brigade's weekly meetings could not have been a better one. Two weeks ago, he had started work again at XS and since Monday was when the club was closed, there was no risk that he might be called upon for an early set. Weekends were another story altogether, and he sometimes had to juggle with the timings of his mixes so that he could join the White Brigade's raids. Clearly, Hendra wasn't over the moon to go back to life as a DJ – and to have to put up with Pak Kelvin's jibes at 'DJ Radikal's latest goatee look' – but he didn't know anything other than mixing to earn his keep.

The other members were already there, sitting on the parquet floor, waiting for Dr Jusuf, when Hendra stepped into the living room and took his place next to Agus. The professor came in soon after and, as usual, they first broke their weekly fast together. Then after the Maghrib prayer, they listened to Dr Jusuf's sermon.

The purdah curtains were drawn closed as was always the

case during their Monday meetings. Often Hendra couldn't help wondering what Dr Jusuf's wives thought about their husband's electrifying speeches in which he unleashed his visceral hatred for bules. For in Dr Jusuf's eyes, just like in Hendra's, the main culprits behind the rampant vice activities in Jakarta were the Westerners and their corrupting influence.

'In the kuffar countries,' said Dr Jusuf, who was now standing and facing the militiamen, 'the sodomites have been given *free speech* but Allah's words are banned. People can walk naked in the streets if they want to, but Muslim women cannot wear the hijab. Their soldiers rape women in front of their husbands, but they say *we* are the terrorists!

'The Western civilization is the ultimate evil, and as Muslims we have an obligation to fight the servants of evil. Jihad against the kuffar is the most direct path to Allah's grace.

' In the surah An-Nisa, He tells us: "Those believers who stay at home – having no physical disability or other reasonable cause – are not equal to those who make jihad in the cause of Allah with their wealth and their persons. Allah has granted a higher rank to those who make jihad with their wealth and their persons than to those who stay at home. Though Allah has promised a good reward for all, He has prepared a much richer reward for those who make jihad for Him than for those who stay at home. They will have special higher ranks, forgiveness and mercy. Allah is Forgiving, Merciful."

'Here in Indonesia, the fornicating bules sell drugs to our children to stupefy them so they can rape them at will. Why don't the police do anything to stop them? Because the bules fatten the wallets of our politicians, who rush to supply them with new victims as soon as the first ones are past their use-by date. But thanks to you, dear brothers, the kuffar cannot rest easy anymore. Although there's still a long way before we are totally rid of them!' His voice had risen a notch to match his enthusiasm and fervour.

He paused for breath and the White Brigade members applauded.

Then Dr Jusuf went on to praise the latest advances of ISIS, who had just seized three new towns. The on-going fight in Syria against the Shias, the Ali worshippers, was the *other* cause that was truly worthy of modern jihad in Dr Jusuf's eyes. And he often liked to remind them that before becoming the leader of the *Nusantara Katibah* of the Islamic State, Agung (now known as Abu Nassim Al Indonesia) had first earned his stripes with the White Brigade.

After finishing his sermon, Dr Jusuf explained that from now on, they would all have to use WhatsApp for written messages and Skype for calls. That was the only way to guard against the risks of phone taping as he had just been informed that apparently all the Saving Hand volunteers had now been placed under surveillance by Densus 88, the national anti-terrorist unit.

'I thought we had the protection of –' started the schoolmaster, Agus.

'Nothing's changed,' Dr Jusuf cut him off. 'We still have the support of the governor's office and the local police. But they have no control over this kuffar-funded police detachment. So, you all need to buy a smartphone and learn to use WhatsApp and Skype. No more regular phone calls or SMS, OK?'

After the sermon, it was time to start preparing for their next raid. Then they would move to the exercise room at the back of the residence, where, led by Sunakin, they learned to box and performed drills with baseball bats.

'Let's attack XS again, they need another beating,' suggested the taxi driver Yatib. With his unkempt hair, rotten teeth and dirty fingernails, Yatib was the only one in the White Brigade who, in Hendra's opinion, had the airs of a thug.

At the mention of XS, Hendra felt his stomach tighten, and to control his emotions he fixed his gaze on the purdah curtain behind Dr Jusuf. He didn't know how much longer he would be able to continue working at XS, but one thing was clear in his mind: even if one day he decided to quit, there was no way he would ever join a White Brigade raid against XS.

'You're right,' replied the professor. 'These degenerates keep taunting us. But now that they have set up this barrier at the alley's entrance, it's impossible to approach the club doors without being searched first.' Then he paused, pensive. 'Hendra,' he said finally and Hendra had to look at him. 'Do you think there could be a way to get in?'

'I don't know. I've never been to that place before.'

'I thought you said one of your friends was a regular there.'

'Yes, but I've never gone with him!'

'Then you might want to start racking your brains about it, my dear brother. XS must have the highest concentration of junkies and prostitutes anywhere in the world. It is the embodiment of this brazen vice which in Jakarta and all over Indonesia tramples the most fundamental values of Islam.'

There was a long silence until Agus, the schoolmaster, finally spoke up: 'Why don't we attack one of these dangdut places where women shake their asses like female dogs in heat?'

'Good idea,' said Dr Jusuf. 'I also hate that satanical music.'

That's when Hendra realised that he had been holding his breath.

***

Hendra noticed the six-year-old boy juggling four balls while their taxi was stuck at a traffic light before the Selamat Datang roundabout. Lowering his window, Hendra beckoned to the youngster and gave him a 10,000-rupiah note. With a large smile on his face, the boy left, limping to the next car to repeat his number.

'That's *also* new,' asked Jasmine, giving him an odd look. 'I thought you never gave money to buskers in traffic jams. You didn't like that they took advantage of the situation or something?'

They were on their way to Mulia Hotel in South Jakarta, where Jasmine wanted to treat him for dinner to celebrate the second anniversary of their first date. She had booked a table at Il Mare, considered to be the best Italian restaurant in town.

'What? I've always given money to street kids, whenever I see one.'

It was adults that he didn't trust. Children were always innocent.

Jasmine turned her head away, sighing. Over the past few days, as soon as she thought she detected a change in Hendra's habits or behaviour, she would remark on it, insisting that he was *different*.

It had all started the week before when she had noticed that in the *Qiyam* position during prayer, he was now crossing his hands on his chest. And when he had explained to her that the Indonesian practice of crossing the hands right above the navel was bidah, she had blown up.

'Is this what you learned at The Saving Hand?'

Hendra had just shrugged.

'Are you sure you aren't with them anymore?'

'I've already told you. I left the Saving Hand when I started work again.'

'Then why don't you shave this goatee?'

'Because I like it.'

And now he couldn't even give money to a kid in the street without Jasmine becoming suspicious.

She was right, of course, he was changing, but how could he confess the truth to her? How could he tell her that he wasn't just a volunteer anymore but had been 'promoted' to the elite White Brigade? The *truth* was that his involvement with the vigilantes had led to a reprieve from his headaches and he had not experienced any more episodes for the last few weeks. He knew it was still too early to celebrate victory; all too often, his hopes of remission had been dashed. But that reprieve meant that since that day when, high on X, he had nearly beaten up his aunt at Palladium, he had managed to remain substance-free – despite the non-stop temptations at XS.

Suddenly, they were hurled forward into the front seats. The taxi driver had slammed on the brakes to avoid an *ojek* cutting in front of them while they were turning into Jalan Gerbang Pemuda, five minutes from Mulia hotel.

'Hey!' said Hendra. 'Can't you be more careful!'

With an embarrassed smile parting his chapped lips, the taxi driver turned around and apologized.

'On that you haven't changed,' Jasmine said, laughing. 'You're still so scared on the road.'

She held Hendra's hand tightly and delivered a kiss on his cheek. How much he loved her, thought Hendra, as a warm feeling spread inside his chest. Maybe one day he would be able to live without Radikal music but he would never be able to live without Jasmine. Whatever his religious beliefs might be then.

The taxi moved along, a tiny ant among the forest of skyscrapers that always made Hendra's head spin. At the entrance of Mulia hotel, a checkpoint blocked the access ramp. After the 2003 terrorist attack at the Marriott, most five-star establishments in Jakarta had set up hydraulic barriers to prevent vehicles from getting too close to the entrance without undergoing a thorough security check first. Unfortunately, five years later, just when people were beginning to get used to this troublesome arrangement, a second bombing had happened, again at the Marriott, after the Jemaah Islamiyah terrorists managed to conceal explosives in a suitcase. Since then, on top of the standard metal detectors used to screen guests, most five-star hotels had added an airport-grade X-ray machine to scan the luggage before check-in.

After carefully examining underneath their car with a small mirror attached to a telescopic pole, as well as verifying the contents of the boot and glove compartment, the security guards let them pass. They drove up a short ramp before pulling up in front of the main entrance. Grooms in white livery rushed to open the taxi doors, delivering an enthusiastic welcome at the same time.

Hendra and Jasmine walked through more security gates and

then into the hotel lobby with its extravagant display of luxury that Hendra always found quite ridiculous if not downright indecent. Built in a rococo style, full of white marble and grand lighting, the five-metre-high lavish lobby seemed designed to look like the antechamber of a European palace, complete with giant mirrors mounted inside sun-topped golden frames, antique armchairs (in which nobody ever sat), gilded chandeliers, inlay chests in Louis XVI style – according to the caption – and potted bamboo plants whose vivid green colours contrasted with the yellow hues all around. A pianist and violinist were playing classical music under the indifferent gaze of businessmen going through the check-in process while a myriad of hotel staff fussed over them. To the right of the lobby, a spiral staircase led to the basement's three restaurants as well as the infamous TC nightclub, one of the most popular pick-up joints among bules travelling on business. (Even better if they stayed at the hotel itself as they only had to press on the lift button if they didn't want to sleep alone.)

Hendra and Jasmine went down a flight of stairs before navigating past a series of imposing jade statues on their way to Il Mare. Such sculptures were highly prized among rich ethnic Chinese whose legendary fascination for jade was a total enigma to Hendra. Could there ever exist an uglier colour than the lifeless green of jade? They arrived at the entrance to the restaurant, where the Italian chef himself welcomed them. Next to him stood a sign: 'All the way from Calabria, meet Chef Luciano Ramazzotti! At Mulia Hotel for one whole month!' The Italian man shook their hands enthusiastically before a waitress showed them to their table.

'Last night,' said Jasmine after they finished ordering their food, 'I was talking to an American clubber who explained to me that Caucasian businessmen now prefer to stay at Mulia.'

In her red tight-fitting dress, Jasmine was quite popular with bules at XS, who liked to chat her up without always realising that she was a waria – especially now that she passed more and more easily

'Apparently,' continued Jasmine, 'it's the only five-star hotel in Jakarta that is hundred percent Indonesian owned – as all the others belong to big American or European chains. So, they think Mulia won't be a target if there's another bombing.'

'Well, for the sake of your Yankee, I hope any would-be terrorists haven't heard the bules' latest craze. Otherwise, it'll make their job real easy when they decide on their next target.'

Jasmine scowled at him. 'That's not funny, ok?' Then, after a pause: 'Speaking of terrorists, have you seen what happened in Canada yesterday? I mean, the attack at the Parliament in Ottawa. I'm sure it's ISIS again.'

'Of course not! They haven't claimed responsibility, and I'm sure they won't. Because they don't engage in terrorism.'

Since hearing Dr Jusuf commending the ISIS fight against 'fake Muslims', Hendra had stopped reading the local and foreign newspaper articles which presented the soldiers of the Caliphate as bloodthirsty psychopaths. To get his information directly from the source, he would browse ISIS' online forums – under the handle 'Radikal_Baru' – or listen to ISIS' Friday sermons, which were broadcast on the instant messaging platform Zello. Now he knew that with the Crusaders' help, the Ali worshippers had planned to slaughter true Muslims by the thousands and ISIS was only defending itself.

'What are you talking about?' said Jasmine. 'And all these bombings by the JI in Indonesia, you think they had nothing to do with it?'

'Do you realise ISIS didn't even exist when the bombings in Bali and Jakarta happened? You're mixing it up with Al-Qaeda, which has indeed always supported the JI.'

'So what? Al-Qaeda, ISIS, JI, they're all the same to me. Why, even the White Brigade! They're all degenerates dragging Islam into the gutter!'

Jasmine's finely pencilled eyebrows made the look of indignation on her face even more striking.

'That's what Americans would like us to believe,' replied Hendra, carefully ignoring the allusion to the White Brigade. 'But Al-Qaeda and ISIS are at war with each other, you know.'

He took his phone out and showed her a recent article in *The Jakarta Post* about the conflict between ISIS and the Taliban in Afghanistan.

'Great news! Better for everyone if they just kill each other, don't you think?'

'The Islamic State's leading a military campaign to rebuild the Califate. It's a political and religious project which has nothing to do with terrorism.'

'Are you really defending these monsters?'

'They don't kill innocents, Jasmine. This is just American propaganda to justify their support of Bashar el-Assad ... in return for oil contracts!'

'Ya Allah, Hendra, we're talking about savages who behead NGO volunteers!'

Hendra knew he should have dropped the argument. But

it wasn't the first time he realised how much Jasmine totally misunderstood what was happening in the Middle East. How much she simply parroted the lies propagated by the Western media. Already a few weeks ago, he had had to explain to her the fundamental differences between the Sunnis and the idol-worshipping Shias. So, no, he couldn't leave unchallenged such bule manipulations. He had to re-establish the facts, even if that meant that he risked ruining their anniversary dinner.

'Do you understand this is brainwashing?' He tried to keep his voice as calm as possible. 'Just like those weapons of mass destruction that were never found because they were just an excuse for the Yankees to invade Iraq and seize their oil reserves. Stop watching CNN. Stop listening to the kuffar media. Or even to Al Jazeera, as it's also ruled by the imperialists!'

'Kuffar, Yankees, imperialists? You're using very fancy words these days ... So, what are you waiting for to buy your air ticket?'

The waitress brought their dishes – *gnocchi arrabiata* for Hendra and *ossobuco* for Jasmine. Hendra started to eat in silence while Jasmine played with her fork.

'See, I've lost my appetite thanks to your stupid theories.' Then, after a while, grabbing his hand: 'What's wrong, sayang? Please tell me! I can see that you're not taking any drugs at the moment. But I don't know ... it's like your mind's always somewhere else. And you're having all these weird ... ideas.'

Hendra felt the urgency in Jasmine's voice. 'You're right, let's change topics,' he said, squeezing her hand.

Jasmine sighed and started eating in silence.

'Tell me ...' she said after a while, 'don't you think we should go back to Palladium and see your aunt again? I don't understand why she never called you back.'

'No, please! She could get upset and turn very … nasty.'

He still hadn't told Jasmine about the intolerable truth he had learned from his aunt. A crippling feeling of shame that he couldn't overcome prevented him from doing so – even though he knew Jasmine would never judge him.

Behind them, a Chinese couple was having an argument, barking some of their insults in twangy Hokkien. As if they couldn't quarrel outside, thought Hendra. Suddenly anxious to leave, he suggested that they take away their dessert – a tiramisu without alcohol – and finish celebrating their anniversary at his flat. Jasmine just nodded and Hendra turned around to get the attention of the waitress. When he faced Jasmine again, he caught her questioning eyes, full of love and concern.

***

'*Assalamualaikum*, Hendra!'

Hendra heard Haji Ahmad's voice calling him from the entrance of Arrahim mosque.

It was 8 in the morning and he had just finished a marathon mix at XS on the occasion of the monthly party 'Re-Live the Dream' – a must-attend event for all Jakarta electro fans. As Violetta had called in sick with food poisoning at the last minute, he had had to fill in for her. Which meant that after the three two-hour mixes he had played consecutively – without consuming any other stimulant than the Red Bulls offered by Jasmine – he could only think of one thing: sleep. So, without pausing, he returned the old man's greeting and pressed forward. In any case, since returning to XS, he had carefully avoided Arrahim mosque and Haji Ahmad, preferring instead to pray inside the XS staff pantry, like he'd done that morning. Umar bin Talib's teachings had opened his eyes to the fact that Haji Ahmad was one of the innovators whose religious opinions had to be ignored.

'Why Hendra, you have no time to even salam your old imam?' asked Haji Ahmad.

Reluctantly, Hendra approached the mosque entrance. He took the old man's hand and brought it to his forehead.

'Come into my office,' said Haji Ahmad. 'I'll offer you some nice Toraja coffee.'

Hendra couldn't shake the feeling that the imam had been out there waiting for him to walk past in the XS back alley. But he did not know how to decline the imam's invitation and grudgingly followed him inside the mosque.

'It's been a long while since I last saw you here,' Haji Ahmad said after they sat in his tiny office and two cups of coffee were served. 'Did I do, or say, something wrong?'

'Not at all ... I just didn't have the opportunity to drop by because, for a while, I wasn't working at XS.'

'I see. And what about this new goatee that you have? What's that supposed to mean?'

Hendra kept quiet. Haji Ahmad knew all too well that it wasn't the latest techno look ...

'It's good to be more observant, Hendra, especially if it helps you stay away from drugs. But ...'

Haji Ahmad paused, as if searching for the right words, while staring at Hendra with an inquisitive look. The imam was well aware of his drug abuse problem as in the past Hendra had sought his guidance and moral support to try and overcome his addictions.

'Let me just be frank with you,' resumed Haji Ahmad. 'Jasmine came to see me the other day. She's quite worried about you. She told me you're hanging around with The Saving Hand. Is that true?'

'I did a bit of volunteering with them, yes, but I stopped when I started mixing again at XS.'

A faint smile formed on Haji Ahmad's lips. The dark circles around his eyes seemed to have grown wider with the shadows seeping into the room. The storm gathering outside promised to be a violent one.

'I prefer that, Hendra. Because these are really the wrong people to mix with. Umar bin Talib might look like a respectable man but he defends outrageously backwards views that can only seed divisions in our society. And his right-hand man, this so-called Doctor Jusuf, he's a very dangerous man who must be avoided at all costs. Rumour has it that he paid with his own money the lawyers who defended the perpetrators of the Bali bombings. And these days, he would be supporting ISIS.'

Hendra couldn't hold back any more. 'But what's wrong with supporting ISIS? Aren't the Islamic State's mujahideen fighting for a righteous cause!'

'Really, Hendra? And which righteous cause would that be, according to you?'

The rain was already pummelling the windows, filling the room with loud, crackling noises.

'The fight against all the enemies of Islam,' Hendra answered, unfazed.

'And who are they, these enemies of our Faith?'

'The Jews who occupy Palestine. The Americans who invade Islam's holy lands. The Shias who kill our Muslim brothers in Syria and in Iraq!'

'The Shias, enemies of Islam? But they're Muslims like you and me!' said Haji Ahmad, his voice quivering.

'Everybody knows that the Shias are heretics!' protested Hendra. 'They're worshipping idols, and on top of that they massacre the real Muslims. ISIS cannot just stand by and watch, they have the right to defend themselves!'

Haji Ahmad had walked around his desk and was now standing in front of Hendra, hands on his hips.

'Is it Jusuf and Umar bin Talib who have put these wicked ideas in your head?' he asked, grabbing Hendra by the shoulders and shaking him with surprising strength. 'The Shias are our Muslim brothers. They have recited the Shahada.'

'Then why are they killing Sunnis?'

'People are fighting for power, Hendra. It's got nothing to do with religion. And why this obsession with jihad in Syria? Please, don't tell me you want to go there! This is *not* how to prove yourself as a Muslim.'

'Isn't jihad an obligation for all Muslim men?'

'But that's not jihad!'

Haji Ahmad repeated what he had already explained in his sermons, about the two forms of greater jihad – the struggle against oneself and the fight for the betterment of society – that Allah encouraged believers to undertake in their lifetime. Then he added:

'As for the *physical* jihad, only a Caliph elected by the

community of Muslims has the right to declare it on an enemy. But Al Baghdadi is only a usurper, a self-proclaimed Caliph!'

Hendra shrugged internally while keeping a straight face. He knew all too well these bidah views.

'Especially in your case, you should really focus on your inner jihad: defeat your own demons and continue along the path of a drug-free life. This has to be one of the toughest battles, and I'm sure Allah will reward you a thousand-fold. Allah is forgiving, merciful.'

No, thought Hendra, it was Dr Jusuf who was right – the spiritual jihad was only an invention of the miscreants to prevent Muslims from fighting back. But there was no point arguing with Haji Ahmad; the corrupt imam wouldn't listen to him.

'You don't seem convinced … Listen, Hendra, I still need to review some quotations that we received from contractors to repair the roof, but can you please come and see me after Friday prayer next week? I'll show you surahs from the Qur'an as well as hadiths from Sahih Al-Bukhari which will enlighten you as to the real meaning of jihad.'

Hendra promised to come back and then stepped out of the mosque, slowly making his way towards his flat under the bright hot sun which had already replaced the torrential rain. In contrast, the ground still bore the remnants of the storm, and his shoes kept sinking into pools of muddy water covering Jalan Hayam Wuruk's broken pavement. Lost in thought, he stumbled a few times into hidden cracks. They were blind to the truth, these supposedly religious men who could not see that the Islamic State fighters were the real mujahideen.

15

'You're screwed, you little DJ cocksucker!' shouted one of the assailants.

A group of five taxi drivers had set upon him as he was walking down the back alley leading to XS and had slammed him against the wall. Among the insults flying at him from all sides, Hendra understood that it was payback time for the attack he had committed on one of them weeks ago. One guy, in particular, was screaming the loudest while pointing with his index finger to the gaping hole in his mouth where his front teeth used to be. But no matter how much Hendra scrutinized the guy's face, he didn't recognize him – in his mind, the taxi driver he had beaten up had been an obese man with a thick neck like a pig's, not a lanky guy like this one. Although, maybe, since he was flying sky-high that night …

Hendra didn't have time to continue in his train of thought as a violent slap hit him across the head and made him sway. He covered his face without trying to defend himself. There was no point fighting back and angering them further when he was so obviously outnumbered. And in a minute or so, the XS bouncers, alerted by the cries in the street, would rush toward the commotion and save his neck.

Hendra managed to fend off the blows until a hard overhand

punch connected with his cheekbone and he started bleeding. Then a sharp knee to the stomach made him double up. What the fuck are these bouncers doing, thought Hendra. He wasn't going to be able to hold out much longer.

At last, he heard quick footsteps followed by the loud voice of the security team's head, Ari:

'Back off, you assholes!'

The taxi drivers stopped hitting Hendra and cleared off, but not before spitting at him one last time. Hendra lowered his hands from his face and wiped the spittle from his knuckles on the wall.

'What took you so long?' he asked Ari, while nursing his cheek.

'Sorry,' replied the bouncer. 'We heard some noise but thought it was just youngsters having fun, you know.'

Hendra thought he could detect a hint of sarcasm in Ari's voice. Could they have deliberately delayed their intervention so that he would take a pounding first? He tried to brush off the thought, but it left a bitter taste in his mouth.

As he massaged his neck, he realised that it felt a bit stiff. Most likely the after-effects of all the slaps and blows, he reassured himself. Hadn't he been headache-free for more than two months already?

He walked the last thirty metres separating him from the XS entrance before taking the lift to the third floor and entering the main hall. As there was still a bit of time before the beginning of his own set at 1 am, he decided to climb to the mezzanine from where, overlooking the dancefloor, he would be able to check the pulse of the club.

DJ Blow-U was performing and his inspiring set mixed

soprano voices with clear percussion that sounded like gamelans. The pure, melancholic music sent chills of pleasure down Hendra's spine, and almost without thinking he started to dance. After a vertiginous musical build-up, a frenzy of bass sounds shook up XS while, simultaneously, lasers drew complex shapes in the smoky air. The stroboscope, flashing like a revolving lighthouse beam, blinded Hendra and he had to avert his gaze. The new carnival-like laser show was the work of Pak Kelvin's latest hire: a VJ, or visual jockey, who occupied a newly installed podium on the other side of the stage.

As a relative quiet descended upon the room, Hendra stopped jumping and, shielding his eyes from the light and the lasers, he observed the activity on the dancefloor. In one corner, a dozen youths thrashed about in an uncontrolled, almost hysterical manner, paying no mind to DJ Blow-U's beat. The boys wore woollen caps and small backpacks, gesticulating wildly with plastic Aqua bottles. One of them was teetering dangerously, his gyrating body forming impossible angles with the ground. Luckily, a medic rushed to his aid just as he was about to collapse onto the dancefloor. That's when Hendra noticed a group of bule predators, well into their sagging fifties, standing in ambush, probably waiting for one of the girls to faint so they could 'rescue' her. Whenever he witnessed disgusting scenes like this, Hendra understood why XS was such a symbolic target for the White Brigade. Yet, he would never … All of a sudden, a searing pain radiated from his neck all the way to his left temple. There was no more question about it: a headache attack was imminent.

Hendra wanted to scream his rage, but what good would that do? There was only one thing for it. He rushed down the stairs, beckoned to a passing mami and asked for a love pill. Looking surprised because Hendra hadn't used in a long while, the mami tried to dissuade him, but he insisted and immediately swallowed the X. Without water. K would have been his first choice but beggars can't be choosers. With a bit of luck, he would still manage to prevent the attack.

While waiting for the pill to start messing with his brain, Hendra decided to sit at the bar at the back, where Jasmine was waitressing. Her perfunctory greeting, when she saw him, made it clear, though, that she still hadn't forgotten their argument from the previous night.

They had just finished making love when Jasmine had suddenly declared, seemingly out of the blue, that Iran was the second country in the world after Thailand for the number of gender reassignment surgeries carried out every year. In fact, right after the 1979 Islamic revolution, the ayatollahs had started allowing transgender women to officially change their gender on their IC, even before they underwent their (compulsory) operation.

'Do you realise, sayang, a Muslim country officially recognizing the rights of transgender women? Isn't it wonderful?'

'The Iranians, Muslims?' he had replied. 'They are Shias, heretics who collaborated with the Crusaders in the 12th century. And still do.'

'Crusaders? Where did you learn that fancy new word?'

Jasmine had gotten dressed and slammed the door, calling him a wannabe Osama. Obviously, she was ignorant of the fact that Osama bin Laden's mother was a Shia – and the reason why, some people said, Al-Qaeda, unlike ISIS, sometimes joined forces with the fake Muslims against the Yanks. But Hendra knew too well that this argument about the Iranians' Muslimness had only served to avoid another dispute, potentially far more distressful, about Jasmine's desire to go for an operation. He was convinced that was her intent, and he didn't want to hear about it. He wanted Jasmine to remain a waria.

Hendra said hi to the two other girls working behind the bar, both of whom wore tight-fitting red t-shirts bearing the Belvedere vodka logo – the latest club sponsor. Didn't Belvedere know that the vast majority of X-wasted clubbers – and so 95% of the XS clientele – only drank water? Well, tonight Hendra would be one of the few exceptions. While Jasmine continued to give him the cold shoulder, he called upon Sally, a ravishing ethnic-Chinese girl who had just joined XS a week earlier, to serve him a large shot of Belvedere. He downed it in one go and signalled to Sally that he wanted another.

Now he was starting to breathe better – thanks to the vodka or the X – and as he began to relax he also cracked a few playful jokes with Sally. How did she find her work uniform? Did her parents know that she was working in such a club? After one laugh too many, Jasmine planted herself in front of Hendra, while informing the newbie that there were lots of glasses to pick up in the room. Hendra knew it had to be the most thankless task for XS waitresses – to grab the empty glasses they had to dodge or push aside the madly hopping clubbers, some of whom danced with their eyes closed. In such conditions, avoiding glass breakage often amounted to a real miracle.

'And so, it would appear that Mister Hendra here drinks vodka but finds that Shias are not Muslim enough to his taste?' she asked with a teasing smile.

Hendra winked at her and took her hand. Then, as he bent over the bar counter, wanting to give her a peck, it suddenly struck him that Jasmine's lips were seemingly painted in a strange orange colour. Was it a hallucination brought on by the combined effects of the X pill and his interminable dreams of his aunt? Or was it, more simply, an effect of the kaleidoscopic LEDs installed by the VJ all over the club? Shivering, Hendra resumed his position in front of the bar without kissing Jasmine. She stared at him suspiciously before moving away to take care of customers.

Luckily, it was now his turn to mix. He decided to take another pill – just in case, even though the attack appeared to have ebbed – and then climbed into his cage. Yes, *his* cage, as during his three-month suspension, nobody had made use of the cage-cum-DJ cabin. That was DJ Radikal's sole preserve.

His first set, from one to three in the morning, went smoothly – except for the non-stop whistling of clubbers marking the beat with their party whistles. Once a source of pride and even inspiration, this practice now drove him insane as he felt that these strident sounds corrupted the purity of his electro music. So much so that these days, when he was mixing, he often tried to cut himself off from the dancefloor by turning up the volume on his DJ headphones. Last week, when he had suggested to Pak Kelvin that they ban these whistles, his boss had looked at him, baffled.

'Are you sure you're quite right in the head, Radikal? People come here to have fun. If they want to blow into a whistle, let them blow into a fucking whistle!'

As Hendra descended from his cage, DJ Mabuhay took over. Despite his dislike for the Filipino DJ's drum and bass selection, Hendra decided to mingle with the crowd rather than go back to the bar, where he was too scared of having to face Jasmine again with her orange lipstick. Straightaway he was accosted by a young female clubber in tight micro shorts who started to jump in sync with him. She kept turning around on herself while smiling provocatively at him. Already quite tall, she also wore platform shoes, which made her dance moves all the more perilous.

DJ Mabuhay was scratching his turntables searching for some inspiration that clearly wasn't forthcoming. In all-too-rare moments, a crisper sound, more electro, seemed to emerge, but it stopped after a few seconds, and the dull jungle rhythm reasserted itself. No matter how much he tried to force himself, after a while, Hendra had to admit that jumping on such a mix was beyond him. He was about to leave the dancefloor when the female clubber clung to him and tried to kiss him. He managed to free himself just in time to see Jasmine barge onto the dancefloor. Under the sharp light of the laser beams, his doubts vanished: yes, her lips really were painted in that horrible, obscene colour that terrified him.

Hendra fled, and at the foot of the stairs leading to the mezzanine he found the same mami as before, hawking her triptych menu to all and sundry. When he asked her for another two Loves, she handed him only one pill, pretending that she was running low and in need of replenishment. Hendra grabbed the mami's arm. 'Don't try to bail on me, OK? I'm waiting for you *here*,' he said before letting her go.

But instead of the mami, it was an incensed orange-lipped Jasmine who presented herself in front of him a few minutes later and told him in no uncertain terms that there was no way he was going to take another X. She had passed clear instructions to that effect to all the mamis and also made sure no waitresses would serve him any more alcohol.

Without replying, Hendra skulked off and sought refuge inside one of the alcoves at the back of the club. Seated on a couch with his head in his hands, he tried to cool the anger rising in him. But to no avail. He was a free man and he could take X whenever he felt like it. Nobody had any right to prevent him from having fun.

Ten minutes later, Hendra began his second set and unleashed his fury like a raging bull. After a non-existent transition with DJ Mabuhay, he played the ultra-violent gothic music of the German band Das Ich, which was famous for including satanical-like screaming in their songs. On the other digital turntable, he started the same track but right in the middle (a technique known as the double mix and invented by one of his gurus, Jeff Mills). Simultaneously, he was shouting into the mic – a first for him at XS – repeating the chorus 'Lügen, lügen, lügen und das ich nicht!', so that there were now three demonic voices in parallel. The few clubbers who were still dancing completely froze but Hendra couldn't care less. He was walking on air.

Unfortunately, his musical high didn't last long; all of a sudden, DJ Mabuhay's moronic jungle music started up again while his own sound was disabled. Who had dared to silence Radikal? Hendra tore the headphones off his ears before punching the command button to bring the DJ cabin back to base.

There to welcome him at the bottom of the ladder was Pak Kelvin himself. It was over for him tonight, his boss said, and if he were him, he would just go home now. Without a word, without informing Jasmine, Hendra took off. For a moment he considered praying in the staff pantry on his way out as it was going to be Fajr very soon but he finally decided against it. Praying under the influence was considered a sin and he was stoned, wasn't he?

He was already starting along the back alley, towards Jalan Hayam Wuruk, when he overheard a discussion between Ari and a group of teenagers who didn't have their KTP, or *Kartu Tanda Penduduk*, their ID cards, with them. Ari was telling them that maybe 'they could work something out'. The youngest in the group couldn't have been more than fifteen and the oldest eighteen …

Hendra walked up to Ari. 'Wait man, you can't let them in! They're all fucking minors!'

'Don't understand what you're saying,' replied Ari. 'Care to articulate?'

But Hendra couldn't unclench his teeth. His jaws were sealed together like a steel trap around its kill.

Coke jaw. It had been a while since he'd last experienced this side effect of X and cocaine causing teeth grinding and jaw clenching. Clearly he was out of practice. Tomorrow he would wake up with terrible cramps all around his mouth, more painful even than the bruising from the taxi drivers, and he wouldn't be able to swallow anything for the next 24 hours.

'They are not allowed to go in,' said Hendra, trying to enunciate each word separately. 'They are kids!'

'Better be careful with XTC, my friend, if you can't hold your stuff … Now listen to me, I'm the one in charge of security here, OK? Your job's just to make these people dance. So, beat it!'

Hendra grabbed Ari by the scruff of the neck.

'Minors are not allowed inside XS, get it? Momo paid the

price because he didn't do his job. And you'll end up like him if you continue to fuck around, OK?'

Perhaps as a result of the rage exploding inside him, his jaws had unclenched all at once.

'The beating earlier wasn't enough for you?' said Ari, angrily wrenching himself from Hendra's grasp. 'Now get the fuck out of here!' And he delivered a sharp slap to Hendra's face.

The force sent Hendra stumbling backwards, but he quickly steadied himself. As he rose, he saw Ari laughing at him. In an instant, the suppressed emotions he'd been harbouring all night surged within him. With a roar, he charged at Ari, landing punch after punch on his face, each hit echoing with the smacking sound of skin against skin. As Ari staggered under the blows, Hendra rolled his arm around his neck to strangle him, oblivious to the kicks the other bouncers were now aiming at him.

'Stop, Hendra!'

That was Jasmine's voice. He felt like a scuba diver disoriented in murky water, catching a faint glimpse of sunlight. The surface, the safe world. He had to listen to Jasmine. He released his grip around Ari's neck.

Then someone grasped him around the waist and Ari seized the opportunity to land a formidable hit to his solar plexus. Hendra sank to his knees – it was as if something had just blown up inside his body. Once neutralized, he was locked up inside a ground-floor room where belligerent patrons were sometimes thrown before the police's arrival.

***

Around 10 am, Hendra was finally back at his flat, together with Jasmine, after spending five hours in the cell-like room with padded walls – and having totally come down in the interval. Pak Kelvin hadn't called the cops on him, but unsurprisingly he had told Hendra that he was definitely fired – and even banned from XS as a customer.

'It's not over yet,' Jasmine was telling him. 'In a few months, we'll try to convince Pak Kelvin to take you back. He's going to lose lots of customers with you leaving XS, especially if you start mixing in another club. You're his star DJ, the flying one. But you need to seek treatment, sayang, you need to stop taking drugs once and for all. Look at the mess you've made of yourself once again.'

'I'm through with all this. I'm just going to stop DJing, that's all.'

'Don't be absurd! Before you know it, you'll have landed a new DJ stint somewhere. With your reputation, everyone in Jakarta will want to hire you!'

'Nobody really cares about Radikal's music. Every time I try something new, people stop dancing. They just go clubbing to get high.'

Jasmine pleaded with him, insisting they should talk again after he had cooled down. But Hendra had already made up his mind. He would find another way to make a living. Hadn't Umar bin Talib mentioned the other day that they would soon need a new paid assistant at The Saving Hand? Why couldn't he apply for that job?

All said, this was probably for the best as he was starting to feel really torn between his quest for purity and this near-daily immersion into the depravity of Jakarta's nightlife. He couldn't go on stifling his religious beliefs every time he set foot in XS. In fact, the more he thought about it, the more he was convinced that such a sinful environment was the root of all his ills. His headache episodes were simply warnings that God had been merciful enough to send to him; he couldn't, he shouldn't ignore them any longer if he wanted to get better.

* * *

In the days that followed, Jasmine stayed with him, trying unsuccessfully to change his mind about quitting DJing. Hendra spent the daytime hours cooped up at home, only going out at night – when Jasmine left to work at XS – to join operations from the White Brigade or The Saving Hand.

Then, one day, while they were having dinner at his apartment, Jasmine announced that she had some very good news. Haji Ahmad had agreed to marry them so long as she went for gender-reassignment surgery. Spurred by her explanations of the Iranian context, the old imam had looked into the fatwas issued by the ayatollahs on the topic of trans women and had convinced himself of their merits. At the same time, a recent court ruling already allowed Jasmine, after getting an operation, to have her gender legally changed on her KTP identity card.

'Do you realise, sayang? We can officially become husband and wife!'

Hendra was speechless. He couldn't help thinking that Jasmine had finally found the excuse she needed to go for her operation. How could she not understand that he loved her just the way she was? And why were all those people now pushing warias to become transgender women? Yet another corrupting influence from bules and Shias!

'I know you find our love less and less compatible with your new religious fervour … Don't lie, Hendra, I can feel the distance growing every day. This is the perfect solution, don't you think?' Jasmine was staring at him intently. 'So, what do you say? Don't get too excited …'

'I … I have a headache coming on,' he replied finally.

And he wasn't lying. That wasn't a neck supporting his head anymore, it was a crowbar. Without any drug on hand, he wouldn't be able to escape the attack this time. The remission he had been enjoying for the last few months was definitely over.

As he rushed to the bedroom to be alone, he heard Jasmine slamming the door. He thought about trying to catch up with her but already his vision was so blurred that he couldn't see anything. As soon as the episode was over, he would call her and apologize. Hadn't she just proposed to him?

***

Jasmine came back a few hours later while he was still lying on the bed, exhausted, crushed by the violent attack which had gone on and on. When he heard the front door open, he quickly put his wristband back on and stood up just as Jasmine burst into the room, dishevelled, livid. And with red-eyes as if she had been crying.

'So, Maia never called you back, you said?'

'Sayang, are you OK? I'm sorry for …'

Jasmine cut him off: 'Answer my question!'

'No ... she never cont–'

'You're lying! Why can't you trust me!'

Jasmine had gone back to Palladium on her own, ready to force Maia to tell the truth. This time, the bouncers had not let her in but had called the mamasan instead. A few minutes later, Maia had come out and informed Jasmine that, yes, she had reached out to Hendra and even met him right after their last visit.

'I've already said too much, despite my promise to Dini. Please leave me alone now,' were Maia's last words before she turned around and re-entered Palladium.

'Yes,' admitted Hendra. 'She came here. But I was so ashamed of what I learned, I couldn't talk to you about it.'

Hendra finally told Jasmine about his meeting with Maia and her revelations – while omitting the part about snorting K together. Jasmine didn't say anything for a while, simply holding and squeezing Hendra's hands. Then she took out her phone, and he saw that she was googling 'Cock & Bull Batam'.

'You're lucky, the bar still exists.'

'But I don't want to go there!'

'Sayang, you can't stop now. You must talk to more people to learn what your mother was doing in Batam, who she was hanging out with.'

'I don't want to continue this search,' Hendra pleaded, vehemently shaking his head.

Jasmine grabbed his hands.

'You have to go all the way, sayang. Fly to Batam and try to discover what happened to your mother while she lived there. Maybe she met someone and ...'

'*Met* someone? My mother prostituted herself, like Maia, and my father is one of her customers. It's crystal clear now! There's nothing else to discover!'

'But she would have sought an abortion!'

'Maybe she became even more popular. Pak Kelvin once told me that pregnant girls can fetch very good prices. It's a thing, apparently.'

'How can you even say such horrible things about your mum!'

Tears welled up in Hendra's eyes and he covered his face with his hands. Jasmine wrapped her arms around him, stroking and kissing his hair for a long while.

16

It was already 5.30 pm when Hendra and Jasmine left their hotel in Nagoya, Batam Island's main conurbation, and started their two-kilometre walk to the city's red-light district, the so-called Nagoya Entertainment District – or NED as the locals abbreviated it.

In the end, Hendra had given in to Jasmine. He knew she would not leave him in peace until they had solved what she now called his family secret. She had read articles on the Internet explaining how this type of lie 'could be so traumatic for children and a source of deep anxiety in adulthood'. He hoped that after this trip, after this last attempt, Jasmine would finally accept that there was nothing else to discover. To cure his headaches, he had to change his life, that was all.

At the same time – although he was loath to admit it – he couldn't help wondering whether Maia had not invented this whole Cock & Bull story. One thing, in particular, puzzled him during that night's course of events: that Maia had already totally recovered when he had come to his senses, even though he had only been unconscious for less than five minutes Could her spectacular K high have just been an act? Could she have lied, tried to hurt him on purpose, to extract revenge for that stupid swing accident? Sure, he knew that sometimes K flashes could be as short-lived as they were violent but what if Jasmine was right? What if in Batam, he did find clues to another story? Some days, though, he felt really upset with himself for still hoping that the truth could be different. Wasn't everything already all too obvious?

Hendra had not told Dr Jusuf about his intended visit to Batam. They had had a falling out one week ago when Hendra had informed the professor that he had left his job at the Plaza Indonesia pizzeria and was planning to apply for the vacant position with the NGO. Dr Jusuf had refused to put in a good word for him with Umar bin Talib, angrily insisting that Hendra continue earning his living *outside* The Saving Hand. It was highly critical, Dr Jusuf had said, for them to have volunteers grounded in civil society. They already had enough full-time religious people who had no idea what was happening in the real world. Since that incident, the professor and Hendra had grown more distant, and Hendra had kept mum about his trip.

They had taken an early afternoon Lion Air flight and after a 90-minute journey followed by a 30-minute taxi ride, checked into the Triniti hotel, located in the heart of Nagoya. (Some Japanese engineers who had come to Batam in the late 70s to work on infrastructure projects had apparently so dubbed the area, Jasmine had informed a disinterested Hendra on the plane, and for some reason the name had stuck, even replacing the official one on maps.) After they had made love, Jasmine suggested that they go on foot all the way to the Cock & Bull to familiarise themselves with the town, and Hendra had silently acquiesced, not really jumping for joy at the prospect of such a long trek in the late afternoon's humid heat.

They were walking in silence, Jasmine observing everything

around her, Hendra helplessly engrossed in his thoughts. Neither of them had been to Batam before. The island, which was only 30 minutes away by boat from Singapore, was mostly a favourite destination for male Singaporeans looking for 'love', who liked to loosen up over the weekend in the red-light district's countless bars. But Batam was not just a prostitution hotspot; it was also one of the largest industrial centres in Indonesia. TMM might have been one of the first foreign companies to open a factory there in the mid-80s but since then many European and American multinationals had followed suit, using Batam as their powerbase for the low-cost assembly of electronic goods designed in Singapore. In the last thirty years, the factory worker population had multiplied by twenty, bolstered by the large contingents of migrants, often women, coming from all over Indonesia.

Which had come first, wondered Hendra, as they continued their walk under the setting sun, the sex or the electronics industry? Well, one thing was sure: they had grown in tandem. They had not even reached NED and were still passing through the main shopping district but there were already dozens of spas lining the street, with young, skimpily dressed girls standing outside the storefronts, smiling languidly at the male passers-by. And judging by the scruffy look of the men walking in, there was no doubt that these establishments offered other services than the chocolate-based massages or aroma treatments advertised on their front doors. In a way, that wasn't much different from his Glodok hometown and given that traffic jams were non-existent and buildings only two or three stories high, Hendra could have been charmed by Nagoya's small-town atmosphere. Yet he couldn't help finding the heat more oppressive than in Jakarta and the people unusually aloof. And everything from taxi rides to bottles of Aqua was so outrageously expensive – more than twice the price than in Jakarta.

Right after Hotel Harmoni they finally entered what on his map was shown as the official Nagoya Entertainment District. As if vice had chosen to scent-mark its territory, the streets were now much dirtier and dotted with heaps of garbage. Reading the addresses of the bars on the signboards, Hendra realised that they all indicated Kampung Bule (bule village) and he guessed that it was the neighbourhood's nickname. It certainly looked fitting. In the near-deserted streets of late afternoon, the only punters were a few Westerners dodging the electrical cables hanging at eye level, while emaciated, haggard-looking mamasans solicited them in English with cries like 'Young Girls!' or 'Fresh from the village!' It wasn't surprising that Maia had decamped to Jakarta, thought Hendra; Batam didn't seem like a good place to grow old as a mamasan.

They crossed a large fruit market – where he lustily breathed in the smell of the day's spoiled fruit as if it was fresh air – before reaching Jalan Imam Boloh. There, along the entire stretch of the street, two-metre-high Japanese-like vertical blinking billboards displayed the bar names. The signs were all perfectly aligned, evoking a forest of red trees that a landscape gardener would have planted in the street. They first passed in front of The Monkey Bar, then The Last Pub, The Red Bar, The Wallabies and finally they found the Cock & Bull, which would have won hands-down the prize for the most dilapidated façade in Kampung Bule. They pushed through the door and walked in.

The place was empty, apart from a couple of girls standing

and smoking at the back of a long, narrow room. Hendra and Jasmine sat themselves at the counter on elevated swivel chairs – the kind which can keep kids entertained for hours – and ordered a Red Bull and a Coke Light. The thirty-something barmaid stared at them in disbelief for a while before turning around to prepare the drinks. Seconds later, a girl who couldn't have been more than twenty planted herself in front of Jasmine.

'Are you operated?' she shot at Jasmine with obvious sarcasm in her voice.

Behind the thick make-up – about as thick as that of Palladium's sad clowns, thought Hendra – one could still make out the freckles and pimples.

'Not yet,' replied Jasmine, unperturbed.

'Then come back after your operation. Our customers only love women.'

'I'm not here to pick up any one,' replied Jasmine laughing. Then turning her head towards Hendra: 'And that one's not a customer. It's my boyfriend.'

The girl looked at them suspiciously. 'Then what do you want? If it's dope, you've come to the wrong place. You'll have to try the big discos in town like Penthouse or –'

Jasmine cut her off. 'My boyfriend's trying to trace an aunt of his. He hasn't heard from her in years, but he knows she used to work in this bar in the late 80s.'

In the final version of the sob story that Jasmine and Hendra had agreed upon, Dini was his aunt and he was looking for her to tell her about her father's recent passing.

The freckled girl stared at them with wide eyes. 'In the 80s? I wasn't even born!'

'But this place already existed, right?' asked Jasmine.

It was the oldest bar in Nagoya, Hendra had discovered on the Internet. Something of an institution if one believed their website.

'Yeah, maybe. You'd need to talk to the boss. Mami Anita. She's worked here since the early days.'

'And she's not here right now?' asked Jasmine.

'She only arrives later, around 9 or 10 pm.'

'Oh, that's pretty late … do you think you could give her a call?'

Hendra let Jasmine do the talking. Unlike him, she was always good at putting people at ease. Anyway, the more he thought about it, the more he was convinced that this visit to the Cock & Bull was pointless because, obviously, nobody would remember anything.

The girl shrugged. 'Don't know …'

'Don't worry,' said Jasmine. 'We have no intention of creating trouble. We're just trying to reconnect with this aunt to tell her that her father passed away. What she was doing here is not our problem.'

The girl seemed to hesitate before moving to the back of the room and taking her handphone from inside her handbag. She made a quick call and then told them that Mami Anita would be there in a while.

Without a word, his lips wrapped around the straw the barmaid had placed in his glass, Hendra slowly sipped the amber-colour Red Bull while observing the bar's comings and goings. Customers were now trickling in, essentially bules in their fifties or sixties, most probably expatriates working at one of the foreign-owned factories located in Batam. Some, briefcase in hand, had obviously come to the Cock & Bull directly from work. Hendra wondered which kind of lies these husbands were feeding their wives to justify why they would be late for dinner. An incident on the production line? A difficult negotiation with a supplier? A last-minute request from their boss? But maybe the wives weren't so gullible and would avenge their husbands' infidelities by going on shopping sprees at Nagoya Hills, the sprawling mega-mall that was only steps away from the NED. All things considered, probably because of the early hour, the atmosphere remained mercifully low-key. Hendra could only hope that they wouldn't have to wait until the rush hour for the boss-mamasan's arrival.

Thankfully, barely fifteen minutes later, a middle-aged woman with cropped hair, dressed in a short skirt and high heels, walked into the Cock & Bull – and judging by the greetings that followed her entrance, Hendra understood that she was Mami Anita. She had a pleasant face and was probably the same age as Maia. After exchanging a few jokes with the girls and filling the room with her hearty laugh, she approached Hendra and Jasmine and shook their hands.

'And you haven't heard from your aunt in so many years?' she asked Hendra after Jasmine finished explaining again the purpose of their visit. The mami's tone was kind, and the timbre of her voice reassuring.

'Yes,' Jasmine replied, 'she really was estranged from her parents. And now her *ayah* has passed away. Hopefully she can still make amends with her *ibu* before it's too late.'

'Her father? So, your grandfather?' she asked Hendra who nodded. 'My deepest condolences, young man.'

'Thank you,' he said.

There was a silence. Mami Anita seemed to hesitate.

'Don't worry,' said Jasmine. 'As we've told your girl just now, what she did here is none of our business.'

'You both seem like nice people. I'm willing to help, but 1988 was such a long time ago! Do you have any photos?'

Hendra felt a heavy weight descend on his chest as he pulled out his mother's photo and handed it to mami Anita. It was the same portrait he had shown to the TMM factory manager.

'No, I'm sorry,' she said after studying the picture for several interminable minutes. 'I don't recognize this face. But I may well have forgotten. Could you tell me more about your aunt and what she was doing here in Batam?'

Hendra explained that his 'aunt' had arrived from Medan to work at the TMM factory.

'Oh, I see, so Dini only came to the Cock & Bull as a freelancer?'

Hendra nodded, almost imperceptibly. He couldn't help shuddering at hearing his mum's name mentioned in the same breath as 'freelancer'.

'The thing is, I only really take care of the girls officially employed by the bar. As for the others, I just ask them to make sure male customers drink a fair bit before they go out with them. So as long as they don't mess around, I don't usually talk to them or get to know them, especially if they only come here very occasionally. I'm sorry.'

Jasmine stepped in. 'Dini was often hanging around with another girl called Maia, her best friend. Maybe you'll remember Maia better as she was probably more of a regular here. Sayang, do you have the other photo?'

It was Jasmine's idea to enquire about his (real) aunt if they drew a blank with his mother, as any information about Maia would potentially unravel clues about Dini's past. At Jasmine's express request, Hendra had had to search through his mother's possessions to find a photo of Maia. Fortunately, he remembered the album with a red batik cover where his mum kept all her photos and he didn't have to unpack too many things out of the near-rotting Cosmo supermarket boxes. One day, though, he would have to open them and retrieve Dini's handmade jewellery and other mementos that he had promised to send to his nenek.

Hendra gave mami Anita Maia's picture. In the colour photo, his aunt, all dressed up and radiant in a blue *kebaya*, was striking a pose in his grandparents' garden.

'Oh yeah, I think I've seen that face before,' said mami Anita. 'Although I don't think I'd have remembered her name. Maia, you said?'

'Yes,' replied Jasmine.

Mami Anita beckoned to the barmaid 'Dwi, give me one double gin and tonic please.' Then, addressing Jasmine and Hendra: 'You know at my age, memory can get a bit rusty, so you need a bit of lube to reconnect all the neurons ...'

While sipping from her glass, she examined the photo again. 'Yes, this young lady freelanced here quite regularly in the late 80s. Often two or three times a week. Not a bad girl. I even wanted to hire her full-time as she was quite popular with customers but she declined. But ... I've not seen her in *years*, as you can imagine!'

'Any friends of hers that you'd remember, who maybe still live here in Batam?' asked Jasmine.

Mami Anita thought long and hard while finishing her drink. 'No, I'm afraid I don't have any idea, unfortunately.'

Hendra couldn't help feeling relieved that this visit to the Cock & Bull was now obviously coming to an end.

'Do you want another drink?' Mami Anita asked them. 'It's on the house.'

'I'm fine, thank you,' said Hendra, while no response was forthcoming from Jasmine.

She was staring intently at something behind the counter.

'You take pictures like that all the time?' she asked, pointing at a cork panel with polaroids pinned on it.

Looking more closely, Hendra realised that the photos, many of them autographed in black marker, were mostly of inebriated customers, occasionally alone, usually in the company of a girl.

'Almost every night,' replied mami Anita. 'It's a tradition since the opening of the bar. My father was one of the first polaroid enthusiasts in Indonesia.'

'And you've kept all the photos from day one?'

'Yes, although sometimes the colours are a bit gone now. They're all at the back, organized by year in different albums.'

'Do you think we could have a look? Maybe we'll find photos of Dini or Maia, which might help lubricate your memory ...'

Mami Anita laughed: 'Sure, while we're at it! So, what years should I fetch? Only 1988?'

Hendra remained silent. He was having a real bad feeling about this.

'Say, from 1987 until 1989,' replied Jasmine.

A few minutes later, Mami Anita came back with six large albums and put them on the bar top. Hendra and Jasmine took one each and started to flick through the pages while Mami Anita, eagerly going down memory lane, browsed another album on her own. From time to time, she would giggle, and the barmaid would lean over to check what was so amusing.

The pictures were quite repetitive storyline-wise, Hendra quickly discovered. The sequence often started with a young Indonesian girl in a mini-skirt (or some other skimpy outfit), standing barefoot on the bar counter and bending over to smile at the camera, offering a glimpse of her cleavage. Then usually followed a picture of a male customer of an advanced age making a drunken face at the girl, and finally the heart-warming denouement of the photo-novel: the man and the girl, locked in a fake amorous gaze, dancing in each other's arms ... Some photos were particularly blurry but one couldn't tell whether this was because of the cigarette smoke, the quality of the camera itself or, just as easily, the intoxication of the photographer.

Hendra was mid-way through his second album when a photo at the bottom of the page caught his eye. He looked closer and froze. Despite all the years, the lips of the girl in the picture had retained their garish orange colour, in sharp contrast with the yellowing already consuming the rest of the image. A bit like those black and white pictures that Hendra had seen in an exhibition on the war in Bosnia where the artist had removed all the colours except for the red of the blood. Heart throbbing, he inspected the next photos, which also featured his aunt. Often smoking, she wore knee-high black leather boots, which made her look like a death metal singer. He was about to call Mami Anita to tell her that he had found pictures of Maia when his stomach sank, and he instinctively gripped the bar counter. Ears ringing, he squeezed his eyes shut for a few seconds before reopening them. The photo of his mum was still there.

Looking even thinner than in his memories, his mother sat on the knees of a man who formed the V sign with one hand while the other was firmly gripped around Dini's waist. Dressed in a red woollen mini-skirt and a see-through sequined top, she stared at the camera without smiling, giving the impression that she couldn't wait for the photo moment to be over and done with.

'What have you got?' asked Jasmine. She had probably noticed his laboured breathing.

Jasmine and Mami Anita came closer, leaning over his shoulder to peer at the photo. He wanted to turn the page, but it was too late.

'Is that Dini?' asked Mami Anita.

'Yes,' replied Jasmine.

'So, she did come to my bar! But I don't remember her, really … Well, the least we can say is that she doesn't really look in her element in that photo! Must have been one of her first times coming here.'

Then she took the picture out of the album, and while she was having a long look at it, a smile pulled at her lips.

'What is it?' asked Jasmine.

'It's the man. Alawi was his name, if my memory serves me. He was working on an offshore oil rig and spent his rest days in Nagoya. He was a regular here for a few years and quite a character who liked to make stupid jokes with me. A very handsome Arab man with green eyes … like yours,' she added, smiling at Hendra.

The mami's words were just rolling down his face while his head spun, faster and faster. This trip was a mistake, he should never have accepted being dragged into this bar.

'I think we're going to go back to our hotel now,' said Jasmine. She grabbed Hendra's hand.

'Yes, sure. Please don't hesitate to come back here if you want to take a look at other photos. And I'll think again about everything you told me. Who knows, maybe I'll end up remembering more things!' She handed Hendra the photo: 'Please keep this picture if it can help you in your search.'

Hendra jammed the photo into his jeans pocket, mumbled a thank you and followed Jasmine into the now darkened evening.

During the short taxi ride to their hotel, she tried to comfort him. She understood that he was shaken, but they had to go further. That's why they had come to Batam in the first place.

'We should try to find more info about this Alawi. I'm sure this woman would help us.'

'To know how much he paid my mother?'

'Sayang, something doesn't add up in this story, and you know it!'

'What doesn't add up? You see how she's dressed in that photo? She didn't enter the Cock & Bull by mistake, like thinking she was opening the door of a mosque!'

'But she also seems so out of place. That's the first thing Mami Anita said, and she's seen many girls in her life, don't you think!'

'Ibu never liked to be photographed!'

Minutes later, while they were already inside the hotel reception, waiting for the lift to their room, Hendra told Jasmine: 'I'm starting to have a headache. I need to go for a walk.'

She proposed to go with him but he turned her down. His neck was already so stiff; he could only do what he had to now out of her sight. He exited the hotel and quickly moved away from the entrance – in case Jasmine was observing him – before jumping into a cab.

'To Penthouse,' he told the skinny young driver. Hopefully, even though it was only 9 pm, the club would already be open.

'But it's just 500 metres away, Pak. Maybe you want to w–'

'Please just take me there,' Hendra cut him off. He certainly had no intention to walk; in his state, there was no time to waste.

Even before the taxi pulled up in front of Penthouse, Hendra saw that he was in luck – the two stocky guys standing in the distance under the streetlights were obviously bouncers and they were there for a reason.

After he stepped into the nightclub –located in the basement of a nondescript low-rise building – Hendra needed a few minutes to get used to the dark, but once he could see, he realised that the freckled cewek at the Cock & Bull hadn't lied. There were essentially two categories of people present at this early hour: dealers and pros. And now one customer. Without hesitating, he walked up to the row of dealers who sat on the sofas at the back and were doing some sort of Morse code with their phone torch to draw his attention. Two girls stood in his way, asking if he wanted company, but he brushed them aside and, cutting to the chase, picked one dealer randomly and asked him for one gram of hero. The guy stared at him in surprise, saying he would never find any smack in Batam but that the K here was very good. Hendra shrugged and bought two doses. Better than nothing.

He rushed upstairs towards the exit, impatient to be back at the hotel. He was going to lock himself inside the bathroom to shoot up that sweet little K! But lo and behold, he caught sight of

Jasmine at the top of the stairs, arguing with the bouncer. He was about to turn back when she saw him and screamed.

'Come here and empty your pockets! You think I'm stupid or what!'

Hendra had never seen Jasmine in such a state, and with the bouncer observing them, it would have been foolish to make a scene here. Pretending to be contrite, he walked out and handed her one of the two K doses. Jasmine swiftly tore the sachet, angrily emptying its content into a puddle of rainwater, which took on a whitish hue under the street lamp.

As soon as they were back in the room after a brisk, silent walk, Jasmine said she wanted to shower. Now was the time, thought Hendra, who pulled out his wash bag where he always hid a syringe. He realised now that it was a good thing that he couldn't find hero as it would have been very difficult to get a quick fix. The K might have impurities, but it had a wonderful advantage over hero in that it dissolved easily in cold water so that there was no need to heat it or add citrus. Seated on the bed and hearing the shower running, Hendra prepared his shoot using the mineral water 'offered with the compliments of the Triniti Hotel'. But no matter how much he tightened his tourniquet after getting the drug mixture ready, no vein would swell enough. Losing patience, he inserted the needle into his forearm anyway and started to press the plunger to release the drug into his blood. All of a sudden, he felt a clot forming.

If the clot travelled to his heart, thought Hendra before blacking out, Radikal would forever return to his roots.

Part VI

Take Me Away

Jakarta, November – December 2014

17

Sitting cross-legged on his living room floor, with the curtains drawn to block all sunlight, Hendra was watching a video of Abu Nassim al-Indonesia, the only emir of Indonesian origin within the Islamic State's top leadership. Since coming across this recording when he had woken up around 1 pm, he had been viewing it on his laptop on a continuous loop.

In the ten-minute movie shot in the Syrian countryside, by the side of what looked like a lake, the former White Brigade member exhorted his blood brothers to join ISIS without further delay. Behind him fluttered a large black banner with the Seal of Mohammad below the inscription 'There is no God but Allah'. (Black, Hendra had now learned, was the favourite colour of the first Muslim caliphates – certainly a much better choice than the green so prevalent in today's Islamic world.) Unlike the other mujahideen around him, who had their faces wrapped in a long chequered keffiyeh, Abu Nassim was unmasked. With a rifle wedged between his legs, the barrel pointing to the heavens, he stared into the camera, fearless, his deep voice trembling under the weight of his rage. Hendra had never seen such pure, unadulterated passion blazing in the eyes of an Indonesian man – except maybe once or twice with an XS clubber experiencing a very powerful trip. Now that the Caliphate had been recreated, urged Abu Nassim, Muslims everywhere in the world had the obligation to do the Hijrah. Otherwise, they themselves would soon become kuffar. What could hold back his Indonesian brothers in this faithless land where Shariah wasn't even enforced, where evil ruled in place of Allah? Was it their families who opposed their departure? Then they ought to repudiate on the spot all these miscreants, whether they were their mothers, fathers, wives or children! Or maybe they were just too weak to give up the material comforts of their sinful life and submit to Allah? Godless infidels! They would eventually pay for their debauchery on the Day of Judgement.

Hendra wiped away the tears running down his cheeks.

The Hijrah was the journey that the Prophet had accomplished, from Mecca to Medina, to escape death and persecution. Hendra too had to flee, run away from everything here that reminded him of his mother or his father and pushed him to take drugs. In order to avoid all temptation, since his return from Batam a few days ago, Hendra had been spending entire days locked up in his flat – most of the time browsing jihadist forums. But soon he wouldn't be able to hold back. The only solution was the Hijrah. Increasingly, Hendra also started to grasp the infallible logic according to which under Shariah law there was no more temptation and everyone ended up submitting themselves to Allah. Enforced purification was what he needed to abolish his suffering.

He had made up his mind after waking up on a hospital bed in Batam, blinded by the bright ceiling light, his face enclosed inside an oxygen mask. For a fleeting moment, he had dreamed that he was a fighter pilot dazzled by the sun before noticing

Jasmine crying at his side. She had found him unconscious after her shower and had gotten the hotel to call for an ambulance. He had been in that state for a few hours apparently, time for the antidote the doctors had injected into his blood to purge the K from his body. For it wasn't because of a blood clot that he had passed out: it was, more prosaically, an overdose. A fucking ketamine OD. Before they left the hospital, the doctor had flat out told him that it was simply suicidal to shoot up such a dose.

On the way back to Jakarta, Jasmine had tried to comfort him, but very quickly he had asked to be left alone in his misery. Not that he was upset with Jasmine on any account. He knew that she had his best interests at heart. And in a way, wasn't it thanks to her that he had finally dispelled all remaining doubts about his mother's past? His family secret was no longer a secret, he had even found a photo ... No, he had rejected Jasmine's sympathy because it was pointless. There was no cure, no possibility to change the past, and his despair was simply grotesque – even more grotesque than the leafless baobab he had seen on the cover of the latest National Geographic issue at Batam airport. He could surrender to it and experience headache after headache. Or he could move into action, cast off and quit this life where there was no happiness. Not even the hope of happiness anymore.

What's more, the photo of his mother a victim of an Alawi was a sign from Allah ordering him to leave for Syria and kill the fake Muslims who dared attack the Sunnis. One just had to google this name that the mamasan had remembered to realise that Syria was full of Alawis, all somehow followers of the apostate Shia sect. At the end of the day, it didn't matter whether the green-eyed Alawi in the photo was really his biological father or just one amongst the faceless customers who had raped his mother: he was guilty and so were all the people of his kind, all the traitors to Allah who worshipped idols and massacred the real Muslims. He was going to join ISIS and fight the enemy, exact revenge on the parasites of Islam who came to Indonesia to abuse its women. Thanks to his jihad, he would transcend his bastard status, and become a *mujahid*. And if he died on the battlefield, if that was his destiny, he would have been more useful in his death that he had ever been in his life.

Only Jasmine held him back. But their relationship was at an impasse, and that also contributed to his torment. For it was she who was right, he understood it too well now: his only choice was between living in sin or living in want (and potentially still in sin!). Torn between the impurity of his attraction for a waria and the imperfection in his eyes of a post-op emasculated body, he had no other solution than to leave her. Already, he was trying to put some distance between them by telling Jasmine that he needed to be alone to nurse his wounds. Every day, she called to check on him and proposed to come and see him, and each time he would invoke his relentless headaches to turn her down. As a matter of fact, these days he did spend almost half of his time in bed resting after one of his three or four daily attacks. Sometimes, even when he acted as fast as possible and made a skin incision on his wrist at the first sign of stiffness in his neck, he didn't manage to defeat the headache. It seemed as if the pain had gotten more pernicious, like a virus mutating into a new, more resistant strain.

Yes, whatever his feelings for Jasmine, there was no time to lose anymore. He had to leave as soon as possible. And who else to ask for help but Dr Jusuf. Wasn't Abu Nassim, one of his former proteges, and hadn't he said a few times that he would support anyone willing to wage jihad in Syria? Hendra hadn't seen him since his return from Batam, citing his painful, repeated headaches to justify his prolonged absence from the White Brigade, but now he couldn't wait any longer. He took his handphone and dialled Dr Jusuf's number.

***

When Hendra reached Masjid Istiqlal around 5 pm, it was already filling up with the faithful arriving for Maghrib prayers.

Located right in the town centre, Masjid Istiqlal was the most famous mosque in the capital and had always been for Hendra a symbolic place dividing north and south Jakarta, the intersection of old and new, where the crumbling Chinese neighbourhood of Glodok gave way to the more modern and sterile city of skyscrapers and airconditioned shopping centres. Together with the Monas monument rising a few metres away on Merdeka square, the Istiqlal mosque was one of those rare buildings in the capital city to be extensively covered in tourist guidebooks – and even visited by Barack Obama himself during his presidential trip to Indonesia five years earlier. Designed in the 60s by the prominent local architect Frederich Silaban to celebrate Indonesian Independence, it was, in its days, the largest mosque in Southeast Asia – capable of accommodating a congregation of up to one hundred thousand – although that record had now been claimed by Brunei.

Hendra had to block his nose as he entered the Masjid Istiqlal compound through one of the eight gates positioned along the outer wall. For the wide wooden doors didn't only let the faithful walk in from all sides, they also took in the noxious smells emanating from the irrigation canal surrounding the mosque, which had long become a sewer system of sorts. After removing his shoes at the entrance of the inner sanctuary, he performed his *wudu* in one of the ground floor's ablution rooms. Then, trousers and sleeves still rolled up, he climbed the stairs leading to the main prayer hall where men sat on one side and women on the other, separated by a one-metre-high aluminium barrier.

It was Dr Jusuf who had suggested that they meet at Istiqlal mosque when Hendra had insisted that he needed to see him as soon as possible. The professor of Islamic law had told him that after prayers, he was to deliver a lecture on the theme: 'Pancasila and Shariah: antagonism or synergy?' at the mosque's madrasah.

Hendra moved as far away as possible from the still sparse crowd before sending Dr Jusuf a WhatsApp message to tell him he was waiting at the back, across from the minbar. In the meantime he decided to perform the customary two *rakaat*. Soon, while low-bowing, he could sense that someone was sitting behind him. He finished his prayer and turned around to see Dr Jusuf seated cross-legged, leaning against one of the twelve aluminium pillars supporting the mosque's one-hundred-metre-high dome.

'What's happening?' asked Dr Jusuf, observing him. 'You've been missing in action for quite a while, dear brother. And I have to say that right now you don't really look good.'

Hendra checked around him to make sure that nobody could eavesdrop on their discussion. But there was no risk – he had chosen a really quiet and isolated corner. They seemed lost in the middle of the immense red carpet covering the floor, like two white spots adrift on a scarlet ocean.

'You always said that if one of us wished to fight jihad, you would help him ...'

An inquisitive smile formed on Dr Jusuf's lips.

'Yes, of course. There's no nobler way to die than as a martyr in the name of Allah. It's the most virtuous act of faith. Once a man asked our Prophet, peace be upon him: "Tell me where I will be if I am killed while fighting in the way of Allah?" He replied, "In Heaven." Then the man threw away the few dates which he had in his hand, jumped into the battlefield and fought on till he was killed!'

The massive ceiling fan whirring above their heads barely managed to stir the heavy humid air. A severe storm was in the making, thought Hendra.

'I'm ready,' he said. 'I want to join them. As soon as possible.'

'Them? Who, if I may ask?'

'ISIS, of course!'

Dr Jusuf's face fell. 'Really, Hendra? I always thought that you of all people would want to fight your jihad here in Indonesia and punish all the fornicating bules who insult our religion every day ...'

'Please, Professor. I have to go there as soon as possible.'

'But what's the rush?'

Hendra hesitated. Dr Jusuf knew nothing about his trip to Batam. They had actually never talked again about his mum's past after that day when he had confided in him following Maia's crushing revelations. But Hendra realised that whatever shame he still felt at the latest discoveries he had made in Batam, baring it all with Dr Jusuf might be the only way to convince him to send him to Syria without delay. And so, he pulled out the photo of his mother with Alawi – which, without really knowing why, he had been keeping in his wallet.

'Because of this,' he said, showing the picture to Dr Jusuf.

'Put that away!' The professor pushed Hendra's hand after a brief glance at the photo. 'May I remind you that we are in a mosque. We'll have to redo our ablutions before praying, simply for laying our eyes on that depraved woman!'

'It's my mother,' Hendra said, putting back the photo inside his wallet. 'The photo was taken in 1987, less than a year before my birth.'

And then he explained what he had found out in Batam.

'I'm really sorry for your suffering, dear brother,' said Dr Jusuf, taking Hendra's hand after he was done. 'I can understand how devastating these sordid details must be for you. Having said that, I still do not grasp why you so urgently need to leave for Syria.'

'Because I was told that the guy on the photo is a Shia!'

'And so what?' asked Dr Jusuf, releasing Hendra's hand. '*Your* enemy is the vice in all its forms, it doesn't matter if the perpetrator is a Shia, a bule or even an Indonesian!'

'Please, Professor, I've watched Abu Nassim al-Indonesia's videos and I want to fight with him. You keep saying that if we want to go to Syria—'

'Maybe, but not you.'

An uneasy silence grew between them.

'If you want,' said Dr Jusuf finally, with a small grin on his face, 'we can plan an attack on the De Leila café in Jakarta. I'm told it's always full of Iranians revelling in their ignominious debauchery.'

'Never mind then,' said Hendra, ignoring the professor's suggestion. 'I'll just go there on my own!'

Dr Jusuf sneered. 'On your own? On paper, it seems so easy, right? Just go to Turkey, cross the border and then onto Raqqa … child's play, isn't it?' Then lowering his voice: 'But that easiness is precisely the problem for ISIS. It attracts lots of wimps and losers who go there on a whim and have to be executed when they suddenly want to leave. Not to mention the spies from various governments, including ours, who infiltrate ISIS in order to eliminate their own nationals and make sure they never come home! So, the leadership of ISIS now wants all aspiring jihadists to be vetted before departure. And here in Jakarta, do you know who is in charge of checking the applicants' credentials?'

Hendra gave a faint shake of his head.

'Yours truly!'

Yes, of course, thought Hendra, who was starting to connect all the dots. But then why refuse to send him to Syria?

'Sorry, Professor, I can't stay here … I need to leave *now*!'

Dr Jusuf sighed. 'Honestly, dear brother, I really don't think it's a good idea for you go there.'

'Why do you say that?'

'First, your relationship with this waria …'

Hendra felt himself going pale. 'What … what do you mean?'

'Don't lie!'

'It … it's finished,' said Hendra with difficulty. How had Dr Jusuf found out about Jasmine?

'And what about the drugs? Is that also *finished*?'

Hendra's pulse was racing. 'How do you–'

Dr Jusuf cut him off. 'In Syria, if you crack, they won't give you a second chance.'

Hendra held his breath. His head was spinning in all directions.

Dr Jusuf smirked. 'You wonder how I know all your little secrets, don't you? I recognized you the very first day when you came to see me, even though you pretended that you were working in a pizzeria. Hard to forget the face of the crackhead DJ who was still mixing, hanging in the air in his cage, while I was beating up that stupid bouncer.'

An intense buzzing had started in Hendra's ears. A white noise, like a long scratch in a DJ Radikal set, drowning out the rising rumble inside the mosque as more and more people arrived for Maghrib prayer.

'At first, I thought you might be part of a set-up by some of our enemies and I had you followed to check who you were hanging around with. Mostly junkies like you, we quickly found out, and that waria of course, but nobody really suspicious. Still, it's only when you told me about your mother's lifelong secret that I finally convinced myself you were truly sincere in your hatred of vice. And I encouraged you to reconnect with your aunt.'

'But why?'

'Because, I thought that once you'd accepted what was obvious to everyone but you, you would have your epiphany, your true political awakening. And I was right, wasn't I? After that meeting with your aunt, you joined the White Brigade. But I just can't for the life of me understand why you still had to go to Batam and then to get fixated on such an ... insignificant photo.'

'Insignificant?'

'In the grand scheme of things, yes!' He was growing more

and more agitated. 'You don't think I invested so much in you to let you slip away to Syria like that, do you? It's here that you have to wage your jihad. Here in Indonesia. Even Agung did something for me before I let him join ISIS. Isn't there so much to do in this country as well?'

There was no mistaking a certain bitterness in Dr Jusuf's tone and he had also raised his voice, drawing the attention of a few faithful who had just sat down nearby.

'The White Brigade is a solid group of good people,' he resumed, speaking more quietly, 'but some days, it seems as if we're just banging our heads against a brick wall. We have to go further and I have a great project for you. Full of meaning and much closer to your own preoccupations than these Shia in Syria.'

Dr Jusuf grabbed Hendra's hand. The XS DJ wanted to flee but he felt like he couldn't move, as though he was glued to the spot, as though he had become one with the red carpet.

'It'll probably be a bit more complicated now that you've left the club,' continued Dr Jusuf. 'But I'm sure that together we'll find a way... I want you to bomb XS.'

Dr Jusuf revealed his plan to Hendra. He had been dreaming about it for three years, ever since his own 16-year-old son had died at the club from an overdose. But with all these metal detectors that had popped up everywhere, including at XS, post-JI bombing – not to mention the new security checks after the White Brigade attack – only an insider could do the job, and Hendra was his gift from Allah Himself. He was to enter XS with an explosive belt, position himself in the middle of the dancefloor, and then, pressing on the detonator, he would put an end both to this Shaytan's den where lives of innocent kids were destroyed every day and to his own junkie existence which he couldn't bear anymore.

Was that why, wondered Hendra, the professor had gotten mad at him when he had mentioned his intention to apply for the assistant job at The Saving Hand? Because his leaving XS risked jeopardizing The White Brigade chief's murderous design?

Hendra was shaking even more than the day when the police had knocked on his door and told him about his mother's accident. How could Dr Jusuf imagine that he would ever become an accomplice to such an abominable crime? Yes, he was ready to kill enemy soldiers on a battlefield, but he would never indiscriminately murder people in a terrorist attack, like the JI had done in 2002 in Bali or in 2004 at the Marriott Jakarta.

Dr Jusuf grabbed his shoulder. 'I hope you realise that only an action of this magnitude can atone for all your past sins.'

By now, the congregation had already regrouped around the minbar. Very soon, the prayer would begin. Hendra had to run from this man as fast and as far as possible. He began to stand up but Dr Jusuf held him back by pulling on his arm.

'Don't forget that it is fate, it is Allah, *subḥānahu wata ʿālā*, who sent you to me because He wants us to band together!'

Hendra didn't reply. Freeing himself from Dr Jusuf's grip, he rose to his feet and made for the stairs. The ground whirled around him. He staggered, stumbled, as if unable to grip the floor under his feet, and began to run, afraid of being swallowed inside the blood-red carpet. After he finally reached the ground floor, it still took him forever long time to locate his sandals.

As soon as he was out, he rushed towards the one taxi that was stationed in front of the mosque and sat in the back without a word.

'Sorry, I'm not free,' said the driver straightaway. 'I've just stopped here because I'm going to pray.'

'Never mind,' replied Hendra. 'I'll wait inside the car until you're done.'

The driver turned around and seemed about to protest. But for some reason – the utter dejection in Hendra's gaze? the trembling of his lips? his heavy breathing? – he must have understood that there was no point trying to get this passenger out of his taxi.

He started the engine, grumbling. 'So, where do we go?'

'Lokasari Square,' blurted Hendra. 'On Jalan Hayam Wuruk Sembilan.'

Lokasari Square, the place where he used to meet Hassan, his former smack reseller. The words had just slipped out of his mouth.

He had entrusted his heart and soul to a man who thought of nothing but to get him to perpetrate a suicide-attack at XS. Now he had to disappear, sever all ties with Dr Jusuf, The Saving Hand, The White Brigade – and relearn to heal his wounds without anyone's help.

* * *

As soon as he reached home after buying one bundle of Afghan, Hendra boiled water and then set to mix half a dose with some of the citric acid graciously offered by Hassan. The smack dealer had seemed very surprised to see him. All this while, Hassan, who only sold heroin, had probably assumed that he had lost one of his most loyal customers. Lost to competition or to OD, not to quitting because, heck, nobody quits smack, right?

At last, Hendra shot up and when the flash ran through his body, he let himself slide across the sofa. Pure happiness was gushing in his veins. Heroin was his guardian angel, the little fairy who could appease all his suffering with a wave of her wand. Life wasn't so difficult, after all. Why get so worked up when you only need one gram of magic powder to make your worries disappear? He fell asleep.

Hendra woke up with a jolt. There was a commotion in the stairwell. Fast-approaching footsteps. Loud voices. It was the White Brigade, they were coming after him! Hendra sat up, panting. An odd noise, like a slow-moving ratchet, echoed through the darkness of the living room. He was about to cower when he realised that it was his own chattering teeth that he was hearing.

Whispering. There was whispering now, right by his door.

He grabbed his phone. He was going to call Jasmine and she would come and rescue him. But he was trembling so much that his fingers couldn't select her number in the contact list. He stopped suddenly, struck by a terrible thought. Jasmine didn't know any of this. He had consistently lied to her all these months. Now it was on his own that he had to face Dr Jusuf. The phone fell from his hands.

He opened his mouth as wide as possible to fill his lungs with strength. Then, still in the dark, he searched for the Lexotan box inside the giant ashtray on the low table and without counting them, put a few pills under his tongue. After some minutes, he started to breathe more easily. The whispering outside his door faded. The shaking stopped. Slowly he managed to reason with himself. There was no Dr Jusuf lurking behind his door. It was just a smack-induced panic attack.

Shivering in his sweat-drenched t-shirt, he went to the bathroom to splash water on his face and saw his reflection in the mirror – his skin white as a sheet, his hair slick with perspiration and sticking to his forehead in sweaty strands, his pupils so contracted they were smaller than pinheads. He pressed his hand against his rib cage, almost surprised when he felt his heart still beating.

Little by little, the panic attack receded.

After a while, he also started to think more clearly about his discussion with Dr Jusuf. What if the professor had bluffed? What if there was no such screening process? Certainly, the Islamic State couldn't afford to reject volunteers as motivated as him. He opened his laptop and logged into ISIS' online forum under his handle *Radikal_Baru*. He waited for the usual pop-up message suggesting a live chat and then clicked the link provided. A new window opened in the top right corner of his screen.

'What can we do for you, today, dear Muslim brother?' asked someone in English.

'I want to join ISIS as soon as possible,' he replied, heart beating.

'*Allahu Akbar*! May I know which country you are from?'

'From Indonesia.'

'Let me connect you with the right person who will assist you with this.'

A short while later, someone took over the chat in bahasa, introducing himself as a member of the Katibah Nusantara which federated all the fighters from Southeast Asia.

'We are so happy about your interest, dear aspiring mujahid.

You can send us your application via email using the attached form. Please don't forget to mention all your acts of bravery. Most importantly, you need to produce a recommendation letter from an ISIS emissary.'

'What if I don't have one?'

'Then we'll put you in touch with one of our local recruiters so that he can interview you and verify your credentials.'

'Who's that person if I may ask?'

'Please, dear brother, just fill out the form with all the relevant information and someone will contact you ASAP.'

The next morning, Hendra saw that he had already received a reply from the recruitment bureau of the Katibah Nusantara.

'Dear Brother,

Thank you for your interest in the Islamic State of Iraq and al-Sham. Praise to Allah for making you want to fight with us.

As per our checks, you are already liaising with one of our official recruiters in Indonesia. He's the only one who can clear your application. Good luck on your path to jihad, dear brother. In sha'Allah, your efforts will soon pay off. We certainly look forward to welcoming you in Raqqa.'

The trap had closed in on him.

18

Hendra inserted his card into the Bank Mandiri ATM at the Lokasari commercial centre, but it was swiftly ejected without giving him a single note.

It was now official: he was broke. Totally broke. Since his failed attempt one month earlier to join ISIS, he had been shooting up heroin like water, and his meagre savings had vanished faster than a reserve of Ketamine in an afterparty. What's more, between injections and incisions, his right forearm was now one giant wound, and like in his golden junkie days, flesh just seemed to be melting off his body.

Hendra had fought until exhaustion. Like a bird trying to set itself free, repeatedly hitting the bars of its cage until it finally crumples to the ground. He had tried many different escape routes but one after the other, the doors had shut in his face: XS, the White Brigade, Jasmine ... Yes, even Jasmine had abandoned him. A few days earlier, during one of her visits to his flat – unannounced, or else he would have told her not to come – she had revealed her decision to 'take the plunge' and get operated – officially so they could get married. he had already scheduled her gender-reassignment surgery for early next year, in Bangkok as it was much cheaper than in Iran. Given how worn out and weak he often was, it had been a while since they'd last made love, but if just the thought of her without her penis made him so sad, he feared that they might never be able to be intimate again. Clearly, the only exit door that was still wide open to him was the one with a large syringe image pasted on it – and he was rushing through it with wild abandon.

Hendra slid to the floor and sat by the side of the ATM.

Last week, he had visited his grandparents. Part of him had wanted to tell them that now *he knew*, and another part still hoped. Hoped that there was more to his mother's secret past than it seemed and that they would finally tell him everything they knew. Yes, his grandfather was sick but wasn't Hendra suffering more than him, he to whom everybody had lied for twenty-six years? While his grandmother was preparing dinner in the kitchen and he was alone in the living room with his grandfather, he had silently placed on the dining table the polaroid photo showing his mother sitting on Alawi's knees at the Cock & Bull. Raising his eyes from his newspaper, his kakek had almost choked on his *kopi* when he had looked at the photo.

'Who gave you this picture?' he had asked, gasping. 'Is it Maia?'

'Maybe … Why does it matter who gave it to me?'

'You must avoid that child of misfortune like the plague!'

Soon joined by Nenek, his grandfather had pretended not to know anything about the man in the photo or the circumstances surrounding when it was taken. Most likely, they had both asserted, Maia had pulled Dini into some seedy bar when they were working together in Batam. But one thing was certain: his dad was Pak Hadi, the former factory manager of TMM in Batam who had died when … Violently kicking the dining table, Hendra had interrupted his grandparents' nice little act and screamed at them, accusing them of feeding him the same lies for so many years. And when his nenek had pleaded with him to calm down and not to make such a scene in front of his ailing grandfather, he had taken off without another word.

These days, he saw prostitution and vice everywhere, whether it was the girls in shorts impudently straddling an ojek, the resellers of cobra meat with aphrodisiac properties, the unisex hair saloons advertising sexy haircuts or this new club, Lolitas, which had just opened a few blocks away from XS. The Glodok neighbourhood where he had always felt home seemed so hostile now and he dreaded even going out to get his refill of smack or to buy groceries. On some nights, he had this harrowing dream where he beat to a pulp one of his primary school classmates for calling him 'son of a whore'. And when he woke up, his head ready to explode under the impending headache attack, he couldn't shake the feeling that it wasn't just a nightmare, rather some buried memory resurfacing after so many years.

An old ethnic Chinese lady approached the ATM, but when she saw him she quickly put her card back into her wallet and moved on without withdrawing money. She must have thought that Hendra was a beggar or, worse, a thief who would try to snatch a few notes from her. And why not? Certainly, sooner rather than later, he would have to find a way to obtain money as he only had enough smack left for a few days. Eighteen months ago, after meeting Jasmine, he was in such a state of grace that he had managed to go cold turkey with very limited methadone support. Yes, he had suffered terrible cravings, but he had found in his new love the physical and moral strength to resist all temptations. These days, he knew that he wouldn't be able to bear up and the mere prospect of having to go through the throes of heroin withdrawal once he ran out of money terrified him.

Dizzy with anguish, his neck already stiffening, Hendra realised that Dr Jusuf was really his only lifeline left now. He had to pull on it on the off chance that it might lead him back to shore. A few days ago, the professor had sent him a WhatsApp message saying that they should talk again, that if Hendra agreed to do his bit, there was, potentially, a solution for him to fulfil his duty here before leaving for Syria. He didn't know what Dr Jusuf had in mind but in this new plan, he was obviously not expected to play the role of a suicide bomber anymore. Who knows, maybe he was not even required to kill anyone?

Without standing up, Hendra took his handphone out of his pocket and called Dr Jusuf. He answered on the second ring, and straightaway suggested that Hendra drop by his house at his convenience.

'It'll be more private than at Masjid Istiqlal,' added Dr Jusuf with – Hendra couldn't help imagining – a large, satisfied smile on the lips.

***

A few hours later, in the taxi taking him to Dr Jusuf's residence – after he had recovered from his headache episode – Hendra had to ask the driver to turn off the radio. Not that he disagreed with the driver's taste. Quite the opposite, the radio was playing Sudirman, a Malay singer from the 80s whose melancholic and swaying voice would usually delight him. But some days, he couldn't bear any sound, not even music.

Hendra presented himself at Dr Jusuf's secure entrance right before sunset. The guards let him pass without question and the professor, in his usual white djellaba, welcomed him on his front porch. He looked radiant. Triumphant even, thought Hendra.

In the living room, the table had been set for two.

'Let's discuss things over a nice dinner,' said Dr Jusuf. 'My wives have prepared a feast.'

They sat on black ottomans around a low table laden with with satay sticks and sambal goreng hati, a Sundanese speciality made of beef liver in coconut sauce, snow peas and diced potatoes.

The purdah curtains were drawn closed, and Hendra could hear the usual chattering voices. For the first time, he noticed that the embroidered batik curtain had small openings and understood that the cloth acted like a giant niqab, allowing the professor's wives to see without being seen.

Hendra was staring at Dr Jusuf, who really seemed to be enjoying himself.

'What's wrong with you, brother?' asked the professor. 'You're not eating?'

'Can you please tell me what you want me to do now in exchange for sending me to Syria?'

'I see … you're impatient to get down to business.' Then after munching on a piece of fried chicken: 'My new plan is quite simple, Hendra. If you don't want to die as a *shahid*, I can find someone else. But I need your help to get the bomb inside XS. Only a former star DJ like you stands a chance to get through the security screening and the metal detectors without being searched. Once you're in the main hall, you'll hand over the explosive belt to another mujahid, and you'll be free to go to Syria or anywhere else.'

Hendra was shaking with rage. How could Dr Jusuf not get it! 'I told you before … I don't want to kill innocent clubbers!'

Dr Jusuf thought for a while before replying. 'Innocence is a very relative concept, dear brother. For instance … who is more innocent, according to you: a Russian soldier conscripted by force in Chechnya or an American citizen who keeps electing a government massacring Muslims both at home and overseas?'

Hendra looked away.

'Now let me ask you: just by paying their entrance fees, aren't all these "innocent" clubbers contributing to the expansion of vice in Jakarta? Are they not supporting the work of Shaytan on Earth?'

'Maybe …' replied Hendra. 'Though you should probably know that the last time I played at XS, I roughed up the head bouncer because he was letting in some underage kid. I'm banned from the club, and if I try to go in, they'll spot me right away and throw me out.'

'*Goblok*!' said Dr Jusuf, rising to his feet. He kicked over a black teak stool, which flew across the room before landing on the marble floor.

***

Hendra looked behind him one last time before inserting the key into the lock. Luckily on a Monday night at 9 pm the XS back alley was really deserted. He swiftly opened the side door and slipped in.

It was Hendra himself – one week after visiting Dr Jusuf and upon failing to borrow money from Jasmine – who had finally thought of a way to help the professor achieve his dream of reducing XS to a pile of rubble – but without any victims. On Mondays, the day when the club was closed, the cleaning crew was at work until late afternoon to clear up the weekend's mess. Then from 6 pm until the following day around 7 pm, the place was devoid of any staff or patrons. That was the timeframe during which Hendra suggested planting a bomb programmed to explode before XS reopened its doors. (As for how to get in since the club was officially closed, he knew that Jasmine, who was sometimes in charge of supplies, had a key to open that side door – used to throw out troublesome patrons like Alessandro but also to take in the drinks' deliveries. He had simply 'borrowed' that key from Jasmine and made a double of it.)

Even though Dr Jusuf had initially insisted that he wanted something more meaningful, he had eventually agreed to Hendra's plan. At least, Shaytan's den would be definitively wiped out. After placing the bomb, set to detonate the next day at twelve noon, Hendra was to meet Dr Jusuf at his home and he would be given his plane ticket before leaving straight for the airport. That meant the blast would occur during his journey from Jakarta to Istanbul – a scenario that was not to his liking as he'd rather have been around until the bomb had exploded. Just in case something went wrong …

'Very bad idea,' the leader of the White Brigade had said. 'Imagine if you're spotted by CCTV cameras entering XS. After the attack, the police would search for you everywhere, and you wouldn't be able to leave the country. Even if you're not captured on camera, you'll be a prime suspect, given your fight with Pak Kelvin and the head bouncer a few months back. No, you have to be far away when the bomb explodes, that's for sure.'

Hendra had only given in to Dr Jusuf's argument after making sure, based on his flight itinerary, that he would already have landed in Istanbul way before the reopening of XS on the Tuesday evening. To that end, the direct Turkish Airlines flight from Jakarta to Istanbul on the Monday night would have been ideal. But Dr Jusuf had insisted that he had to avoid it at all costs because Indonesian customs officers had been instructed to scrutinize any single male in his twenties with a brand-new passport travelling alone to Istanbul. Indeed, one month earlier, President Jokowi had promised to do everything in his power to prevent Indonesians from swelling the ranks of ISIS. In the end, Hendra was to board a 1 am Emirates flight to Dubai, and after a two-hour transit, a Pegasus Airlines plane would take him straight to Istanbul. According to Hendra's estimate, he would be flying over the Persian Gulf when the bomb was meant to explode. Four hours later, when he landed in Istanbul, if it still hadn't gone off, he would immediately raise the alarm.

As for the date of the attack, he had wanted to wait until Jasmine was away in Thailand for her operation. But Dr Jusuf had insisted that the XS elimination had to happen symbolically right before Christmas – so on Tuesday 23 December 2014 – whereas Jasmine would only leave after the New Year.

With the explosives stuffed in a black backpack on his shoulders, Hendra climbed the stairs that led straight from the drinks' storeroom to a landing at the back of the central bar. Then he headed towards the ladder that gave access to his DJ cabin.

When Hendra and Dr Jusuf had discussed together where to put the bomb, the professor had convinced him that to cause maximum damage, the best was to hide it in his former cage (which, according to Jasmine, had not been in use since his departure, as Pak Kelvin couldn't convince any of the other resident artistes to become the next flying DJ). After concealing the backpack under the mixing console, Hendra climbed back down and activated the safety switch by the side of the dancefloor (installed in case the DJ got stuck) to position the cabin right above the centre of the room.

As he cast a final glance at this place that would soon disappear and take with it a whole part of his life, he felt no grief. Instead, a fleeting thought made him smile. This would be DJ Radikal's last performance and, by all accounts, the most striking one. Then he rushed down the stairs from the central bar and exited by the side door after checking through the peephole that the field was clear.

He got into the first free Bluebird taxi passing by and asked the driver to wait for him at the bottom of his building while he went to pick up his luggage. He was travelling light, only carrying with him his MacBook and enough clothes for one week – plus, a Bahasa translation of the Qur'an and two pill bottles of buprenorphine – more effective than methadone, Hassan had advised – to help him get over the withdrawal symptoms. His apartment would still be full of his stuff for a while, but he was quite sure his landlord would have no qualms about getting rid of his belongings once he stopped paying the rent … Or maybe Jasmine would want to empty the flat herself. One way or the other, the last traces of his life in Jakarta would soon be erased. Needless to say, Jasmine was still in the dark about his plans.

He'd been avoiding her for the last few days, pretending when she knocked on his door before or after work that he wasn't around. Only upon arriving in Raqqa would he inform her of his irrevocable decision to start anew, far away from wretched Jakarta.

After loading his suitcase into the taxi boot, Hendra gave the driver Dr Jusuf's address in Menteng.

'Another piece of luggage to pick up,' he explained to the driver, 'and then straight to the airport.'

Barely twenty minutes later they reached Dr Jusuf's villa and, for the first time, Hendra saw him waiting outside the steel gate by the side of the road. As soon as Hendra got down from the taxi, Dr Jusuf gave him an envelope which contained his flight ticket, a number to call (only once he was in Istanbul) and 1,000 USD in cash to cover his expenses until his arrival in Raqqa. The professor also clarified that Hendra's credentials had been passed to the Islamic State's authorities a few days earlier, and his passage was already pre-approved.

'Oh, and I almost forgot,' Dr Jusuf added as Hendra was about to get back inside the cab. 'Let's imagine for a second that, for some reason, the bomb doesn't explode. Just a supposition. I would then send instructions to ISIS to detain you, should you still attempt to cross the Syrian border. And believe me, you don't want to spend time in their jails ... So just play along until the end and don't alert anyone, OK?'

One hour later, Hendra arrived at Terminal Two, Soekarno-Hatta International Airport. Right next to the Emirates counter, a large group of enthusiastic pilgrims was checking in with Saudi Airlines for their Umrah journey. Like them, Hendra should have felt overjoyed – wasn't he after all on his way to jihad? But an intense fear still gnawed at him, and he knew that he would only be able to experience any sort of happiness after clearing the last few hurdles, not least of which was the smooth bombing of XS.

After passing through customs, Hendra went to the toilet and shot up the last dose of the heroin he had bought a few days ago with Dr Jusuf's money.

***

Inside the transit hall in Dubai, Hendra perused the information screens and learned that his Pegasus airlines flight was delayed by four hours. They wouldn't take off until 3 pm Jakarta time. While the other passengers around him started ranting against these low-cost airlines who 'treated their customers like cattle and couldn't even be on time', Hendra straightaway realised that as far as he was concerned, this delay was good news as he would be able to follow the XS explosion in real time.

To kill time as there were still two hours to wait before the blast, he lay down on a wide bench seat in the departure hall. Remnants of the heroin's soothing effects were still flowing inside his body and soon he started to doze off.

'Mama, there's free WIFI,' a little girl screamed next him, begging her mother to connect her iPad to the airport network.

Hendra sat up and checked his watch: 11.45 am in Jakarta. XS would soon be razed. Adrenaline rushing through his veins, he switched on his mobile phone and after connecting it to the WIFI, opened WhatsApp while making sure he appeared offline. The news of XS bombing was bound to go viral in an instant and he would start receiving a torrent of messages, from Jasmine of course, but also from all his fans who still contacted him from time to time even after his departure from XS and his announcement that he had retired from the DJ scene.

At 12.30 pm, he still hadn't gotten any messages and he began browsing news websites but there was no mention of a blast anywhere in Jakarta. Next to him, the little girl asked her mother in a low voice why 'the *man*' was breathing so loudly.

At 1.25 pm, the deafening silence of both the Internet and his phone became too much to bear and he decided to contact Jasmine.

'Hello, sayang, how are you?' he wrote for lack of a better opening after not replying to any of her many messages over the last 24 hours.

'Hi ... finally. Can I come and see you after work?'

'You working today?' Usually, Jasmine was never on duty on Tuesdays.

'Yeah, Pak Kevin asked me to replace one waitress at the last minute. It's a private corporate event for Beer Bintang. Something like a pre-Christmas lunch party for their staff from 1 pm until 8 pm. So, I can be at your place around 8.15 pm, OK?'

'You mean you're at XS as we speak?'

'Yes, sayang, that's what I just wrote ...'

Hendra sensed his bowels turn to ice. The bomb ... it could explode any time now. He had to ask Dr Jusuf to deactivate it. His heart racing uncontrollably as if wanting to break free from his rib cage, Hendra tried calling him on Skype, but he didn't pick up.

'Not sure why the bomb hasn't exploded yet,' he wrote on WhatsApp, 'but you have to call it off. There's a private party going on!' He was typing frantically on his screen and from the corner of his eyes, he saw the little girl and her mother standing up and moving away from him.

'You're not on the flight from Dubai to Istanbul?' replied Dr Jusuf seconds later.

'Still at Dubai airport. Next plane delayed. You MUST call this off. NOW!'

'The bomb is set to explode soon … once that private party you didn't know about is in full swing.'

'NO!! YOU MUST STOP THE BOMB!'

'Brother, you should have been on the plane right now and never learned about this party and the explosion until you landed in Istanbul. But never mind … Just don't alert Pak Kelvin or anyone else, or I'll have you arrested by the ISIS police. In sha'Allah, we'll soon deal a fatal blow to Shaytan in Jakarta.'

'YOU MUST STOP!' typed Hendra. He had stood up and was pacing like a demented man, attracting curious stares of passers-by.

But Dr Jusuf's status said that he was now offline.

Terror engulfed Hendra. He had to warn Jasmine right now. Make sure she saved herself and evacuated XS! He sent her a message on WhatsApp but he didn't receive the second tick which would have informed him that his message had been delivered. Most likely, after not getting any more news from him, she had cut off the 3G data access on her mobile phone, as she sometimes did – pointlessly – when she was working, to minimize the consumption on her Telkomsel package. There was only one solution: he had to buy a local SIM card and make a standard overseas call.

He dashed into a stationary shop that stood a few metres in front of him but the young Arab woman with a multi-coloured veil who was behind the cashier informed him that he wouldn't find any local SIM cards inside the transit zone. He would only be able to buy one after going through customs.

Hendra let out a small cry and plunged his head into his hands.

'Is there anything wrong?' the young woman asked him.

'I'm just in transit,' said Hendra, looking at her with pleading eyes. 'I absolutely need to make a call to Jakarta. If I give you fifty dollars, can I ... use your phone?'

'Go ahead.' She grabbed her iPhone from her handbag and passed it to him. 'And keep your dollars!'

He composed Jasmine's number, but she didn't pick up. Smiling embarrassedly at the young woman, he tried again, and at last, after five rings, she answered.

'Please check my messages on WhatsApp!' he almost screamed.

'Is it Hendra? Why are you calling from an overseas number?'

'No time to explain! Go to WhatsApp!'

He hung up and returned the phone to the young woman.

'I'm sure things will work out for the best,' she said, giving him an encouraging smile.

'Thanks,' replied Hendra. He rushed out of the shop and pulled out his Samsung.

Unfortunately, as Jasmine didn't have a Skype account, he couldn't place an Internet call and the only solution was for them to chat over WhatsApp. He had never typed so fast in his life.

'There's a bomb hidden inside XS,' he wrote, 'and it'll explode in one hour. You have to evacuate the club ASAP!!!'

'If that's a joke, it's a very bad one, Hendra!'

'This is not a joke! There's a bomb at XS! Please tell Pak Kelvin and evacuate everyone!'

'And where are you now?'

'In transit in Dubai.'

'What???'

'Please Jasmine, believe me. The White Brigade planted the bomb. There's no time to waste! I'll explain later.'

At 2.15 pm, he finally received a message from Jasmine: 'XS evacuated. Now are you going to tell me what's happening and what you're doing in Dubai??? How did you even know about the bomb? Please don't tell me you have anything to do with this!'

Hendra didn't reply and switched off his phone, exhausted.

A few minutes later, he heard that his Pegasus flight to Istanbul was about to board. Despite Dr Jusuf's threats, he was going to continue his journey. Because it was jail for sure that awaited him if he U-turned and flew back to Jakarta. At least in Syria, he stood a chance of persuading ISIS of his good intentions – and of the savagery of their Indonesian emissary – before being locked up.

19

The Turkish Airlines internal flight from Istanbul vibrated like an overdriven subwoofer as it began its descent through a dense layer of clouds. Hendra jolted in his seat and clutched tightly at the armrests. Moments later, the Boeing 737 touched down safely in Sanliurfa, 800 miles southeast of Istanbul and close to the border with Syria. Seen as the birthplace of Prophet Abraham in the Muslim tradition, the city had become in more recent times a primary gateway from Turkey into the Islamic State.

As soon as he had cleared customs in Istanbul earlier that day, Hendra had bought a local SIM card and after first getting confirmation on *Kompas.com* that the bombing of XS has only caused material damage, he had sent an SMS to the number given to him by Dr Jusuf (strictly no calls, had said the professor). He had initially feared that, alerted by the professor, the nameless intermediary wouldn't reply to his message. But Hendra was immediately given instructions in English by John – that was how he had chosen to name the man in his phone directory – asking him to take the first plane departing for Sanliurfa. Once there, Hendra was to pretend he was a Muslim tourist on a spiritual quest and wait for further instructions at a local hotel. Someone would contact him to arrange for his passage to the other side of the border. And from there, Raqqa, the Islamic State's capital, was only a hundred kilometres away.

At the airport in Sanliurfa, Hendra asked the taxi driver to take him to Kirim Guesthouse – one of the three hotels that he had seen advertised in the arrivals hall – and forty minutes later he was walking through the guesthouse lobby. Looking up from his book, the sole receptionist on duty observed him with suspicion. Just as much out of a desire for actual information as an effort to portray himself as a genuine pilgrim, Hendra asked if it was true that the famous Pool of Abraham was only five minutes away from the hotel on foot. The receptionist didn't even bother to reply and just placed a room key on the counter after photocopying his passport. Then he went back to his book without paying any more attention to Hendra.

Once in his room, Hendra sent a message to John to tell him the name of the hotel he was staying at, before taking a shower. Eyes closed, his head right under the jet of wonderfully warm water, he tried to just relax but his mind kept returning to the shocking claim made by Jemaah Islamiyah that they were behind the bombing of XS.

All the Indonesian news websites that Hendra had checked upon landing in Istanbul talked at length about the powerful blast that, at 3 pm Jakarta time, had rocked the four-storey building where the notorious XS club was located. Fortunately, an anonymous caller had tipped off the management just in time to evacuate the place and prevent carnage, as the club was hosting a private party. So far, so good, except that the JI had also released a statement claiming responsibility for the attack while demanding the immediate closure of all places dedicated to the 'cult of Shaytan' in Jakarta. Was this just a bluff from JI, Hendra kept wondering, or was there really a connection between them and the White Brigade? During his six months with the militia led by Dr Jusuf, Hendra had never heard him praise the JI. Quite the contrary – despite Haji Ahmad's claim. But he also acknowledged now that the professor was a master of manipulation and dissimulation. Anything was possible.

After his shower, Hendra saw that he had received a message from Dr Jusuf on WhatsApp – the first one since their heated exchange at Dubai airport.

He who took up arms against us is not of us and he who acted dishonestly towards us is not of us (Muslim, 101).

This time, there was no doubt left: Dr Jusuf had every intention of trying to convince the Islamic State that Hendra was a traitor. Maybe he had even already informed them.

Well, it didn't matter – Hendra was prepared to take the risk. Now that he was so close to his goal, he would see it through, whatever the consequences. Besides, given the claim by JI and their official allegiance to ISIS' sworn enemy, Al-Qaeda, Hendra thought it now even more likely that the ISIS leadership would side with him and agree that he had been right to do everything in his power to avert the spilling of innocents' blood.

The song of a bulbul briefly filled the room, alerting him that he had received an SMS. For a second, Hendra thought it might be from Jasmine – he would probably forever associate this ringtone with her and might soon have to change it. But no, it was John – the only person who actually knew his local number – asking him to send a photo of his passport, which Hendra did so immediately.

Then his phone chimed again, but with the WhatsApp ringtone. And this time it really was Jasmine. She kept on messaging him, asking him why he had left Jakarta, where he was, whether he had anything to do with this terrorist attempt ... but Hendra remained quiet. He would only reply to her once he was in Raqqa.

Hendra was already starting to experience muscle cramps, which was hardly surprising given that his last heroin fix had been more than 24 hours ago. He grabbed one of the pill bottles of buprenorphine from inside his luggage, swallowed a tablet and quickly fell asleep.

***

Around 4 am, Hendra was jolted awake by a thumping sound, as if someone had dropped a very heavy object in the room above him. He jumped up to check his phone but there was still no message from John. Perhaps it was a network issue, thought Hendra, who rebooted his phone a few times. But no, John hadn't even acknowledged receipt of the copy of his passport. What the hell was that guy doing?

As Hendra tried to sleep back, he soon realised that he couldn't bear the eerie silence in the middle of the night of a room without a fan or air-conditioning. He plugged his earphones in and listened to Laurent Garnier for a while. But to no avail; sleep didn't return.

At 5 am, he sat up in bed and started browsing *Kompas.com* on his phone. He was shocked to learn that The White Brigade had now issued an official statement on its Twitter account to condemn the XS attack and express relief that there hadn't been any casualties. Further proof that Dr Jusuf really was one of the most devious and manipulative persons on Earth!

Soon the first rays of sunshine seeped round the room's shutters and, after performing Fajr prayer, Hendra decided to walk around town. He really needed to stretch his legs because despite the buprenorphine that he kept taking the cramps were getting increasingly painful.

It was only 7.30 am but the streets were surprisingly lively with lots of people en route to work or to the market. All the men, young and old, wore a weird kind of baggy trousers, taken in at the ankles and with a drop crotch, which reminded Hendra of the bloomer pants sported by MC Hammer and other American rappers.

After twenty minutes of wandering aimlessly, Hendra headed towards Balıklı Göl, the so-called Pool of Abraham. He found a table on a tree-shaded terrace at a café overlooking the famous pool and ordered a mint tea.

According to the legend on the tourist information board, King Nimrod had thrown the bearded Abraham into a pyre because he wouldn't stop preaching belief in one God as opposed to Nimrod's polytheistic faith. But God had intervened and saved Abraham by transforming the fire into a pond and the wooden logs into fish. These days, the pool was home to enormous sacred carp that locals and tourists alike liked to feed, especially kids. And there were already a few children around, accompanied by their pilgrim parents, squeaking every time one of the giant fishes appeared right below the surface before gulping the breadcrumbs. Hendra remembered his childhood when Kakek used to take him to a river close to Medan, where villagers were known to emit guttural sounds to bait freshwater eels. Hendra would watch in amazement as these long, slender fishes suddenly emerged from the depths and gobbled up the egg yolk that the 'eel whisperers' were dangling a few centimetres above the water.

A powerful bulbul song pulled him out of his reverie. He quickly grabbed his phone, but there was no SMS from John, let alone a message from Jasmine. Probably a real bird then, decided Hendra. Unlike in Jakarta, where only pigeons had managed to survive the catastrophic pollution, Sanliurfa's trees might still be home to songbirds.

Noticing that his neighbours were smoking a shisha, Hendra was initially tempted to give it a try, if only to relax a bit, but he eventually told himself he'd better save his money until he was safely in Raqqa in case of any unforeseen events. He paid for his coffee, stood up and resumed his exploration of the town, heading towards the city centre. At 10 am, the sun was already high in the sky, and although it was winter the air felt warm on his face.

Away from Sanliurfa's main tourist attraction, Hendra quickly realised that the atmosphere was noticeably less welcoming. People often looked sternly at him when he met their gaze, and a few shopkeepers standing in front of their stores rushed inside as he walked past and shut their doors on him. But Hendra wasn't really surprised by such open hostility as he had read online that Sanliurfa was a bastion of the PKK, the Kurdistan Workers' Party. The outlawed extremist organisation fought an armed struggle against Turkey for Kurdish independence, while ISIS also considered the Kurds as its enemy. How could foreign fighters like Hendra waiting to cross to the other side have been welcomed here?

Once back in his room at Kirim Guesthouse, Hendra performed his ablutions and started reading the An-Nur surah, one of his favourites. But as the hours went by, cold sweats and increasingly stiffer cramps made it more and more difficult for him to focus on the words on the page – much less catch their meaning. He decided to take another buprenorphine pill and then sent a new message to John, on WhatsApp this time.

'What's happening???' he wrote without trying to hide his impatience. 'Why no news?'

As indicated by the blue tick that he got a few seconds later, John had read his message without bothering to reply.

It suddenly dawned on Hendra that there was another scenario that he had not contemplated; the possibility that based on Dr Jusuf's mudslinging, the pre-approval for his passage into Syria might have been rescinded. What would he do then, alone and stuck in Sanliurfa? As if cramps weren't bad enough, his teeth started to chatter. Maybe a hot shower would do him good, he told himself. He went to the bathroom and sat on the shower floor, while the warm water rained down on his head.

Before leaving Jakarta, he had convinced himself that the buprenorphine pills would counteract the most painful withdrawal symptoms while the exaltation of being in Raqqa and the prospect of soon fighting jihad would lift his spirits. But buprenorphine itself was not as effective as Hassan had promised it would be, and worst of all there was no excitement, just an excruciating, uncertain wait compounding the craving and messing with his brain. He'd never imagined that he would be made to languish in an obscure hotel room in Turkey. Just how long was this ordeal going to last? What if it was *forever*?

Following his shower, Hendra took two more buprenorphine pills and soon, for better or worse, he started to drift off.

He woke up slightly past midnight, shivering, the bedsheets soaked with sweat. He checked his phone. Nada, not a single message from John! What was the fucker doing? He was about to bust his phone against the wall, but at the last minute he grabbed the bedside lamp instead and smashed it to the floor. Soon, strong spasms wracked his body. He swallowed three pills but he couldn't even lie down in bed anymore.

He kept gasping for breath as if caught inside the rolling waves of a swollen sea, and whenever he managed to raise his head out of the water, he was swept away by the next wave. He started to pray but even his faith couldn't anchor him anymore. Slowly he was drowning, feeling as if his lungs and head were soon going to burst from the pressure of the depths. That was the end, the ultimate downfall.

Suddenly he went into convulsions and rushed to the toilet where he vomited and voided himself both at the same time. He was just standing up from the toilet bowl when he realised that he was also experiencing a headache attack. Probably because of his agonising withdrawal symptoms, he hadn't felt it coming. He knew the risk was always there, especially with the heroin craving and all, but still he was caught off guard. For fuck's sake, he had been headache-free for two weeks!

He called reception, asking for a bottle of water – a glass one, he specified – and as soon as the night duty manager brought him a large Evian, he broke it against the toilet sink without drinking a single sip, before making an incision on his wrist. After a couple of minutes, the attack was thwarted, and Hendra was finally able to lie down in bed again. Remembering and comforted by the idea that he was in the same place where Abraham was born, he fell back to sleep.

***

The loud singing of a bulbul startled Hendra. Dazed and breathless, he grabbed his phone and saw that at last John had replied, directing him to be at a city centre café called 'La Storia' at 12.30 pm. There, someone named Ahmet would meet him to discuss his passage into Syria.

It was only 7 am but it was already quite bright inside the room. During his short sleep, Hendra had stained the bedsheets with blood from his wrist. He tried to clean the mess but only managed to spread the blood further. In the end, he gave up, covered his wound with toilet paper and went back to sleep for a few hours.

When he woke again at 11 am, he immediately took a cold shower which somewhat shook him out of his comatose state. Based on his reflection in the mirror though, there was no doubt that he looked more like a craving junkie than a future mujahid.

Before leaving his room, he took half a pill of buprenorphine, as he was really trembling too much, and thrust the bedsheets into his backpack. He would rather discard them on the way to the café – and refund the hotel for its loss – than face the questioning stare of that obnoxious day receptionist over the origin of the blood. As for the bedside lamp, he would apologize for the 'accident'.

Ahmet was an elegant Turk in his twenties. Born in Istanbul, he was affable and thoughtful, and if he had been given any instruction to be wary of the new Indonesian recruit, he gave nothing away. He explained to Hendra that they would cross into Syria the next morning, simply exiting Turkey through the official border post located in the small town of Akçakale. According to Ahmet, despite the border closure, one only had to bribe the Turkish officers there to convince them to close one eye and let a mujahid pass into Syria. Then, directly on the other side, they would already be in friendly territory, as the Syrian border town of Tal Abyad had been conquered by ISIS in June 2013, and there would be a truck waiting to take him to Raqqa. A walk in the park, so to speak ...

'Tell me,' said Ahmet, once he was done with his explanations, 'did you spend the night wrestling with a ghost or what? Because you look as pale as one, you know!'

'It's just that I don't have any money,' he lied. 'Haven't had a real meal since I arrived here.'

'You should have told me! You'll need all your strength when you're in Raqqa tomorrow!' Ahmet ordered two full plates of shish kebab.

Hendra forced himself to eat despite the nauseous spasms that jolted his stomach like electric shocks every time he swallowed a morsel of lamb. While he was eating – and doing his best to prevent his hands from trembling too obviously – Ahmet explained that he himself had rallied to the ISIS cause because he thought that was the only way to annihilate once and for all the Kurdish independence movement. He considered President Erdogan to have made far too many concessions to the PKK.

As much as the local political context interested Hendra, it was a real effort for him to just listen to Ahmet's words and he simply couldn't wait for the lunch to be over so that he could go back to his room – and sleep until the following day.

***

On his return to the guesthouse, the receptionist asked where he had put the bedsheets. Hendra talked about an accident during the night which had forced him to throw them away, at once proposing to refund the hotel. For a moment, the employee gave him a weird look before accepting his offer. Thankfully, no mention was made of the bedside lamp.

Once in his room, Hendra lay down on the bed. Clearly, the idea of being in Raqqa as early as the next day was already helping offset the worst of the withdrawal symptoms, and despite the trembling he now felt much better. The turmoil of the previous night had given way to a precarious calm; he wasn't safe yet from Dr Jusuf's possible retaliation, but at least hope was back.

***

The next morning, around 7 am, Hendra paid his bill with the Turkish lira Ahmet had given him in exchange for his American dollars and then went to find the young Turk who was waiting for him in front of the hotel, seated behind the wheel of a battered red Renault 5.

Chain-smoking cigarettes, Ahmet initially drove in silence, and Hendra didn't try to make small talk. Sometime after leaving Sanliurfa they ended up in a sort of no-man's land, travelling along a meandering road that crossed fallow fields. Enormous black clouds loomed on the horizon, echoing the feeling of ominous loneliness that the scenery conjured.

'I'm sure you could grow anything in these fields,' remarked Ahmet, breaking the silence in the car, 'but people are too scared of the land mines that the PKK would have placed around here. Has to be a paradise for hunting now!'

Hendra politely smiled at Ahmet and then closed his eyes, pretending to be asleep. His own thoughts were quite remote from such agrarian considerations. He was only starting to realise that he would soon be alone in a new world, cut off from his roots and the few people still close to his heart, without any possibility of going back.

Lightning lit the sky and thunder rumbled. The clouds were finally making good on their threat. After the storm, thought Hendra, remembering instances of such liberating downpours in his grandparent's rural village, nature would look resplendent, rejuvenated in its newfound serenity. Quite unlike in Jakarta, where heavy rains and mud often turned the streets into a mess that lasted long after the deluge was over.

After one hour of driving under a torrent of rain, they finally reached Akçakale. The small border town had long been deserted by its habitants after one ISIS bombing too many targeting the Kurdish resistant fighters holed up inside the houses. To keep up appearances, the Turkish government would usually strike back but in reality, explained Ahmet, the ISIS attacks couldn't be more welcome.

Soon they saw a large Turkish flag flying high above a red tin panel straddling the road with the words 'AKÇAKALE – SINIR – KAPISI'.

'That's your border, brother,' said Ahmet. 'Just wait inside while I pay the bill.'

Seated inside the old Renault 5 that reeked of cigarettes, Hendra observed Ahmet as he smoked and drank tea with the guards as if they were having a reunion. After about ten minutes, Ahmet came back with a big smile on his face.

'I didn't have to pay a single cent. They're chaps from Istanbul. Their way to support the fight against the Kurdish vermin, they said.'

He drove on through the rain and, as they passed in front of the border guards, slowed down and lowered his window. He shouted a few words – in Turkish, Hendra guessed – and the officials raised their right hands in the air, making the V sign.

A few hundred metres down the road on the other side, a military truck was stationed right before the entrance into Tal Abyad. As they approached, two armed men jumped out of the vehicle and barred the road. Ahmet stopped the car and he and Hendra got out very slowly into the rain, their hands clearly visible in front of them. Ahmet handed Hendra's papers to the ISIS soldiers, presenting him as a latest recruit from Indonesia. The two men initially looked askance at him, inspecting his passport in detail and ostensibly comparing his photo with the thinner, emaciated version in front of them. They exchanged a few words in a foreign language that wasn't Arabic and then, in very clear English, instructed Hendra to climb into the truck with his luggage.

Hendra thanked Ahmet, who briefly hugged him, exclaiming: 'Good luck, brother, In sha'Allah!' Then, heart racing, he took a seat at the back of the empty truck on one of the two side-facing metal benches, and they set off under a glorious sun which had already replaced the rain.

Was he the only recruit today? wondered Hendra, as he watched the bitumen pass before his eyes through the holes in the green jute tarp. An unknown existence was awaiting him in Raqqa, but one that was full of promise and hope of redemption. Yes, he would miss Jasmine and his grandparents but that was the price that he had to pay if he wanted to leave behind his life of suffering and sinful wanderings.

He had almost forgotten his cramps when the cold wind that seeped inside the truck made him shiver, reminding him that he still had a few days of withdrawal to go through.

Part VII

The Tender One

Syria, end of December 2014

20

Hendra pushed open the door to his assigned dormitory, announcing his arrival with a vigorous 'Assalamualaikum'. A dozen faces turned towards him and replied as one: 'Waalaikumsalam, waraḥmatullahi wabarakatuh!'

Hendra quickly scanned the rectangular room where two rows of four bunk beds faced one another, realising with relief that his allocated space on the upper level was at the far end, close to the sole window.

After driving for a good hour through deserted war-torn villages, they had finally arrived at their destination: Raqqa, the Islamic state's capital – sometimes nicknamed 'The Tender One' because, as Ahmet had explained to Hendra, ar-Raqqah الرقة meant tenderness in Arabic. Hendra's first impression while he sat in the back of the truck was of a dusty, lively town bathed in yellow hues. The streets were teeming with bearded men in sarouel and scurrying women shrouded in black burqas. His vehicle had eventually pulled up in front of a large beige-coloured brick building with an ISIS black flag flying high above it. A young red-haired man with a long goatee so bright that it looked like it had been dyed orange had taken his passport and allotted him a place in dormitory A2. He was supposed to slip into the ISIS military tracksuit handed to him and be ready in one hour to start the onboarding and orientation process.

Hendra got acquainted with Rachid, the new French recruit sleeping below him. Rachid, who had a large scar on the left cheek, kept snapping selfies, telling Hendra that he planned to post them on Facebook (as soon as he was given Internet access) to prove to his friends that 'he had done it, man, he was *here*!' He had a waxy complexion and hair full of dandruff, and with his gaunt body floating inside the ISIS tracksuit he already wore, he looked in rather poor shape.

'So, how do you like Hotel ISIS?' he asked Hendra while taking a last photo from the window.

Without waiting for Hendra's reply, he explained that the building they were hosted in was a former guesthouse, Hotel Turismo, converted into barracks for recruits.

Unlike the French clubbers that Hendra sometimes met at XS, Rachid spoke a perfectly intelligible English. Which, he was given to understand, was the result of the two years Rachid had spent working as a waiter in Brighton, the vibrant seaside resort town on the south coast of England. Brighton, thought Hendra fleetingly, the place where it had all started for the most brilliant house DJ of the 90s, Fatboy Slim.

Rachid told him he was so happy to have met someone to talk to as the other aspiring mujahideen in their room all hailed from Central Asia and couldn't string together more than two words in English. He had Algerian Kabyle roots and was, at least in theory, third-generation French, his maternal and paternal grandparents having arrived in France from Setif in 1962, after the war against the French colonizers.

'My family, they're all *harkis*, traitors who fought against the

Algerians!' he said, spitting on the floor.

By his own account, Rachid had never really studied at the Republic's school.

'What for? The *bougnoules*, the sand niggers like me, will always be screwed by the Gallic. Ever heard of their slogan, "Liberty, equality, fraternity"?'

Hendra nodded.

'Well, it's pure BS man, just a smokescreen so that we continue to suck up to them like minions.' Then he started to hum.

Tu m'dis la France un pays libre
attends mes détenus, attends-toi à bouffer du calibre.

'It means "You tell me, France is the country of freedom. Wait for my fellow captives, and be ready to suck their gun!" It's from Booba, the best rapper ever. You know I wanted to give back my French passport but the Gallic told me: not possible, sir!'

From the age of 14, he had been dealing drugs to earn money as they were often strapped for cash at home, especially after his father, a labourer, had become an invalid following the collapse of a scaffold he was standing on. But three years ago, during one of his stays in jail, Rachid had had a flash, a real mystical experience: Allah himself had appeared in front of him and warned him that drug trafficking was a great sin. After that, Rachid had started to pray and upon his release from prison, he did not resume selling dope. Not even to the kuffar, not even to the Jews in his *cité*! His parents had always practiced their faith in secret, hiding it from the French colonisers who wanted them to eat pork and drink pastis and make their women go naked on the beach. But

Rachid was so proud to be a Muslim that he had let his beard grow and often roamed the streets in Paris in djellaba. Yet, after taking a few religious classes at a mosque on Saint-Maur Street, he had concluded that the Salafs' reclusive lifestyle wasn't for him. Too much of a snooze-fest for him, like watching paint dry. His mission on Earth was to wage jihad in Syria and save his Sunni brothers butchered by the Shia vermin. One of his cousins was already here, and he had decided to join him.

'So ... what are you going to tell the physios you want to do?' Rachid asked.

'The what?'

'The *physionomistes*. You know these SOBs who decide who can and who cannot get into nightclubs in Paris and never let the *bougnoules* in? Well, good news, bro: here the physios love us!'

'I see,' said Hendra. 'To be honest, I don't know much about this selection process.'

Indeed, he was totally clueless. All this while, he had naively believed that as soon as he was in Raqqa, he would just start fighting alongside the other Indonesian mujahideen of the Nusantara Katibah – provided, of course, that he wasn't thrown into jail on Dr Jusuf's orders ...

Rachid told him they would first be submitted to a series of intellectual and physical tests before going for an interview with a captain, probably someone called Abdullah according to his cousin here. In the end, depending on their test results and own interests, they would normally be assigned to a specific combat unit, while some were also sent to a shahid squad – but only the volunteers, clarified Rachid. According to the French recruit, the Islamic State's military comprised four large battalions which were named after the geographic region of origin of the first combatants even though anyone could now join them: the Libyan battalion, the most prestigious as it headed up all the special operations; the Maghreb and Gulf battalion, which was in charge of the protection of the ISIS leadership, most of whom lived in the vast desert at the border between Syria and Iraq; the Syrian battalion, which was responsible for the defence of the territory around Raqqa; and finally the so-called Mosul Liberation Brigade, the largest battalion, which fought everywhere to protect or expand the Islamic State's borders. Rachid said that he hoped to join the ranks of the Maghreb and Gulf battalion like his cousin, but above all he wanted to avoid the support functions (like inventory and administration of the war trophies, tax collection, weapons transport, etc) where new recruits assessed to be unfit for combat usually ended up.

'Those public servants,' explained Rachid, 'they won't be considered as real mujahideen on the Day of Judgement. Their reward won't be the same.'

'If you're assigned to one of these support functions, is it final?' asked Hendra.

'Not necessarily. My cousin told me that if you want to, you can still train and the day when you're ready physically and mentally, they send you for jihad. But anyway, touch wood, that's never gonna happen to me, bro. You see, before coming here, I trained like crazy.'

Really? wondered Hendra.

'So ... bro, what're you going to tell the physios?' asked Rachid.

'I ... I'd like to fight alongside Abu Nassim al-Indonesia, the leader of the Nusantara Katibah, the Southeast Asian unit.'

'You'll have to ask which battalion that unit belongs to, bro, because I really don't know.'

Would they let him join Abu Nassim? wondered Hendra. Or had Dr Jusuf already warned the Islamic State's physios, exhorting them to send him to jail instead of jihad?

**

It was 2 pm when, full of apprehension, Hendra knocked at the door of Captain Abdullah's office. Now was his turn to be interviewed by the 'head physio'. One hour ago, he had finished taking all the tests together with a dozen other new arrivals.

A dozen was, according to the red-haired soldier in charge of the front desk, the average number of daily enrolments.

'And we still have to reject some chiefs as too many people want to join us!' Daniel, alias Al-Iskutlandi, who was originally from Glasgow, had commented. As far as he knew, Hendra had been on his own in the truck simply because the road from Sanliurfa was much less in use these days: it had become so well-trodden that it was now under close surveillance from the Iranian Secret Services who didn't hesitate to kidnap or even kill the future combatants before they could cross into Syria.

A commanding voice ordered Hendra to enter.

Captain Abdullah was seated behind an old wooden desk with an ISIS flag behind him next to a portrait of Caliph Abu Bakr al-Baghdadi. The captain himself was also Iraqi, from Fallujah, as he had explained in his brief introduction in front of the new recruits before they started the orientation and selection process.

The walls of his office were totally bare, except for a few surahs, hand-written in black ink one metre above the ground, making a frieze of sorts around the room.

Hendra saluted before coming to attention.

'Stand easy,' ordered Captain Abdullah after a few seconds. 'So ... tell me, why did you come to Raqqa, Hendra?'

'To fight jihad, Captain.'

'I see.'

Captain Abdullah took a grim, solemn air while perusing a list of names and numbers. Probably their test results, thought Hendra. He hadn't particularly shone during the endurance run. Right before the race, he had again started experiencing severe withdrawal symptoms and, because of the cramps, had only managed to run two kilometres in ten minutes, coming second last – still ahead of Rachid by a wide margin.

'Given your condition,' said Captain Abdullah after a while, 'forget armed struggle. If I were you, I'd apply to be a shahid.'

Hendra kept silent. He fixed his gaze on the ISIS flag behind the captain, while he felt his hands clasped behind his back becoming markedly clammier.

'Just kidding,' Captain Abdullah said finally, with a straight face. 'Although you're certainly no marathon runner either ... OK, let's not beat about the bush. We've been told that you might be a *kafir*.'

Hendra felt the ground spin under him but still found the strength to reply.

'That's not true!'

'We received an email asking us to cancel your visa to ISIS because, apparently, you helped patrons from a nightclub in

Jakarta escape a bomb attack. Do you confirm this information?'

'Yes, Captain. The attack would have caused lots of Muslim fatalities.'

'People who drink alcohol and do drugs are not Muslims.'

'But the JI's claimed responsibility and the JI is allied with the Al-Qaeda enemy!'

'So what? If they do something righteous, we don't have to–'

'But–'

'Do not interrupt me. You may only speak when I say so. Understood?'

'Yes, Captain.'

'Indeed, it's not in our plans to set up attacks on Indonesian soil ... for the moment. Because first we have to rebuild the Caliphate here in Syria and Iraq.'

The captain rose from his chair, looking across the window on his right for a while before continuing.

'But after Syria and Iraq, we'll expand the Caliphate to other countries, and in every town, in every village, in every house, we'll stamp out immorality in all its guises! Will you be with us, O brother Hendra, to wage this ultimate jihad against Shaytan?'

Hendra didn't reply straightaway, which didn't go down very well with Captain Abdullah.

'You see, you're not even sure! To tell you the truth, some people here wanted to deny you entry into the Islamic State. Or rather, let the Iranians take care of you in Sanliurfa. But I personally insisted that you be given a chance.'

He made a pause, and Hendra understood that he had to thank him.

'Thanks for your trust, sir,' he said.

'Usually, after two weeks of basic military training and physical reconditioning, we send the recruits to the battlefield. But considering the circumstances, we must submit you to one more test first to make sure that you're really one of us. Understood?

'Yes, Captain.'

'We'll decide on the nature of this test as and when the opportunity arises. Until then, you're assigned to the Raqqa prison under the responsibility of Major Waheeb. So as not to waste time, you'll also get started on your military training in the company of other recruits who like you have to prove their worth. Understood?'

'Yes, Captain.'

'Dismissed.'

What was this test going to entail? wondered Hendra as he left Captain Abdullah's office. Part of him felt fretful, but he also realised it could have been much worse. At least they were giving him another chance, and if the objective was just to check whether he was truly 'one of them', he should have nothing to worry about.

***

When Hendra returned to the dormitory, Rachid was already there, looking quite cheerful. He had been selected to join the secret services, which was part of the Libyan battalion. This wasn't what he had hoped for at the beginning, but on the other hand it was more prestigious than the Maghreb and Gulf battalion of his cousin.

'You mean you'll be like a spy?' asked Hendra.

'That's right.'

'But what do the Islamic State's spies do exactly?'

'Top secret, bro.'

'Oh, I see.'

'Just kidding, bro. ISIS spies infiltrate those countries in the West considered enemies and plan bomb attacks there.'

'But I thought ISIS only fought against the Shia in Syria and Iraq?'

'And what should we do when the Gallic colonizers who already looted Algeria fifty years ago dare attack Muslims again? Don't we have the right to defend ourselves when they launch terrorist air strikes on Raqqa and butcher hundreds of women and children?'

He added that he didn't know yet where he would be sent for his spying mission – although France was high on the list for sure; he would only learn about it after three months of specialised training in a camp located an hour's drive to the south of Raqqa.

Hendra just shook his head. He couldn't help wondering whether Rachid had not actually been chosen to become a shahid …

'And you, where are you going?' the French recruit asked Hendra.

'I've been assigned to the Raqqa prison.'

'Oh, I see, support function … Don't worry, bro, am sure in a few months you'll get to fight the real jihad!' And he gave him a friendly tap on the shoulder.

After discreetly swallowing a buprenorphine pill, Hendra lay on the bed and plugged in his iPod earphones. Closing his eyes, he let himself be carried away by 'Wake-up' from Laurent Garnier until suddenly he felt someone shaking him vigorously. When he opened his eyes, he saw Rachid staring at him, looking even paler than normal. Hendra pulled out his earplugs.

'What're you doing, man!' said Rachid.

'I'm listening to some techno music, to relax …'

'You're fucking stoned, man! Music's forbidden here. Anyone caught listening to anything other than Qur'an recitations is to be punished with a hundred lashes!'

Hendra just shrugged and put away his iPod.

'Else, I'd already have made you listen to Booba. But it's verboten, bro. Really.'

Sitting up in bed, Hendra saw that Rachid was getting ready to perform *salat*, having already spread a praying mat on the floor by the window.

'You're praying for Asr?' asked Hendra.

'No, bro. For Maghrib.'

'But the sun won't set until four plus, you know?'

'I know, bro. I'm just praying in advance. I'm a bit fried, so am gonna get some shut-eye until dinner time.'

Praying in advance? Hendra thought about contending that this was certainly not allowed either, but all the day's events had drained him, and he had no energy left to argue with Rachid.

21

The next morning at 4.30 am, Hendra was woken up by the muezzin's powerful singsong voice calling the faithful to pray for Fajr. He walked to the shared bathroom to perform his ablutions and while he was washing his forearms, his sarong slid to the floor. As he was picking up the multi-coloured cloth and tying it up again around his waist, Rachid laughed:

'What's this thing? A skirt?'

'It's not a skirt, it's a sarong!'

'Well, anyway you should stop wearing that. All these bright colours, don't you think it clashes with our flag?'

Hendra shrugged, thinking that if Rachid had pictures of Zinedine Zidane pasted inside his locker in the room, why couldn't he keep his sarong if it made him happy?

After breakfast, Daniel Al-Iskutlandi, Kalashnikov slung over his shoulder, escorted him to the Raqqa prison, which was located only two streets away from Hotel Turismo. A bit odd, reflected Hendra, to open a hotel so close to a jail but maybe the hotel had been built first. On the way there, Daniel told him that once done with the day's classes, he was authorized to come back to the dormitory on his own. But he needed to be mindful that until his recruitment into the ranks of the Islamic State army was confirmed, he wasn't allowed to mix with, or even talk to, the local population.

Hendra nodded. Anyway, the opportunities to mingle seemed rather limited as all the civilians whose paths crossed theirs quickly turned their eyes away.

Once inside the jail, he was directed to a small classroom and sat there waiting for Major Waheeb in the company of two other recruits: Dhakir, a Uighur in his forties, and Sameer, a young Pakistani who had just arrived from London. So, if Hendra understood correctly what Captain Abdullah had said to him yesterday, these two military hopefuls were presumably in the same boat as him. For what reason? He would probably never know.

A few minutes later, a middle-aged officer with a bald, wrinkled skull limped in with a stick in his left hand. The three of them rose to their feet, standing at attention.

'Why are you smiling like an idiot?' the man, who had to be the major, immediately shot at Hendra. 'Do you think you came here to have fun? We are Allah's soldiers, never forget that!'

Hendra lowered his eyes. Like most Indonesians, Hendra naturally smiled – and he apparently smiled much less than the national average, if he were to believe Jasmine. The smile was like the stationary point for an Indonesian, the neutral position from which all face expressions started. When an Indonesian did not smile, it was already an indication that he or she wasn't happy. But one bule clubber at XS had once told Hendra that foreigners, especially non-Asians, sometimes interpreted such a smile as a form of mockery, especially when it came in response to a reproach or a mark of displeasure.

'Relax!' Major Waheeb finally ordered. 'And sit down.'

Then, without introducing himself, he dived head-on into his lesson, beginning with the organization of the Raqqa prison.

Three types of inmates were detained here, he explained: common criminals, apostates and prisoners of war. The latter were held in solitary confinement until their execution – or potential release in exchange for ISIS soldiers captured by the enemy – while the other two types of inmates were often jailed together.

In each and every cell, there existed a strict – albeit unofficial – hierarchy, comprising three ranks: the chiefs, the aides and the 'new-borns' i.e. those who had just been interned. During their first days in jail, the new-borns were generally submitted to heavy beatings by the chiefs while the aides restrained them. For that was most often the only way to get them to comply with their key responsibility, which was to clean the squat toilets after each use and then cover them with their bodies to block the pestilential smells.

'It stinks like a soiled diaper in these cells, you'll soon realise,' said Major Waheeb. 'We haven't cleaned the drains since the beginning of the war against the butcher of Damascus. So, you can imagine what kind of stuff festers inside …'

In those mixed cells, only the 'commons' could eventually rise to the position of chief; at best, the 'apostates' could only hope to 'graduate' from new-born to aide. Overall, it was very important for wardens to know the respective ranks of the inmates and, stressed Major Waheeb, under no circumstances were they allowed to disturb this informal organization. It was such autoregulation that guaranteed peace inside the prison.

Next, after a brief exposé of their warden duties, they were introduced to Anwar Imran who was in charge of the executions and would teach them how to wield a sword or a knife to perform amputations and decapitations. A practical example had already been scheduled for the following afternoon, he announced. Tall and rather good-looking, the Thai national in his thirties spoke a nasal, staccato English that sounded like a vinyl record playing too fast.

Then came the lunch break during which Hendra and Anwar chatted together in a mix of Indonesian and Malay – the two Southeast Asian languages being closely related and, generally, mutually intelligible. For the executioner, born in Yala, belonged to the minority Malay-Muslim population living in Thailand's Deep South who had been fighting for its independence ever since its land had been unlawfully ceded to the Thai king by the British colonizers in 1909. Because the means of the Islamist guerrilla were limited, the militants had opted for a strategy of maximum terror: decapitating Buddhist monks. And it was in this context that he had learned to swing the parang to lop the heads off his victims. Anwar made fun of the new recruits whom he nicknamed 'mujahideen made in China', bogus combatants who fainted at the sight of blood.

'Hopefully, you're not like that!' he said.

'Of course, not!' replied Hendra. 'By the way, brother, what made you leave Thailand?'

Anwar explained that he was part of the group of militants who were occupying the Friday Mosque in Pattani in 2007 when the army, on the order of Prime Minister Thaksin, had stormed in. He had managed to escape over the border to the Malaysian jungle and then thanks to local accomplices in the town of Kota Bahru, he had taken a fishing boat which had dropped him off on the Indonesian island of Natuna – somewhere in the middle of the South China Sea. From there, he had travelled to the Mindanao province in the Philippines and rallied to the cause of the Moro Islamic Liberation Front, fighting alongside the Abu Sayaf militants in the town of General Santos. But disappointed by their lack of discipline, he had finally decided to offer his skills and experience to the 'Islamist International' based in Raqqa. And thanks to his military feats, he had been appointed chief executioner of the central prison.

Hendra couldn't help wondering why Anwar had not requested to join the Nusantara Katibah but he would ask him another day. Time was short now as before the resumption of classes, he intended to send an email to Jasmine from the shared computer that he had seen at the wardens' cafeteria.

Until his arrival in Raqqa, Hendra kept receiving messages from Jasmine, and while he never replied or even read the messages, he always opened them. The blue tick that she would automatically receive was his way of giving her news. But after crossing into Syria, he had lost all access to the Internet on his phone and would only be given a code to log into the Hotel Turismo's WIFI network after being confirmed as an ISIS soldier. Hendra could only guess that since he had been totally silent for more than 24 hours, Jasmine was already starting to imagine the worst. But on top of reassuring her, he also finally intended to tell her where he was – as well as seek her help about something really important he had forgotten to do before leaving Jakarta.

Hendra excused himself from Anwar and headed towards the wardens' cafeteria. He wasn't sure whether he was already allowed to use the PC there, but he just sat behind it and logged into his Gmail account. Quite a few messages from Jasmine awaited him of course, but he had no time to read them and straightaway composed his own email instead.

Sayang,

It is from Raqqa, Syria, that I am writing to you. Yes, I have joined the ranks of the Islamic State. It had really become too painful for me to stay any longer in Jakarta. Sayang, I'll be forever grateful for all the things you've done to help me, but please do not try to convince me to come back. You must now move on with your life, go through with your operation and forget me. Please.

May I ask one last favour from you though? My landlord in Jakarta will probably want to get rid of all my stuff as soon as he realises I'm gone. But before that, could you please make sure that my mother's belongings are sent to my grandparents? You'll find everything in a Cosmo box inside my cupboard.

This is their address:

Pak Taslim Chaniago

Pasar Rawa, Kec. Gebang,

Kab. Langkat, Sumatera Utara 20857

Please just send the items to them and don't say anything about me or where I am. I'll inform them soon.

Forgive me.

Love,

Hendra

* * *

In the afternoon, they followed a history class taught by Daniel al-Iskutlandi. For the occasion, the young Scot had donned a pair of John Lennon glasses with a thin black frame that contrasted starkly with his smooth white forehead dotted with a smattering of freckles.

The sacred mission that Allah *subhānahu wata'ālā* had bestowed upon ISIS, Daniel first explained, was to restore the Caliphate which had ended in 1517 with the Ottomans' unlawful overthrow of the Mamluk Sultanate. At long last, Abu Bakr al-Baghdadi, the first Caliph of the Islamic State, had re-established the broken lineage of political successors to Prophet Mohammed.

Daniel then launched into a brief overview of the Middle East's late pre-colonial history, before dwelling on the so-called Sykes-Picot agreements signed in the 1920s between the French and the Brits. The kuffar had basically split between themselves the whole Arab region and in doing so shattered the unity of the Muslim world, the Ummah intended by Allah. But already the army of the Caliphate had taken down the sand wall which in the middle of the desert used to separate Syria and Iraq. And that was just the first step towards the reunification of the two peoples who would embark together on the reconquest of the entire Arab world – and even beyond, In sha'Allah. All Muslims would eventually have to accept the truth or die. As for the Shia, except if they converted to the real Islam, they belonged in the same category as the crusaders and the miscreants opposed to the divine project.

Daniel continued his class by mentioning a major prophecy which would soon be fulfilled, In sha'Allah. Reported in one hadith, it predicted that the Last Battle between the Muslim forces and the 'Roman' armies – 'under eighty different flags' – would unfold between the towns of Al-Amaq and Dabiq, now in ISIS territory close to the Turkish border. The Armageddon would be unleashed and the world would see the victory of Islam, followed by the advent of Judgement Day. The wrath of God, the divine intervention ... Hendra was now convinced that it was Allah himself who had delayed his plane from Dubai to Istanbul so that he could save Jasmine and all the innocent clubbers.

He really enjoyed Daniel's history lesson, although by 4 pm when it ended he was all too happy to return to Hotel Turismo so that he could pop another buprenorphine and alleviate the muscle aches and cold sweats that he was starting to experience again.

***

After Maghrib, Hendra had to rush back to the prison because the execution that they were supposed to attend the following day had been brought forward.

He, Dhakir and Sameer joined a group of thirty soldiers and inmates inside the prison's central courtyard, which had been lit for the occasion. There, a Swiss member of Action Against Hunger, captured a few days ago in Aleppo, was kneeling with his hands bound behind his back and a black blindfold covering his eyes. The scene looked exactly like the decapitation that Hendra had watched on Indonesian TV a few months earlier, with the prisoner wearing the same orange jumpsuit. That jumpsuit, Hendra had learned today thanks to Imran Anwar, was the one worn by Iraqi prisoners on the infamous photos taken in 2004 inside the Abu Ghraib jail. Forcing the captive kuffar to put it on, Imran had explained, was very symbolic; it was a way to avenge the abuse and humiliation that Muslims had suffered in Iraq and elsewhere at the hands of Americans.

The filmed execution started with a sermon in English in which a masked imam justified the punishment by quoting a hadith from Sahih Al-Bukhari. Two ISIS soldiers then grabbed the howling NGO worker from behind and forced his upper body to the ground. A long butcher's knife in his hands, a hooded Imran Anwar stepped forward and slowly severed the infidel's head. As metal sliced through bone, muscle and cartilage, screams of pain and terror – not drowned out by techno music this time – filled the air. Wracked with tremors, Hendra had to hide his hands behind his back. At last, Imran brandished the man's head in the direction of the camera before throwing it into a wicker basket. Then two soldiers dragged away the decapitated body while blood still spurted from the neck.

That's when the imam asked the cameraman to stop recording and a boy was brought in, who couldn't have been more than ten. The masked imam removed his black balaclava before announcing that the child had been sentenced to the amputation of one full phalanx for stealing fruits at Raqqa's central market for the third time. How could that be? thought Hendra, horrified. Weren't the Hudud punishments prescribed by the Shariah only supposed to be meted out to adults?

When Anwar's knife plunged into the flesh of the screeching child, tied to a chair with black leather straps, Hendra was suddenly overcome with nausea. In front of everyone, he stood up and left the courtyard before seeking refuge inside the nearest toilets where he vomited his guts out.

He could only hope that chopping a kid's finger wasn't the

kind of the test that lay in store for him.

**

Later on, all the prison personnel – about twenty of them – gathered for Isha inside the jail's mosque.

The day before, Captain Abdullah had said that praying together was one of the best military drills that existed, a most powerful show of unity – much more powerful than the Shaytan incantations sang by the kuffar armies. As for Hendra, since his arrival in Raqqa the daily prayers had quickly become his favourite moments of the day, the time when his mind stopped wandering and he really felt at peace with himself.

After the prayer, the middle-aged Arab imam – the same one who had presided over the executions earlier on – stood up and proceeded to deliver a sermon.

'Tonight, as we have new recruits amongst us, I'd like to start with the historic words pronounced by our Caliph Abu Bakr al-Baghdadi during Friday prayer last week.'

And then he read from a paper:

'Soon, by Allah's permission, the Muslim man will walk everywhere as a master, revered, holding his head high, his dignity restored. Nobody will dare attack him anymore, for any hand that will reach too close to his face will be cut on the spot.

'The time has come for those generations that were drowning in oceans of disgrace, nursed on the milk of humiliation, and ruled by the vilest of all people, the time has come for them to rise. The time has come for the Ummah of Muhammad (peace be upon him) to wake up from its sleep, remove the garments of dishonour, and shake off the dust of humiliation and disgrace, for the era of lamenting and moaning has gone, and the dawn of honour has emerged anew. The sun of jihad has risen. The glad tidings of good are shining. The signs of victory have appeared.

'So, listen, o Ummah of Islam. Listen and comprehend. Stand up and rise. Free yourself from the shackles of weakness and stand in the face of tyranny, against the treacherous rulers – the agents of the crusaders, the atheists and the protectors of the Jews.'

Hendra shuddered as a shiver of pleasure ran down his spine.

The imam folded his paper before continuing with his sermon. 'Captain Abdullah told me today that some of you here are reluctant to take part in bombing attacks because that would be terrorism.'

Hendra thought the imam's gaze lingered on him and instinctively he turned his head away.

'Now, let me tell you what is terrorism. Terrorism is nothing more than the anger of the oppressed, pouring out by force into the world of the privileged. The kuffar think that they're protected by their armies and antimissile defences, that they can continue sipping their coffees, nice and warm in their little bistros, listening to Shaytan songs, while millions of people starve to death at their doorstep. But we have bad news for them: they cannot do anything against our shahids who sneak through their porous borders.

'Terrorism is to refer to Allah's law for judgement. Terrorism is to worship Allah as He ordered you. Terrorism is to refuse humiliation, subjugation and subordination. Terrorism is for the Muslim to live as a Muslim, honourably with might and freedom.'

The imam paused for a second and when he resumed, a faint smile parted his lips.

'But of course, terrorism does not include the killing of Muslims in Burma and the burning of their homes. Terrorism does not include the dismembering and disembowelling of Muslims in the Philippines, Indonesia and Kashmir. Terrorism does not include the killing of Muslims in the Caucasus and expelling them from their lands. Terrorism does not include making mass graves for Muslims in Bosnia and Herzegovina, and the slaughtering of their children. Terrorism does not include the destruction of Muslims' homes in Palestine, the seizing of their lands, the rape of their wives and the violation and desecration of their sanctuaries and families! Terrorism does not include the filling of prisons everywhere with Muslim captives. Terrorism does not include the waging of war against chastity and hijab in France and Tunisia. It does not include the propagation of betrayal, prostitution, and adultery. Terrorism does not include the insulting of Allah, the cursing of Islam, and the mockery of our Prophet (peace be upon him). Terrorism does not include the slaughtering of Muslims in Central Africa like sheep, while no one weeps for them. No, of course, all this is not terrorism. Rather, it is freedom, peace, democracy, tolerance!'

There were some suppressed laughs in the room. Then the imam continued: 'Always remember what our Caliph said: "The world is divided into two camps, and there is no third one! The camp of the Believers and the camp of the Infidels; the camp of the Muslims and the camp of the Jews, the crusaders and the kuffar." You must make sure that you are always on the side of Truth. If you are asked to die as a shahid, you must be grateful and thank Allah for having chosen you for His divine mission.'

The imam ended his speech. Everyone shook hands and the

three new recruits received praise and encouragement for their jihad in the name of Allah. Just then, Major Waheeb approached Hendra.

'Soldier, I want you to come with me to my office before you head back to Hotel Turismo.'

'Yes, Major,' replied Hendra.

Heart beating, he followed behind the major, anxiously wondering if the head of the prison had noticed him slipping away earlier on, while that poor child was subjected to hudud punishment.

Despite leaning on a cane, the major walked briskly along the cold, narrow corridors. After a few minutes, they reached a door with his name on it, engraved in black letters on a white plate. The major pushed it open, while Hendra stayed behind.

'Come on in!' ordered the major.

Hendra took a deep breath before walking in.

'Congratulations, soldier!' the major said after sitting behind desk. 'Now your face looks like a real mujahid's!'

'Thanks, sir,' Hendra replied, still standing at attention.

No Quranic calligraphies or photos of Caliph Abu Bakr al-Baghdadi in this office, he noticed, only one old, dog-eared almanac from a local detergent brand. Also, unlike in the entire prison and in the rooms at Hotel Turismo, a pleasant heat prevailed, which emanated from a small portable heater by the side of the desk. From what Rachid had told Hendra, the electricity was strictly rationed in Raqqa so that most of the megawatts produced by the Baath Dam on the Euphrates River, twenty kilometres upstream from Raqqa, could be sold to Turkey to help finance the Islamic State's war efforts. Patently such rationing didn't apply to Major

Waheeb or he simply didn't care.

'Relax, soldier!' said Major Waheeb, laughing. 'I mean, chill. This morning I just wanted to spare you some nasty comments and bullying from other recruits if they see you smiling like this in the prison. But with me you can smile.'

Hendra was still on his guard. Although now standing at ease, he remained expressionless and looked at the major in silence.

'Would you like to chew some *khat* with me?' Major Waheeb asked.

And without waiting for Hendra's answer, he opened a drawer and pulled out a package wrapped in white cloth. Opening it on the table, he revealed shrub-like branches knotted together with a string. Hendra had heard about khat before but this was the first time he saw some in front of his eyes.

Major Waheeb removed one branch. 'First you must carefully clean the leaves because you never know where they might have been lying around before landing in your hands. If you don't, you could be in for some terrible diarrhoea, believe me! Then, you pluck a few leaves and stems starting from the base, you roll them into a small ball in your palm and you put everything into your mouth! You can also chew the leaves one by one, it's your choice. What matters is that over time you grow a sizeable quid inside your cheek.'

Matching words with action, he pushed the ball into his mouth.

'You keep chewing as long as you can, without swallowing, to get all the juices out.'

Hendra remained motionless.

'Don't worry!' said Major Waheeb. 'You won't go to jail! Go, take khat, that's an order!'

Still on his guard, Hendra took one shrub and detached a few leaves before inserting them into his mouth. At first it felt like he was chewing paper, but very quickly a bitter juice flooded his mouth as if he was drinking a strong gin and tonic – without the gin.

'Normally you sweeten it with Coke except that here, Coke, even the imitations, is forbidden. On the other hand, maybe it's for the best, because as a result of drinking so much Coke to cut the bitterness, you end up losing your teeth, soldier. So, for us, it'll be tea today.'

Hendra now understood why the major had all these cavities in his mouth. He tried his best to hide them but, especially when he smiled like now in the privacy of his office, it was hard not to notice them.

After a while, Hendra started to experience a light floating sensation, mixed with excitement, but barely stronger than if he had drunk two double espressos. Certainly nothing to write home about but not unpleasant either. And given the lingering effects of his heroin withdrawal, every little bit helped, didn't it? A bargain of sorts that he couldn't refuse ... But Hendra still remained cautious, not really sure why Major Waheeb wanted to chew khat with him. Had he detected in him a fellow drug user. Or had Dr Jusuf also warned the ISIS leadership of his junkie past and this was a trap? Hendra just stopped plucking new leaves.

'This is what I thought,' said Major Waheeb, who was getting more and more talkative, 'you are more fun than the average new recruit here. You'll see, there's nothing like a bit of khat to unwind with at the end of the day.'

'Is it allowed here?' asked Hendra.

'Of course not. Like so many things here, it's forbidden, but don't worry, there's no risk.'

The major explained that although khat was officially banned in the Islamic State, it was widely available – courtesy of its heavy consumption by combatants coming from Yemen and Djibouti – and on the whole, the religious police tended to close their eyes as long as users remained discreet. Anyway, given his own position within the ISIS leadership, he, Abu Waheeb, was untouchable.

'What's happening?' he asked. He was now talking with a funny elocution due to the growing bulge in his left cheek. 'Why you don't take any more leaves? You don't like it?'

Hendra didn't need too much persuasion to grab another branch of the alkaloid plant. The sensation of wellbeing spreading to his entire body was getting more and more potent – and undoubtedly enjoyable.

The major started to tell him his own story. Born in 1967, shortly after the Golan Heights' invasion by Israel, he had spent his childhood hiding behind his mother's skirt inside Aleppo's famous covered market where she ran a textile shop. His parents belonged to the majority Sunni community and fiercely hated Hafez al-Assad, the leader of the Alawi minority which subjected the entire Syrian population to its political and economic yoke. (Hendra felt his stomach tightening at the mention of 'Alawi'.) The major's father had been arrested in 1998 because he was (wrongly) suspected of having joined a terrorist enterprise aimed at overthrowing the Alawi government. He was never tried and like so many other political prisoners, never reappeared from the Damascus jail where he had likely been tortured to death. No body was ever released to the family.

When the Syrian civil war had broken out in 2011, the major hadn't thought twice about joining the ranks of Al-Nusra Front as the group tied to Al-Qaeda had quickly established itself as the most disciplined resistance movement, the only one capable of toppling the Alawi tyrant. Over time, Al-Nusra, with the military support from the Islamic State in neighbouring Iraq, had extended its control over larger and larger swaths of Syria. And then, in 2013, the breakup, the unthinkable, inexplicable schism between Al-Qaeda and the Islamic State, had happened, at which point the major had chosen to side with the stronger Islamic State and its new allies in Syria. In mid-2014, he had been severely injured by mortar shells near Aleppo, and though the surgeons had managed to remove most of the shrapnel lodged in his flesh, he was still left with one leg three centimetres shorter than the other. Having become unfit for combat, he had been assigned to Raqqa as the central prison commander, while his wife and three daughters had finally left Aleppo, totally devastated by the civil war, and sought refuge in Turkey. The major hoped that one day, his hometown would be conquered by the Islamic State army – or at least freed from the tyrannical rule of Bashar, whom he nicknamed the 'butcher of Damascus'.

While listening attentively to the major's story, Hendra was working hard to grow the khat quid in his mouth, and soon his left cheek became even more swollen than if he were suffering from a really serious toothache. When, after two hours of chewing, the major bid him good night, Hendra was feeling delightfully light-headed like after smoking a great joint. Before he left the office, the major recommended that he keep the ball in his mouth for another two hours – just sufficient time for all the juices to be extracted.

Upon entering Hotel Turismo, Hendra realised that he desperately needed to take a piss to get rid of all the tea he had drunk, and he headed for the common toilets near his room. As he switched on the light by the toilet door, he gave a start, spooked by the sudden, strong whirring noise of the ventilator, imagining for a fleeting moment that a plane was taking off next to him. Yeah, he was a little stoned and that was doing him a whole world of good – more good, in fact, than Hassan's buprenorphine pills.

22

Hendra had spent the day barefoot in the middle of the red sand dunes that surrounded Raqqa, learning to use a Kalashnikov. Barefoot, to boost endurance, like the Companions of the Prophet when they were training for combat. Come evening, he found himself returning to the prison for watch duty, a role he was now expected to perform every second night.

As Hendra opened the door to the wardens' cafeteria, he noticed Sameer and Dhakir talking together near the coffee machine. Because the three of them slept in different rooms at Hotel Turismo, their interactions were limited to work and classes, but their encounters were increasingly tinged with unease. Looking into Sameer and Dhakir's eyes, Hendra saw the same question that he kept asking himself: why was there a need for another test to prove their worth?

'*Assalamualaikum*, dear brothers,' said Hendra.

'*Waalaikumsalam*, Brother Hendra!' they replied with unmistakable excitement in their voice.

'Anything happened?' he asked.

'Yes, we got a new POW today,' replied Dhakir. 'A fighter pilot from Jordan.'

F-16 pilot Hazem Al-Rawabdeh had intended to bomb Raqqa but, *Alhamdulillah*, a ground-to-air missile from the Islamic State had downed his plane before he could fly over the town. Indeed, while Hendra was learning to shoot barefoot in the desert, sirens had sounded, followed shortly afterwards by a powerful detonation which his instructor explained must have been caused by ISIS' Saudi-supplied anti-aircraft batteries.

'The pilot managed to eject before his plane crashed,' said Sameer. 'But he was caught and brought here an hour ago.'

'The instruction is to keep a close watch over him to make sure he doesn't try to kill himself,' added Dhakir. 'Abu Bakr wants to leverage his capture to force the infidel King Abdullah II into freeing some of our own. So, we must check on him every thirty minutes. You wanna go now? He's in cell 12.'

Hendra left the cafeteria and walked along the bare and chilly prison corridors until he reached the single cell where Hazem was held captive. Curled up on the bed with his back to the door, he didn't move when Hendra opened the grille.

'Look at me!' Hendra screamed.

Slowly, wearily, the pilot turned around, but he avoided Hendra's gaze. His tanned face and cropped hair were covered in wounds and burns. Had he sustained his injuries during the downing of his plane, wondered Hendra, or had they been inflicted by ISIS soldiers following his capture? It could also be both, he realised. And so that he couldn't hang himself, he had been stripped of his military fatigues, with only a pair of boxers on and not even a cover to wrap himself in. But despite the cold of the winter evening, he wasn't shivering. As if, thought Hendra, his body was too numb to feel anything.

At last, he raised his head, looking at Hendra with absent, empty eyes.

The next morning, the Royal Jordanian Air Force pilot was paraded around town, and Hendra was authorised to go out and watch the procession. Abu Bakr al-Baghdadi himself was leading the cortege along dusty streets swarming with people in black clothing who gave the scene an air of a funeral party.

In a kind of mock crucifixion, the pilot's half-naked bloodied body was tied to a large standing cross, itself fastened to the back of a tipper truck. He barely flinched whenever a stone hurled by an onlooker hit him, he just kept staring in front of him, his eyes wide open, full of terror. Women in niqab had also joined the procession, some with children in tow gripping their mothers' abayas, and Hendra saw one or two kids pick up stones and throw them at the pilot with the same confidence as if they had been skimming pebbles by the river.

The mixed crowd of locals and foreign mujahideen were screaming their hatred in both Arabic and English.

'Kafir! May you burn in hellfire forever!'

'Chop the Zionist's head and feed it to the dogs!'

'Skin him alive!'

'Crucify the infidel!'

At some point, the caliph started to speak into a mic. 'Sleep in peace, dear brothers! For those who betray their religion are destined to a terrible death ... I have decided that the swine shall be killed with fire.'

Suddenly slipping out of his stupor, the pilot jerked and murmured a few words, drowned out by the crowd's cheers.

'Shut up, Jew!' yelled Abu Bakr. 'Since when do the enemies

of Islam have the right to talk?'

The pilot's head fell back on his chest, and from where he was standing, Hendra thought he could see tears rolling down his cheeks.

Upon his return to Hotel Turismo, Daniel told him that he was to see Captain Abdullah immediately.

Had they already decided on a test of loyalty for him? wondered Hendra, full of apprehension as he knocked on the captain's door.

'Come in!' he heard, and as soon as he opened the door he was confronted by the same rancid smell as on the first day: a mix of cigarette smoke and poorly dried clothes.

'Our Caliph, may Allah be his shield,' started Captain Abdullah, 'has decided that the Jordanian pilot shall perish by fire. And together with Sameer and Dhakir, under Anwar's guidance, you'll be in charge of carrying out the execution. That will be your test, and I do hope you'll pass it hands down. For you cannot claim this time that you'd be killing an innocent. The Jew was ready to drop a bomb on Raqqa and slaughter hundreds of unarmed civilians.'

***

Towards the end of the day, after joining the congregational Maghrib prayer at the prison's mosque, Hendra asked Major Waheeb if he could see him in his office. The major winked, probably thinking that Hendra wanted to chew khat again. But the former XS DJ had something much more important on his mind than trying to allay his lingering withdrawal symptoms.

During the day, he had done some research on the Internet using the shared computer at the wardens' cafeteria and he had discovered that death by fire wasn't one of the capital punishments prescribed in the Qur'an or in the Sunnah. In fact, the Prophet himself had specifically forbidden it, saying:

> Kill the enemy but do not burn him. For no one punishes with fire except the Lord of the Fire. (Abū Dawūd)

Now Hendra could only think of one thing: why had the Caliph chosen such a horrific sentence for the Jordanian pilot even though it was clearly haram? He had first considered asking Rachid, with whom he still shared the same dormitory at Hotel Turismo, but his gut feeling was telling him that the major was probably the only person in Raqqa with whom it would be safe to raise such a question. And even then, he would have to tread carefully.

'They have chosen our test, Major ...' began Hendra, standing in his superior's office.

'So, what will it be?' Major Waheeb had already unwrapped a few khat branches and was starting to wash them thoroughly.

'We've been appointed to execute the pilot.'

'I see, scratch the match or something ...' And the disgust that Hendra heard in the major's voice encouraged him to press further.

'May I ask you a question about this, sir?'

Having finished cleaning the khat, the major raised his eyes. 'Go ahead, Hendra.'

That was the first time the major was calling him by his name.

'Why is the pilot going to be burned to death? I mean, why not decapitate him like the other war prisoners?'

The major sighed.

'I tried to oppose Abu Bakr's decision but according to him, death by fire is such a vicious sentence that it'll convince the Americans and their allies not to attempt any land invasion for fear of the atrocious fate that we reserve for POWs. That's the strategy: terror marketing. Maximal terror.'

'But ... if I may ...'

'Yes, Hendra?'

'Isn't it forbidden by Islam?'

'If I were you, I wouldn't repeat this around me. I mean ... if you want to stay alive.'

'I'm sorry. I didn't mean to–'

'But to answer your question: yes, it's forbidden by Islam. Except that Abu Bakr doesn't give a shit about that small detail. Or rather, he thinks the foundation of the Islamic State is such a pivotal moment in the history of Islam that he has full authority to issue his own fatwas, which will become references for future generations of Muslims. And in this new Islam, death by fire for infidels will be an accepted practice.'

Hendra remained silent while Major Waheeb paused before inserting a ball of khat inside his mouth.

'Now I'll tell you what I think,' continued Major Waheeb. 'All this heinous slaughtering works against us. And if Abu Bakr makes good on his new threat to carry out bomb attacks in Europe, he will drive us to our ruin. Without September 11, the Taliban would still be in power today.'

He plucked a few leaves and placed them on the desk in front of Hendra.

'Go on, chew. It'll help you relax.' Then, after Hendra absentmindedly picked up the leaves and put them in his mouth: 'I'll make another shameful confession. I would be unable to burn this pilot. I'm a soldier, not a psychopath like this Anwar ...'

As he pronounced the name of the executioner, the major spat out his quid of khat with such a rage that it flew across the room and landed on the wall opposite his desk.

'It's like this pathological obsession with the Shariah, it's such a huge waste of time and energy. Our only goal should be to eliminate the butcher of Damascus.'

'You mean you do not want to apply the Shariah here in Syria?'

'It surprises you, doesn't it? When I was your age, I was a communist, you know. Here, I just pretend to believe in God because it makes everyone happy.'

Hendra stared at the major without trying to hide his shock.

'Now you must be wondering what poor old Major Waheeb is doing here ... As I told you the other day, I think only ISIS can rid us of the butcher of Damascus, and right now that's the only thing that matters to me. One day, when I was your age, I saw my mother pull her hair out with her two hands because she understood we'd never be able to bury my father. That day, I swore to myself I would kill that beast before I died, whatever the price. All the other resistance movements, even with American support, cannot succeed. They're just too corrupt to achieve anything ... But now maybe even ISIS will also fail because of all these fanatics.'

The major prepared a new ball of khat in his palm.

'Abu Bakr knows my opinions. But he won't do anything against me, at least for now, because thanks to me, he has the support of the Tay tribe all over the country. What will happen when Bashar and his minions are defeated? Will I still stand behind Abu Bakr? Maybe not. Maybe we'll become enemies ...'

He pushed his chair back.

'This is where I keep my lucky charm,' he said, opening a drawer. Then he pulled out a black string necklace from which hung a white tube, the size of a human finger. 'A cyanide pill. To die with dignity if Abu Bakr turns his nutjobs against me. To open the tube, you just have to yank on it. And after you've swallowed the cyanide salts inside, the curtain falls quickly.'

A long silence ensued, punctuated only by the rhythmic sounds of Major Waheeb's chewing.

'But this is my country I'm fighting for, Hendra,' the major resumed. 'Frankly, I don't understand what you and all the other foreigners are looking for in Syria.'

'We're ready to die on the battlefield in the name of Allah. That's why we're here, to defend Islam against the fake Muslims and the Jews.'

'Well ... all I'm saying is that it's not your war here, and if you feel you're incapable of taking part in this immolation perhaps you should go home. There are people who can exfiltrate you, you know.'

'Thank you, Major,' Hendra said, somewhat shaken. 'I think I'll go back to the dormitory now.'

'But you barely touched your khat!'

'Sorry ... I'm a bit tired, Major.'

'Your place is not here,' were Major Waheeb's last words as

Hendra closed the office door.

As he wasn't on duty that night, Hendra's day was over and he planned to go straight to Hotel Turismo, take two pills of buprenorphine and sleep right after performing Isha. No dinner. He wasn't hungry anyway.

Hendra left the jail's main building and walked across the interior courtyard where Shariah sentences were carried out. Above his head, the clear sky shimmered with countless stars, while a full moon cast a chillingly beautiful luminescent glow. Shivering and unused to the light mist that formed in front of his mouth every time he exhaled, he buttoned up his woollen military jacket. It was only the beginning of winter, but it already felt freezing to him. He saluted the guard on duty and exited the jail.

Despite the early hour – it was only 5 pm – the streets were already dark and deserted, except for a few kids playing football under the weak light of tired streetlamps and a handful of burka-clad women gracefully gliding between buildings.

Even confirmed foreign mujahideen, Hendra had been told on his first day, were forbidden from talking to local women. To satisfy their sexual urges, Captain Abdullah had casually informed the new recruits during the orientation process that infidel slaves were at their disposal. And if it was a spouse they were after, it was quite easy for them to find one (or more) from among the many Muslim women who came the world over to get married to a mujahid. If one were to listen to the wildest rumours circulating at Hotel Turismo, a dedicated space had been set up in town where the new women arrivals paraded, naked, in front of senior female cadres who ranked them according to their beauty with the youngest and sexiest being offered to the most deserving combatants.

But Hendra couldn't care less about the prospect of such 'rewards'. He hadn't made it to Syria to find a bride; he was here because he wanted to fight jihad! Yet, could the major be right when he said that his place wasn't in Raqqa? Even if he managed to pass his test in a few days, even if he took part in the execution of the pilot, what guarantee did he have that he would be allowed to join Abu Nassim al-Indonesia's unit afterwards? For all he knew, he might end up being teamed up with Imran Anwar and asked to commit new crimes forbidden by Allah.

He thought about Jasmine. For the last 48 hours, he had been unable to access his Gmail account and check for her reply to his message. Earlier that afternoon he had tried again while consulting the hadiths on immolation but to no avail. Supposedly, Raqqa's Internet traffic was routed through one of Syria's official internet service providers, and firewalls controlled by Bashar often blocked Facebook, Gmail and any known VPN server.

Amplified by a nearby loudspeaker, the muezzin's clear, strong voice broke the silence of the cool evening. Soon it would be time for Isha, and he'd better rush back – as every man caught in the street during prayer time could be punished with ten lashes. Even the kids had already picked up their football.

***

That night, for the first time since his arrival in Raqqa, Hendra experienced a crippling headache episode and had to make an incision on his left wrist to stem the excruciating pain.

Then, the next morning, during breakfast at Hotel Turismo,

he was so worried people might notice the plasters or his lingering tremors that he ate on his own. But he overheard a conversation between Sameer and Dhakir in which Dhakir explained that in fact the execution would not be an immolation as the pilot would first die from smoke asphyxiation. And so, the argument went, the punishment wasn't against Islam. Dhakir saw Hendra listening to the discussion and a knowing smile briefly parted his lips.

Right after breakfast, Hendra went to work at the jail and as he walked past the wardens' cafeteria, he saw that the room was empty and the computer was free. Could ISIS' IT support team have already found a new VPN workaround to access Facebook and Gmail? Since there was still time before the morning roll call, he decided to try his luck and sat behind the old IBM PC.

And yes, this time he was able to connect to the Gmail server.

A few hours after he had sent his email two days ago, Jasmine had replied with a long message. Telling him, among other things, that she had gone to his flat and taken Dini's stuff but also his belongings – his clothes, his vinyl, his turntables, his sound system, etc – just in case the landlord decided to repossess the apartment 'before Hendra returned'. She concluded her email by asking for his grandparents' phone number so that she could contact them before dispatching Dini's things to them.

Over the next three days, she had sent him five or six more emails to get his grandparents' contact number, each time sounding more frustrated and worried. The most recent message, received just one hour earlier, was not from Jasmine but from a certain *Taslim Chaniago* ... Hendra felt his chest tighten as he opened it.

It was indeed his grandfather, and he quickly understood who had taught his kakek how to create an email account ...

Hendra, my dear cucu,

Your friend Jasmine is here.

She arrived this afternoon and told us everything: your meeting with Pak Hadi Harsono, what Maia told you, how you found this photo. Jasmine also said that you might have had a hand in this bombing at a nightclub in Jakarta last week. And that you would now be in Syria to fight with terrorists? You, my cucu?

Who is your father, Hendra? How much I wish I could answer this question for you. Unfortunately, I only know what your mum always told us. When she came back from Batam in July 1988, you were already born and she said that your dad was the former manajer umum of the TMM factory there. I understand now, based on the discussion you had with Pak Hadi Harsono, that it was a lie and that there was never any deadly fire at this factory. Hendra, I can't say I or your nenek ever totally believed your mum's story. I think we chose not to question her too much because we were too afraid of a different truth. I can see now that we should have demanded more answers. Please forgive us, Hendra.

Could your father be this green-eyed man called Alawi on that photo? Maybe. Only your mother knows. But whatever happened that day, I'm sure it was an error of judgement and I can't believe Maia dared telling you Dini worked in that bar! It is such a horrible, heartless lie. I can only imagine she wanted to get back at me by hurting my only cucu.

I'm also sure of something else, Hendra. Dini always

loved you like a mother loves her son and so much more.
You were what was most precious to her on this earth.
Please come home, Hendra. My days are counted. Once
you're back, you can scream at me as much as you want,
for as long as I'm still alive, but I beg you, don't stay with
these terrorists!
Your Kakek

Yeah, sure, thought Hendra when he finished reading. How could his grandfather not know whether Alawi was his biological father and yet be so adamant that it was a one-off, that his mother had never worked at the Cock & Bull? Either he knew much more than he was letting on, or he didn't know *anything*. Either way, he was just feeding him lies, new lies. Why? Didn't he, Hendra, deserve to know the truth by now?

While he was reading his grandfather's email, he had received a new message from Jasmine seeking to reassure Hendra that she hadn't said anything to Pak Kelvin or the police about his bomb warning. She had simply claimed that an anonymous caller had tipped her off, and so he shouldn't be afraid of getting arrested on his return to Indonesia. Jasmine – who was going to sleep at his grandparents' house tonight – concluded her message by saying that, for the moment, she had put her reassignment surgery on hold. The only thing that mattered to her right now was that he come back to Jakarta as soon as possible.

Without responding to either Jasmine or his kakek, Hendra closed his Gmail account and left the wardens' cafeteria.

* * *

The next day, during their now nightly khat chewing session, Major Waheeb informed Hendra that, much to Imran Anwar's chagrin, the ISIS leadership had changed its mind about him supervising the immolation. The role had finally been given over to someone called Al-Turkmani.

A native of Merv, Turkmenistan, Al-Turkmani was a member of the Shura, Abu Bakr's own cabinet, and a Turkmen political refugee who, after escaping from the Ashgabat jails, had initially enrolled in the army of Saddam Hussein before fighting alongside ISIS. Abu Bakr wanted Al-Turkmani to oversee the Jordanian pilot's execution – which had to be perfectly scripted as it would be live-streamed on the Islamic State's Twitter account – because the Turkmen was a fire expert. In his youth, he had trained as a chemical engineer and had been involved in several missions to try and extinguish the fire that had been burning inside the Darvaza craters in the Turkmen desert for forty years.

The major repeated to Hendra that he didn't have to take part in this immolation and that he could introduce him to people who would be able to exfiltrate him. But Hendra just chewed on without replying, clinging to Dhakir's reasoning – however weak it sounded.

***

Two days later, after breakfast, Hendra, Dhakir and Sameer gathered in the prison courtyard to receive their instructions from Al-Turkmani, freshly arrived from Mosul.

The pyrotechnician had a ruddy face covered in scars and greying cropped hair. Despite being in his fifties, he still had the stocky physique of an elite soldier and wore immaculate battle fatigues along with shining commando shoes. Speaking with a hoarse voice, he kept squinting as he addressed the three recruits. Standing behind him, Imran Anwar looked on, at times yawning, clearly annoyed that someone else was stealing the show.

Al-Turkmani first explained that he had decided to change the place of the execution because a fire in the prison courtyard was too dangerous. And he had already found an ideal spot in the middle of the desert, ten kilometres from Raqqa, where they would set up a cage inside which the pilot would be locked up during the immolation. Sameer was in charge of sourcing twenty litres of the best quality kerosene, while Hendra and Dhakir were tasked with digging a one-metre-deep trench around the cage, which would be filled with water to contain the fire. Standing on top of the nearby dunes, the ISIS leadership would watch the execution – planned for noon the following day, right after Dhur prayer – while soldiers would be posted around to secure the site.

Al-Turkmani then assigned a role to each of them for the actual execution: Hendra would douse the prisoner's body with the fuel; Dhakir, getting his order from Al-Turkmani, would start the fire; and Sameer (who apparently used to be a professional cameraman) was to film the entire scene.

'Should I cut and change the view as soon as the pilot faints?' asked Sameer.

'Call him by his name, the Jewish dog!' replied Al-Turkmani. 'And I don't understand your question, soldier.'

'I mean, with all the smoke that he will have inhaled, the … Jewish dog will quickly pass out, and he'll already be dead by the time his body starts burning. Should I keep focusing on the cage after he collapses and before the fire reaches him?'

'You fool, why do you think I came here? Our mission is to guarantee a flash fire so that the Jewish dog roasts alive. So, make sure to soak it all in with your camera!'

Part VIII

The Bulbuls

Raqqa, 3 January 2015

23

Tortured by repeated headaches, Hendra spent most of the night locked in a toilet cubicle. Then, right before dawn, after the last episode, he went to the shared bathroom, sarong tied around his waist, to perform his ablutions for Fajr prayer.

'I start my *wudu* in the name of Allah,' recited Hendra. 'All praise is due to Allah, Who made water purifying, and not impure. May Allah's peace and blessings be upon Muhammad and the family of Muhammad.'

But he had to repeat the *dua* a few times as no matter how much he tried to focus on the sacred words, his thoughts kept wandering back to the execution and he would miss the meaning of the invocation – a distraction contrary to Islam which required a submission to Allah in full consciousness. He was becoming increasingly terrified at the idea that he might be about to commit a major sin, one that he would never be able to expiate even by leading the exemplary life of a mujahid.

After prayer, Hendra didn't follow his dorm companions when they went for breakfast at Hotel Turismo's main dining room. Instead, he went directly to the jail. He wanted to have time to use the shared PC before the morning roll call and get to the bottom of another distressing thought that had been eating him up inside since the previous night.

After dinner, Rachid had wanted them to pose together for a selfie.

'It's for my best friend, Alawi,' he had said. 'I told him I had an Indonesian pal now and he's really big on Bali, you know. Says it's the best place on Earth. After Raqqa, of course.'

'Your friend's a Shia?'

'Are you on something, man? You know it's forbidden here …'

'But you just said your friend's name is Alawi.'

'Hallo, my bro's Moroccan! Alawi is a very common name there. And by the way, he should be arriving here very soon … I suggest you don't go ask him if he's a Shia or he might rearrange your face!'

How could a Sunni ever be called Alawi, literally a follower of Ali? But at the wardens' cafeteria, it only took Hendra a few clicks to realise that Rachid was right. Yes, Alawi could refer to a disciple, a worshipper of Ali – like the members of the Alawi Shia sect in Syria – but it could also simply mean 'Descendant of Ali' and was a relatively frequent name even among some Sunni Muslim communities, especially in Morocco where it was the name of the ruling dynasty since the end of the 17th century. Simply put, not all the people called Alawi were Alawis. How could he have been so blind?

He was about to leave when on an impulse he decided to log into his Gmail account, which he had intentionally not checked since reading his kakek's message a few days ago. He saw that he had seven unread emails from Jasmine, including a latest one titled 'URGENT – please read this!!'. He clicked it open.

Sayang,

Please stop tormenting us with your silence!

Yesterday, when your nenek finally decided to unwrap Dini's belongings, she found four thick notebooks. You know, the kind with a batik cover and a small gold-plated lock … ?

Well, we all wondered if they were her personal diaries and if yes, whether they might reveal anything about your mum's time in Batam. After much hesitation, your grandparents decided to break the locks and we discovered that your mother had indeed been keeping a journal from 1995 until 2001 …

Sayang, you MUST read these pages that your kakek is going to send you. After that, there'll be no more lies. No more secrets.

Please come back before it's too late. There's nothing for you over there, you're not one of them.

I love you,

Jasmine

As a matter of fact, Hendra's grandfather had just sent him an email:

Hendra, my dear cucu,

We found this journal amongst your mum's old papers. What a shock for me and your nenek. I can't say we ever imagined that this is what had happened in Batam, although it probably explains a lot of things.

I was initially reluctant to send this to you but Jasmine

*convinced me that whatever the truth, it was better than
the torture of the secret.*

*May these words appease your soul and convince you to
come back.*

Love,

Your Kakek

Pulse racing, Hendra double-clicked on the document which took a while to download. More than 200 pages had been scanned into a single pdf file. He immediately recognized his mother's handwriting, neat and cursive like a little girl's, the same with which she used to correct his Bahasa compositions. Closing his eyes for a while, he tried to calm himself down. The knot in his stomach was so tight that he had difficulty breathing. At last, he started reading the journal extracts which began on the 1st of December 1986.

*Alright, I'm already in Batam! I arrived last night,
exhausted by the journey but so happy to be here. The
only disappointment is that Maia works in a different
workshop, five kilometres away from mine. Which means
we don't sleep in the same dorm. Never mind, we'll meet
up on weekends, then!*

*Today, I completed my first day on the job. I've been
assigned to a production line where parts of the famous
Sony Walkman are assembled. Our boss, the factory
head, is Pak Hadi, a young Chinese Indonesian born in
Batam ... probably the only one in the factory who is
from here! He's a nice man although I don't really like*

the way he flirts with some girls when he walks around the workshop. Especially with Yati who is in the same team as me. A pretty girl, Yati, with very large eyes and a beautiful skin white as milk, like a Hollywood movie star.

Hendra quickly flipped through the next pages, where his mother described at length her work at the factory, only slowing down when the names of Maia or Hadi were mentioned. He would read everything in detail later, after the execution. Then he stopped at the 5th December entry:

It is Sunday today, my day off, and I saw Maia for the first time. She took me to a coffee shop in Nagoya and we just sat there chatting for hours. I was so happy to see her, though I have to say I didn't really like her new look.

She wore high-heels, which made her one head taller than me when we walked side by side in the street, and she had so much make-up on her face! Like this strange, orange-coloured lipstick. But most shocking of all was her short skirt that stopped right above the knee! Oh, and she smoked these clove cigarettes with a sickly sweet smell that Ayah used to smoke.

When I asked her about her clothes, she replied that I didn't know anything, that was how girls dressed these days. For sure, men around us kept looking at her and it seemed to amuse her.

One month later:

We've received our first pay today. What a disappointment! I thought I was going to get 150,000 rupiah per month, but I've just discovered that they deduct 50% to pay for our lodging and food! Maia never told me that! I'm so sad. How am I going to send to Ayah and Ibu all the money I promised?

I went to see Pak Hadi in his office after lunch, and he tried to cheer me up. He said that he could help me and give me a raise, provided I become a good model worker. So, I'm going to work extra hard on the production line. No more chatting with Yati!

Then a few days later, under the 20 January 1987 entry:

I feel so ashamed.

As it was my day-off, I went to see Maia at her dorm, and she insisted on taking me out after I told her how sad I was about my pay. My treat, she said.

Before we left, she put on a pair of knee-high black leather boots and a woollen red skirt that was even shorter than the other day. So short that while we were both riding ojeks *into town, it slipped, and I could see her underwear. People kept staring at us as we drove through Nagoya. I almost wanted to ask the driver to U-turn.*

Then we stopped in front of a bar called Cock & Bull, and Maia pushed me inside. They were playing some super loud music which made the ground shake, and the place was so dark and there was so much smoke everywhere that for a few minutes, I couldn't see anything.

After a while, Maia grabbed my hand and guided me towards the back of the bar. What a terrible sight there! What a disgrace! All these girls sitting on the knees of foreign men who kept kissing and groping them. I had to close my eyes. Then Maia ordered a beer (a beer!) and I couldn't take it anymore and told her I wanted to leave. She said she wanted to stay a bit longer and so I left on my own. Just at the door, I bumped into Pak Hadi who gave me a very funny look. I ran away and hailed the first ojek I saw to go back to the dorm.

What is Maia doing in these bars? Ayah and Ibu would be so upset if they knew how she is behaving here.

In the next entries, Hendra learned that his grandmother had become sick. Indeed he remembered, based on old discussions with his mum, that it was around that time that Nenek had to be operated on for breast cancer. Dini sounded desperate as she couldn't remit enough money home to pay for the hospital bills, and Kakek kept sending her reproachful letters where he accused her, like her sister Maia, of not keeping her word. Hendra also read that Yati had fallen pregnant and Yati's father had barged into the factory and made a big scene in front of everyone. A few days later, Hadi Harsono had apparently been transferred out. Then one month on, Dini had met with Maia again:

I am so sad and disgusted. Today, Maia revealed to me her 'secret' to earn more money. On weekends, she meets foreigners at the Cock & Bull and sleeps with them for money. She said that it's not too difficult as long as you choose a nice guy, and that the money's good. Something like 300,000 rupiah for the night. 'Imagine, one-month salary for a few hours of work!' she said. And she mentioned that because I have a whiter skin than her, I should be even more popular, especially with Arab expats. She asked me why I didn't give in to Pak Hadi's advances. As he could be quite generous ...

Hendra continued to scan through the journal. Kakek had implored Dini to send more money, or else, they would have to sell the house to pay for Nenek's medical bills. When Hendea reached the pages written in September 1987 – nine months before his birth – his heart started to pump so hard that the pulsations echoed into his ears. The 17th September's entry was longer than usual:

Maia came to pick me up around 8 pm.

To get dressed before going out, I had locked myself inside the toilets, so that the other girls couldn't see me. Over the leather skirt and sequin top that Maia had passed to me yesterday, I had slipped on the black abaya offered by Ibu on the day I left for Batam. Maia screamed at me when she saw me dressed in that 'coat' but I told her that I would only remove it before getting into the Cock & Bull.

When I finally took it off in front of the bar's entrance, Maia told me that I looked damn sexy and that all men would be fighting over me. She was going to check who was around tonight and, for my first time, choose someone she knew to be very gentle.

Maia kept telling me that I needn't worry, that everything would be OK. Then she said I should drink some of her beer to relax a bit. I don't know what came over me, I was so terrified that I drank two sips in one go, and felt like vomiting after that. Then at some point, Maia grabbed my hand.

'You're lucky, Alawi's here today. You'll see, he's a nice guy, funny and all. I think he's from Morocco or another Arab country. He works on one of these huge oil rigs that we can see blinking at night off the coast, and on weekends, he comes to Nagoya to have fun!'

The man had noticed us and came to sit at our table. He kept staring at me with his green eyes and that made me feel so uncomfortable, so ... dirty. Then Maia took him aside and whispered some words into his ear, while winking at me. Finally, she said to me in Bahasa:

'All settled. Alawi's going to bring you back to his hotel room. I told him that he'd better be nice with you or I'd bust his balls tomorrow! You stay with him until morning and you'll see, he'll be generous for the taxi money when you want to go home ...'

Before leaving the bar, Alawi made me sit on his knees while some people took photos. When I got up, my legs were like jelly and I was shaking all over. That's when I suddenly realised I'd never be able to do it. I freed myself from Alawi and ran out of the bar, ignoring Maia's cries asking me where I was going. I ran and ran until I finally found an ojek to go back to the dorm. As I had *forgotten my abaya in Maia's handbag, the other girls saw me coming back dressed like a ... but they didn't say anything.*

Will I see Maia again? I don't know, I just don't want to go to that disgusting bar ever again.

What? But what had happened then? Hendra's mind raced in all directions as he kept flicking anxiously through the pages, learning that for a long while after that night at the Cock & Bull, Dini had stayed away from Maia. And then he stopped at the 2nd Feb 1988 entry:

Maia came to my dorm today. She sounded so distraught and was crying all the time. She told me that she had started seeing Alawi more and more often until she thought they were officially dating and she stopped taking the usual precautions. Then one week ago, he had suddenly left for Morocco and that's when she discovered she was pregnant! But the doctors that she saw refused to give her even a secret abortion because she's already into her fifth month of pregnancy. She said she had no choice now but to go and see one of these dukuns[4].

All this feels so wrong, so dangerous. And so against God's will ...

In the next journal entries, Hendra read that Dini had sought guidance from a local imam who had confirmed that at this age, killing the foetus would be a crime, an unforgivable sin. And so,

---

4 Witch doctor.

she had talked Maia into giving her baby for adoption instead of seeking an abortion that would be both haram and unsafe for her. During these discussions, her mother mentioned touching Maia's stomach several times and feeling a 'growing connection' with the unborn baby. Then on 15 April 1988, two months before his birth, Dini had written:

> Whatever happened, this baby is a gift from Allah, and I can't stand the idea that he or she will be handed over to an unknown family and maybe never be loved. What should he or she pay for Maia's sins?
>
> My decision is taken: I will raise this child.

His mother would have been perfectly aware of the difficulties ahead, including the hurt that she was going to cause to her parents and the fact that it might be difficult for her, in the future, to find a husband as a single mother. But she had been determined, and in the next entries Hendra learned how, drawing her inspiration from Yati's affair, she had decided to invent a story about a secret liaison with Pak Hadi. (Why had she chosen Hadi Wijoyo for his fictional dad's name instead of Hadi Harsono itself or, on the contrary, a totally made-up name? Maybe the answer was somewhere in the rest of the journal, which he would read after the execution.) He was born with the help of a private midwife, whereupon they had gone to the town hall and declared Dini as the mother. Shortly after his birth, his mum had quit her job at the TMM factory, returned to her parents' house and told them her green-eyed-factory-manager story.

All of a sudden, Hendra's stomach contracted under violent

spasms and he rushed to the toilets where he vomited like a fountain, completely emptying his guts out. He had never vomited like this before, not even in Sanliurfa. Was he now going to experience a headache episode? He stood up and, as he cautiously bent his head backwards, he felt his neck crack but instead of the usual pre-headache stiffness blocking his head, he found himself staring at the blinding light of the ceiling lamp.

Hendra closed his eyes and let himself slide to the floor. He heard Dini's voice whispering in his ear, he smelled her alcohol-free perfume, he felt her hands wiping the tears rolling down his cheeks. Alawi, Maia … All was falling into place now. Most probably, there were more green-eyed Dutch ancestors on Maia's biological parents' side than on his grandparents' …

Hendra stood up and looked at his watch: already 7 am. In thirty minutes, it would be morning roll call, after which the preparations for the immolation would continue in earnest. That's when he finally accepted that Major Waheeb had been right all along. His place wasn't here; he had to leave Raqqa as soon as possible. The major had said he could help exfiltrate him, but would he be able to remove him right away from the execution team? Regardless, Hendra had to inform the major of his decision immediately.

He exited the toilet and headed straight for the jail's officer mess where he knew the major could usually be found before the morning call. On the way, he had to walk past the pilot's cell. Instinctively, he stopped and the Jordanian stared at him in silence, his bloodshot eyes full of terror. Hendra averted his gaze just as a deep sense of guilt washed over him. How could he let him endure such an odious end without trying to come to his aid? But even if he opened the grille, the pilot had no chance of escaping! What if he gave him all the buprenorphine pills that he had left, would that help numb his body and soul before the execution? Hendra froze. Of course, he knew of another kind of pill that would suppress *all* pains! Please Allah, let the door be unlocked, prayed Hendra as he rushed towards Major Waheeb's office.

He gave one hard knock on the door and waited for a few seconds. No reply. He squeezed down on the door handle and, yes, the door opened. Hendra slipped into the room and pulled open the drawer. Next to a white cloth wrapped around khat shrubs lay the cyanide capsule, oddly illuminated in a ray of morning sun. Hendra grabbed the necklace and hurried out. He would first take part in the execution, but save the pilot from the torments of hellfire, and then he would approach Major Waheeb for the exfiltration.

***

11 am: It was time for Hendra to fetch the pilot from his cell and escort him to the truck that would take him to the place of immolation.

Hendra brought with him the orange jumpsuit that all prisoners sentenced to death had to wear during their execution. Without opening the grille, he threw it onto the ground through the bars. The pilot didn't move.

'Put this on, you Jewish dog!' screamed Hendra.

The pilot stood up, mechanically, almost lifelessly, and picked up the jumpsuit.

Hendra looked around him to make sure no one was within earshot before leaning in closer to the bars. 'I have a cyanide pill for you,' he whispered, showing the necklace, while the pilot slipped into the jumpsuit. 'You just pull on the tube and swallow what's inside, OK?'

The pilot lunged forward and passed his arms through the bars, trying to grab the necklace but Hendra pulled away.

'Not now! I'll pass it to you at the last minute.'

'Why?'

'Because if I give it to you now, I know you'll take it on the spot. And then I'll be the one they'll want to burn alive instead of you.'

**

12 noon: The red sands shimmered under the amber sun hanging large in the impossibly blue Syrian sky. The pilot knelt in the middle of his cage, crying and begging for mercy. His orange jumpsuit had taken an even more ochre hue after Hendra had doused his body with kerosene right before locking him up. The three of them – Dhakir, Hendra and Sameer – were positioned around the circular, water-filled trench, waiting for Al-Turkmani, standing a few metres behind with the imam, to launch the execution. Abu Bakr and the rest of the Shura weren't far away, their silhouettes clearly visible on top of a nearby dune.

It was incredibly hot under the hood that Hendra, like all the other ISIS soldiers present, had donned to prevent identification by foreign secret services. So much so that large beads of perspiration rolled down his forehead. Yet he was shivering. How had he found himself here, about to become an accomplice to such an infamy? Hopefully, after the 'successful' execution of the pilot, it would be easy for him to leave Raqqa. Maybe ... maybe he wouldn't even have to be exfiltrated by the major as he would have passed his moral test and he could then just request to go home for personal reasons ...

Al-Turkmani gave the go-ahead and Sameer started filming, focusing first on the prison's imam who read an extract from the surah Al-Anfal:

Muster against them all the military strength and cavalry that you can afford so that you may strike terror into the hearts of your enemy and the enemy of Allah, and others besides them who are unknown to you but known to Allah. Remember that whatever you will spend in the cause of Allah, shall be paid back to you in full and you shall not be treated unjustly.

Then the imam went on to justify the punishment meted out to the infidel. Yes, the Prophet (peace be upon him) had expressly forbidden death by fire but the interdiction only applied to humans and by choosing to attack Raqqa, the new sacred city of Islam, the pilot had excluded himself from humankind.

With a quick shake of the head, Al-Turkmani signalled to the three executioners that they should start the fire. That was the moment, thought Hendra, just as he met the pilot's crazed, pleading eyes.

'Wait,' he told Dhakir who had already grabbed a torch. Then screaming in Al-Turkmani's direction: 'I'm going to pour more kerosene on him! The Jewish dog has been standing too long under the sun, some fuel might have evaporated.'

Without waiting for Al-Turkmani's reply, Hendra rushed across to the cage with a jerrycan in one hand and the necklace concealed in the other. He ordered the pilot to come closer to the grille and kneel, and slipped the cyanide capsule into his hand while he emptied the content of the jerrycan onto his body.

'Just wait a bit before taking the pill, please ...'

The pilot whispered back between sobs: 'My parents, my wife ... please tell them I didn't suffer.'

'Don't ever take this kind of initiative again,' barked Al-Turkmani when Hendra returned to his position on the other side of the trench. Then, addressing Dhakir: 'Now get on with it! We've already wasted enough time!'

His terrified eyes shining though the hood, Dhakir approached the oil trail which set ablaze as soon as he lowered his torch. The flames gushed forth, devouring the kerosene in the sand, but even before they reached the cage, the pilot collapsed face first, and his body did not so much as flinch when the fire gripped his orange jumpsuit.

Hendra felt the sweat freeze on his back. The pilot had popped the pill too fast. Hendra now risked being discovered.

The fire had not even finished burning that Abu Bakr al-Baghdadi emerged behind them, a pair of binoculars in his hand, and marched towards Al-Turkmani.

'What the hell happened, Al-Turkmani? Why was the Jewish dog already dead when his jumpsuit caught fire?'

'I don't know, O Caliph. But I think it's quite possible that massive stress could have triggered a heart attack.'

'That's totally messed up! Next time, make sure to give the kuffar a relaxant or something! I want them to roast alive!'

***

Alone in the dorm – as the other new recruits were attending a training session – Hendra was lying on his bed, waiting for Isha after which it would be time to join Major Waheeb for their khat chewing session and to tell him about his decision.

They had come back two hours earlier from the execution and everyone in the truck seemed to have accepted Al-Turkmani's explanation that the pilot had probably died from a heart attack.

All of a sudden, the door burst open and the major barged into the room.

'I have orders to arrest you, Hendra!'

'What?' said Hendra, sitting up in the bed.

'They watched the video of the immolation and saw you handing something to the pilot while you were dousing him in fuel. They zoomed in and they're convinced you gave him a cyanide capsule. No wonder mine has disappeared!'

'Death by fire is forbidden in Islam!'

'This is so fucked up, Hendra! I told you to leave! Now it's you that they want to burn alive.' He paused, then said: 'I've brought two guns. I'll put one in your hands and say you tried to shoot me when I came to arrest you, and then I fired back and you died on the spot.'

Hendra was staring at the major. Dazed. Paralyzed. The major grabbed his shoulders and shook him. 'Do you understand? There's no choice!'

Hendra was frozen to the spot.

The major slapped him. 'Do you also want to end up in a cage, waiting for someone to give you a pill?'

Fast-approaching footsteps echoed in the corridor.

'We're out of time!' screamed the major, who fired a first shot into the wall and then brought the barrel of his other gun to Hendra's temple.

Everything froze for Hendra. Final visions flashed before his eyes. His mother's dimpled smile ... the green eyes of the father he would never see other than on a Polaroid ... Maia's orange lips ... Kakek and Nenek playing angklung together ... Jasmine's loving hands on his face ... bulbuls singing in the wild ...

Hendra heard a series of fast beeps, like a high-speed build-up in a set from DJ Radikal, and felt one last sharp pain in the head when his skull exploded under the impact of the bullet.

Inna lillahi wa inna ilayhi raji'un. To Allah we return.

Acknowledgements

I would like to express my profound gratitude to Gope Editions who first believed in this story and published the French version in 2017. Without Gope Editions' unwavering support and encouragement, I would never have carried on with my writing journey.

I would like to thank my wife, Juliana, for her insights into South-East Asian culture. Any remaining errors are mine and only mine. I should also acknowledge her patience with my bouts of mental absence whenever I was too engrossed in my writing.

This book would not have been possible without the guidance and editorial help of all the early readers who gave their feedback on the initial drafts (in French and in English): Cédric Baudouin, Laetitia Baufine-Ducroq, Clémentine de Beaupuy, Alain Castaignède, Nicole Castaignède, Martine Chaberty, Emmanuel Clerc, Renaud Garrigues, Maryline Geisler, Alain Jaubert, Arnaud Méjane, Peter Morgan, Laurent Perdiolat, Jean-Baptiste Rossi (alias Tino), Prachi Topiwala Agarwal, Christine Vu Thien, Stéphanie Zoccola, Yannick Zoccola.

And finally thanks to Phil Tatham from Monsoon Books for taking on such a challenging story.

Books set in Indonesia,
published by Monsoon Books